Ramsey's Gold

Russell Blake

Published by

Reprobatio Limited

Chapter One

Southwest of Cajamarca, Peru, A.D. 1532

Lightning flashed through the anthracite clouds that roiled over the rainforest as an explosion of thunder shook the earth. A long line of llamas, their matted fur drenched from the constant downpour, shambled along a trail deep in the rainforest. The animals staggered under heavy loads strapped to their backs, hooves slipping in the mud and pulling free with a sucking sound.

Thousands of the unfortunate beasts had been conscripted into duty on the far side of the Andes Mountains, their drovers trudging beside them to see to it that none wandered off with precious cargo. Inkarri, the head of the expedition, had made it clear that this was a sacred mission, with the destiny and survival of the Inca Empire at stake.

Only two months earlier the Spanish conquistadores had betrayed Atahualpa, the Inca emperor, whom they'd captured through trickery. After hundreds of loads of ransom had been delivered to the Spanish leader in the Inca city of Cajamarca, the conquistadores had broken their promise and executed Atahualpa. Word had spread through the Inca world of the treachery, and an edict had gone out: the prosperous Inca nation's treasure was to be safeguarded, away from the invaders.

Inkarri had traveled for many weeks, first crossing the Andes and then tackling the western jungle's swollen rivers. He'd braved impossible terrain to put as many natural barriers between his people and the invaders as possible. Now, hundreds of miles from home, the procession was running short of resources. Many of the animals had perished along the way, and every surviving beast now bore an insupportable burden.

Inkarri knew his trek couldn't continue. The latest attack on his group by the hostile Amazon natives had taken its toll – hundreds of his men had died repelling the assaults. He slowed at the head of the column and cocked his head, his bronze features haggard from the trip's demands, and listened intently.

From the thick underbrush ahead came Lomu, his second in command, who'd been scouting with a small advance party for possible new routes. Inkarri held his hand over his head to signal a stop.

Lomu wiped rain from his face before leaning in close. "I found a promising site an hour away. It has streams – tributaries to the big river that winds through the area, so there will be plentiful fish," he said in a quiet voice. "And I saw an auspicious omen. A jaguar, standing in the center of a small clearing. It's what we've been waiting for. As clear as the gods could make it."

Inkarri looked to the sky. "An hour, you say? Very well. We have another few left before it gets dark. How difficult does it look to defend?"

"If attacked, we would have the high ground. And there's a small river that runs along the northernmost section, which will serve as a natural barrier."

Inkarri nodded. "Pass the word down the line. We're headed to our new home."

Lomu rushed to share the news with the men. They were close to their journey's end, and the beginning of a new, secret life in an inhospitable wilderness. Their mission was clear – to establish a new city away from the Spanish, where the wealth of the nation would be safe, a cradle for the fresh start of the civilization. When they had done so, Inkarri would return to the empire with news, leaving a trail of false clues and deceptive directions to confound any would-be pursuers. He'd seen the avarice of the conquistadores, and witnessed their duplicity, and knew their lust for gold and emeralds would never die – that he and his kind would never be safe.

It would take months to create a habitable enclave, but when he'd done so, he would set up small camps along the trail to help new arrivals find the city. Once he was back among his people, he would recruit women and more able-bodied men to colonize the area and build a new capital.

Inkarri watched Lomu disappear down the column of tired llamas, communicating the tidings to men who had been through an ordeal unlike any in their people's history. The jungles east of the mountains had been the limit of the Inca world, and it was only a compulsion to survive that had driven Inkarri's group into its reaches.

At last they arrived at the site. The sun broke through the clouds – the first pause in the rain in three days. Inkarri eyed the trees, taking the measure of the area. After several moments of silence, he moved to the center of the clearing and stood, his arms spread, the sun's dimming rays warming him as he offered a quiet prayer of gratitude for bringing them safely to this spot. When he faced his warrior brethren gathered in a large ring around him, he beamed confidence and conviction.

"Our quest is over. Remove the treasure from the animals and let them rest. Organize patrols to ensure our safety this night, for tomorrow we begin building a new future in this place." Inkarri paused, taking in the men's expressions. "Oh, Inti, god of sun and light, and Apocatequil, god of thunder, thank you for leading us to this blessed spot. We shall honor you with a city the likes of which has never been seen. It shall be called Paititi, after the jaguar father you sent as a sign. Its riches shall be legendary – the stuff of which dreams are made."

Lomu gazed at the hundreds of bags the men were placing on the wet ground, brimming with gold and jewels, and his eyes came to rest on the pride of the Incas: a massive chain crafted from thousands of pounds of gold, its gemstone-crusted serpentine links glowing orange in the waning light, so heavy that it had taken a hundred men to carry it. Even with all the other riches in the clearing, it was breathtaking to behold, and Lomu felt justifiable satisfaction in spiriting it away to safety.

The road ahead would be hard. But they would do it, and survive as a people until the Spanish were driven from the shores. Temples would be built, babies would be born, trade routes established, the empire would flourish, and their deeds would be spoken of in hushed tones of awe and respect.

They would achieve the impossible and be remembered in their culture until the end of time. Stories would be told around fires, and the name of their city would be known far and wide as the crowning jewel in the Inca crown – the great promise of its future, the legendary new center of the noble and ancient civilization's universe: Paititi, the City of Gold.

Chapter Two

Patricia hurried from her flower shop to the car. Night had fallen hours ago and traffic had dwindled to nothing, leaving the downtown deserted. She normally didn't stay at the store after dark, but it was the end of the month and there were accounts to be balanced. Times were hard now, and she'd been handling the bookkeeping herself. She considered herself lucky that she still had a business.

Her sensible heels clicked on the sidewalk, her breath steaming in the frigid night air, and then she heard the sound again – something or someone was gaining on her. She struggled to stay calm as she reached into her purse for the can of pepper spray she'd hidden there years ago, praying that it still worked.

Patricia's hand fumbled in the bag, a knock-off Coach she'd gotten on a Mexican cruise in better days, and her trembling fingers felt the distinctive cylinder. She tried to remember the effective range, but all she could think of was that she should run. Run as fast as her feet would carry her, run to safety, to her waiting car.

She hesitated at the junction of two gloomy streets, ears straining for any hint of a pursuer. A scrape from behind her, no more than twenty yards, reaffirmed her worst fears before she forced them away and slowed her breathing. That could have been anything. A cat. One of the heaping garbage bags she'd passed rustling in the breeze. Something shifting inside them, or a rat burrowing for buried treasure. Anything at all.

When she rounded the corner, she sprinted for the parking lot, all pretense of calm gone as she ran on tiptoes to avoid the sound of her heels alerting whoever was behind her that she was in full flight. Because now, in spite of her inner dialogue, she was sure someone was tailing her.

Visions of serial killers played through her imagination as she reached the waist-high concrete wall that encircled the lot. She pushed through the gate, wincing at the groan of its corroded hinges, and made her way to her car as she fished in her overcoat for her key ring. God, she hoped it would start on the first try. She cursed silently at how she'd been putting off taking the old Buick to the dealership for months.

A decision she prayed wouldn't prove her undoing.

Patricia fumbled with her keys and got the door open. She wasted no time sliding behind the wheel and throwing her purse on the seat beside her before twisting the ignition. The doors locked automatically as the starter ground.

"No. Oh, God, no. Come on. Come on!" she murmured.

Two black-gloved hands slammed against the driver's side window. Patricia screamed and wrenched the ignition again. With a phlegmy roar, the engine coughed a cloud of black exhaust. She shifted into gear and floored the accelerator just as she registered the unmistakable shape of a pistol in her side mirror. Patricia swerved toward the street, ducking in panic as she saw the orange blossom of a muzzle flash and her rear window blew out in a shower of safety-glass fragments.

The old vehicle bounced over the curb with a jolt as she cut the driveway too tight, and then she was speeding down the empty street. Behind her, a pair of headlights blazed to life and grew frighteningly large. She gazed in spellbound horror in her rearview mirror as the shooter's vehicle pulled after her, and she spun the wheel, hurtling toward the highway that led to the safety of her modest home ten minutes outside town.

Patricia blew through the red light at the base of the onramp. Panic replaced her momentary relief when the glare of headlights reappeared behind her, gaining on her even as she strained to drive the gas pedal through the floorboard, pulse pounding in her ears, a band of pressure tightening around her chest.

"Come on. Come on…" she hissed, willing the aging Buick to greater speed as she raced by the old gas station that marked the town periphery, the arched windows of its fifties-era building as dark as the night sky.

A cold wind tore at the trees along the highway as the speedometer needle inched past eighty, faster than she'd ever forced it, but insufficient to pull away from the vehicle closing on her. Her gaze darted to the mirror again, where she could see the other car a hundred yards behind.

Patricia was doing ninety-six miles per hour when she missed the curve just before the river bridge. Her tires screeched like a wounded animal, and then she was sailing through space in a graceless arc.

The sedan chasing her slowed until it rolled to a stop halfway across the bridge's span. The passenger reached up with a gloved hand and flipped the interior light off, and then opened his door and stepped out into the freezing gloom. His head swiveled right, then left, verifying that he was alone. He approached the edge of the bridge and stared into the darkness at the inky rushing water of the river hundreds of feet below. There, at the base of the gorge, was the Buick, partially submerged, mangled beyond recognition.

He shook his head and pulled his overcoat around him, slim protection against the chill wind as he returned to the waiting car.

"Nobody could have survived that," he said, swinging the door open.

"Now what?" the driver asked, hands loose on the wheel.

The passenger glanced at the moon grinning crookedly from between the clouds.

"Now it gets hard."

Chapter Three

Drake Simmons peered over the dashboard of his Honda Accord at the row of clapboard homes across the street and took another sip from his lukewarm can of cola.

He hated stakeouts. Endless hours watching and waiting for the perp to appear, which often never happened, rendering for naught his patient vigil living off caffeine and peeing into a Gatorade bottle. He ran a hand over the dusting of dark beard on his lean face and wondered again how he'd wound up in this business rather than using his journalism degree.

The job market had gone from bad to worse since he'd graduated five years ago. Finding criminals who'd skipped out on their bond wasn't quite in the same league as being an investigative reporter, but it required many of the same attributes: patience, dogged determination, research skills, and a certain crazy recklessness that had defined his character since childhood. It was just a lower-rent version of how he'd imagined himself, playing out his Woodward and Bernstein fantasies as the star of a major newspaper.

The door to one of the squalid houses opened and a tall man with the jaundiced pallor of an addict sauntered down the stairs, eyes scanning the street. Drake slumped down behind the steering wheel and pushed a long lock of dark brown hair off his forehead, and then adjusted his Oakley sunglasses before sliding up just enough to see.

No question that was his boy. Alan Cranford, two-time B&E loser up for his third count, a junkie, a thief, a cheat, and now a fugitive after he failed to appear at his arraignment last week. But most importantly, Cranford meant five thousand dollars in Drake's pocket as his fee – ten percent of the bond's value, which the scumbag had allowed his aging mother to post before kicking her, and the bail bondsman, to the curb.

Cranford had a rep for being violent, Drake knew from Harry Rivera, his sometimes employer and longtime friend.

"Be careful, kid. He's mean as a reservoir dog and twice as dangerous," Harry had warned in his distinctive gravelly voice tempered by two packs a day of unfiltered Pall Malls and an affinity for Jack Daniels. "Last time he was in the joint he almost killed his cell mate. You don't wanna play him wrong."

"Sounds like my kind of fella," Drake had said as he'd studied the photographs Harry handed him. "A sweetheart, really. I'll just ask him politely to come in with me – that should do the trick."

"Drake, don't go overboard. I can't afford any more complaints. Do you read me?"

"Complaints? Of course they're going to complain. I drag their asses back to justice. What do you expect?"

"No unnecessary force. I'm still taking heat over Jarvis." Mel Jarvis had been a drug dealer who'd skipped on an eighty-grand bond. He'd tried to remove most of the top of Drake's skull with a two-by-four when Drake had caught up with him after a three-day meth binge at one of his girlfriends' houses. Drake had tackled him and Jarvis had hit his head on the sidewalk when he'd fallen, resulting in a concussion and more than a few stitches. Of course the girlfriend had lied and said Drake had beaten her boyfriend unconscious. The police were still looking into the matter, although no charges had been filed – they had slim patience for dope dealers who skipped on bail.

"Jarvis was a fecal speck. He tried to brain me. What was I supposed to do? Frown? Give him one of my scary looks? Guy was trying to kill me."

"That's not what his squeeze said."

9

"I love it when you use that old-time talk. I think they call 'em 'shorties' now."

"Just bring him in without any broken bones. All right? You don't want the contract, I got guys knee deep begging for work."

"I'll bring him in soft. I promise. Maybe I'll use passive aggression. Perps looking at their third strike respond well to that. If he gets snotty, I'll scowl disapprovingly or something."

"Okay, smartass. Just go find him and stop breathing my air."

Drake was pulled back to the present as he watched Cranford return to the door. Someone inside handed him a backpack. Cranford threw the street another predatory glare and began walking toward the main boulevard two blocks away.

Drake reached over the passenger seat and grabbed the bulky pistol grip of his stun gun, and then exited the car, the weapon's bulk hidden in the oversized gray hoodie he favored for stakeouts. Patting the steel handcuffs in his pocket, he locked his doors with a chirp and sauntered across the street, pretending to talk on his cell phone as he beelined for Cranford.

It was looking like an easy takedown until some part of Cranford's reptilian brain sensed he was being followed. He broke hard right across a ramshackle house's brown lawn, accelerating with surprising agility for a dope fiend. Drake gave chase, his Converse Chuck Taylors pounding the ground as he turned on the speed. Cranford vaulted over a four-foot-high chain-link fence and into the home's yard, and Drake hesitated, but only for a second, any worries about trespassing overshadowed by the five grand Cranford represented.

He landed on the far side of the fence in time to see his quarry darting across the back lawn, which was littered with dog droppings and trash. Cranford threw his hands over the top of a wooden fence at the rear of the lot and pulled himself up and over. Drake was just about to follow him when the back door of the house creaked open and an old woman's sandpaper voice called out.

"You. What are you doing in my yard? Filthy punk. Brutus! Get him!"

10

Drake gripped the fence and cursed under his breath at Cranford for making this hard. He was scrambling up, feet trying for a grip as he hoisted himself, when Brutus made all hundred and ten pounds of his Rottweiler presence known with a chomp on Drake's left leg. Drake screamed and kicked at the monster as he boosted himself over the fence, his ankle radiating pain.

He landed in another yard and winced. After confirming that the dog's teeth hadn't penetrated his skin, Drake took off after Cranford, who was fumbling with a tall iron gate at the side of the house. He reached him just as Cranford was turning toward him, a sneer on his face, the metal trash can by his side emanating the telltale stink of a recent fishing expedition on the bay.

Drake pulled the stun gun from his pocket and held it aloft.

"It's over. Only question is if you want to do this the easy way, or the way that zaps the crap out of you. All the same to me."

Cranford responded by ducking to the side and lifting the garbage can in front of him to block Drake's shot. Then he charged him, using the can for cover. Drake dodged to the left, but not enough to completely avoid the container, and found himself covered in fish guts and beer dregs as it struck his ribcage, knocking him backward. He landed on the ground with a grunt, and by the time he'd rolled and gotten the stun gun aimed, Cranford was swinging a leg at him, trying to kick his teeth in.

Cranford's work boot struck him a glancing blow on the side of his head. A starburst exploded behind his eyes, and then he had the punk's foot in his grip and the gun pointed at his crotch. He fired and heard a howl of agony as he shocked Cranford, who dropped next to him like a sack of twitching rocks. Drake sat up and shook his head, trying to clear it, and zapped Cranford again, just for good measure.

"There. You like that? That what you had in mind?" Drake stood unsteadily and tossed the cuffs at Cranford. "Put those on. Try anything and you get another dose."

A man's voice boomed from the rear of the house. "What's going on? I've got a gun."

Great. Just what he needed. Drake looked over his shoulder.

"I'm apprehending a criminal, sir. Please don't shoot me." Drake returned his attention to Cranford. "Put the cuffs on or I push the button. Now."

All the fight had gone out of Cranford, and he grudgingly snapped the cuffs in place. The man approached carrying a shotgun and stood a safe distance away.

"Why are you in my yard?" he demanded.

"This scumbag jumped the fence and was trying to get your gate open. I followed him over."

The man's eyes narrowed. "You a cop?"

Drake shook his head. "No, he's a bail skip."

"So you're a bounty hunter?"

"I much prefer fugitive recovery agent."

"Well, Mister Fugitive Recovery Agent, my brother's in the joint doing hard time, and I don't like the law. Especially bounty hunters. So I'm gonna call the cops while you two wait, and then I'm filing trespassing charges. Now don't you move," he ordered, and pulled a phone from his pocket.

Drake swore under his breath. He wasn't supposed to trespass. That was one of the cardinal rules of his trade and a very real legal issue. Harry would be livid, and worse, the charge was likely to stick, if the man couldn't be dissuaded from pushing it.

"Yes, sir. Of course, I wouldn't have had to enter your property if this dangerous felon hadn't been there first."

"Shut your pie hole. You play this way for a living, you take the hits."

A small voice called out from the open doorway. "Ew. You got fish guts on you, mister."

Drake sighed, trying not to gag at the reminder of the rotting leavings soaked into his hoodie.

"I know, kid."

The man snarled over his shoulder. "Shut up. Bailey, go back into the house. Git. Now."

"I ain't outta the house."

"You want a strapping? Talkin' back like that? Get back inside. Now."

"You gonna shoot 'em?"

The man grinned, an ugly display of marginal dental work that chilled Drake's marrow. "Never know, son. Now git."

Sirens greeted them several minutes later, and Drake stood by patiently while the disgruntled homeowner insisted on swearing out a complaint. A second squad car arrived and carted Cranford back to jail as the officer finished filling out the form and had the owner sign it.

"All right, Simmons. You know the drill. We gotta take you in and book you."

Drake shook his head. "Tell me this is a joke."

"Wish it was. Sorry. Let's go. Oh, and I need your Taser."

Drake handed it over as the homeowner watched, a smirk on his face, and Drake got another waft of fish stink rising from his shirt.

"Christ. What is that? Smells like an open sewer," the cop complained as they walked together to the car.

"You ever have one of those days?" Drake asked.

The cop stopped by his cruiser, opened the back door, and nodded. "All the time, man. Watch your head."

Chapter Four

The afternoon light faded to amber as dusk approached. Harry paced in the small area behind his desk, gazing through the window at a copse of trees behind the office, the stub of an unlit cigar clenched between his teeth. Obviously agitated, he finally stopped and faced Drake, who was sitting in one of two dilapidated chairs in front of the desk.

"I'm sorry, man, but I warned you. I can't have this kind of crap associated with my company."

"What crap? I nailed him. Dead to rights," Drake protested.

"While trespassing on private property. You're lucky the old lady didn't jump into it and file, too."

"She's lucky I don't sue her for the dog bite."

Harry shook his head and sat in his worn executive chair, his nervous energy finally dissipated, and leaned over to open his bottom desk drawer. He extracted a locking metal box and lifted the lid.

Drake caught the bundle of rubber-band-wrapped hundreds in midair.

Harry smiled. "Good catch."

"Thanks. This the five?"

"Yup. Listen. Drake. We go back a ways, so let me make a suggestion. Lie low. Take some time off. Go find a girl or get drunk or something. Take a vacation. And consider a different line of work. This isn't for you. You're too smart to be a bounty hunter. You've got your whole life ahead of you, a degree…you're wasting your time with this."

Drake's eyes fixed on Harry's face. "You firing me? For real?"

"You don't work for me. You're a free agent. So I can't fire you. But if you're asking, I'm not going to hand you any more jobs, at least not for a while. I don't need the grief. You know better than to chase a perp through private property like that. And Cranford's complaining that you used cruel and unusual subjugation techniques. He may press charges, too."

"What? I Tasered him."

"You got him in his family jewels."

"While he was trying to kick my face in."

"Still. It looks bad." Harry's gaze wandered to his message pad. "Dude, you're the best I've ever seen at figuring out where these mugs are hiding. It's eerie – like a sixth sense. But you don't follow the rules, and that's a big problem. So even though you're great at the tracking part of the job, you suck at the obeying the law part, and I can't have that reputation associated with me." He squinted at the writing on the pad. "Oh. Hey. I almost forgot. This came in earlier. Some guy looking for you. An attorney, he said." Harry tore off the message slip and handed it to Drake, who read it with a puzzled expression.

"Did he say what he wanted?"

"Nope. Maybe somebody else wants to file charges against you. Been a full day even by your standards, hasn't it?"

"Very funny. Can I use the phone?"

"Sure. And then make yourself scarce. If you still want work, call me in a month. But for now, you're off my approved list. Nothing personal, of course."

"Of course." Drake stood and walked to the office door. "I'll use Betty's phone, okay?"

"*Mi casa*, baby. Sorry to cut you off at the knees."

"No sweat. Maybe you're right. Time for some sightseeing someplace warm and sunny. Maybe Mexico. You can live pretty cheap there, I hear."

"That's the spirit. Get a tan. Have too many beers. Find a *señorita* to lie to. You're a young man. Live a little."

"Not that young."

"What are you, twenty-five? I got stuff in my freezer older than that."

"Twenty-six. Not that I'm counting."

"Course not."

Drake sat behind Betty's receptionist desk and dialed the number. Washington State, judging from the area code. It rang three times and then a musical female voice answered.

"Baily, Crane, and Lynch. May I help you?"

"I think so. I'm returning a call from a Michael Lynch?"

"Certainly, sir. And who may I say is calling?"

"Drake Simmons."

Music on hold waltzed in his ear for thirty seconds and then a refined baritone boomed over the line. "Michael Lynch."

"Mr. Lynch, this is Drake Simmons. You called today?"

"Oh, yes, of course. First of all, let me extend my sincere condolences."

"Condolences?"

"Yes. Your aunt, Patricia Marshall, passed away the day before yesterday."

"I'm sorry. Patricia Marshall? You say she was my aunt?"

"That's correct. I gather you weren't close?"

"There must be some mistake. I've never heard of Patricia Marshall."

"Mmm. Apparently she was your father's sister."

"My father didn't have a sister, as far as I know."

"Well, be that as it may, as executor of her will, her instructions were very clear. I have a package here that I'm to hand to Drake Simmons, currently of San Antonio Road in Mountain View, California, in person. Your employer was kind enough to confirm that's you. I've also been authorized to purchase a plane ticket to get you to Seattle, as well as pay for accommodations for two days. And of course, compensate you for your time."

"Compensate me?" Drake echoed, his ears perking up.

"Yes. A thousand dollars a day. Apart from what she left you, of course."

"She left me something besides the…package?"

"Correct. Twenty-five thousand dollars. All the money she had in the world."

"Mr. Lynch, I'm afraid there's been some sort of mistake. I don't know this woman, and as sorry as I am to hear she passed away, I'm not sure what to make of this. How do I know you're legit?"

"You called the firm's offices. If you like, go online and check us out – verify that I'm a member of the bar, that we've been here for over twenty years, whatever you like. You should be able to do that quickly." Lynch paused. "Mr. Simmons, there's twenty-five thousand dollars with your name on it in my account, and a package that requires you to sign for it in my office. Do you have something so pressing that you can't make it here to claim your inheritance?"

"See, that's the problem. It's an inheritance from an aunt I didn't even know I had."

"If you say so. That's not my concern. But it's your money, assuming you show up to claim it."

Drake thought about the odd set of circumstances. "And there are no strings attached?"

"Correct. Show up, confirm your identity, sign, collect your cashier's check and the package, and you're done."

Drake picked up one of Betty's pens. "Fine. I can fly in tomorrow. I'll verify your bona fides, and if it all checks out, I'll be on the first plane out tomorrow. How do I get a ticket paid for, and will you be there around lunchtime?"

~ ~ ~

When Drake arrived at Lynch's building the following afternoon, he was impressed by the baroque décor and wood-paneled offices on the firm's floor. The suite smelled like prosperity, of weighty matters and important men. The receptionist was a perfectly manicured

Chinese woman not much older than Drake, who peered over the rims of designer glasses at him with the glacial composure of a surgeon. One look at her severe suit made him feel instantly underdressed in his dark gray cargo pants and blue polo shirt, his North Face jacket clenched in one hand as he waited for her to alert Lynch of his arrival.

A tall bearded man in a charcoal suit with a leonine head of graying hair approached from the back offices with an outstretched hand and a somber expression.

"Drake Simmons? Michael Lynch. Good of you to come. I trust your trip was uneventful?"

"Yes. It wasn't bad."

"Excellent. Would you be kind enough to follow me to the conference room?"

"Sure."

They moved through the hushed suite to a large room with a rectangular table. A bookcase filled with legal tomes occupied one entire wall, with a panoramic view of the Seattle skyline through the picture windows that ran its length the main attraction. Lynch offered Drake a seat by the window.

Lynch moved to the head of the table, where a small package wrapped in brown paper sat next to a check and a heavy green leather-bound signature book.

"Let's dispense with formalities. Do you have identification?" Lynch asked.

"Of course. Driver's license okay?"

"Certainly."

Drake slid it across the table to the attorney, who pressed a button on the intercom box mounted on the corner of the table. "Would you please come in and make a copy?"

Twenty seconds later a blonde in a black business suit entered and wordlessly took Drake's license. She offered a polite smile and departed as quietly as she came, exuding high-priced professional discretion.

Lynch made small talk until she returned with a photocopy and deposited it in front of him. He studied the license like it held nuclear launch codes and then opened the big ledger and slid it, and the ID, to Drake.

"Sign there, by the X, if you would," Lynch instructed. Drake did so and pocketed his license.

"Well. There we have it. All done. This, young man, is yours," Lynch said, presenting him with the cashier's check. "And this is also yours." He handed him the package. "Oh, and I'm afraid there's one tiny caveat. It's nothing, really."

"A caveat?" Drake repeated, instantly suspicious.

"Yes. You're to open the package while seated in this room, and read the note inside. After that, if you choose to do nothing else, I will return with another check for your two thousand dollars of expense money, and you may leave the contents of the package with me. I've been instructed, if that's your choice, to forward it on to the largest museum in New York, and you may leave, your part in the matter finished."

"Wait. All I have to do is read a note from some lady I never heard of?"

"Your aunt. Recently departed."

"Sure. Okay, go get the check. This won't take long."

"As you wish. I'd suggest you be careful with the wrapping. You don't want to tear the note," Lynch said with a frown, and then stood. "I'll be back shortly."

Drake waited until the heavy door had closed and smiled to himself. Fine. He'd humor the old codger. Play along, pretend interest, and then take the money and run. Twenty-five big ones. No, counting the extra two, twenty-seven. Added to the five he'd just gotten for Cranford, that was enough to lounge around on the beaches of Baja for a good year, if not longer.

He leaned forward and began tearing at the brown paper, which to his eye was an old sandwich bag hurriedly sliced up and used for wrapping, and then remembered Lynch's warning about going easy. He folded back the flaps, the cheap tape yellowed from age, and found a single creased sheet of binder paper sitting atop a five-by-seven battered brown leather book held closed with a grimy piece of twine. Drake gave it a cursory glance and opened the note. A flowing, clearly feminine hand filled the ruled page in blue ballpoint ink.

Dear Drake:

If you're reading this, I'm dead. How or why isn't important. What is important is that you know some things about your past. Important things. About your father.

My brother.

After his death, I moved from Portland, leaving everything behind. I did so because the men who killed him would be looking for me. As they would for your mother, who was a saint. By the way, I'm sorry she passed away. She'll be missed.

Where do I start? Best at the beginning.

I was at your baptism. At your first four birthdays. At countless outings, picnics, dinners. Then everything changed. Your father went away and never returned. But I'm getting ahead of myself.

Do you know the story of your name? You're named after one of the greatest adventurers of all time: Sir Francis Drake. Your father admired his courage no end, which was probably his undoing. And your real last name is Ramsey. Drake Ramsey. Your mother and I changed our names after your father died, and yours, too. Why you don't use the Ramsey name is one of the topics of this letter.

Your father loved you more than life itself. Words can't describe his joy when you came into the world. It breaks my heart that you never really knew him.

Your father, Ford Ramsey, was an adventurer. A treasure hunter. He was a good man, but with a wild streak that couldn't be tamed. Your mother knew it when she married him, and she did so willingly.

He was killed searching for a lost Inca city said to contain the greatest treasure ever known. The journal contains his notes and his reasoning, up until he left for South America. Word arrived later that he'd died in the jungles there. Murdered, although the details are muddled. I know this because his trusted friend, who also changed his last name and is now using the name Jack Brody, returned from that trip with the news of his death.

I have left you whatever money I've managed to cobble together in my new life. And the most precious gift I can offer – the words of your father, in his own hand, chronicling his thinking, and ultimately, his journey to his fate. Read it and guard it well. Its value is substantial.

Your loving aunt,
Patricia Ramsey

Chapter Five

Drake reread the note three times, wondering if it was for real. He had no memory of his father – or at least, nothing concrete. A vague recollection of a man at the first birthday party he could remember. Drake was four years old, wearing a red cowboy hat, playing pin the tail on the donkey. A hazy figure, male, tall, was there with his mother, but beyond that, he couldn't form anything more. That was it for his dad, whom his mother had claimed had died in an accident. Beyond an insistence that he'd loved Drake and been a good man, she'd been reluctant to talk about him. When she did, it was always generalizations: that he'd been a writer and photographer, very smart, engaging. And that Drake shared some important qualities with him – a photographic memory and an ability to organize seemingly random data into patterns that were obvious to him, but eluded everyone else.

The few photos she'd shown him were of a handsome man in his early forties with a full head of Drake's longish brown hair and a twinkle of merriment in his eye. Their resemblance was strong, but it was one that elicited nothing from Drake but an ache in his gut at the lost opportunity to know his dad.

And now, here was a connection with the past, his father's thoughts and observations set down on paper in his own hand.

Ultimately, his curiosity got the better of him, and he unwound the string with a trembling hand before cracking the worn cover open to the first page.

Lynch returned, and seeing Drake reading the journal, left him to commune with the ghosts of the past in peace. Drake didn't notice, so engrossed was he in his father's account, and barely registered the passage of an hour. When Lynch entered again, Drake looked up from the journal as though surprised.

"I see you elected to read what Patricia left for you," the attorney said.

"I...it's really remarkable. What do you know about it?"

"Absolutely nothing beyond what I've told you. I was to arrange for you to come here, give you the check and the package, and give you Patricia's final instructions. Which brings me to the next point. Have you decided whether you wish to keep it, or leave it with me for donation to the museum?"

Drake shook his head, pushed back from the table, and rose. "I'm taking it."

"Then I have a further instruction that was based on your choice. Patricia had an insurance policy. Not a fortune, but substantial. I've been authorized to release the funds to you when they're paid by the company."

Drake hesitated. "Substantial? How substantial?"

"I believe the amount is seventy thousand dollars."

Drake sat down again. He'd been broke yesterday, chasing scumbags through sketchy neighborhoods, and now he'd come into almost a hundred grand...and the most fascinating account he'd ever read, even though he was only halfway through it.

"Really? When will the policy pay out?" he asked.

"I'm waiting for the death certificate. Once I have that, it shouldn't be more than five to ten days."

Drake nodded mutely. He leaned forward, his hands folded in front of him on the table, the journal next to him. "How well did you know...Patricia?"

Lynch looked like he'd been expecting the question. "She was referred to me by another client. I handled some small legal matters for her. Contract review. That sort of thing. And of course, her will and estate planning, such as it was."

"You say she died. How?"

"A car accident. The coroner said she died instantly on impact, so she didn't suffer."

"Where did she live?"

"In Idaho." Lynch didn't elaborate, and Drake sensed that he wouldn't be forthcoming with any more information. But he had to try.

"Do you have any idea why she'd have changed her name?"

Lynch shook his head and cleared his throat. "You now have all the information I do. Perhaps you could leave me your banking details, and I'll arrange for a wire transfer when we receive the insurance payout?"

Drake closed his eyes and recited his bank details from memory, which Lynch dutifully recorded on the ledger's signature page. When he was done, Lynch rose and cleared his throat.

"That's it, then. I'll contact you before we send the funds so you know they're on their way. Thank you for coming in. Oh, and here's the check for the two thousand, along with three hundred dollars for your hotel."

Drake took the check. The firm had paid for his airline ticket, so that concluded their business, other than the insurance. Lynch shook hands with Drake and then showed him out to the waiting area. Drake asked the receptionist to call him a taxi and took the elevator to the ground level, his father's journal in one pocket and a small fortune in the other.

He had the driver take him to the nearest branch of the bank that had issued the checks, and waited patiently in line before cashing them, ignoring the suspicious look of the porcine teller at his request for the entire amount in hundred-dollar bills.

The cab was still in the lot when he came out of the bank, wads of hundreds in the pockets of his cargo pants. He gave the driver his hotel name and settled into the seat. His mind raced at how his day had gone thus far: He now had a stack of Benjamins two inches thick, no urgent plans, and his father's legacy to pore over.

Drake ate a late lunch, treating himself to a beer with his hamburger as he read at a quiet table at the back of the hotel restaurant. When the waiter arrived to take his empty plate, Drake was surprised – half an hour had flown by like seconds as he'd been sucked into the little book. He paid the bill, returned to his room, and spent the rest of the day reading. By evening he'd finished, and the hotel courtesy pad was filled with scribbled notes.

According to Ford Ramsey, in the 1600s, persecuted by the invading Spanish, the Incas had spirited away the empire's collected wealth to a new capital in the jungle where it would be safe: Paititi, the Inca city of gold. For a century, the city prospered, and then something changed – as near as Ramsey had been able to put together, the water that fed the metropolis became tainted and the population lost the ability to reproduce. Ultimately the last inhabitants passed away, leaving a ghost city in the jungle. Since then, for hundreds of years, adventurers had gone in search of it, returning empty-handed…when they returned at all. Ramsey had collected every bit of data from even the most obscure sources and cobbled together a rough idea of the city's location, somewhere in the eastern jungles of Peru, or the westernmost edges of the Brazilian Amazon rainforest. He'd isolated a spot where a meteor had struck at some point in the 1700s, possibly contaminating the water table, and had narrowed his search to that region.

The journal described in detail the logic his father had used to arrive at his deductions, which included his conviction that a set of outposts had been set up by the Incas along the route to Paititi to guide travelers to the city. Find the remaining outposts, and Paititi was within reach. Drake's father believed he'd figured out where the final outposts in the chain were, after his penultimate trip to Peru.

When Drake got to the final chapter, the story took a more ominous turn. In dispassionate language, his father described being approached by an unnamed American intelligence service and been made an offer he couldn't refuse, a secret conscription he'd been forbidden to share with anyone.

That entry was the last in the journal.

Drake sat back and eyed the little book. His investigative reporter instinct was aroused, and by the final pages he better understood why his father had felt compelled to go in search of the lost city. Not only because Paititi would have been a once-in-a-lifetime find, but because he'd apparently been forced to cooperate in the interests of national security – although why an Inca city was of interest to the U.S. government was perhaps an even greater mystery than Paititi itself.

Drake stared at the notes and gathered his conflicted thoughts. He'd just gotten a glimpse of how his father's brain worked – the familiar gathering of seemingly disparate information and recognition of a symmetry nobody else had seen – and in spite of his better judgment, he felt himself getting sucked into his father's world. After studying the scrawled names and circling several, he activated his iPad, did a search for Paititi and found numerous sites. He read about the legend of the lost treasure, and even as he did so he realized that he, too, felt the tug of the city of gold.

Not that he was planning on actually searching for any Inca treasure. That was idiocy. But he couldn't see any harm in trying to locate his father's closest friend to learn what he knew about Ford Ramsey's last days. Drake certainly had the spare time to do it, now that he'd lost his job and had money in his pocket.

The first step would be to use his skip-tracing skills to track the man down. Drake loaded a website he used to locate fugitives and typed. The interface flashed at him twice. He sat back as it churned, the letters blinking hypnotically onscreen. A window popped up and he studied the readout and then entered more information. Another menu illuminated, and it quickly became obvious that it wouldn't be as straightforward as he'd hoped. There were hundreds of hits, and Drake had little else to go on other than the man's new name, which was as vanilla as they came.

Jack Brody.

That's all he had.

But with perseverance, it would be enough.

Chapter Six

The sun was setting by the time Drake landed at the San Jose airport, the afternoon flight from Seattle having been delayed for two hours. He exited into the parking lot and made his way to his car, anxious to spend some serious computer time running down the right Jack Brody, which he'd failed to do on his tablet, adding to the frustration of being stranded at the airport.

Pink and orange ribbons of high clouds marbled the twilight sky as he pulled out of the lot. When he rolled down his window to pay the attendant, the air felt heavy and moist with the approach of a springtime storm. The ride home was typically slow as the tail end of rush hour clogged the freeways, and he was seized by an unexpected bout of melancholy as he inched past endless anonymous strip malls and car dealerships, altars of commercialism in a land that worshipped consumption.

Two days of newspapers had collected on the stoop of his apartment when he eventually made it home. He kicked them aside and pushed the door open before stepping inside and glancing around. Drake paid too much rent every month for his one-bedroom unit in Menlo Park, where the local economy was driven by Silicon Valley economics that had spread like a metastasizing tumor, making the entire southern peninsula impossibly expensive for those not involved in software or the development of specialized electronics. He flipped on the light and moved into the laughably small section of the apartment allocated to dining.

Drake retrieved the three bundles of hundred-dollar bills from his pockets and set them on the table, pausing to consider how little space almost thirty thousand dollars occupied. Eyeing the princely sum, he was struck by how inconsequential the pile of currency appeared. It seemed like a cheat. It would have taken him six to eight months of skip-tracing and apprehending felons to make that much – the better part of a year risking his life, and that's all it looked like.

He left the money and walked into the kitchen. After a quick scan of his bare cupboards, he pulled the refrigerator open and studied the contents with dismay: a loaf of moldy wheat bread, four high-caffeine sodas, a bag of leftovers from an Italian meal from four days ago, and seven bottles of Rolling Rock beer. He retrieved the white polystyrene container and eyed the half lasagna inside skeptically. After a few cautious sniffs he slid it into the microwave with a shrug and opened one of the beers.

The damned journal had put him in a morose mood he couldn't seem to shake. Compared to his father's life, his was as mundane as a fry cook's. While Dad had been planning a journey into the Amazon jungle every night after work, what did Drake have to show for his efforts? A dead-end job chasing derelicts, a car on life support, and a nonexistent love life. A fine state of affairs for a promising student who'd graduated near the top of his class, 'a gifted writer with a keen analytical mind,' as one of his professors had enthused. All that had done him zero good in the real world. He couldn't even get a job writing copy for one of the ad agencies in the Valley, and his freakish ability to spot patterns hadn't translated into any career advantage, even if it had enabled him to coast through his math and science classes.

The *ping* of the microwave pulled him from his reverie, and the odor of questionable Sicilian surprise wafted through the space. He unceremoniously pushed the money on the dining room table aside and sat down with his feast, which he consumed with plastic utensils provided by the Lebanese couple who'd bafflingly chosen Italian cuisine as their specialty.

He chewed the tough layers of suspect pasta with mechanical determination, his mind elsewhere. As he swallowed the last bite, he checked his watch and considered his options for the evening. The choices were hitting one of the local watering holes and throwing some of his newfound wealth around in the hopes of attracting female company, or settling in for a long evening of plodding research as he attempted to triangulate his father's friend. An image of himself standing in a darkened bar, hundred-dollar bills plastered all over his naked body, sprang to the forefront of his imagination. Perhaps he could construct an elaborate fan of hundreds, like a strutting peacock's tail, announcing his mating availability to the willing hens...

The visual convinced him to opt for research, although he rewarded his diligence with another beer, the green bottle his companion for another tedious night of solitude in front of a flickering screen.

~ ~ ~

Lynch yawned as he finished with the pile of paperwork on his desk and stared at it like it was toxic waste – always a reliable indicator it was time to call it a day. He'd attended to all his pressing matters, having arranged for an automatic transfer to Drake and executed the remainder of the instructions in Patricia's will.

He'd been less than forthcoming about his relationship with Patricia, true, but he saw no reason to complicate a simple transaction with irrelevant personal history. The truth was that he and Patricia had been an item two decades ago – a long time by any measure.

It had been forever since he'd seen her. He'd helped her change her name when she'd moved to a small town in Idaho after her brother had died. But maintaining their long-distance affair had grown increasingly difficult over the years, made more so by Patricia's dawning awareness that Lynch was never going to leave his wife and children for her, and that any hope he would was as misguided as

29

many of the other choices that had sculpted her life. He'd been surprised that she'd kept him on as executor of her will, but it made a certain sense, he supposed. He was good at his job, even if possessed of considerable moral elasticity in his personal affairs.

His secretary ducked her head in to say goodnight, and he admired the fit of her skirt as she left, as he found himself doing more often – always a dangerous sign, he knew from prior entanglements. No matter how tempted, he wouldn't poach in his employee pool. It was one rule he made sure to never break, even if she did have the easy glide of a tigress with the smoldering looks to match.

Lynch shook off his mental meandering and rose. The work could wait. He was tired, and his longsuffering spouse would be waiting at home, a delicious meal prepared, a passable Bordeaux open on the table. He ran his fingers through his hair, thankful that unlike his father he still had most of it, and moved to the door, where his tailored suit jacket hung on a hook.

The offices were still as he walked through the suite. He was turning off the last of the lights when the front door opened and two men entered. Lynch regarded them, his briefcase in hand, taking in their cheap suits and rugged features.

"I'm sorry. We're closed," he said.

The taller of the two, around the same age as Lynch, perhaps a little younger judging by the amount of gray in his crew-cut hair, offered a smile as warm as a cadaver's.

"Michael Lynch?" he asked, the two words thick with an accent – Russian, Lynch thought fleetingly before responding.

"Yes, that's right. But I'm afraid you'll have to come back during business hours."

The shorter man moved surprisingly quickly, covering the distance between them in a blink, and Lynch barely had time to register the blow to his abdomen before a wave of nausea washed over him and the room spun.

When he regained consciousness, it was dark. It took him several moments to realize he was in the conference room. His stomach felt like he'd been hit by a car. He tried to move, intending to probe the tender area, but found himself immobilized. He heard a rustle to his left, and turned his head to where one of the intruders was sitting, staring at him. The man leaned forward and cleared his throat.

"Mr. Lynch. This is not a robbery. I am here to obtain certain information. As you may have guessed, I am willing to do whatever is necessary to get it."

The accent was definitely Russian, the voice cultured but menacing. Made more so by the fact that Lynch had been tied to the chair. Testing his bindings, he quickly calculated the time: The cleaning crew would be there by nine; he'd been preparing to leave at seven thirty. So depending on how long he'd been out, if he could stall them...

He looked at his captor. "I'm an attorney. There's no money here other than a petty cash box. No stock certificates, no bonds," he sputtered.

"Perhaps my English is not as good as I imagine it to be. I said this is not a robbery."

Lynch looked at him, confused, noting the scarring on his face, the nose broken numerous times, his eyes wide set, the cheekbones high, typically Slavic. "Then I don't understand."

The man scowled and shook his head. "I will attribute your confusion to having lost consciousness. This one time. But I must warn you that my associate here will not display such patience. So again. I am here for information, not to rob you."

Lynch felt a stab of fear. Whatever he was, the man was clearly dangerous – as if his current predicament wasn't sufficient evidence.

"Information?"

"Yes. You are handling the affairs of a Patricia Marshall. Or should I say, Patricia Ramsey?"

Lynch tried to control the flit of his eyes, but couldn't.

The Russian nodded. "I see the name is familiar to you. Let us dispense with any further games, Mr. Lynch. I know you are handling her affairs. I require information about her. Everything about her. What she bequeathed, and whom she left it to."

"I...Patricia Marshall? I don't...that's a nothing case. A simple will. Winding up her business and her leases on her home and shop. There's nothing to tell."

The conference room opened and the shorter man entered carrying a paper cutter and a pair of scissors, the blades glinting from the hallway light. He set them on the table.

"Mr. Lynch, allow me to introduce ourselves: I am Vadim and this is Sasha, who you met earlier, but I fear not under the best of circumstances. Sasha is expert in interrogation. And after twenty years in the Siberian prison system, more so than any man on the planet. Sasha and I have experienced things I will not burden your soul with." He paused, allowing his words to sink in. "I mention this because I do not want our discussion to be more unpleasant than it has to be. You *will* tell us what we need to know. Everything. You will beg to tell us things we have not even asked for. Your deepest secrets. Those of your clients. Passwords, account numbers, crimes. In the end there will be nothing between us."

Lynch refrained from commenting, the blood draining from his face.

"*Da*, you will talk," Sasha echoed with assurance.

"This is your opportunity to make things easy on yourself. Tell us everything about the will. Start with telling me where it is. After I have read it, I will know exactly what questions to ask."

"What do you want to know? Tell me, and maybe I can help you," Lynch tried, hoping to drag out the discussion.

"As I just spelled out to you, I want the will. Where is it?"

"I...it's in a safe deposit box at the bank."

The Russian sighed, an exhausted sound like a winter wind, containing the weariness of the world. "It is obvious you do not fully comprehend your situation. Sasha? Start with Mr. Lynch's left hand. When he has lost those fingers perhaps he will think twice about trying to delay the inevitable."

"No. Really. I'm not lying," Lynch insisted, his tone now panicked.

"Perhaps. But perhaps you are still playing games with us. Say goodbye to your little friends. It is regrettable that it has to come to this. Because you *will* tell everything."

Twenty minutes later, Lynch had.

Sasha rooted in the office refrigerator for a bottle of cold water then moved to the sink to rinse the blood splatter off his face, taking care not to touch anything – not that it would have mattered much, since his fingerprints weren't on any records in the U.S. Still, it was better to be prudent than foolhardy.

Vadim glanced at his watch and spoke softly in Russian before gesturing to the entry doors. After a final sweep around the suite, they slipped out of the office and down the emergency stairs, soundless as wraiths, leaving the unlucky attorney's mangled, lifeless body to be found by the janitor.

Chapter Seven

Drake came to with a start, a metallic taste in his mouth from the dubious cuisine and the beer, and realized he'd fallen asleep at his computer station at some point. He coughed as he sat up, ignoring the pain in his sacroiliac and the tingling as blood and feeling returned to the arm he'd rested on. He stood and stretched before padding to the kitchen to get a glass of water and some aspirin – a commodity he always had on hand, no matter how barren his larder.

He eyeballed his watch and blinked. It was seven a.m., so he'd slept for three hours. No wonder he felt like the floor of a rest-stop bathroom. He took a cautious sniff of his armpit and winced. Time to clean up, no doubt.

The warm spray of the shower revitalized him, and his mind began replaying where it had left off. He'd narrowed the field to twenty-two men who were in Jack's probable age range. Now it was a matter of doing the grunt work, calling each to see how they reacted to a few key questions. A process he was more than familiar with.

Ignoring the pungent odor of fish rot from the prior day's disastrous chase wafting from his dirty clothes basket, he pulled on a fresh shirt and a pair of dark brown cargo pants. In the kitchen, he double-loaded his coffee maker and stood like a contrite penitent waiting for it to spurt forth alertness.

After his second cup of coffee, he munched on a stale breakfast bar he'd been avoiding for months and returned to his computer, where he pulled on a headset and opened his voice-over-IP software.

The first Jack he called was in Trenton, New Jersey, three hours ahead, so it was more than past wake-up time. The man answered on the third ring.

"Hello?"

"Yes, hello. I'm Frank Lombard, with the Nellis law firm. How are you this morning?"

"Who?"

"Frank Lombard. With the Nellis law firm. Is this Jack Brody?"

"Uh, sure. Whaddaya want?"

"I'm handling an estate, and I'm looking for the Jack Brody who's named in the will."

"Will?"

"Yes. If you wouldn't mind, can I ask a couple of questions?"

"That's one."

"Yes, it is. Thanks for helping out. Do you know a Patricia Ramsey?"

Drake listened attentively, every fiber of his being keying in on tone, word choice, volume, breathing, timing.

"Who?"

"Patricia Ramsey. Or does the name Ford mean anything to you?"

"I drive one. Hell of a truck. Although I've had a few crap ones the first model year."

"Thank you for your time, Mr. Brody."

Drake hung up and scratched the first name off his list. Forty-five minutes later, he struck pay dirt. A woman's voice answered the phone, and he asked for Jack. Her voice sounded young.

"Who's calling?"

"Frank. Frank Lombard. Is he there?"

"I don't know any Frank Lombard."

"No, I wouldn't expect you to. Who am I speaking with?"

Long pause.

"His daughter."

"Ah. Very good. Is he home?"

"What can I tell him the call is regarding, Mr. Lombard?"

Drake sighed, hoping the exasperation of the long-suffering cog in the machine carried over the phone line and engendered sympathy, or at least kinship. "It's a personal matter. A legal matter, actually. I'm with the Nellis law firm." He paused. "Long distance," he added, hoping to hurry the process along.

"You should get a calling plan. Hang on," she said, and then the phone clattered as it struck a hard surface and bounced. A minute later a gruff male voice picked up.

"Yeah? What's this about?"

"Jack Brody?"

"You got him. Now answer my question."

Drake went through his introduction and began his interrogative. At the first question, he got what he was looking for. A hesitation. An instant too long to be innocent.

"Patricia? Mmm, no, can't say as that rings any bells. Where was she from?"

"Idaho."

"Idaho? Son, Texas is a long way from Idaho. Sorry I can't help you."

"You're sure you never heard of her? The estate's rather significant."

"Story of my life. You got the wrong Jack, Jack. Good hunting," he said, and hung up.

Bingo.

Drake had been doing skip-tracing long enough to recognize the subtle tells. This was his Jack. Drake checked the address on his computer screen and executed a Google Earth search to find the nearest airport to Flatonia, Texas.

Which was Austin.

Fifteen minutes later he'd packed an overnight bag, stuffed all his money in his pockets, and called the airline to book a flight departing in three hours, which he could just make out of San Jose if traffic wasn't bad. He took the stairs to the parking area two at a time, energized in spite of his lack of sleep. As he started the car and let it warm up, he called Harry.

"New Start Bail Bonds," Betty answered, her voice perennially cheerful.

"Betty. It's Drake. Harry there?"

"He just got in. Hang on a moment, mmkay?"

Harry's voice came on the line after a brief pause. "What – are you in jail?"

"No. I'm taking your advice. Heading out of town for a few days."

"Wow. Look at you. Where you going?"

"Texas. I've never been there."

"Why Texas?"

"Looking up old friends around Austin. Taking some time off. Wasn't that what you advised?"

"Yeah. Have a good time."

"I will. And I wanted to ask you straight. Will there be a job for me whenever I decide to return to lovely Menlo Park?"

The extended silence on the line said everything.

"Look, kid…"

"No problem, Harry. We had a good run, didn't we?"

"Sure. Sure we did. Hey, when you get back, I'll buy you a beer. We can talk about it. That's all I can promise. I gotta see what happens in the meantime."

"Yeah. Absolutely. Hopefully you don't get sanctioned or investigated or anything."

"Too late. They're already nosing around."

"I'm sorry, Harry. Really."

"Goes with the territory. Safe travels, okay? Have a couple for me."

"You bet."

The freeway flowed like cold molasses, cars creeping forward in fits and starts. Drake was reminded of his lowly position in the food chain as Teslas and Mercedes sedans battled for advantage in the migration south, the late rush hour the province of the wealthy and privileged making their way from multimillion dollar estates in Palo Alto and Atherton, long after their underlings had migrated lemminglike in pursuit of their daily bread. A neon billboard announcing a sporting event at a corporate-named stadium caught his eye, and he wondered absently whether there had ever been a time when things had just been things, and not advertising opportunities.

He parked at a discount lot and rode the shuttle bus to the terminal. After being frisked, X-rayed, and eyed suspiciously, he was on the plane, waiting to take off, his seatmate a hirsute woman of generous proportions who was reading a romance novel with all the intensity of a mullah studying scripture.

Then the engines kicked in with a roar and he was pressed back into his seat as the plane leapt forward, rocketing down the strip of black and vibrating like it was going to come apart before hurtling into the cloudy sky.

Sasha and Vadim sauntered down the concrete path toward their destination. The grounds of the complex were deserted, everyone at work or at school. When they arrived at the unassuming door, they knocked and affected pleasant expressions. Nobody answered. They tried again, and when their second attempt met with silent indifference, Vadim blocked the exterior patio with his bulk while Sasha went to work on the lock. They were in thirty seconds later, and after a quick glance through the condo, Vadim shook his head – their target wasn't there.

"Search it," he growled in Russian.

Sasha took the bedroom while Vadim went through the living area, but neither found anything.

"We missed him," Sasha said, his voice quiet but intense. He moved to the kitchen and opened the fridge, then snorted in disgust. "This place is a right dump. Are you sure this is our boy?"

"You saw the contact information. It's him all right. What kind of a name is Drake, anyway?"

Sasha removed a soda, eyed the ingredients, then put it back. Vadim raised one eyebrow and pointed at the computer. He moved to it and sat down, and then opened the Internet browser with a black-gloved hand.

Ten minutes later they left the apartment as silently as they'd entered, their pace unhurried, to any observers two gentlemen without a care in the world, their suits out of place for the casual chic of the area, but not so much as to draw close scrutiny.

Chapter Eight

Drake's first impression of Texas was that it was cold. This surprised him, given how warm it was in California in April. For whatever reason, he'd always thought of Texas as arid and hot and dusty, but what greeted him as he drove south from Austin was a lush, green, and freezing landscape, a cold snap having hit several days before. His coat was barely adequate for the unexpected chill, and he found himself muttering soft encouragement to the rental car heater as he rolled onto the highway leading to Flatonia, which as far as he could tell was population close to nothing, its industry largely agricultural, judging by the endless fields of crops he passed on the way.

He hadn't developed a real plan for confronting Jack, but he didn't think he would need one. Drake didn't understand why Jack was denying knowledge of his father and Patricia, but the answer might provide further insights into what he was getting himself into. Not that he was necessarily doing anything but following up on some loose ends, learning about his family tree, he told himself.

After a late lunch at a highway fast-food restaurant, he drove the remaining few miles to Flatonia, which was even more underwhelming than he'd expected, little more than a forlorn two-block strip of brick buildings with garish façades fronting on the old Highway 90. Drake pulled past the pharmacy and the hardware store and the florist, feeling like he'd traveled through a wormhole and wound up in the 1930s, so quaint and quiet was the main drag.

He continued south and, after a series of turns, found himself at a rusting iron gate at the end of a gravel road. A faded placard that had seen better days announced the property as the Buckeye Ranch, and an imposing padlock secured the barrier in place. A "No Trespassing" sign with the outline of a rifle beneath the lettering trembled in the light breeze, which smelled like wet dirt and hay as it blew through his open window.

He parked in front of the gate and stepped out of the car. At the barbed-wire fence that ran along the front of the property, he stood and gazed across the field at three buildings several hundred yards away: a barn, a garage, and the main house, all painted with discount earth tones and in serious need of a touch-up.

A man in a heavy brown coat worked in the adjacent field, riding a tractor that was dragging something across the ground. Drake waved at him. After ten seconds with no reaction, he wasn't sure the tractor driver had seen him, so he cupped his hands and yelled.

"Hey. Hello! Over here. At the gate."

The tractor operator kept going. Drake yelled again, waving his arms over his head. "Hey. You, on the tractor. Over here."

The engine ground to a halt. The man climbed from behind the wheel and, after a quick study of the field, made his slow way to the gate. He was short and stocky, built like a fireplug, his skin tanned the color of tarnished copper. Drake could make out wisps of silver hair at his temples under the Stetson that shielded piercing hazel eyes from the sun – eyes that were clear and lucid, the whites seeming backlit as he approached.

"Can I help you?" the man asked, his voice seasoned by the years, but lacking the twang Drake had been hearing since his arrival in the Lone Star state.

"Maybe so. I'm looking for Jack Brody."

The man blinked, but held his gaze. Drake could see a muscle in his jaw tighten as he clenched his teeth, but other than that, he could have been carved from stone. He slowly pulled his heavy leather work gloves off and held them by his side as he shifted from foot to foot.

"Why?"

"I need to talk to him. Are you Jack Brody?"

"Who wants to know?"

Drake had considered this moment for halfway across the country, and now that it was here, wasn't sure which approach to use. Did he launch into a story, try a routine, or answer honestly? He studied the web of lines on the man's face and made a snap decision.

"The name's Drake. Drake Ramsey." Drake watched for a reaction, but wasn't expecting what came next.

The man sighed, a doleful sound that contained more than fatigue or resignation, and spoke in a soft voice. "I always expected you'd show up here one day. How did you find me?"

"Jack?"

"Good guess, Sherlock."

"I…I did some skip-tracing. Took some doing, but you're a lousy poker player. You gave yourself away on the phone."

"Of course. The call. I knew I should have packed up the truck and headed for Mexico. Damn near did."

The two men stared at each other in silence. A frigid gust of wind cut across the road, carrying with it a small dust devil that spun giddily along the red dirt shoulder. Jack's eyes followed the dervish before returning to Drake's.

"So now what?" Jack asked.

"I've got some questions."

Jack nodded. He rubbed his hand across his face and then leaned to the side and spit onto a meager patch of weeds by one of the gateposts. "I expect you do," he said noncommittally.

"Should I ask them out here, or can we go inside?"

"How about I tell you I'll shoot you if you set foot on my property?" Jack asked, his tone reasonable. He spit again, almost as a form of punctuation.

"I'll just wait you out. Park here for the duration. Eventually you'll have to leave."

Crow's feet deepened as the corners of Jack's mouth tugged upward in a wan smile. "I'm self-sufficient. Not planning on leaving for a long time."

Drake nodded and put his hands in his pockets to counter the chill. "I don't have to be anywhere. I've got time."

Jack stared off at the horizon, where the trees at the edge of his property line shivered in the wind before falling still, standing like cardboard cutouts against the crisp blue of the clear sky. He grunted and returned his attention to Drake, who was waiting patiently for him to say something more.

"You'll have to use the bathroom at some point," he observed.

Drake smirked. "I'm pretty good with a Gatorade bottle."

"Man's got to have skills. Where did you learn to skip-trace?"

"It's a long story."

"I could shoot you by mistake. Nobody around here would convict me if you got hit by a stray shot."

"Probably have to shoot me more than once. Blows the whole stray thing out of the water."

The older man grunted again. "Well, then, I suppose you might as well pull your car up to the house."

Jack dug in a pocket of his faded jeans and extracted a brass key. He moved to the lock and sprung it open with a click. The gate protested as he pulled it inwards. Drake returned to the car and put it in gear. Gravel crunched under his tires as he rolled across the cowcatcher and onto the drive. He watched in his rearview mirror as Jack closed and relocked the gate before turning to follow Drake.

Drake shut off the engine and waited by the hood for Jack to arrive, the heat of the motor feeling good against the backs of his legs. A recent model Toyota sedan was parked by the side of the house, and a thirty-five-year-old truck near the barn. The front door of the house opened with a creak, startling him. As he turned his head, he was even more surprised by the woman who emerged – medium height, black hair, dressed in jeans that fit her like a second skin, hiking boots, and a multicolored flannel shirt that did little to conceal her gentle curves. She looked to be in her early twenties.

"Who are you?" she asked, her tone unfriendly as she moved to the porch railing.

"I'm here to see Jack Brody."

She frowned. "That didn't really answer my question, did it?"

"Oh, sorry. My name's Drake."

Jack arrived, his breath steaming the crisp air, the tip of his nose pink as he regarded her.

"Allie? This here's Drake Ramsey. Drake, my daughter, Allison."

Allison's face divulged nothing, but her piercing blue eyes widened slightly as Drake approached with his hand outstretched. She took it and shook, looking over his shoulder at her father and then back at Drake.

"Nice to meet you. Everyone calls me Allie," she said with a nervous smile.

"Allie. I guess that's what I'll call you too, then," Drake said. He realized he was still holding her hand and released it.

Jack cleared his throat. "Well, come on in out of the cold, Drake. I suppose you have a lot of questions, so this could take a while." Jack pushed past him and mounted the three stairs to the porch. "Allie, could you make up a pot of coffee for us? Hopefully this weather will turn soon, but right now it's creeping into my bones."

"Sure, Dad. It'll be ready in a few minutes," she said, her eyes still locked on Drake.

An energy passed between them, and Drake reluctantly broke away and followed Jack inside, trailed by Allie.

The interior of the house was exactly what was promised by the exterior – a sparsely furnished working man's home, devoid of most feminine touches, the furniture comfortable and worn. Jack shed his heavy jacket and hung it on a coat rack and moved to a tan leather reclining chair near the department-store couch. He motioned to Drake to have a seat, and removed his hat and set it on the coffee table in front of him. His salt-and-pepper hair was cut short, a no-nonsense style, probably for ten bucks at a barber – no frou-frou hair salon for him.

Drake cleared his throat and began with a question he already knew the answer to.

"Why did you change your name?"

"Is there any law against it?" Jack fired back.

"No, but it seems like everyone involved with my father did it. My mother, Patricia, you..."

Jack's eyes narrowed. "That's right. You know about Patricia. How?"

Drake saw no reason to lie. "Her attorney got in touch after she died."

Jack looked surprised. "Patricia died? God rest her soul. She was a good woman. I haven't heard that name for years. How did she go? She was still pretty young. No more than fifty-something..."

"A car accident."

"Accident? A shame. World's a poorer place for her passing."

"I'll have to take your word for that. I never met her."

"You did, as a baby, but I don't expect you'd remember that. What did the attorney want?"

"She left me some money."

"That's how she was. Good heart." Jack paused. "So how did you find me, and how do you know I changed my name?"

"She passed on some personal papers about my father, and apparently she'd been keeping track of you. I guess she was still interested in keeping in touch. She mentioned you were using a new name."

"I'm surprised. She never reached out." He stopped as Allie entered with two cups of coffee and placed them on the table.

"Hope you like it black. We don't have any milk. Sorry. You want any sugar?" she asked.

"No, black's fine," Drake said.

She stared at him for a moment and then left them to their discussion, returning to the kitchen.

Both men took appreciative sips of the rich hot brew before setting the cups down to cool. Jack leaned back in his chair and resumed talking.

"You say she left some papers?"

"Right. About my father. His history. About you and him going to South America. Where he died."

Jack nodded. "That's correct. Another sad day."

"I want to hear about it. She says he was murdered."

Jack looked away, seeming to drift to another place, then took another gulp of coffee. "That's right. Killed in the jungle. In Peru."

"How did it happen?"

"You want the long version or the short one?"

"I just flew hours to hear it. Might as well take the scenic route."

Jack exhaled and nodded again. "Like I said. I always knew this day would come. You know, I recognized you from twenty yards away. You look that much like him. A young version, but still, you got his build and his face. Eerie, really. Like a carbon copy."

"I've seen photos of him. We do look a lot alike."

"Yup. Well, I suppose there's no point in beating around the bush. Patricia was right. He was killed like a dog by Russians."

Drake's eyes widened. "Russians? What were Russians doing in the South American jungle? And why kill him?"

"That's where the story gets complicated."

"Complicated or otherwise, I want to know everything…"

"Then I'll start at the beginning. With two men. Vadim Olenksi, formerly of the KGB, and his sidekick, Sasha Berekov. Two of the worst miscreants to ever walk the earth. Dangerous as diamondbacks and twice as mean. They were looking for the same thing your father was. I guess they wanted to eliminate the competition. So they killed him." Jack gave him a bleak look, tormented, as though the wound he was opening was as fresh as the morning frost. "They killed him without a second thought. And the reason we all changed our names and moved the hell away from wherever we were, dropping everything, leaving whatever we had behind, was because we were all worried they'd do the same to us."

Chapter Nine

"I don't understand. Why would two former KGB operatives want to kill everyone connected to my father?" Drake asked.

"Because of what they thought one of us had. Your father's journal. The key to finding the treasure they were after."

"His journal?"

"Yes. Your father had a nearly photographic memory, but he was a writer, and he liked to set things down on paper. He laid out all his reasoning, including the result of his research, which took him years. Almost a decade, actually. This was before the Internet, so you had to go to libraries and museums in whatever country had the resources you were looking for. He must have taken a half-dozen trips to Peru and Bolivia and Brazil before the final one. He was like a man with a disease." Jack stopped, considering his next words. "Your dad ditched the journal before he went south. He never told me where he hid it."

"I inherited his memory, too, I guess. It's not eidetic, but it's close. Why would he hide the journal?" Drake asked.

"Even then he understood it contained a lot of information some might do anything to get their hands on."

"Sounds paranoid."

"Paranoia becomes prudent planning when a threat appears. He learned that from me. You learn to live by that maxim in Special Forces."

"I expect you do," Drake said, trying to be polite.

Jack took another pull on his coffee. "What do you know about what he was looking for?"

"What I learned from Patricia's notes. Something about a lost Inca city of gold. You mean he actually thought it was real?"

"Not at first. But over time, he became convinced of it. Paititi. Where the pre-Columbian treasure of the Incas was stored, lost forever to history when the Spanish systematically eradicated their culture. But he wasn't the first to believe that the legend was based in fact, so not as crazy as it sounds. Plenty of bright minds have gone in search of it, only to come up dry. From all over the world. As recently as in the last few years."

"Maybe because it doesn't exist. Like the El Dorado. Or any of the other treasure myths."

"Perhaps, but your father didn't believe that. And he was the smartest man I've ever known. And the man was like a lamprey once he latched on to something."

Drake paused. "How did you know him?"

"Met in high school and were buds ever after. Only he went to college and I went into the service. When I left after seven years, it was like nothing had changed. Except, of course, for the bullet wounds and scars. I was in the Rangers. Caught the tail end of 'Nam. Trust me – the movies got that completely wrong. Even the most realistic can't capture what it was like. It takes a lifetime to get over that kind of thing. I'm still working on it."

"How did you wind up hooking up with him to go to South America?"

"It was a natural fit. He needed someone who knew his way around the jungle and was combat hardened – someone who could handle a gun and a knife in case we ran into trouble. Don't get me wrong. I trained him to be about as good as anyone could get, but his heart wasn't in it. He wasn't a fighter. He was an explorer. Anyway, I spent a couple of months in the rainforest with him. It's my deepest regret that the Russians got to him when I was making a supply run. Only a three-day trek roundtrip, but it was enough."

Drake leaned forward. "How? How did he die?"

"It was probably painless. Do you really want to hear this? Why? What's it going to change?"

"I need to know. Everything," Drake said softly.

Jack shook his head and then shrugged. "All right. When I got back to our camp, I found him by a stream. He'd been shot in the head, execution style. I don't know whether he'd been beaten or tortured...the animals had gotten to him."

"How do you know it wasn't the natives?"

"I'm confident it wasn't them. Early on in our jungle days he rescued a small Indian child who was drowning and returned her to her father. From that point on, he was untouchable to them. I wouldn't say they were in love with him, but they let him do his thing while they went about their business. Plus, deep in the Amazon, the Indians don't have guns. They use bows and blowguns. And back then, the drug cartels hadn't moved in – Colombia was the primary cocaine-growing region, so the jungles of Brazil and Peru weren't infested with killers like I hear they are now. That leaves the Russians. Your father and I knew they were in the area, looking. But obviously, we misjudged what they would do to find the treasure."

Drake studied Jack's face. "Tell me more."

"Not much to tell. Cutthroats. Vicious. No conscience. Ex-KGB, they were trying to find the treasure for their employer, an oligarch – one of the bosses that wound up running the filthy place. The only positive is that seventeen years ago both of them wound up in a Siberian prison. So they got what was coming to them, even if it wasn't for your father's death."

"How do you know?"

"I have friends in the intelligence community. We still talk, although not as much as we used to since I quit drinking alcohol. They were willing to do me a favor. You never know when you'll need one in return. Last I heard, the Russians were in for the duration in an arctic wasteland – a frozen hell nobody could survive for long. The life expectancy in that camp is five years. Need I say more?"

"They never found the city?"

"No. If they had, they wouldn't have returned to the mother country and fallen low enough to get arrested." Jack finished his coffee. "All ancient history."

"But you still changed your name, so the threat couldn't have been completely neutralized."

"Even if the two scumbags wound up in the gulag, there was about a two-year period when we didn't know what would happen. It wasn't worth the risk."

"How do you know about the Russians?"

"They approached your father on that last trip and suggested joining forces. Actually, it was more like they threatened him if he didn't help them. I was at the meeting. Let's just say it got tense. Two things you need to know about your father: he was stubborn as a mule, and he didn't take kindly to bullying. Like I said, it got tense." Jack looked at Drake appraisingly. "I'd say you take after him in respect to being stubborn."

Drake ignored the observation. "My father stared down two former KGB killers?"

"You've never seen anything like it. You'd have thought he was bulletproof. The man didn't know what fear was, unfortunately. Guns came out, and looking back, it was only because they needed him alive that it didn't escalate. Anyway, that's how I knew I was still at risk after the expedition. Following that meeting, your father made me promise that your mother and Patricia would go into hiding if anything happened to him. Gave me notes to hand-deliver to them. It was like he knew…"

"I understand why the name changes. But I still don't get how grown men could believe that some golden city has remained undiscovered for centuries."

"Many believe the legend's true. I still follow all the latest developments. In fact, after your dad died, an Italian researcher discovered a report by a Spanish missionary squirreled away in the Jesuit archives in Rome. I think that was 2001 or 2002. The report talked about a hidden city in the jungle overflowing with treasure – precious gems, gold, you name it. The Spaniard had been on good terms with the Indians and they'd shared the story with him, if not the exact location."

"Do you believe it's real?"

"You know, I started off skeptical and wound up a believer. Mostly because of your father's conviction – that it was real, that he had a good idea of where it was, and that not only was it possible to find it, but that he'd be the one to do so. Does that mean it is real? Hell no. Would I bet the farm on it? No. I'm too old for that kind of gamble. But if you're asking me whether somewhere in the jungle at the ass end of the world there are ruins of an Inca city with unimaginable treasure in it, the answer's a cautious yes."

"Cautious? Why? That hardly seems consistent with a commando's nature."

"You take enough risks when you're a kid, you see enough, and you start to appreciate your own mortality. How old are you?"

"Twenty-six."

"Yeah, I remember those days well. You're only a couple of years older than Allie. When you're young, you think you're invulnerable and have all the time in the world to live out your life. Once you're an old fart like me, you understand there are no guarantees, and if you see the sun rise tomorrow, it's a gift, not a right." Jack cleared his throat. "Now you can answer some questions for me. How do you know how to skip-trace well enough to find me? I'm pretty much unfindable. No criminal record, not even a traffic ticket. I've kept my nose clean. I live in the middle of God's country. My nearest neighbor is a half mile down the road. How did you do it?"

Drake explained about his career as a bounty hunter and the painstaking process he'd gone through to locate him.

Jack appraised him with a knowing eye. "See? The apple doesn't fall far from the tree. Your father was convinced he could find Paititi – that he could find anything. Whether you know it or not, you're the same."

Drake shrugged, the praise uncomfortable. "It's a living."

"I'm sure it is. But given how smart your old man was, I'm surprised you're not a doctor or a lawyer or something. How did you wind up in the bounty-hunting game?"

"It's just one of those things you fall into."

"Being a short-order cook or a car salesman's the kind of thing you fall into. There aren't many bounty hunters. Did you go to school?"

"Yeah. I've got a journalism degree that's good for lining the bottom of a bird cage. It's tough out there these days. No jobs. Newspapers folding right and left. Christ, there are lines for openings at fast-food restaurants. It's crazy."

"We've certainly made a mess of it, I'll give you that."

"So I got a tip from a buddy that his brother needed some help with his bail bond business, and after talking to him, I interned there for a few weeks – unpaid, of course – and learned the ropes. I nailed my first perp at month number three and pocketed six grand, and then another the next month and made four. Following month, took home ten. That was it for me."

"Doesn't seem like the kind of thing you'd be good at. No offense, but you're not exactly the type to take on a three-hundred-pound fugitive."

"You'd be surprised. I used to wrestle in school, and took some martial arts courses. I'm not saying it's easy, but like I said, it puts food on the table."

Allie entered, looking at her watch. "Speaking of food on the table, is he staying for dinner?" she asked Jack.

Jack eyed him. "Well? You heard the lady. You staying for dinner?"

Drake tried his most winning grin on Allie and got polite indifference in return. He decided not to let it faze him.

"I'd love to. You need any help in the kitchen?"

"I was just going to microwave a couple of TV dinners. I think I can handle it." She spun on her heel and left.

Jack shook his head. "Don't take it personally. She's had a rough patch lately. Same as you. No jobs. A bum for an ex-boyfriend. So she's a little angry."

"No offense taken."

"Atta boy. Now tell me about everything you've patched together about your dad, and I'll try to fill in the gaps for you."

Chapter Ten

Contrary to Allie's verbal menu, dinner consisted of thick, juicy steaks and garlic-sautéed spinach that would have been the envy of any high-end restaurant. The dinner discussion centered primarily around Drake's father and his exploits before leaving for South America, with Jack providing a running commentary throughout the meal. When they were done, Drake insisted on helping Allie with the dishes. He donned a pair of rubber gloves, stood next to her, and dutifully rinsed in the huge double farm sink after she washed.

"That was a wonderful meal, Allie. Thanks again," he said as he ran water over a plain stoneware plate.

"You're welcome. It was my pleasure."

He placed a matching dish in the rack beside him. "What's it like living on a farm?"

"A ranch. We have sixty head of cattle."

"Is that how your father earns his living?"

"No, he's retired. Collects social security and his army pension, and has some savings from his security-business days. He does all right. Has everything he needs – he's driven the same truck since forever and has lived here for twenty years. Everything's paid for, and he doesn't want for anything. It's not a bad situation."

"I'll say. He seems content."

"I'm not so sure about that, but he's not hurting. And the ranch gives him something to do. He'd be bored out of his mind just sitting around all day."

"When did he retire?"

"About five years ago. Sold the company to his employees."

"You mentioned it did security?"

"That's right. Based in Austin. Did corporate work and some celebrity and diplomatic stuff. Bodyguards, that sort of thing."

"I wouldn't think there'd be a huge demand for that in Austin."

"You'd be surprised. And he was statewide. Did a lot down in Houston. Some in Dallas and San Antonio, too. It was a good living. Enabled him to pay off the ranch and put me through school, and still retire at fifty. Not a terrible deal."

"No, not bad at all. What did you major in?"

"Archeology, believe it or not. I should have taken a harder look at what being an archeologist pays, though, before I put in all the work. And maybe considered how many slots there are any given year for each wave of new grads."

"No luck?"

"Not even a bite. I've been out of school for three years, beating my head against the wall. I finally wound up doing clerical work to make ends meet. Dad invited me back home when he heard about it. He said I could do just as well applying for positions from here as from my apartment in Austin. Basically, I was just working to pay for the rent, my car, and my expenses. By the time the tax man took a bite and I'd fed myself each month, I was back to square one."

"I know that feeling."

"It sucked having to move home, but what was the point in working at a job I hated just to run in place? Now I do some bookkeeping for a few of the businesses in town, and freelance on research jobs whenever they come up over the web. Way less stress, and I've got more to show for it in the end. The only part that doesn't sit well with me is having to live with my dad, which makes me feel like a loser sometimes."

"You shouldn't. A lot of people are in the same position. I probably contacted every paper in the country looking for a gig, with no takers. The last few years haven't been kind."

"You can say that again. And he was right about one thing – I have a lot more time to apply for jobs, maybe ten positions a week. It's only a matter of persistence until something pops."

"What about teaching? Can't you do that?"

"I'm not interested in regurgitating what I learned for a living quite yet. I'd hoped to work for a museum or, better yet, in the field on a dig somewhere. Right now that's just a dream." She gave him a sidelong glance. "What about you? Are you thinking about going to South America and following in your dad's footsteps?"

Drake stopped rinsing and turned to her. "What?"

Allie gave him a small smile. "What, what? Don't tell me it didn't occur to you."

"It actually hadn't. I don't do stuff like that. It's crazy. Plus, how would I even go about it? I don't know anything about finding lost cities." He shook his head. "Nope. Not for me. I'm in the same boat you are. Filling out apps for a reporter job. My degree's in journalism. I'm not cut out to be some kind of adventurer living off roots and berries in the bush."

"It's not like that. Although it's funny because that's exactly what I did study to do. But different strokes. What do you do to make ends meet?" she asked.

He told her about his bounty-hunting sideline, and it was her turn to be incredulous. "No way. You mock hunting for lost treasure, and you chase felons for a bounty? Are you kidding me?"

"It's not that hard."

"Are you going to get your own TV show? Drake the Bounty Hunter? That's too funny," she teased, genuinely amused. "So, fill me in. Do bounty hunters do well with the chicks? Is it like being in a rock band or something? Do you go all Clint Eastwood on the ladies? Give 'em the steely eyed squint and pretend you're shooting them in the bar?" She pointed her finger at him and made a *pow* sound when she brought her thumb down like a hammer. "Hey, baby. They call me 'The Hunter.' And I'll take you down."

Drake had to laugh at the merriment dancing in her eyes – she was clearly delighted with herself, and it was infectious.

"You should try stand-up comedy instead of archeology. You're a natural."

"Maybe. But you didn't answer my question."

"I do all right," he said, hating how defensive he sounded.

"That's not what I meant. It was just a joke. Did I touch a nerve?"

"Not at all. I've got a whole harem of hoes. 'Cause that's how I roll."

She returned to washing the last dish. "I have no doubt."

"How about you? Line of suitors outside the gate?"

She chuckled good-naturedly. "Hardly. Around here, a classy pick-up line is asking whether I'd like to do beer bongs in the back of some yeehaw's truck. Let's just say I'm keeping my options open while I'm in transition."

"You don't like beer bongs?"

"Back to the subject. No girlfriend?"

"Just the hoes."

"Besides them."

"Can't tie me down…"

She eyed him with amusement. "That's actually pretty popular these days, looking at the bestseller lists." He almost choked on his tongue as he struggled with a comeback. She waved him off. "I think my dad's waiting for you in the living room. Probably wants to talk about old times some more."

"Oh. Right. Sorry for taking up so much of his day. It's just…I never knew my father, so finding his best friend…I'm just being greedy, I guess."

"I don't know about that. Seems natural to me. Go on. You've kept him waiting long enough, regaling me with your bounty-hunting stories."

"I didn't tell you any."

"We can save those for another time. Should I call you Hunt? Hunter? Which do you like better?"

"'Hey you' works pretty well."

Drake returned to the living room, where Jack sat with a photo album in his lap. He looked up when Drake settled into the couch again, and passed it over to him.

"There's some shots of me and your dad in there. Back in the day. A few from South America. Not many. We weren't playing tourist."

Drake opened it and went through the pages. There, and there, a photograph of his father. Grinning as he held up a fish. Another where he was toasting the camera with a half-empty beer. On the next page, Jack and Ford standing by a pair of Harley-Davidsons, wearing bandannas and sunglasses.

"You're welcome to take any you like. I've looked at them all enough. About time they made it out of here."

"That's…I'll probably take you up on that, Jack. Thank you."

"Think nothing of it. Oh, and I almost forgot. I have something for you. Something of your father's I've been keeping for over twenty years. His pride and joy."

"Really?" Drake said, looking up from the album. "What?"

Jack rose and crossed the room to an armoire. With a nod to Drake, he swung the two wooden doors wide. Drake caught a glimpse of a row of rifles as Jack leaned over and slid one of the drawers open. When he turned, he had a cloth-wrapped bundle. He returned to the coffee table and handed it to Drake, who took it, staring at it with open curiosity.

"He never went anywhere without it down in South America. Called it his equalizer," Jack said as Drake unrolled the cloth.

Inside was the largest knife Drake had ever seen, with a black wooden handle smooth as glass. He slid the blade free of the sheath and held it up to the light, the stainless steel shiny as chrome, the top of the blade a line of wicked saw teeth, the curved cutting edge sharp enough to shave with.

"That's a survivor Bowie knife an old friend of mine custom made for him back in the day. The man was a master, long gone to his reward. Twelve-inch blade, Pakkawood handle. You could practically use it as a machete. Indestructible," Jack said with reverence. "Feel the heft? Balanced. Fits neatly in your hand, and all business."

"This was his?"

"He loved that knife. Had a thing for it."

Drake slipped it back into the sheath and inspected the hand tooling.

"Your dad stamped that himself," Jack said.

"What do the initials stand for?" Drake asked, noting the stylized script.

"He named it after the two most precious things in the world to him. His son and his wife. DAR. Drake and Anna Ramsey. He used to parade around the campfire, waving it like a pirate after a few drinks, saying it over and over. Dar. *Darrr*. It was funny, but it got old. Anyway, there it is. DAR's yours now. Which is as it should be."

Drake set the knife on the table and sat back against the soft sofa cushions. "Thank you, Jack. You know my mom passed away six years ago?"

"I heard through the grapevine. I'm sorry. She was a saint."

Drake swallowed hard. "She was. Cancer got her, but for a long time I thought it was heartbreak. She never got over him. You could tell. She had plenty of offers, but she wasn't interested. I used to hate my dad for it. I blamed him. And now that I know that he abandoned us to go chase after some stupid dream…"

"It wasn't a stupid dream. He believed he knew where the treasure was, and that it would secure your family's future for generations. He made a sacrifice. And he did it for you. That was all he ever talked about. You and your mother, and how different your lives would be once he'd found the treasure." Jack glowered, and then his expression softened. "You probably see it as a selfish decision. It was anything but. I understand how you feel, but you couldn't be more wrong."

"It doesn't feel wrong."

"It should now that you have all the information." Jack paused. "Son, I've been around for a while. Let me tell you something. You don't have the right to judge others. You can only judge yourself. I know at your age you think you know it all, but you're not the absolute barometer of good and bad, and you got your dad plain wrong. Was he perfect? Hell no. But he was a good man, and you can take that to the bank."

Drake didn't say anything. He reached up and rubbed his eyes, tired from only three hours of sleep the prior night and the long day.

"I should go. I would like some of the pictures, thank you. And thanks for keeping the knife for me, and for giving me a feel for who my father really was. It means a lot to me."

"He would have wanted you to have it. Drake, he loved you more than you can imagine. Both of you."

A crash sounded from the kitchen, followed by a muted curse from Allie.

"Honey, are you okay?" Jack called, pushing himself to his feet.

Allie's voice rang out. "Yes. Sorry, Dad. Damn slippery fingers. I dropped a dish. Don't worry. Everything's fine."

Jack lowered himself back into the chair, and they sat quietly as Drake paged through the photo album. After a few minutes he set it down next to the knife.

"Jack, thanks for the hospitality. If it's all right, I'll be back in the morning. Is there a decent motel around here?"

"Hell, boy, you don't need to go to any motel. If you don't mind a little dust and Allie's snoring sawing through the walls, you can take the third bedroom. Got plenty of space."

"I feel like I've imposed on you enough."

"No skin off my back."

Drake smiled. "I thought you were going to shoot me earlier?"

"You try to sneak into Allie's room, you can damn sure bet that prophecy's going to come true. Knife or no knife, a double load of twelve-aught buck'll stop you dead."

"I can hear you threatening the guest, you know. I'm not deaf," Allie called from the kitchen.

"You mind your beeswax. I was just laying down the ground rules."

The kitchen doorway darkened as her slim form moved into it, the warm glow of the lights behind framing her like a soft halo.

Her brow scrunched as she frowned. "Right. I heard. No rape. Good rule. We should have it stamped on the soap. Or I could embroider it on the pillows. *Y'all come back now, but no rapin', ya hear?*"

"Maybe this isn't such a good idea–" Drake started, but Allie cut him off.

"No, now *I* insist. And you better bar your door. Double lock it. Because those Texas women can eat you alive, like a black widow. Wanton lust on the plains. Isn't that right, Dad?"

Jack regarded Drake with a tired expression and shrugged. "You may need that little knife of yours."

Drake looked at Allie and grinned. "I'll be fine. I know karate."

Chapter Eleven

The night crawled on as Drake tossed and turned, his mind running at hyper-speed to process Jack's revelations about his father. He eventually drifted off at two a.m., no soft knock on the door and invitation to romantic interludes forthcoming.

He awoke to pans clattering in the kitchen and the mouthwatering smell of bacon and coffee. After a hurried shower in a claw-foot antique tub, he ran a comb through his wet hair, pulled on a shirt and jeans, and made his way down the hall to Allie in the kitchen. Jack was watching her go about her chores from the dining room table, a steaming mug of coffee before him.

"There he is. How did you sleep?" Jack asked.

"Fine. Like a baby," Drake lied, surreptitiously eyeing Allie as she broke three eggs into a bowl and expertly whipped them with a fork.

"Hope scrambled's okay. It's the only thing I know how to make," Allie said.

"I love scrambled eggs. Especially with bacon."

"Then you're in luck. Coming right up."

Breakfast was delicious. When Jack had finished, he moved into the living room with his second cup of coffee and took up his familiar position in the easy chair. Drake joined him after being shooed out of the kitchen, his offer to help with the dishes rebuffed. He sat down across from Jack and went through the photo album again, carefully removing a half-dozen snapshots before closing the cover.

"I'll get these copied and bring them back. I'm sure there's some place with a scanner around here," he said.

"No need. They're yours. With my compliments, young man. Your father would have wanted that."

"No, really. They're just as much yours as mine. A part of history." Drake paused, having grappled for most of the night with whether to come clean with his father's friend. He took a deep breath before continuing. "Jack, I haven't been completely honest with you. When I told you that Patricia left a few notes, I mean. She left a lot more than that. I've…I've also got my dad's journal."

Jack stared at him and leaned forward, his tone hushed. "The journal? You have it?"

"Yes. Patricia left it to me. I just didn't understand its significance until I spoke with you. I didn't realize that it was anything more than the notes of a deluded man chasing a dream."

As Jack took a pull on his coffee, Drake could have sworn that his hand shook, just a little.

"So you've read it?"

Drake nodded. "I have. Taken in context, it's a remarkable document. What was missing was context, which you provided." Drake hesitated. "But there's more to the story than just Paititi. Which might explain why ex-KGB thugs were in the mix." Drake told him about the government forcibly recruiting his father, and when he was done, Jack looked like he'd been gut-punched.

Jack set his cup down. "I had no idea your father was working for the government. That's almost impossible for me to believe. I wonder what they wanted, and why he never said anything…" Jack squinted at Drake suspiciously. "Why are you telling me this?"

"It was his last entry in the journal." He stopped, unsure of how to continue. "And I'm telling you because I wanted your take on it…and because I'm thinking that having the journal may present an opportunity."

"An opportunity?" Jack repeated. "What kind of opportunity?"

"I know this will sound crazy, but a chance to fulfill my father's vision. To succeed where he failed."

Jack frowned and shook his head. "No. Absolutely not. Your father was killed chasing that phantom. I'd say that's enough Ramseys sacrificed on the Inca altar."

"I agree. Which is why I'm not sure what to do. Part of me is looking at my life up until now, and realizing it's a big fat zero. I live in a society I don't particularly like, doing a job I hate, and I have no…nothing to work toward. I thought I wanted to be an investigative reporter, but now I'm beginning to think that's just another side of the same coin my father was living. He was researching where the greatest treasure of all time was hidden, and I chose a career researching big stories. The point is, it's all research. But until I read the journal and talked to you, I didn't know why I'm so drawn to it. Maybe it's genetic. Something in the Ramsey blood. I don't know."

"Son, I'm going to tell you straight. Paititi has killed more men than Everest. It's not something you just sort of try to do because you're bored. That jungle takes no prisoners. It's filled with every variety of toxic threat on the planet and then some. Snakes, spiders the size of your fist, alligators, jaguars, Indians who would just as soon cut your throat as spit, drug traffickers, smugglers, thieves…it's the most dangerous place on earth. Nobody in their right mind would go in there. Nobody."

"Maybe I'm not in my right mind. Maybe my father wasn't, either. But at least he felt alive. I don't. I feel like I'm sleepwalking through the only life I get, like I'm playing a part where they got the casting wrong. I couldn't have put my finger on it before, but it's taking shape now."

"Your father's dead because of that damned treasure, boy."

"No, he's dead because he was murdered by Russians. You said it yourself. I think we've got it wrong. Blaming his objective for something that happened along the way."

Jack snorted derisively. "Why are you telling me this?"

"Because if I decide to go after Paititi, I'm going to need help."

Jack stood. "You're gonna need more than help. You're gonna need a thorough psych workup, because you've got a screw loose. I knew I should've shot you when I saw you."

Drake met his gaze without flinching. "Maybe you should have. But it's a little late now."

"Don't bet on it."

"Look, I'm not saying I want to go charging into the jungle. I'm saying that I'm thinking about it. I've got some money and a lot of time. That seems like a good start."

"You've got exactly none of the survival skills you'd need to last even a week."

"Maybe. Or maybe you're underestimating me. I'm a quick learner." Drake rose and collected the photo and the knife. "I just thought I'd see how you reacted. You obviously think it's a bad idea."

"Where's the journal?" Jack asked.

"In a safe place."

"Maybe not safe enough." Jack took a slow sip of his coffee and studied some spots on the carpet by his feet, obviously weighing what to say. "I was on the phone this morning. Talking to my buddies in the intelligence community. You weren't the only one doing a lot of thinking last night. I started doing some of my own, and at about one a.m., I got on my computer and looked up the details of Patricia's death. That crash…it looks sketchy. They estimate she had to be going a hundred when she sailed off the road. A hundred. The woman owned a flower shop and drove a frigging Buick. That's not someone who joyrides at triple digits at night."

"What are you saying?"

"That I smelled a rat. I got a bad feeling in my stomach, so early this morning I called one of my buds. The one who works with an alphabet agency agreed to check on something for me."

"What?"

"Whether those two Russians are still alive."

"And?"

"I'm waiting for a call back."

"That's it? You're waiting for a call?"

"What is it with you? Yes. That's it. But if they're alive, and anywhere but in the middle of Siberia, you've got a real problem. Or maybe I should say, we do. You were able to track me down in only a couple of days, so that means I could have a problem, too."

"You can't possibly think–"

"I don't jump to conclusions. I plan. I prepare. But I'll tell you – on its face, that accident is just plain wrong. That's the canary in the coalmine. I could ignore it and be surprised, but that's not the kind of surprise I like. Or I can put out feelers and see what comes back. That's what I did. Now I'm waiting. A smart man takes small but significant actions and waits to evaluate their effect."

"Nobody knows I've got the journal."

"Who gave it to you? How exactly did you come by it?"

"An attorney. In Seattle."

"Then he knows. And so does anyone he's talked to about it."

"No, he only knows I got a package. That's all." Drake stopped. "Except...you're right. He saw me reading it, so at the very least he now knows I got a book from Patricia."

"Look. It could be nothing. Could be Patricia decided life wasn't what it should be, and took that way out. Could be she was drunk, or high, and got her thrills in a way that wasn't wise. But that's not the Patricia I knew. That woman was conservative, deliberate, and very smart. The obituary says she owned a flower shop. That says it all. Does that sound like the kind of person who guns it to a hundred on a dead-man's curve?"

"Not really."

Jack's tone hardened. "Who knows you came to see me?"

"Nobody."

"Nobody knows you're in Texas? You're positive?"

Drake stared at the ceiling, a sense of dread creeping through him. "Crap. My boss. I told him I was coming to Austin."

"Then we already have two people who could compromise you. The attorney and your boss. What else haven't you told me?"

"Now you're being seriously paranoid."

Jack ignored his comment. "What was the attorney's name?"

"Lynch. Michael Lynch. In Seattle. Why?"

"You got a number for him?"

"Sure. Let me double-check it on my phone." Drake pulled up his calls and thumbed through them until he found the number. He gave it, along with the address, to Jack.

Jack grunted. "Stay put. I'm going to go do some research. You want some more coffee?"

"Sure. What do you mean, some research?"

"Call it a hunch. If I was running an op to find the journal, I'd be looking for whoever handled Patricia's affairs."

"How could they even know that?"

"How would you do it if you were skip-tracing someone?"

Drake blinked twice. "I'd talk to her landlord. See if someone put a stop on the mail. Nose around to see who requested a death certificate."

Jack nodded and reappraised Drake. "Huh. Maybe you do stand a chance, after all. Look, I'm not saying anyone's after you. But it never hurts to be cautious. I told your dad that a hundred times. Now I'm telling you. Always expect the unexpected. It's like playing chess. All strategy. Predict what your opponent will do next, and then prepare for the move. Know your options. Think two moves ahead so you can block him. And be proactive once you understand your opponent. Otherwise you'll be reacting, which means he's controlling the pace and the direction of the game."

"Remind me not to play chess with you."

"I'm the least of your worries if those two are on the loose – or worse, if they told someone and it's a new player."

"Why? Why would new players be bad?" Drake asked.

"Better the evil you know. And I know these two. Again, if you can cut the learning curve down and understand what you're dealing with early, you have an advantage. Anyway, I'll be back in a few. Might want to touch base with your boss to see if anyone's been looking for you – suspicious calls, that sort of thing. Tell him to get in touch with you if anything weird happens."

"Weird."

"Right."

Jack trundled back to his bedroom and Drake went into the kitchen. Allie stared at him without expression as he set his cup in the sink.

"I heard some of that. Are you really thinking about trying to find the treasure?"

"There's a big difference between thinking and doing."

Her high-wattage blue eyes seemed to bore holes through him. "That sounds like it would be incredible. Really cool. I mean, it's what I dream of doing, you know? Hell, it's what I studied to do."

"It sounds like your dad doesn't think it's a good idea."

"You let other people make your decisions for you a lot?" she asked.

He eyed her. "So you think I should do it?"

She gave him a smirk. "You're a big boy. If you're afraid to try on Dad's shoes, I don't blame you. Bail skips sound a lot more interesting than treasure hunting for billions."

Drake bristled at her tone. "I'm not afraid."

"Right. Obviously."

"Don't hold back if you have an opinion."

"What do I know? I'm just a disinterested bystander. The kitchen help. That's all. Now if you'll excuse me, I think it's time to mop the floors. Then I'll go milk the cows and sew some shirts. You know what they say – woman's work and all…"

"I'm not saying you don't have a point."

"I'm sorry. Would you like anything else to eat or drink? Or maybe your clothes washed?"

Drake held up his hands. "Can we call a truce? I don't know why you're upset, but whatever I said or did, I'm sorry."

She folded her arms across her chest. Her ample chest, he noted, the buttons of her flannel shirt straining to contain the swell of her breasts. "I'm sorry too. It's just that nothing like this ever happens to me, and here you are, with no training or education, with the opportunity of a lifetime dropped in your lap, and you're waffling. If it was me, I'd have been packing my bags at first light. But hey. It's not my choice. It's yours. I accept that."

"Thank you." He offered her a smile.

"You're welcome." She turned away and opened the pantry, muttering, almost inaudibly, "Even if you're being a pussy."

Drake elected not to push it. He sensed that whatever was bugging Allie was bigger than her opinions about how he should handle the journal, and he didn't want to get in the middle of it. He decided on a graceful retreat to the living room, and pretended he hadn't heard her.

Thinking through Jack's concerns, he retrieved his phone and called Harry. Betty answered on the second ring.

"New Start Bail Bonds," she chirped.

"Betty, it's Drake. Can I speak to Harry?"

"Sure, hon. Just a sec."

Harry's voice boomed from the tinny phone speaker. "Well, if it isn't the prodigal. How's it hanging, my man?"

"Going well. Day two in the land of big. How about you?"

"More crooks need another shot at life than usual. Thank goodness. And they're all innocent! I'm the luckiest guy on earth – every single one of 'em's as free of guilt as a newborn. They tell me so. And I believe them. The system's just keeping them down. Oppressing them, and all."

"Yeah, well, I'm glad business is good. Listen, has anyone asked about me?"

"What, you feeling unimportant? Like who?"

"I don't know. Have there been any calls asking for me? Trying to get info?"

Harry turned serious. "This have anything to do with why you got out of town?"

"No. Nothing like that."

Harry paused. "You sure, kid? You can tell me."

"Nah. I just wanted to know if anyone's sniffing around. I can't say why, but it's nothing illegal. I promise."

"You and every other derelict that walks through my doors."

"Harry…"

"I'm just busting your chops. No, everything's copasetic. Nobody's asking about you. Remember, you're not an employee, so you don't show up on most records."

"I know. Hey, if anything weird happens with the computers, or if anyone noses around, would you try to get as much info as possible and call me?"

Harry didn't say anything for a long beat. "Now you got me worried. What are you into here, Drake? What did you do?"

"I didn't do anything. I swear."

"That's your story…"

"…and I'm sticking to it," Drake said, finishing his sentence for him.

"Then I'm cool with that. Will do on calling you. Meanwhile, go get some of that Texas hospitality. Austin's a college town. Lots of coeds." The leer in Harry's voice was exaggerated. Even though he'd been happily married for fifteen years, he liked to live vicariously through Drake.

"I hadn't noticed."

"Take care, kid."

"You too, Harry. And thanks."

Relieved, and reconsidering Jack's alarm, he wondered whether maybe the old man had been in one too many firefights and was seeing danger behind every tumbleweed. Sitting in the living room, miles from anything, with the biggest threat to him noisily cleaning the kitchen, it all seemed a little…overblown.

Of course, there was the open question about Patricia's accident, but he suspected that was unanswerable. He'd never met the woman, so how could he possibly know what demons she was battling? Maybe she'd grown tired of waking up every day and drawing breath. It happened, he knew. Each morning some people decided they can't go on, and while most would find a reason to continue, there would be a few who felt the struggle just wasn't worth it. Perhaps Patricia had been one of those, where the future was more frightening than eternal nothingness.

By the time Jack returned, Drake had just about convinced himself that this was all drama created by a bored man with time on his hands. One look at Jack's face told Drake that he'd gotten that badly wrong. Jack sat down and tossed a single piece of paper onto the coffee table.

"That your boy?" he asked gruffly.

Drake picked up the paper and began reading the article Jack had printed out. As he did, the color drained from his face, and for a moment he thought he was going to black out.

Chapter Twelve

When he was finished skimming the article, he placed the paper back on the table and took several deep breaths. Jack raised one eyebrow and said nothing, waiting for Drake to comment. Eventually Drake regained his composure and did.

"Yes, that's him."

"That's what I was afraid of. That's the Russians' style. Brutal, obvious, and completely unconcerned about the law. Unless you think a torture-murder, as the papers are calling it, is unrelated."

"I...I don't know what to think."

"Well, I do. I don't need to wait to hear back from my spook friend. Whether it's the same two or their newer twins, they're coming after the journal. Which makes you nothing but a liability."

Drake bristled. "Then I'll leave."

"That won't solve anything. Guys like this just keep coming. You weren't at the attorney's, and that didn't stop them from slicing him up like a Christmas turkey, did it? Do you really think they'll come in, ask Allie and me some polite questions, and then apologize for the bother and leave when we tell them that we have no idea what they're talking about?"

"I just talked to my boss. Nobody's asking about me."

"That's your first lucky break. Maybe the trail stopped at the attorney. Did he have your address?"

Drake thought about it. "Yes."

"Then you are, as they used to say in the game, blown. You can't go back home. They'll be waiting." He hesitated, calculating quickly. "Damn. You have a cell phone, don't you?"

"Of course."

Jack held out his hand. "Give it to me."

"Why?"

Jack scowled. "Drake, let's get one thing straight. Not to be rude, but when I tell you to do something, do it. Your life may depend on it. This is not make-believe. You're in very real danger. Two people have died so far. I say 'so far' because I can guarantee that this is only the start. If you want to stay alive, don't ask questions. Just give me the phone. Now."

Drake bit back the surge of anger at the older man's tone and told himself that it wasn't personal – Jack was used to issuing terse commands, he could tell, and had probably never learned to soften his style. He handed Jack his cell, and Jack flipped the back open and removed the battery. "I don't know if these have a secondary power source in them, but we have to assume so. You can be tracked with your phone. Anywhere in the world. You say you've got a photographic memory?"

"I said almost photographic."

"What does that mean? Almost?"

"It means it's almost photographic. I don't know how to explain it. I can see a document I read once, clearly, but it will fade over time."

"Can you memorize your phone contacts and email lists?"

"I already have. It's not that big a list."

"All right, then. Come with me."

Drake followed Jack to the rear door and out into the sunshine. They moved to the barn, and once inside, Jack went to a tool shed and opened it. When he turned back to face Drake, he held a sledgehammer.

"What are you going to do?" Drake asked.

"What do you think?"

They walked back outside into the brisk morning air. Jack tossed the phone onto the hard-packed dirt and with a single powerful swing, crushed it. Plastic pieces flew everywhere, and Drake watched as his lifeline to the real world disintegrated before his eyes.

"Did you really have to do that?" he asked.

"Depends. Do you want your appendages cut off and fed to you, one at a time?"

"Let's assume that's a no."

"Did you read the article? That's what they'll do if they find you. Or maybe they'll be more creative. A blowtorch. Acid. Broken glass. Bleach. Depends on how much they believe you when you tell them where the journal is. Of course, they'll still kill you when all's said and done, but by the time they do, you'll be begging for death, so they'll actually be doing you a favor."

"You aren't kidding, are you?"

Jack leaned aside and spat. "Drake, do I seem possessed of a whimsical nature?"

Drake studied his expression. "Not really."

"Then you can assume I don't kid."

"What…what do I do now? I mean, assuming these guys are looking for me?"

"Oh, I think that's a safe assumption. But that's a good question. The problem, as I see it, is the same as your father had after he told the Russians to go to hell. There's only one way you'll ever be safe. And you're not going to like it. Hell, I don't like it."

"You…you can't be thinking…"

"We need to get out of here and head to South America. The only way they're going to quit is if you find Paititi and the treasure's out of their grasp. As long as they think it's there and that you have information that could get them to it, you're dead meat. And unfortunately, so am I. And so's Allie. That's just the way it'll play. It's not right or wrong. It just is. But my biggest problem is that you're not ready. How much do you know about hand-to-hand combat?"

"Some. Like I told you, I did take martial arts."

"Ever been in a street fight?"

"A couple of times I got into it with bail skips."

"How about weapons? You ever fired a gun?"

"No."

"I don't suppose you've had any survival training."

"Nope."

Jack sighed and then went back into the barn and put the sledge away. When he came out, he waved a hand towards the black plastic pieces all over the ground. "Pick those up. Don't leave any, or when they get here, they'll find whatever you missed, and they'll know we're onto them."

Drake watched him walk back toward the house. "What are you going to do?" he called after Jack.

"Try to explain to Allie why she's in mortal danger, and then load a bunch of guns before I pack a bag and empty the safe. I want to be out of here in twenty minutes."

"Where are you going?"

"We. Where are *we* going." Jack turned and studied Drake. "You'll find out when we get there."

~ ~ ~

A kit of pigeons flapped from the sidewalk in front of the downtown building's tired green façade. The New Start Bail Bonds sign blinked on and off, its "Open 24 Hours" tagline not entirely accurate since the option after seven at night was to contact a call center that would in turn take a message and forward it to Harry's phone. Scattered clouds drifted lazily across the turquoise sky, the prior day's storm having hit with full force in the afternoon and spent itself by midnight. The air smelled like wet grass and exhaust from the nearby freeway, and the birds flapped higher before turning as one and shooting south.

Betty had been out to lunch for ten minutes when the front door chimed, alerting Harry that someone was there. That was always how his day played – business came on its own schedule, and it was always a big hurry, someone's freedom at stake.

"Just a second," he called from his office, and when he didn't hear a response, he put down his pen and rose. "Hello?"

Nothing.

He opened his door and stepped out to find two men in long overcoats standing by Betty's desk.

"Can I help you?" Harry asked.

Vadim grimaced slightly, and Harry realized as his face cracked that it was his attempt at a smile, the effect as inviting as the toothy grin of a moray eel.

"I certainly hope so."

Chapter Thirteen

Drake hoisted his bag, his new knife clutched in his free hand, and followed Jack to the vehicles. Allie was already in her Toyota and would accompany him to the car lot in Austin to drop the rental off before driving to meet her father at an undisclosed location. Jack had warned him that he wanted to sever all ties with the system immediately, and cautioned against using his credit cards on the off chance the Russians were tracking them.

The landline had rung when Drake had joined him inside the house, and after a hurried discussion, Jack had set down the receiver and turned to Drake, who'd taken his usual position on the sofa.

"The Russians were released from Siberia seven months ago. Unbelievable. They served almost twenty years, and their sentences were for life, but apparently a tribunal is reexamining all the trials from that period, and determined that the sentences were overly harsh."

"So they're on the loose."

"That's correct. They're out and want the journal. Makes sense, because without it they weren't able to find Paititi."

"Then what are we going to do?"

Jack studied Drake's face, noting the resolve in his gaze. "We need to put some serious distance between ourselves and them, because there's not a doubt in my mind they'll find us eventually if we let down our guard. Do you have a passport?"

"Sure. But it's in my safe deposit box back home."

"Well, hell. Let me think about that some. In the meantime, drop off the car, don't call anyone or even hint at where you are, and maybe, just maybe, we'll all get to live to see tomorrow."

"How much did you tell Allie?"

"Enough. She's wildly bright and knows me well, so she's up to speed and understands we've got to take action. And she's not a bad shot."

"She's got a gun?"

"Yup. I gave her one of the SIG Sauers. She's had a lot of time on it, so she knows how to use it." Jack smiled. "She was a tomboy growing up, and a girl in Texas learns how to shoot if she lives on a ranch."

"That's good to know."

"Just don't piss her off. She's packing."

Drake glanced at her sitting in the car. "Noted."

Jack stopped at the truck and dropped his duffel in the bed next to the three gun cases he'd toted out earlier. He slipped a bulging backpack off his shoulder and slid it onto the passenger seat. "Drive the speed limit. Don't attract attention. Get rid of the car, be pleasant to the counter clerk, and get out of there. We're probably ahead of the game, but that won't last forever. If we're lucky, we just bought ourselves enough breathing room so that I can get you at least halfway ready before we take off. This isn't the kind of job you want to learn on the fly if you can help it, because any mistakes once we're in the field could cost you, or me, or Allie, our lives."

Drake shook his head. "You're really planning to let her come?"

"Try stopping her. I thought she was going to shoot me when I suggested she stay in the States. I'm serious. This, other than the murderous psychos stalking us, is her fantasy adventure."

"Other than that."

"Boy, you're going to have hours to talk to her on the road, and you're welcome to try to talk her out of it. My money's on her."

"That's encouraging."

"I haven't lied to you yet. You got everything?"

"Yes."

"All right, then. No point in dawdling. Get going. She'll tail you to Austin." He held out his hand.

Drake shook it, noting the hard calluses – they were a workingman's hands. He climbed behind the wheel, twisted the key and put the car into reverse, and then executed a three-point turn and followed Jack's truck out to the road.

Jack kept going past the on-ramp, bound for parts unknown, as Drake and Allie pulled onto the highway. Once up to speed, Drake checked every few minutes to make sure that Allie was still behind him. A vision of her flashing blue eyes and sultry looks filled his thoughts. He couldn't figure her out – one minute she seemed friendly, and then the next she was cold and distant. But whatever was going on in her head, Drake couldn't afford to spend much time worrying about it.

They were headed to a mystery destination that Jack had simply described as 'someplace safe,' with a truckload of guns and little else. Drake had already decided that he wasn't going to tell Jack that he had the journal with him. That was his only ace in the hole, and he wasn't going to give it up easily. The truth was that its actual whereabouts weren't as important as the information in it, which he needed more time to pore over. His read had been cursory, and he hadn't been as interested in the minutiae of his father's reasoning about which patches of jungle were the most likely candidates as he had in the overall sense of the man he'd never known, and never would.

The rental clerk was sunny and efficient, and Drake was out of the office in less than five minutes and pacing to Allie's waiting car. He'd paid cash, and the attendant had torn up the credit card form in front of him, so theoretically the trail ended at Austin airport, assuming the Russians could even access credit data. He'd done enough skip-tracing to know that many private investigation firms skirted the edges of the law, and that one could get banking records, phone records, and whatever one wanted if the money and motivation were sufficient. All it would take was one meeting, and within forty-eight hours his whole life would be laid out on someone's table, his every financial move tracked by a system that frowned on cash.

Drake slipped into the passenger seat, noting that Allie smelled great, as he'd noticed she did when washing dishes. Her face looked as tranquil as an angel's, with not a care in the world, for which he envied her no end.

"No complications?" she asked as she coasted out of the lot.

"Other than my life being turned upside down by this? No. All good."

They drove in silence for five minutes, the radio on low, an insipid pop tune crooning about timeless love and shaking that groove thang.

"Where are we headed?" Drake asked.

"My dad's got a friend with a spread between San Antonio and Corpus Christi. Only uses it maybe four months a year to dove and pheasant hunt. He's some kind of Richie Rich type. It's about the size of Connecticut. No exaggeration."

"Wow. That's convenient."

Allie shrugged. "My father knows plenty of government types that seem to have an awful lot of money. I don't ask questions. I learned that from him." She sneaked a peek at his profile. "How are you set up for cash?"

"Actually, right now, great. Probably for the first time in my life. I got almost thirty grand from Patricia, with another seventy coming. So I'm good for a while."

"You should talk to my dad about what it's going to cost to fund a jungle exploration. It can't be cheap."

"I will. I'm still kind of hoping there's a way out of this."

"Right. And I keep hoping for gelato that's good for you and tastes awesome."

He laughed. "How's that going?"

"My odds are better than yours."

The trip took several hours, and when they pulled off a narrow strip of pavement onto a dirt road, it seemed like civilization was a thousand miles away. The tops of mature groves of trees rustled in a lazy breeze, and the flatlands seemed to go on forever, the green of the earth blending hazily into the crystal blue of an endless sky. They bounced down the rutted lane for a quarter mile and dead-ended at an elaborate iron gate suspended from two brick posts. Chain-link fence ran as far as they could see along the property on either side.

"A big place," Drake commented as Allie climbed out of the driver's seat and approached the barrier. The padlock was open, and she unfastened the chain and pushed the gate wide before returning to the car and pulling through.

"Close it and lock it up."

"How do I know you won't leave me here?" Drake teased, but only partially.

"Don't tempt me."

He did as instructed and returned to the car. Allie eased it down the road, now little more than a track with two ruts in the grass. Ten minutes later they saw a brown two-story log structure nestled among tall oaks. Jack's truck was already parked at the side.

Jack materialized at the edge of the trees with a reel of fishing line in one hand. Allie parked next to the truck and they got out after she popped the trunk.

"Good. You made it," Jack said as he neared.

"Yup. No complications." Drake eyed the line. "What are you doing? Is there a stream around here?"

"Nope. I'm stringing a perimeter line so we know if anyone gets within a hundred yards of the house."

"You really think that's a danger here?" Drake asked skeptically.

"Rule number one: Never rely on luck. Prepare as though you only have a short amount of time before all hell breaks loose. If you're wrong, no harm done. You just got some practice. If you're right, you might have just saved your own life."

"How does it work?" Allie asked.

"I'm just finishing up. I've taken ten-yard lengths of line and secured them to the trees. Crude but effective. If anyone tries to sneak up on us at night, they trip the line, make a racket, and we're warned rather than sitting ducks. I'd prefer if I had a few dozen claymores, but you make do with what you have. Which is rule number two: There's always something you can use to defend yourself. Always. You just have to be resourceful."

"What about the drive?"

"That's next. We won't be leaving for a while, so anything that trips the line can be considered a threat."

"And then what?" Drake asked.

Jack smiled at Allie and turned to Drake. "My response to threats is to shoot first and ask questions later. That brings me to the next of today's chores. We have about five hours of light left. After you get settled, you'll be getting your first intensive shooting course."

Drake and Allie hauled their bags inside the lodge, which was primitive but serviceable, consisting of a large main area downstairs with a second story of open loft. They climbed the stairs and Drake stopped.

"There are only two beds up here."

"It won't matter. One of us will be downstairs on guard duty while the others are sleeping. That's how this kind of thing works. Three shifts of three hours apiece once we all tuck in," Allie explained.

"How do you know?"

"I've had to listen to his war stories all my life. After a while it rubs off."

Jack's voice called from outside. "Drake? Come on out here. Might as well learn how to string a decent trip line."

Allie nodded at him. "You heard the man. I'll blow the worst of the dust off things in here. Go do manly-man stuff. This is your chance to bond with Pops."

Drake joined Jack and watched as he carefully wound the monofilament around two tree trunks at knee height and tied crosspieces of line to either end. Satisfied with his work, he took empty soda cans and dropped some pebbles inside, shook them to confirm they would make suitable noise, and secured them to the crosspieces so they were resting on the ground, but the line was taut.

"A guy sneaking up on you in the dark, thinking he's got the upper hand, he's not going to be scouting for trip lines in the woods. Go ahead. Walk like you're headed to the house."

Drake did so, and when he connected with the invisible line, the two cans rattled.

"Nice. I get it."

"You hear that noise, you don't second-guess. You immediately get your ass in gear, because they'll know what it was too, and that they're blown. But it gives you an advantage, because instead of sleeping like a log, now you're up, armed, and ready to shoot."

"And you believe that there's any chance at all someone could find us here? How?"

"Son, if I try to second-guess everything my adversary knows, and I get even one thing wrong, I'm making assumptions that can get me killed. Sure, it's a slim chance, but it's still a chance, and all I've lost stringing these rigs is an hour of my time. See the logic? No assumptions. Just preparation."

Drake nodded. "It just seems like overkill."

"With preparation, there's no such thing. There's simply prudent measures, and laziness – and laziness gets you dead. So does complacency. An enemy knows that. They'll wait you out if they're smart and they have time. Wait for you to let down your guard. For you to believe it's all a big fat waste of energy. Next thing you know, you're holding your guts in your hand. I've seen it. You don't want to be that guy."

They moved back to the house. Jack reached into the truck bed, lifted out one of the rifle bags and handed it to Drake, and then retrieved a large metal suitcase.

"All right. Let's go for a walk. There's an area about two hundred yards from here that should do."

Jack led Drake to a clearing, where he arranged two sandbags on an old tree stump with paper targets taped to them. He set the suitcase on the ground, popped the lid, and glanced up at Drake.

"Go ahead and put the rifle down. We'll start with handguns."

Jack studied the four pistols in the foam-lined case, each with its own compartment, and lifted one out. He held it up and inspected it, ejected the magazine and verified that it had ammunition, and then slipped the magazine home and hefted it in his hand.

"This is a SIG Sauer P226 pistol. The magazine holds thirteen rounds of .40-caliber ammo. Now, a couple of things you need to know…"

The couple of things lasted half an hour, with Jack checking and rechecking Drake's understanding of safety measures and the mechanics of the gun. Drake was an apt pupil, following Jack's every word as if his life depended on it—since it did.

Satisfied that Drake respected the gun and could load and arm it, Jack next showed him the basic shooting stances, explaining the positives and negatives. Four magazines later, Drake had relaxed and was hitting the targets more often than not. When Jack remarked that he was beginning to find his primeval self, Drake eyed him skeptically.

Jack grunted. "You can doubt all you want, but I've been in shit enough times to know what I'm talking about. You've done karate; you told me so. Isn't there a point in the match when you allow your training to take over, and you leave yourself out of it? That's the secret to all the practice. You want this to become automatic, so when you're in a pinch, you can simply *do*, rather than think. In sports, professional athletes call it being in the zone. This is no different. To perform at peak, you need to be in the zone."

The afternoon went by quickly, and by the time Drake had been through his second box of ammunition, he was hitting the targets at twenty yards most of the time. Taking a break, Jack moved them back another twenty yards. Now the sandbags looked like dots.

"This is about as far away as you'll ever be when firing, if you expect to hit anything. The weapon will be accurate to fifty yards, but the chances of you actually hitting your target are slim to none unless everything's ideal. Remember – pistols are good for close-quarter shooting, but if the target's more than twenty or thirty yards away, go for a rifle every time, assuming you have the choice."

Rifles came next, and Jack showed him the basic operation of an AR-15 semiautomatic assault rifle. Drake's accuracy with that weapon was much higher at longer range, and he was feeling pretty good about himself when Jack burst his bubble.

"Something to remember. Most shots fired in combat don't hit their target. If we get into trouble, I'll do the shooting that will take out the bad guys. You shouldn't wait for the perfect shot. Just start blasting away when I tell you."

"Why? This seems pretty accurate to me."

"It is. Against a sandbag. But in an actual combat situation, everything happens fast, your nerves are tightly wound, you're probably shaking, the enemy is moving, it could be dark, sweat in your eyes…there are a lot of variables. The best advice is to avoid situations where it'll come down to shooting. If you do have to shoot, do so to get away, not to play hero. Because the chances of you doing any better than a combat soldier are pretty slim. And all due respect, you're not a marksman."

Jack saw the flare of anger on Drake's face. "Look, almost nobody is. That's why the perfect weapon for home defense is the pump-action twelve-gauge shotgun loaded with double-aught buck. It has a decent spread, which increases your chances of hitting something. For our nightly guard duty we'll be using those and our handguns. But the handguns are mostly for last resort, because if they've gotten close enough for you to stand a chance with one, they probably have a better chance with theirs."

Dusk was approaching when they called it a day and headed back to the lodge. The air was cold, with a mild breeze that rolled in waves across the tall grass, and the darkening sky was streaked with veins of peach and rose as the sun dropped into the horizon. Drake's shoulder ached from the hundreds of rifle rounds he'd fired, and he was dizzy from the ocean of information Jack had thrown at him. But in spite of that, he felt a confidence that had increased through the practice, and he resolved to spend the following day honing his gun skills, so that if he ever did have to use one, he'd be more than potentially dangerous.

The one takeaway he'd gotten from Jack's demeanor was that he was expecting the worst, and Drake had spent enough time around him already to understand why his father had placed so much stock in his abilities. Whatever Jack's faults might be, he was lethal, and his business was that of the warrior. If a battle-hardened fighter was worried, then Drake had every right to be, and wouldn't let down his guard, no matter what.

Chapter Fourteen

For the next two days, Drake drilled intensively with Jack, with Allie joining them to refresh her skills. By the second evening, Drake was able to hit any target Jack could. That night, after a relaxed dinner, they settled in for sleep, and Drake dozed dreamlessly until Allie woke him with a cautionary finger held to her lips and her SIG Sauer pistol clutched in her hand. Drake quickly shook off his drowsiness when he saw the fear in her eyes.

"What?" he whispered.

"I already woke my dad. One of the cans rattled. Get your stuff and be ready to move."

Drake sat up, fully dressed, as Jack had insisted they all sleep, and groped around in the dark for his shoes and backpack. He pulled them on and shouldered his bag, and then grabbed the Ruger shotgun he'd been assigned and flipped the safety off. With his free hand he lifted the SIG Sauer from the nightstand and quietly chambered a round, then decocked the hammer and slipped it into his waistband as he followed Allie down to the ground floor, feet feeling for each step, his eyes adjusting quickly to the near-total darkness.

Jack was near one of the windows at the front of the house, staring into the night, his weapon the modified AR-15, with an aftermarket burst mode, steadied against the back of a heavily stuffed chair. When he heard them approach, he leaned to the side and murmured.

"Something's out there. Allie, you take the rear of the house with your shotgun. Drake, you take the window on the right side by the vehicles."

"Wouldn't it make more sense to take one of the windows up on the second floor? Better visibility of the area," Drake murmured, and Jack shook his head.

"No. If all hell breaks loose, then you're trapped up there. This way, you can make a break for it. Just do as I say. If you see anything move, shoot it. Don't think, don't hesitate. Just blow it in two. But don't go off half-cocked. Make sure it's a human. No point in starting a war with a raccoon."

"Do you think it's a raccoon?" Allie whispered.

"No. Get to the back. If I was doing this, fifty-fifty chance I'd try to come in the back once the can went off."

"What are you going to do?" Drake asked.

"Once you're in position, I'm going to hit the exterior lights before they have a chance to cut the power. Assuming they haven't already. Maybe we'll get a look and be able to take them out." Jack swallowed hard. "Barring that, on my word, run for the truck and jump in the bed. Assuming I'm alive, that is. If I am, I'll drive us out of here. If I'm not, Drake, you do the driving, and Allie, you take the bed. Anyone tries to follow you, empty the shotgun at 'em. Understand?"

Drake and Allie nodded. Jack swallowed again. "All right. Go. Both of you. Now."

Allie trotted to the rear of the house and Drake moved to the right side, where there were two windows. He could make out the vehicles in the moonlight, but nothing else.

They listened for any hint of movement, but didn't hear anything. After a full two minutes of this, Jack lifted his rifle and stepped softly to the light switches. He took a deep breath and whispered again. "Here we go."

The lights illuminated the exterior area of the house for roughly forty feet, and when Jack ducked back to the window, he saw a fleeting human shape running away into the gloom. His rifle sounded like a howitzer in the confined space of the house, the window pane shattered from the first shot, and he fired half his magazine into the night using controlled, steady bursts.

"See anything?" he called out after he'd finished shooting.

"Negative," Allie said.

"No," Drake replied.

"I spotted one. Looked like he was carrying a pistol."

"Did you hit him?"

"Probably not, judging by how fast he was moving."

"So what now?"

"Two choices. We stay put, call the cops, and hope they arrive before these guys take another run at us; or we make a break for the truck and get out of here."

"What should we do?" Allie asked.

"I'd say go for the truck. Staying put, we're sitting ducks. If they cut the power, we're hosed, because then we're stuck in the house without options. By the time the police could be out here, anything that could have happened already would have. And there would be a lot of questions I don't feel much like answering – like what I'm doing with an automatic assault rifle."

Drake nodded. "Fine. How do we do this?"

"I go first. If I make it to the cab, I'll signal you, and then you come running and jump into the bed. Bring the guns. Anyone tries to follow, blow them to pieces."

"Won't they be waiting for us on the road?" Allie asked.

"If they are, they're screwed. There's a second gate about four miles through the property. It lets out on a completely different road. By the time they figure it out, we're history."

"And my car?"

"We can send someone for it once we're safe."

Allie nodded. "What if they shoot you?"

"Then you barricade the door, call the cops, and blast anything that moves. Besides, I'm betting they're high-tailing their way out of here right now. If I was sneaking up on a house and encountered not just a tripwire but automatic weapons, I'd be out of there. I thought I caught the flash of a pistol in the light. If that's all they've got, they'd be insane to try to take us on. Remember – they were thinking this would be easy, and now they're in a war and completely outgunned. Same situation, I'd rather live to fight another day instead of doing a kamikaze run."

Drake caught Allie's eye. "I hope you're right," he said.

"That's why I get the big bucks. Okay, here's what I'm going to do. I'll go to the kitchen door, and when I give the word, shut off the exterior lights. Then, when you hear the engine start, come running and jump into the truck bed. You hear any shooting, you stay put. Understand?"

"Yes," Drake said from his position at the back of the house.

Allie nodded again. "Be careful."

"All right. Here we go. Allie, you take the lights. On my signal."

Jack backed away from the window and, once clear of it, moved quickly to the kitchen door. With a last look at the rear of the house, Allie hurried to the lights, and Drake crossed to where Jack was standing, peering out the glass in the door through a gap in the curtain. Jack reached down and twisted the deadbolt open, and then turned to Allie.

"Now."

The lights extinguished, plunging the grounds into darkness. Jack swung the door open and stepped into the gloom, then bolted to the truck, which was twenty feet away. He scanned the area, confident that any watchers would be temporarily night blind from staring at the brightly lit house. With his free hand he pulled his keys from his jacket pocket and slid them into the door. The lock made a soft thunk as he opened it, and then he was in the cab, the overhead light having burned out long ago.

The engine started on the first try, a tribute to his regular meticulous maintenance, and then Allie and Drake were running for it. He felt their weight land in the bed, and at the second thunk, put the truck into reverse and accelerated toward the rear of the house.

Muzzle flashes exploded from near the barn, and a slug hit the front fender. Jack floored it, knowing that the more distance he gained, the harder he'd be to hit. He twisted the wheel and stood on the brakes, causing the big Chevy to pirouette on the loose dirt. When he'd spun 180 degrees, he slammed the shifter into drive and punched the gas again. The all-terrain tires gripped and the truck shot forward, but not before two rounds pounded into the tailgate. One punctured the rear of the cab, and Jack felt the burn of a bullet – a searing he knew too well. He reached down and felt his hip where the slug had gotten him, and when he brought his hand up, his fingers were shiny with blood. Ignoring the pain, he rolled his window down and called out.

"Anyone hit?"

Allie's yelled "no" was immediately followed by Drake's, and he exhaled a sigh of relief and illuminated his headlights, now far out of range of the pistols. The beams found the track, and he pulled onto the two ruts and gunned it for the far side of the property.

Every bounce felt like a hot poker to his hip as he watched in the rearview mirror for any signs of pursuit. He was just about convinced that they'd gotten clear when he saw a glint of moonlight off metal several hundred yards behind them. He sped up and dust flew up from the tires, leaving a thick cloud for the darkened chase vehicle to fight through.

Jack called out again, the wind whistling through the window. "Allie, we've got company. Get your shotgun ready. You too, Drake. If they get close, open up on them."

"What?" Allie cried, unable to hear.

He slowed and repeated his instruction, and when she signaled she understood, sped up again.

Gunfire sounded from the pursuit car, the shots starbursting in the gloom, but nothing hit the truck. Allie sat up with her shotgun and fired at the pursuers, pumped the gun, and fired again. Drake wedged himself against the side of the bed and swung his weapon around and added his to the mix, the boom deafening as the big gun slammed into his shoulder.

More shots barked from the car, but farther back. Drake and Allie blasted away at the bright flashes, and then they saw the red glow of brake lights as the car slowed. Drake kept firing and had almost emptied his shotgun when Allie's hand grabbed his shoulder.

"Save it. They've stopped. Either we hit them, or they decided this was a bad idea. In any case, we're out of range now. If they come at us again, you'll need the ammo."

Drake was gritting his teeth so hard that his jaw hurt. He lowered the shotgun barrel and clicked the safety back on, his eyes never leaving the trail behind them, and stayed that way until they reached the far gate eight minutes later.

Jack pointed the hood at the wire fence and blew through it, and then they were on a gravel road, the more even surface feeling like ice after the jarring they'd received on the track. He accelerated to fifty and then sixty as he put distance between them and the shooters.

Two miles later he saw the intersection for the larger artery that would take them north to San Antonio or south to Corpus Christi. He probed his wound again and came away with more blood. Daring a glance down at the seat, he saw that the cloth next to him was stained red. He knew he'd need to get a dressing on sooner than later, and opted to head north.

Three miles beyond the junction he pulled into a bar parking lot, its life-size neon cowboy sign blinking a garish welcome, and eased to a stop. Allie and Drake hopped out of the bed, and Allie approached the driver's side window as Drake moved along the passenger side.

"Why are we stopping here?" she asked, and stopped when she saw Jack's drawn expression.

"I'm grazed. Doesn't hurt too bad, but I need to get a look at it. See if you can find something we can fix a bandage out of, would you? Doesn't have to be elegant, just functional."

Drake opened the passenger side and stared at the blood. "Jesus. You're hit…"

"Keep your voice down. I know I'm hit. Go inside and buy a bottle of the strongest booze they've got. Vodka, preferably. I'll need to sterilize this." Jack caught his look. "Drake, I'll live. It's just a flesh wound."

Drake nodded and jogged to the bar entrance while Allie dug through the backpacks and extracted one of Jack's white undershirts.

"Will this work?"

"Looks like it. We can stop at a drugstore once we're in San Antonio. It's only got to hold for an hour or so. Can you drive?"

"Of course I can. You're the one who got shot."

"Then I'll slide over."

"Okay."

He took the shirt from her and moved to the center position on the bench seat and tried not to think about sitting in his own lifeblood. Drake returned with a bottle of rotgut vodka and handed it to him. Jack twisted the top off and poured the alcohol on his side, wincing as the vodka did its work, and then loosened his belt and slid the folded undershirt into place over the wound.

"There. That should do it," he said. He pulled his belt free before re-strapping it around his upper waist so it would hold the shirt in place. "Let's get moving."

Drake had stepped away from the truck and was peering beneath it. When he returned to the passenger door, he had a grim expression.

"We've got a problem. A bullet must have hit the radiator. Looks like we've lost most of the coolant."

Allie slid behind the wheel and looked at the dash. The temperature gauge was three-quarters to the red. She turned to look at Jack, who shrugged.

"We can stop and get more water later. Right now, keep the speed down and an eye on the gauge. It's cool enough out that we should be able to make it. As long as it doesn't get much hotter, we should be okay. But sitting here, it's not getting any cold air blowing on it. Let's go."

Drake climbed in and shut the door after himself, trying to stay away from Jack so as not to jostle his wound. Allie reversed out of the lot and pulled off. San Antonio was a good hour away, assuming they made it.

Allie settled in at fifty, and the temperature needle crept upwards before stopping a few millimeters below the top of the range. Drake studied Jack's profile and saw he was sweating in spite of the chill.

"I don't understand one thing. How did they find us?" he asked.

Jack winced. "Do you have another cell phone you didn't tell me about?"

"Of course not."

"Damn. Then it must be Allie's. I don't have one. That's the only possibility. Nobody knew where we were going. They must have put two and two together and somehow gotten hers. I should have thought of that."

"They're tracking my phone?" Allie asked.

"I think so, honey. Pull over."

She did and raced around to the bed to retrieve her cell from her bag. When she had it, she returned to the cab and removed the battery. "What do I do now? Is this good enough?"

"Nope. Put it on the ground and run it over. And the first road we come to heading south? Take it. They're tracking us, so they know we're on this road. Probably thinking we're headed to San Antonio. So now we're not going to do that. We'll head to Corpus. If necessary, we'll hotwire a car to get there if the truck gives out."

Drake could see the conflict in her eyes as she placed the phone on the asphalt and returned to her position behind the wheel. She pulled forward and heard a sickening crack as it shattered, and then the rear tire rolled over it. She braked and put the truck in neutral, and got out again to inspect her handiwork.

She was back in ten seconds. "It's history."

"Good girl. Now let's make ourselves history as well."

Back on the dark two-lane road, they came to an intersection and took a right, and found themselves driving through more farmland, the engine in the danger zone as they drove south. Drake looked through his window at the landscape moving by and considered that they'd crossed an important point of no return. There was no way to pretend that this was all a big mistake or that Jack had been unduly paranoid. The Russians were on their tail and wouldn't stop until Drake had found the treasure, or died trying.

Which it would be was anyone's guess. But he didn't intend to go down without a fight.

They'd find he was tougher to take out than they'd assumed. He might not know everything there was about guns, but he'd dropped enough felons to feel confident in his abilities, and he could always learn to shoot better.

Now he just needed to figure out how to survive in a hostile jungle while looking for an impossible-to-find lost city, and he'd be golden.

He took another look at Jack and was glad the man was on his side.

Maybe they actually had a chance. Between the three of them, maybe it could be done.

He sighed, tired, the adrenaline burnt out of his system, nothing left but fatigue. He rubbed his eyes, and when he looked up again, he was no longer hesitant about what he was going to do.

If there actually was a Paititi, he'd figure out how to locate it, Russians or no Russians. He had the journal, so he had an edge, even if it was a slim one.

The question was whether it would be enough.

Chapter Fifteen

Vadim and Sasha trudged down the road, their rented sedan dead a mile behind them, the windshield shattered from a shotgun blast, the driver-side front tire flattened. Vadim's face was bleeding from safety glass that had sprayed across his cheek, and Sasha had his tie wrapped around his left arm where he'd been nicked by a few shotgun pellets that had winged their way through the car.

"What now?" Sasha asked in gruff Russian, his breath steaming before him.

"We find a vehicle. We take it. Then we continue until successful," Vadim said angrily. "What do you think we do?"

"I was thinking about how the girl's phone stopped transmitting. Looks like they worked that one out."

"Only a matter of time."

"Yes, well…which brings us back to question of what we do now."

Vadim's eyes narrowed to slits, rage building in him, driving him forward as his blood dried on his face. "I don't know. But we will think of something – just as we always do."

"I wish we had accessed some heavier artillery," Sasha complained, patting the Ruger 9mm in his jacket pocket. "I, for one, did not expect the boy to travel with an arsenal. The only things missing were grenades and a bazooka."

"A mistake we will certainly not make again."

A frigid gust blew across the adjacent field, carrying with it the scent of freshly plowed soil. Tendrils of ground fog seeped over the furrows, the land stretching as far as they could see in the gloom, the only sound in the quiet night their footsteps crunching on the gravel underfoot and the hiss of their labored breathing.

"The larger oversight was underestimating their resourcefulness…that they were onto us. That changes the situation. But it also tells us something – they either have the journal, or they know where it is."

"The lawyer already told us the boy has it."

"But the boy probably does not understand its significance. Now that his father's associate is involved, we have to assume he does. And that he also realizes that no place is safe for him. For any of them." He paused, thinking. "What would you do if you knew that the devil was coming for you and you couldn't go home?" Vadim asked rhetorically.

"I would go after whoever was hunting me."

"Ah, but that is impossible for them. We don't exist. The old man isn't stupid. He knows the stakes. The only thing we can assume is that they'll try to find the Inca city themselves."

"But can we be sure of that?"

"It is the most probable outcome."

Sasha spit. "I hate that jungle. Hated it then, and I hate it even more now."

"As do I. But it holds our future. And this time we will prevail."

~ ~ ~

Allie emerged from the twenty-four-hour drugstore on the outskirts of Corpus Christi with a roll of gauze, a bottle of iodine, tape and pads, two liters of orange juice, and a container of Pedialyte. Jack gulped the juice greedily, his body depleted by blood loss, and downed the Pedialyte by the time they'd rolled out of the lot.

The engine was still holding out, although strained to its limits. Drake was relieved when they eased to a stop in front of a fleabag motel that wouldn't care much about formalities like identification as long as their cash was green. He went in with Allie and got two rooms from a sleepy East Indian clerk listening to a radio broadcast that sounded like cats rolling down a slope in a barrel.

Drake helped Jack to the first room as Allie backed the truck into a dark recess by a dumpster so that the bullet holes in the tailgate wouldn't be obvious. Upon her return, she stripped the clotted T-shirt from Jack's side and examined the damage before twisting the cap off the iodine.

"This is going to hurt. It's a flesh wound, but deep. Looks like it cut through one of your love handles," she warned, and Jack nodded.

"I'm not using them for anything. Do your worst."

His sharp intake of breath hissed as the liquid bubbled into the wound, and Drake could see moisture well in his eyes, an involuntary physical response to the pain. Allie fished a small first aid kit out of Jack's bag and poured another dollop of iodine onto the bullet hole – thankfully a clean entry and exit that had missed any organs. After blotting it, she squeezed two drops of Dermabond adhesive into the entry wound, and Jack reached down and held it closed with his fingers. She went to work on the exit hole and repeated the procedure, pressing the flesh together until it had sealed.

"That's pretty amazing stuff," Drake said as she returned the tube to the kit.

"A friend of mine who works in the ER got me some. It's prescription, but it's basically superglue without the compound that generates heat. I use it for mountain biking spills. It can be a lifesaver out in the boonies," Allie explained.

"Only a graze, it was the blood loss that was worrying me," Jack said, and looked up at Drake. "I suppose we should add some basic first aid to the bag of tricks I teach you. If we hadn't had the Dermabond and we'd been in the jungle, you might have had to heat your dad's sword up and cauterize it. Trust me. I've had to do that, and you never forget the smell."

"I'll take your word for it." Drake looked around the shabby room, whose sickly cream-colored walls reminded him of pus. The carpet was stained and threadbare in places, and the bathroom door hadn't been properly repaired where a prior guest had punched a hole in it. The impressionist print of a woman staring off over a field of wildflowers made him unaccountably sad, and he realized that it was lack of sleep more than anything that was wearing at him. He checked the time and saw that it was 4:20 a.m., and couldn't help but yawn. "Sorry. I'm beat."

"I think we all are. Let's get a few hours of shut-eye and then figure out what we're going to do," Jack suggested. "Figure nine we'll hook up?"

"Fine by me. I'm right next door if you need anything."

"I'm just going to get the rest of our stuff so nobody steals it out of the truck. I'll be back in a second," Allie said.

Drake caught Jack's worried look. "I'll go with you."

Allie didn't argue, and as they walked to the darkened form of the Chevrolet, Drake instinctively scanned the lot. Nothing. All quiet.

"How much time do you think we have before they find us?" he asked.

"Who knows? Hopefully my dad has some idea. He usually does. It's his world, not ours."

"It's ours now."

Drake helped her with the shotguns and backpacks. They carried the bags back to the room, and Drake saw the dark circles under her eyes when the light hit her face. The night had been hard on all of them.

He hung out the Do Not Disturb sign and locked his door before setting his backpack onto the bed. How had it all spun so out of control so quickly?

Drake brushed his teeth, shrugged out of his clothes, and set the alarm clock for eight thirty. He laid the SIG Sauer next to it, within easy reach. After a quick look around the room, he moved the lone wooden chair to the door and leaned the back against it, wedged under the knob, as additional insurance against intruders. He was so tired it didn't even strike him how odd that would have seemed to him just a few short days before. Now, it was just something he did.

Automatic. Reflexive. As he drifted off to sleep, his last thought was to wonder how much else about his life was going to change before this was over.

His dreams were uneasy. Silent figures lurked in the shadows outside his room and, before he could come fully awake, were inside and pointing the ugly snouts of silenced pistols at him, the SIG Sauer now useless only a foot away. Both had stockings pulled over their heads, distorting their features. The nearest one, with a body like a bear, swung his pistol and slammed the butt into Drake's head. Drake saw pinpoints of light.

Drake bolted awake, the sheets soaked with perspiration, his heart trip-hammering in his chest, his hand groping for the SIG Sauer. It took him a few seconds to realize he was still in his bed, the chair undisturbed, his only companion the slow ticking of the heater grate.

Drake stood, shaking his head, and shuffled to the bathroom half asleep. The tap water was icy cold and tasted like metal and chlorine, but he didn't care. He drained the cup in two gulps and peered at his watch. 5:47.

The rest of his slumber he spent tossing and turning, a headache pulsing behind his eyes as his body tried to get the sleep it needed. When he cracked a lid open to check the time, warm sunlight streamed through a slit in the curtains, and he saw it was 8:00. He threw the covers aside with a sigh and switched off the alarm before heading to the bathroom, any further chance of sleep lost to the day's advance. He caught a glimpse of himself in the mirror – his red eyes, face drawn with fatigue, three day's scraggly growth on his normally chiseled jaw – and a single word sprang to mind to describe his reflection.

Hunted.

Chapter Sixteen

The interior of the restaurant was jarring, all bright yellow and orange veneers apparently deliberately chosen for their perkiness. The other patrons were also travelers – grizzled truckers with weary scowls, families in transit – all looking out of place and ill at ease, counting the minutes until their time was up in the cheery purgatory and their journey could continue. Jack sat next to Allie on one side of the booth, Drake on the other, drinking bottomless cups of mediocre coffee, after they ordered from a waitress who'd greeted them with a toothy smile and vacant eyes.

Of the three, only Jack looked better; his color had returned along with his trademark steely determination in his gaze. Like Drake's, Allie's face showed signs of the stress, her easy grin nowhere in evidence, replaced by a thin humorless line as serious as a firing squad.

The server arrived with their meals and set platters of artery-clogging lumps before them before strutting off to the next patrons with a swish of her ponytail. Allie's fruit plate was probably the only thing that hadn't been churned out of a slaughterhouse, but at that moment it all smelled heavenly, and Drake attacked his meal like it owed him money.

Once they finished with breakfast, Jack cleared his throat and began to speak in a low voice.

"I've given this a lot of thought. A private investigator might have done the phone tracking, and could probably, with enough time, get bank records and credit card statements. So we should assume they'll do exactly that. We can use that to our advantage by creating a false trail for them to follow to oblivion."

Drake nodded. It made sense.

"Here's what we're going to do. How much money do you have on you?" Jack asked him.

Drake eyed the ceiling and did a quick calculation. "A little over thirty grand."

Jack looked surprised. "With you?"

"Yeah. It's a long story."

"Doesn't matter. That's a stroke of luck. With that kind of cash, you can do whatever you want, within reason. It buys you a lot of flexibility, so you don't have to use your credit cards at all unless you're deliberately leading them on a goose chase."

Allie finished her coffee. "How much do we have?" she asked Jack.

"I've got almost fifty thousand in gold coins, and fifteen in cash. I can convert the gold wherever. For now, we're set. If this goes longer than a year, then it gets sticky."

"But your pension payments go into the bank during the interim, right?" she asked.

"Correct."

Drake sat back. "I've also got seventy grand coming from Patricia's estate. For all I know, it's already in my account."

"Then you're set. But getting it out without leaving a trail could be difficult."

"Yeah, but I'm going to have to go to the bank anyway to get my passport. Like I said, it's in a safe deposit box there. I can always withdraw a bunch of cash when I pick it up. Now that I'm carrying thirty around, I can see that it's not as bulky as I'd have thought. Two pockets in my cargo pants. Piece of cake."

"The good news is that there are no forms to fill out or boxes to check leaving the U.S. So if you don't declare it, you'd only be in violation of your destination's laws. And my experience is that places in South America aren't doing full body searches on arriving passengers," Jack said.

"That's good to know."

"So here's what you're going to do, Drake. Book a flight home, paying cash. Take a taxi to the bank. Pull the money and the passport, and then get the hell out of there. Hightail it to a border city and walk across. From there, you can get to wherever. Peru. Brazil. Bolivia."

Drake nodded. "What about you?"

"We have different issues. The truck's going to need to be repaired. Fortunately, I can easily find a radiator to replace this one. That'll be my errand for the day. I'll buy some tools, slap one in, and she'll be as good as gold. I'll use my credit card to do it, so they're looking for us down here. By the time it shows up anywhere, we'll be long gone. Same with you. You can buy something here – anything – either a jacket or shorts or whatever, and that will put you in Corpus. Of course, right after you buy it, you'll be heading to San Antonio to fly home."

"I'll just wait for you to get the truck fixed, then. I can help. I'm pretty good mechanically."

"No. I want you out of here. They'll probably be looking for three people. The sooner we're two, the better. But one thing, son, and I'm not kidding about this. Don't go anywhere near your apartment. That's dead to you. Stay away. Do you understand? Because the odds are good they'll be watching it. Waiting for you to make a rookie mistake. So don't do it."

"There's nothing I can't replace."

"Exactly. Grab the cash and your passport, and either fly, or hitch, or take a bus to Tijuana. Once you're out of the U.S. system, I'll have a lot more confidence."

"Fine. What else?"

"Buy a disposable cell phone. Don't call anyone you know with it. Use it only to call ours."

Drake's eyes narrowed. "You still have one?"

"Not yet. But that's going to be our first purchase while you're still here, so we have each other's numbers – two phones. Once you call us, toss it. Buy another phone somewhere else before you call. Give us that new phone number and lose the one you called on."

"Okay."

Jack studied his face. "When was your passport issued?"

"Two years ago."

"So it won't be expiring any time soon. That's good." Jack took another sip of coffee. "Now to timing. The sooner we get to South America, the more of a jump we get on the Russians. It's only a matter of time until they figure out our end game. I'd propose hooking up in Brazil in five days. Think you can manage that?" Jack asked.

"I don't see why not. I'll call you when I've gotten my passport to confirm."

Allie exchanged a glance with her father and pushed her coffee cup aside.

"Now let's pay and get phones. Then you're on the first bus to San Antonio after buying a jacket somewhere." Jack waved for the check.

Drake caught Allie's eye, then looked back at Jack.

"Where in Brazil are we going to rendezvous?"

Jack pulled his wallet from his back pocket, wincing slightly as he did so, the wound still tender.

"Rio."

Chapter Seventeen

Drake verified his bank balance from a computer at one of the Internet cafés in the arrival area at San Jose International Airport and was relieved to see a deposit the day before for seventy thousand dollars. Which only left getting in and out of the bank without being killed to contend with. Sitting in the busy airport, that seemed easy; but the memory of his nocturnal gun battle was still fresh, as were Jack's warnings.

He'd been forced to check his backpack due to the big knife in it, and waiting for the carousel to deliver the luggage had eaten a solid half hour of his time. He checked his wristwatch and did a fast calculation – it would take him forty-five minutes to make it to the bank if traffic cooperated, and the branch closed in two hours. That posed no problem, but the niggling detail he'd left out of his discussion with Jack did – he couldn't get into his safe deposit box without the key, and the key was in his apartment.

Drake hadn't remembered the key until he'd been buckled into his plane seat with the journal in hand, ready for several hours of in-depth study. With the combination of sleep deprivation and anxiety, he hadn't been thinking clearly. Now it was too late. Before checking his bank balance he'd researched emergency passport issuance within twenty-four hours, but it wasn't practical due to all the documentation required. He'd tried to figure a way around it, but nothing seemed reasonable, so now he would have to risk doing exactly what Jack had warned against – trying to sneak into his apartment.

The taxi line was short, and he was speeding north toward Menlo Park in less than five minutes. Rush hour hadn't gotten ugly yet, and the cab took the car-pool lane once they were on the freeway, trimming valuable time off the trip.

He had the driver drop him off a block and a half away from his place. After shouldering his backpack, he donned his sunglasses and the baseball hat he'd bought at the airport and began strolling along the sidewalk to his complex. The units were built around a courtyard with a pool, with a driveway along the outside of the L-shaped building and parking for one car beneath each unit. His was a ground-floor apartment. He'd never met his upstairs neighbor, preferring to avoid contact with anyone in favor of privacy, and had actually dodged him several times by dawdling when he'd seen someone going upstairs in his section.

Drake's nerves were close to the surface, tingling, but he sensed nothing out of the ordinary. The street was a busy one, and there were no suspicious black vans with antennas announcing surveillance, no sedans with crusty PIs sipping coffee. Nothing.

He passed the entry gate to the complex and kept walking, doing his best impersonation of an uninterested pedestrian. When he reached the driveway, after a quick scan of the surroundings, he ducked down the side of the building and moved along the empty stalls until he reached the stairway that led to his unit from the parking level. Drake paused at the bottom of the steps and listened for anything unusual, but only heard the peals of delighted children laughing from the pool area, accompanied by muted splashing.

As he mounted the stairs, his anxiety gave way to relief. There was nobody waiting for him, no watcher with a sniper rifle, no figures in the shadows. Just Jack's overly cautious paranoia, even if well founded, and the contagious fear it bred.

At his door he stopped a final time, fished his key out, and ducked inside, feeling foolish for the elaborate approach and unnecessary subterfuge. He made a mental note to not allow Jack's flights of fancy to color his view of the world too much, but still twisted the deadbolt closed behind him, just in case.

Across the courtyard on the other side of the centrally located pool, a new tenant raised his cell phone to his ear and made a call from his position on a poolside chaise longue, the temperature still moderate enough for sunbathing even in the fall.

"The target just appeared at his apartment. What action should I take?"

The voice on the phone cursed in Russian, and then after a hurried discussion with someone in the background, issued instructions. "It will take us at least six hours to get there. Do whatever is required to contain him. But do not kill him. Do you understand? He is of no use to us dead."

"*Da.* You're the boss," Anatoly Radisov said, hanging up. As a member of the Russian mafia, he was more accustomed to shaking down shop owners in East Palo Alto or collecting gambling debts from yuppies with a taste for the wild side than conducting surveillance, but his latest duty had been the easiest cash he'd ever made. Two shifts, round the clock, five hundred dollars per man for a twelve-hour shift, and all he'd had to do was worry about getting fat from inactivity.

He stood and collected his towel before ambling back to his unit, newly rented by his organization from one of the numerous available in the complex, and hastily donned trousers and a shirt. He slipped his pistol into the pocket of his windbreaker and pulled it on, all the while watching the unit across the way through the window, and then made for his front door, an expression on his face that would have stopped traffic.

Drake quickly found the safe deposit box key and took the opportunity to pack some more clothes that would be appropriate for tropical climes, including a set of sturdy hiking boots and lightweight shirts. He had no idea whether he'd ever see any of his belongings again, but realized that the sum total of his life's acquisitions hadn't amounted to anything he would really miss, which made him both sad and relieved. As he was preparing to leave, his eye caught the red of his mountain bike, and he made an impulsive decision to ride it to the bank. He shouldered it, and with a final glance around the apartment, he opened the door and stepped out, pausing to make sure he relocked it before toting his bike and backpack down the stairs to the parking level.

As he was throwing his leg over the seat of his bike, he detected movement on the stairs. A tall, muscular man headed toward him in a hurry, reaching into his pocket. Some part of Drake recognized a threat, and he pumped the pedals with all his might, leaving the man standing by the stairwell fifteen yards behind him.

The distinctive whistle of a ricochet greeted him as a silenced slug gouged a chunk of concrete out of the retaining wall that ran along the driveway. Drake immediately swerved and increased his pace, his calves burning from the sudden demand. Adrenaline flooded his system and he hunched over the handlebars, presenting a smaller target as he raced a weaving course for the street. Another ricochet pocked the wall, but this one farther away. Accuracy was falling off as he neared the sidewalk, but he kept pumping for dear life – a lucky shot could still drop him.

Drake was doing at least thirty when he hit the street. A car stood on its horn and locked up its brakes with an earsplitting shriek as it narrowly avoided sideswiping him. Drake ignored it and swerved around an oncoming truck, the behemoth missing him by so little he could feel the heat from its front fender as he brushed by it.

More horn honking sounded from behind him, and he dared a brief look over his shoulder, where a green sedan was trying to pull out of the driveway. He shifted gears to buy more speed and blinked sweat out of his eyes as he passed a strip mall on his right. A car engine revved behind him, signaling bad news. He dodged right and shot down a service alley that ran along the side of the complex. The car followed him, its oil pan slamming against a speed bump, and he turned the corner behind the stores as another gunshot tore a divot from the asphalt just in front of him.

Drake had no idea how he was going to escape, but he wasn't going to make it easy for his pursuer. He heard the car take the turn, and then slammed on his brakes, nearly going over the handlebars as he twisted his front wheel. To his right was a three-foot-wide pedestrian entrance in the high concrete wall he could make – and that more importantly, a car couldn't.

He barreled through and rolled across a small field, industrial buildings on the far edge. He heard a door slam from the lot, but he was easily seventy-five yards away from the shooter. From what Jack had said, that would be an impossible shot even for a marksman: a moving target alternating speed over rough terrain, and zigzagging to boot.

A puff of dirt exploded to his left, but not close, confirming his belief. Now he needed to get to the nearest structures and he'd be clear.

He reached the buildings and edged between two, shielded from any gunfire. But it would only be a matter of minutes before the gunman drove around and found his way into the industrial park – assuming he wasn't working with a team. Drake forced himself to greater effort and swung onto a residential street with small homes nestled among mature oak trees. At the next block he took another turn, and at the next, another.

After five minutes of hard riding, he found himself close enough to the El Camino Real to ditch the bike and walk. He leaned it against the side of an apartment building, out of sight, and after rummaging through his backpack, changed his top. Anyone looking for him would have his description, which wouldn't track with his dark gray T-shirt. He pulled his baseball cap on backward and inspected himself in a nearby car mirror – it wasn't perfect, but it would hopefully be good enough.

The bank was six blocks away. By the time he arrived, he only had ten minutes. A harried-looking assistant manager escorted him to the hand scanner, which quickly verified his identity and granted him access. Drake entered the vault and moved to the section with his box, unlocked the door, and pulled the long metal drawer from its resting place. He didn't bother carrying it to the table in the small room next to the chamber, preferring to open it there and retrieve his passport. After a moment's hesitation, he reached into the zipped pocket of his backpack and retrieved the journal. He placed it in the box and closed the lid, and then slid the drawer back into the compartment and locked it.

Finished, he left the secure area and approached the teller. The manager seemed annoyed when he withdrew thirty thousand dollars in cash, and checked his balance twice before approving the transaction and going back into the vault for the money. The doors were closing when he walked out with his cargo pants stuffed with hundred-dollar bills. He made a right and walked along El Camino Real while scanning his surroundings for watchers. Luxury cars whizzed by him on the street as he made his way toward an electronics store, and within minutes he'd bought a second disposable cell phone and activated it. He asked the woman behind the counter to call him a taxi, and he used the waiting time to dial Jack's cell.

"You get it?" Jack answered, no attempt at preamble or greeting, the muted rumble of motor and tires on the road audible in the background.

"Yup. But I had a little complication." Drake told him about the key and the near miss. Jack didn't respond with more than a grunt, so Drake continued. "I'm going to catch a flight for San Diego and walk across the border there. Hopefully I can get a night flight to Mexico City from Tijuana. If not, first thing in the morning. How're you doing?"

"Radiator's fixed, a can of Bondo covered the bullet holes, and we're on our way to Austin."

"How's the graze?"

"I don't recommend it, but all things considered, it could be worse."

Drake paused. "And how's Allie holding up?"

"Fine. She's excited about going to Brazil. Go figure."

"With any luck I should be there in two days. Where should we meet?"

"I'll check into the Mar Ipanema Hotel down by the beach. Under the name Jack Keller. Stop in once a day until I'm there."

"Got it. Jack Keller. Mar Ipanema. Easy."

"Let's hope so. Safe travels and good luck. Oh, and Drake? Don't under any circumstances underestimate these guys. You're damned lucky you're alive. That could just as easily have gone the other direction."

"I know."

He disconnected and decided there was nothing to lose now by calling Harry, which he'd avoided based on Jack's warning. The line rang and Betty picked up, sounding out of breath.

"Betty, it's Drake. Is Harry there?"

A long silence greeted him, and then a choking sound.

"Oh...you don't know. He was murdered. A few days ago. In broad daylight. While I was at lunch," she said, ending with a sob.

"What? Someone killed him?" Drake's stomach sank. "What do the police think?"

Betty pulled herself together. "They're investigating some of his bail skips, and anyone that could have held a grudge. You know the kinds of psychos he dealt with. It's a full roster."

"Who's running the show?"

"Harry's brother is helping out, but unless someone wants to buy the business, he's saying he'll wind it down. This isn't what he wants to do for a living. He's got his construction business. I don't blame him. I'm looking for another job. It's creepy coming into work. I...I found him..."

Drake swallowed hard, shock setting in at the realization that his longtime friend was dead – because of him. Or more accurately, because of the murderous thugs who'd targeted him. "I'm so sorry, Betty. It must have been horrible."

"You have no idea. What kind of animals...never mind." She paused. "Did you want to speak to Harry's brother?"

"No...no need. I was just checking in. Nothing more. I hope things go okay for you." Betty had serious health issues and limped along from paycheck to paycheck, so Harry's death would affect her more profoundly than most. She was highly competent but too long in the tooth for most to hire, and it would be rough finding another job that paid a living wage for her receptionist skills.

"Thanks, Drake. Please stay in touch."

"Will do," he said, knowing he wouldn't. Everyone he came near seemed to be in mortal danger. No point adding poor Betty to the list.

The taxi arrived shortly after he hung up, and he asked the driver to take him to the San Jose airport. He jettisoned the phone outside the terminal and paid for his one-way ticket to San Diego in cash, relieved that he'd be there by nine o'clock at night. It had been years since he'd been in Tijuana on a hazy spring break during his college days, but he suspected it hadn't changed much and that there would be plenty of foot traffic crossing over from the U.S. for the evening's festivities.

Once across the border, a beat-up taxi took him to the airport, but there were no more flights to Mexico City until the next day. He booked one departing at ten o'clock in the morning, and after getting a recommendation from the ticket agent, took another cab to a nearby moderately priced hotel. He finished his evening with dinner and two Pacifico beers in the restaurant next door, and fell asleep by midnight, the low hum of the air-conditioning masking the traffic noise below his fifth-story window.

The flight to Mexico City was bumpy but tolerable, and he was able to buy a ticket on Avianca to Rio, with a layover in Bogotá. He just made the flight before the doors were closing, and as he took his seat, he felt a palpable sense of relief.

Almost fourteen hours later the plane's wheels smoked on the tarmac in Brazil. Drake rubbed his dry eyes as it taxied to the terminal, body sore from so many hours in a narrow seat. The turbulence over South America had been too severe to sleep on the night flight across the continent.

Drake's knowledge of Brazil wasn't encyclopedic, but he knew that Rio de Janeiro was on the opposite side of the country from the Peruvian border. When he'd questioned Jack's decision to use Rio as a rendezvous point, he'd told Drake that he had an old acquaintance with a ranch an hour north of the city, and who he was sure would let them use it as a base camp while they prepared to go into the jungle.

"I've still got a thing or two to show you before we head into the wilds. My buddy's place is perfect for you to practice survival skills. It's huge, remote, and nobody's going to mess with us. Best of all, it's off the radar. I'll call him later and clear it, but it shouldn't be a problem. He's only there in the winter months. Has a full-time staff operating it year-round," Jack had explained.

"How many buddies with ranches do you have?" Drake had asked skeptically.

"Enough."

Drake sped through customs and took a taxi to the Orla Copacabana Hotel at the southern end of the famous beach of the same name. The day was just beginning, and as the car rolled along the strand, every imaginable shade of skin was on display, most of the sun worshippers wearing little more than string for their morning on the sand. A trio of spectacular young beauties in thongs that would have been illegal back home scampered across the street in front of the car. The driver caught Drake's eye in the rearview mirror and grinned, words unnecessary for the universal moment.

The staff at the hotel was courteous and efficient. Five minutes after arrival he was in his room, stuffing wads of rubber-band-wrapped hundreds into the room safe. Once he was done, fatigue hit hard in a wave of dizzy disorientation, and he opted for a nap before going out and exploring Rio's attractions. He pulled the curtains closed against the bright glow of the morning light and lay on the bed, and within two minutes of his head hitting the pillow, he was out cold.

~ ~ ~

Vadim simmered, his anger barely contained as he drew heavily on his cigarette. Sasha knew his moods and stayed silent, preferring to allow him to brood in peace.

"What did I tell him? What were my instructions? That he was not to shoot unless it was a last resort. Where do they find these idiots?" Vadim spat.

"It looks like it is even harder to find good help in America than back home."

"As things stand, we have lost him, and now he will be on full alert. Any element of surprise we could have hoped for is gone, assuming we ever pick him back up."

Sasha didn't have a reassuring rejoinder. Vadim was right. It was a disaster. First the Texas nightmare, and now this. "I think we can expect them to be forewarned. There is no way around it now."

Vadim stood and crushed his cigarette underfoot. "I refuse to pay for this."

"Nobody in their right mind would expect you to." Sasha sighed. "But what now?"

"We seem to be running out of options. I had been hoping to avoid doing this the hard way, but it appears we have no choice."

"Then off to Peru."

"Exactly. It will only be a matter of time. We can use that knowledge to stay one step ahead of this boy, instead of trailing him, as we have been doing. And it will be much easier to deal with all of them in the jungle than in civilization."

Sasha eyed him. "It sounds like you have something in mind."

"Always."

Chapter Eighteen

Drake's nap turned into sleeping most of the day. After a lazy dinner at the hotel he was still wiped out, so he returned to his room and slept solidly all night. The next morning he rose early and went for a run on the beach before the sun's heat hit, and he found himself one of numerous joggers slogging along the sand.

The two-mile stretch of beach took more out of him than he'd expected – when he got back to the hotel he was soaked through with sweat and dehydrated. A long shower and two liters of water rejuvenated him, and after shaving and running a brush through his hair, he slipped into a light shirt and shorts and was ready to face the day.

He spent the morning rereading the notes he'd taken while studying the journal to ensure he hadn't missed any nuance, but for the life of him he wasn't sure how to interpret many of the obscure references that would hopefully lead them to the treasure – his ability to spot patterns unfortunately hadn't kicked in, based on the data his father had left in the journal. That Jack was going into the jungle with him was a lifesaver. If Jack could remember where he and Ford had made their camp, it would eliminate a lot of the time they'd spent on false trails twenty years ago.

Their biggest problem was that there were no step-by-step directions, only anecdotes and hearsay from unreliable sources, and rumors whispered by the natives, none of which had ever been verified. The rainforest they would be in was vast, unexplored and teeming with lethal hazards of all kinds – the area had become a major drug-trafficking area in the last two decades, rivaling the infamous Golden Triangle in Asia for danger. The army left the region alone, preferring to focus where they stood a remote chance of policing effectively, as did their Brazilian counterparts across the border, who viewed the rainforest east of the Andes as a lawless no-man's land best left to the hapless tribes that inhabited it.

Jack had told him that in the last few days of his life, his father had been convinced that they were on the brink of locating the fabled city. He'd been secretive about why, which wasn't unusual – Ford Ramsey always played his cards close to his chest. But he'd let slip that he'd gotten new information from the indigenous tribes in the area: information that he believed held the answer he'd been looking for.

Jack had gone back to civilization for more supplies, so he never knew what the elder Ramsey had been thinking or had discovered – he'd alluded to having a meeting planned during Jack's absence, but that had been it. Jack had registered a difference in Ford's tone, though, and believed that his attitude had become more optimistic, and that they were only days away from their journey concluding successfully.

The satellite footage on Google Earth was of no help. The canopy of the Amazon was far too dense to make out anything other than a sea of green with rivers snaking through it. He tried looking for the waterfalls rumored to be near the lost city, but it was no good.

Frustrated, he realized his stomach was growling and that it was well past lunchtime. He tore himself away from his iPad with a resigned sigh and went to a seafood restaurant a block away that he'd seen on his run, where he ate incredibly fresh fish prepared in a spicy sauce that had his eyes watering by the time he was halfway through his meal.

The sidewalks were clogged with beachgoers, and he found himself carried along by the crowd as he walked south. Glittering skyscrapers lined the waterfront, yet only footsteps away, shantytowns clung to the sides of the mountains, their alleys narrow and treacherous, graffiti covering the buildings. Bootleg electricity cables crisscrossed the alleys like black spaghetti, the wiring's tentacles snaking along streets the police didn't dare go into, day or night. The hotel had warned him against leaving the premises after dark, and cautioned him against going anywhere near the *favelas* – the local slums that housed the armed drug gangs at perpetual war with the law and military: hotbeds of trafficking, both of narcotics and humans.

He'd seen enough photos on the web of machine-gun-toting thugs on motorcycles firing indiscriminately at each other to understand that the slums were beyond dangerous, but that world seemed a million miles away as he meandered down the beachfront. Beautiful women and fit men were the flavor of the day, all golden-brown skin and white smiles and endless summer expressions of carefree ease.

The Mar Ipanema Hotel wasn't on the beach, but rather two blocks from the Atlantic, surrounded by other towers with apparently no thought to city planning. Drake entered and was scrutinized by two burly security men, whose no-nonsense expressions signaled zero tolerance for mischief, and approached the reception desk. A young woman with a thousand-watt smile and passable English checked for Jack and pointed to a house phone. Allie answered after three rings, her voice musical.

"Hello?"

"You made it," Drake said.

"Yeah. We just got in a few hours ago. How's Rio?"

"I haven't been out much. Mostly hibernating. The trip wiped me out, and I've been online most of today."

"I hear you about it being a bear of a flight. I'm pretty beat as well."

"Yeah, but you didn't have to escape gunmen to get here. That takes a little more out of you."

"So I'm told. Where are you?"

"Downstairs."

"Okay. I'll be right down."

"What about Jack?"

"He went out after checking in. Said to stick around until he got back."

"Did he say where he was going?"

"To look up some friends. That's all he would let on."

"You eaten?"

"Plane food."

"Can I buy you a drink?"

"You're on. Be down in five."

When Allie stepped out of the elevator she looked like every bit of a million dollars. Her mane of dark hair shimmered in the light, and her blue eyes flashed like sapphires. Drake took a moment to appreciate the way her shorts showcased her sculpted, tan legs as he moved toward her. He almost hugged her, but something about her body language warned him off, and instead they stood awkwardly facing each other, waiting for the other to make the first move. Drake grinned and waved at the en-suite bar.

"You want to stay here, or go down to the beach?"

"I promised him I wouldn't leave."

"Ah. Right. Well, then, I'd say happy hour at the Mar Ipanema just got underway."

The beer was cold, the music soft, the booth comfortable, and they laughed easily as they discussed the adventure to come.

"So what made you interested enough in archeology to want to major in it?" Drake asked, savoring his icy Brahma beer, studying her face.

"I think it was the stories my dad told me as a child. About his trip here. His time with your father. It sounded so…exotic, and important. No, that's not the right word. More like the kind of thing most people never get to do – discovering the secrets of the past. I think I was hooked by the time I was ten years old."

"What does your mom think about it?"

Allie grew quiet and took a sip of her beer. "She died when I was very young. When I was twelve. A traffic accident."

"I'm sorry to hear that."

"It was a while ago, but I still think about how proud she would have been. She always encouraged me to pursue academics in a big way. Not that my dad wasn't supportive. But she was over the top…"

They finished their drinks, and Drake held two fingers aloft to the bartender, who nodded. Allie picked at the bar snacks in a bowl between them, and then sat up, eyeing the hotel entrance. "He's back."

She rose and moved into the lobby. Jack saw her and nodded, then spotted Drake and followed Allie into the bar.

"Can I buy you a drink?" Drake asked. Jack gave him a sour look, and he kicked himself mentally, having forgotten that Jack didn't imbibe.

"Sure. How about a Coke?" Jack said.

"Coming right up." Drake slid out of the booth and walked over to the bartender to relay the order. Jack sat next to Allie and plowed into the bowl of treats like a starving man. Drake returned, followed by the bartender with their beverages. When they were alone, Jack leaned forward.

"I've been out making calls. I met with a friend who comes to the U.S. every four or five years – owns a vitamin manufacturing company. Anyway, to make a long story short, he gave me some leads."

"Leads? For what?" Drake asked.

"Someone who knows the area we're going into and can arrange for anything we need."

"Sounds promising. And he has somebody?"

"Brazil is the kind of place where everybody knows somebody. That's why I hit the ground running and went to work."

"Speaking of which, when do we go to your buddy's ranch?" Allie asked.

"Tomorrow. I've already hired a car and driver to take us there," Jack said. "I want to get our preparation over with as quickly as possible so we can stay ahead of the Russians. They'll figure out soon enough what we're up to, and I want to be long gone by the time they do."

"Won't we need our own car?"

"We can't rent anything or we'll show up on a computer. So we're going to pay a little more and have a local ferry us around. Which isn't the worst thing that can happen. I remember from last time I was here…if you're not used to driving in Brazil, you're better off leaving it to the natives. Take my word for that."

After a few more minutes of discussion, Drake finished his beer and rose. "I'm going to get some fresh air and check out the beach, since we're leaving tomorrow. You two want to come along for a walk?"

Jack shook his head. "Not for me. That's a young man's game. I'm headed upstairs for a *siesta*."

Allie smiled and nodded. "I'd love to see the beach. Being cooped up in a plane and a hotel room has me going a little stir-crazy."

Jack looked concerned, but seeing Allie's face, his expression softened. "Just be careful. Rio's a dangerous city, even in the tourist areas. Watch yourselves."

Drake waved the bartender over and handed him money. "We will. It's way safer here than in Texas or Menlo Park, apparently."

They pushed their way through the double steel and glass doors and the humid swelter settled over them like a blanket. The sidewalks were jammed, the afternoon a popular time for those out of school or taking a late lunch. Rio boasted two world-class expanses of sand, Ipanema and Copacabana, both two miles long, sun-drenched and justifiably famous. In the distance, the iconic statue of Christ the Redeemer's open arms watched over the city. Opposite, Sugar Loaf Mountain jutted into the sky at the northern end of Copacabana.

"You can really hear the Portuguese influence. It's so strange that the other countries in South America speak Spanish and Brazil doesn't," Drake said.

"No huge surprise. The Portuguese pretty much ran the place for five hundred years, one way or another. Even after independence the two countries were locked at the hip. But the polarization between the rich and poor is a lot more obvious than you typically see elsewhere. It's the kind of social situation that can't last."

"They've been saying that for decades, yet it just keeps on keeping on," Drake observed. A group of rowdy teens approached down the sidewalk, their girlfriends laughing drunkenly, flashing endless expanses of flawless bronze skin, and Allie moved closer to Drake. As they pushed by, he took her hand, and while he thought she tried to pull away at first, soon they were strolling along like a couple, an important connection made and maintained. Neither wanted to interrupt the simple pleasure of the moment, so they walked in silence until they came to a volleyball net near the northern end of Ipanema, where young men and women were competing athletically in spite of the afternoon heat.

They paused, looking out across the sand at the crashing waves of the Atlantic clawing at the beach, the young Brazilians vigorously swatting the ball back and forth across the net. Drake squinted at Allie looking untamed as the breeze tugged at her hair, an eagerness in her eyes, as though she was considering joining the good-natured contest. He returned to his study of the players, noting that they were all in exceptional physical shape, and then Allie gave a cry. Two street urchins, maybe eleven or twelve, were running across the wide Avenida Vieira Souto, one of them with Allie's purse clutched in his grasp.

Allie held up her hand, red with blood.

"Damn. They slashed the strap with a razor, and it got me."

"How bad? Let me see."

She turned and he could see a small red stain on her shirt, spreading slowly, but not alarmingly.

"Are you okay?" he asked, his eyes tracking the boys. "Do you have anything in your purse that can't be replaced?"

"Oh, God. My passport. I only had a few dollars, but my passport and wallet..."

"I'm going after them. Get back to the hotel and have them call a doctor. Or find a cop. You probably need stitches," Drake said.

Without waiting for a response, he tore off after the thieves across the wide boulevard, dodging honking cars as he made for the far sidewalk. The boys had a good head start, but his longer legs equalized much of it, and in three blocks he was only thirty feet behind them. They raced up the street toward one of Rio's infamous hillside slums, where red brick hovels sprawled up the steep face of the mountain, narrow alleys running in front of them, garbage littering much of the unclaimed open areas, which stank of sewage and rot.

The pair darted to the right of the massive elevator that had been built as a concession to the residents during one of the city's modernization drives, and disappeared up a steep concrete staircase that would have challenged a mountain goat. Drake took a deep breath and took the steps two at a time, intent on not allowing them out of his sight. He knew that all it would take was a few seconds and they'd be gone for good, and with them, Allie's passport, creating unknown hardship and placing them squarely on the radar with the Embassy – a situation to be avoided at all costs.

The stairs twisted to the right, and he caught a flash of cut-off jeans as one of the two twisted up an even narrower path carved straight into the dark brown dirt, flanked by a wooden handrail improvised out of cast-off lumber from broken pallets and shipping crates. His calves were burning like he'd run a marathon, and he wondered as he pushed himself how much longer the kids could keep up the pace. He was rewarded when the one with Allie's purse lost his footing and slid down the hill toward him, only ten feet from Drake. His companion grabbed him and pulled him to his feet, a straight razor clutched in his other hand as hundred-year-old eyes stared at Drake from an adolescent face.

The pair bolted laterally along the dirt walkway scarcely three feet wide, and Drake drove himself harder. The boys were almost in his grasp. He sprinted with all his remaining energy and dove at the one with the purse and got his hand on it. Drake ripped it free as the boy kept going, neither of them quite up to tackling a full-grown man, even if the one with the razor had clearly been considering it before he'd locked eyes with Drake and seen something that had made him think twice.

Drake sat panting for several seconds, winded. A rustle behind him came from one of the shanties of crumbling red brick with a blue tarp for a roof, and a young man stepped from its entrance. His clothes were filthy, but the nickel-plated revolver in his hand looked clean enough.

The gunman pointed the pistol's barrel at Drake and said something in rapid-fire Portuguese. Drake shook his head, and the man drew closer, his intent clear – he was robbing Drake and wanted the purse.

When he was only a few yards away, Drake twisted and simultaneously threw a baseball-sized chunk of brick he'd palmed at the would-be thief. It connected solidly with the thug's forehead and nose, making a sound like a melon being hit with a bat, and then blood gushed down his shirt.

But he didn't drop the pistol.

He was bringing it up to fire even as he bellowed in pain, and Drake launched from the ground and tackled him as he pulled the trigger. The shot missed by a hair, and then he was on top of the gunman, slamming his wrist against the ground with all his might in order to break his grip on the pistol. He felt it loosen and caught the man on the jaw with his elbow while he smashed his wrist again. The pistol fell harmlessly a few feet away and Drake lunged for it, making it a split second before the mugger.

Drake slammed the gun butt into the man's cheek and his eyes rolled into his head, his face ruined as he blacked out. Drake lay panting by him and then caught movement up the hill. More youths – at least three, and all carrying weapons.

Drake leapt to his feet and sprinted down the alley, the gun gripped in his hand as he ran, his heart hammering in his chest as he fought to get some distance between himself and the thief's friends. He was just turning to take the dirt path back down the hill when an explosion sounded from behind him and part of the wooden rail shattered. Drake didn't like his odds, trying to make it down the hill with the punks shooting at him from higher ground, so he spun and dropped, simultaneously slowing his breathing. With Jack's words reverberating in his head, he cocked the hammer back, drew a bead on the first gunman, and squeezed the trigger. The little revolver bucked like a panicked animal, and he fired again. The second pursuer grabbed his abdomen and dropped his gun, and Drake used the opportunity to throw himself down the hill, sliding down the path.

He began rolling and tumbling, and his downward trajectory was only stopped by a brick wall – another shanty. The collision knocked the wind out of him, but he quickly recovered when he saw the remaining two attackers at the top of the alley, pointing their weapons down at him. Four shots rang out. The rounds hit the wall behind him as he brought the barrel up and emptied the revolver at them, remembering Jack's warning about how hard it was to hit someone in a combat situation with a handgun. None of his shots found a home, but they did seem to take the enthusiasm out of the thieves. In any case, they didn't follow him as he rolled and lunged for the stairs, bolting down them three at a time, figuring the tradeoff of risking a shattered ankle was more than warranted by the circumstance.

Thirty seconds later Drake was crossing the garbage-strewn field at the base of the hill. He tossed the useless revolver into the heaping bags of refuse as a shambling vagrant dug through a nearby pile, oblivious or unmoved by the sound of nearby gunfire – likely an hourly occurrence in his life. Drake's ribs were throbbing from the encounter with the brick building and his ears were ringing from the gunfire, but he had Allie's purse, and he was alive.

Drake glanced back up at the hillside, but he didn't see anyone chasing him. The predators had returned to their familiar haunts to prey on easier victims, or perhaps to help their downed friend. He jogged to the street and continued at that pace until he reached the beach – a world, with its G-strings and heady aroma of coconut suntan oil, as distant from that of the nearby hillside as night and day. Several passersby looked at him with alarm, and he realized he was filthy, his clothes torn from his fall down the hillside, dirt smeared on his sweating face and arms. Something about the situation made him grin and then laugh out loud as he moved along the famous strand toward the hotel. His fellow pedestrians gave him a wide berth, his lunatic smile and unaccountable mirth as disturbing as the gun would have been if he'd been brandishing it and screaming.

The security men barred him from entering the hotel until he was able to convey to them what had happened. Even once Jack emerged from the elevators and approached, they hovered close by, as though he might attack the other guests at the slightest provocation. Jack took one look at him and shook his head. Drake held the purse aloft in triumph.

"You weren't kidding about this being a rough place," Drake said.

Jack eyed him expressionlessly and then steered him to the elevator. "Come on. You've got a cut over your eye. I'll patch you up after you return Allie's purse."

"Is she okay?"

"He sliced her pretty good, but it's not critical. We'll get a couple of stitches later. The hotel already called a doctor. Should be here in a few minutes." Jack turned to look at Drake as he stepped into the elevator. "Maybe we can get a two-for-one deal. Looks like you could use a stitch or two, too."

"I won't even tell you about the gun battle."

Jack's eyebrow rose as the door slid closed. "Tell me you're kidding," he said, then saw the look in Drake's eye. "You're lucky to be alive."

"At the rate things are going, you're right."

"Kid, you only have one life. No more stupid risks, okay?"

"Says the man who's about to go into the jungle with me."

Jack chuckled in spite of himself. "Touché. But seriously. Ease up. This will be dangerous enough as it is."

"The lady needed her purse back. Tell me you would have done anything different."

They rode up in silence, and when the floor indicator pinged, Jack sighed and shook his head. "Just like your father."

"Maybe. Only I'm going to walk out of that jungle. That's a promise."

Jack eyed him. "You know what? I believe you."

Drake nodded.

"Bank on it."

Chapter Nineteen

The driver picked them up the next morning at ten, and by eleven they were on the road to Teresópolis, north of Rio. The highway was modern until they turned off onto the smaller road to Cachoeiras de Macacu, where it became a two-lane strip of asphalt winding through open fields, the rainforest held at bay by the hand of man. The sky was brilliant blue, the road framed by vivid green on both sides, and the air humid, redolent of wet earth and pollen.

An hour more and they arrived at their destination: a small winding dirt track leading through a clearing to a gate a quarter mile off the road. An ancient man, wearing a black baseball cap and brandishing a shotgun, sat in a security hut. After several moments of back-and-forth with the driver, the guard swung the gate wide and beckoned to them to enter.

The driver revved the motor and the little car lurched forward. Ten minutes later they neared the foothills, where a large two-story house hulked near a cluster of trees, a guest cottage and service quarters near the separate four-car garage. The home's bright yellow paint had faded in spots, and a young man worked near them with a brush. He turned as they eased to a stop, curiosity in his eyes as they opened their car doors and stepped from the vehicle.

"Paolo?" Jack asked as he approached.

"Yes," Paolo answered in heavily accented English.

"I'm Jack. Solomon should have called you to let you know we were coming."

"He did. I've prepared rooms in the main house for you. Let me get your bags and I'll show you the way," Paolo said, closing the paint can and balancing his brush on the lid.

"That's okay. I've got it," Drake said from the trunk, hoisting his backpack and putting it on before lifting Jack's and Allie's bags free. Jack reached out and took one from him, and they followed Paolo inside through the front door.

The house was simply furnished with heavy pieces crafted from native wood, rustic and sturdy, in keeping with the locale. Paolo led them up the wide stairway to their rooms, which looked comfortable, if basic.

"Let me know if you need anything," he said. "I've filled the refrigerator with food and drinks, and was told to assist you with whatever you want."

"Thank you, Paolo. I'm expecting a visitor tomorrow or the next day. I'll give you his information later. Other than that, we're not to be disturbed. I'm conducting training exercises with my pupils here. Other than my single guest, nobody is to be allowed on the grounds," said Jack, his tone eliminating any argument before it started.

Paolo nodded assent. "Enjoy your stay. I'll be painting most of the day, so you'll know where to find me."

They quickly unpacked and, after stowing their gear, met downstairs, Drake with his father's knife, Jack with a small black nylon bag.

"Come on. Grab some water and let's go for a walk. I see no reason not to start on this now. The sooner you understand the basics of what I'm going to show you, the sooner we can begin our search," Jack said.

They set off down a trail that led from the rear of the house into the brush, and ten minutes later emerged into a wide clearing surrounded by tall trees, a stream running through it fed by the nearby hills. Jack set his bag down and, after scanning the periphery to ensure they were alone, turned to Drake and Allie.

"I'll begin with hand-to-hand combat techniques. We'll start with defensive, then move to offensive. Allie already knows most of this, but there's no time like the present for a refresher course. Most of this is based on street fighting, my Special Forces training, and Krav Maga – an Israeli specialty that combines the best of all worlds." Jack considered Drake's sweating face. "You said you studied karate? To what belt level?"

"Black. Second Dan. Not a master, but I was the best in my class. I know the pressure points, the various strikes and blocking techniques, kicks, punches… I participated in some competitions, but that was years ago."

"Okay. And how useful did your training prove in the real world? I'm gathering you had to get physical with some of your bail skips."

"I did, and the answer is, of limited help. The problem was your opponent doesn't react the way you're taught he will. And sometimes he'll have a weapon. I'd say my wrestling skills did me more good. A full nelson usually quiets down even the most agitated skip."

"That's right. All the theory's fine, but what typically happens is you have an adversary who'll do anything necessary to survive or escape. What I'm going to teach you is what you should master in a few days. Which isn't much."

"Then why don't we take more time?" Drake asked.

"Because it wouldn't make any difference. To really see any improvement, you'd have to practice for years. So it's the basics. The first is that in any engagement, survival is your priority. I know that sounds obvious, but believe me, when some crazy SOB is coming at you like they're going to kill you, all your training can get forgotten in a heartbeat. So rule number one is that everything you do should be oriented toward surviving. Not on the best way to disable your opponent. Not on some specialized technique that will work every time." Jack gave Drake a hard stare. "Instead, on doing whatever you can so you can get the hell out of there and live to fight another day."

Drake nodded, as did Allie, who'd obviously heard it all before.

"The best way to survive is to avoid the fight altogether. If you can't do that, then you have to focus on ending it as quickly as possible while inflicting maximum damage. That often means attacking preemptively and disabling your adversary before he knows what hit him. Krav Maga focuses on strikes to the most vulnerable areas of the body – the eyes, groin, neck, face, knees, solar plexus, and so on. But the overarching idea is to destroy your opponent in seconds, and discard any notions of a fair fight. What's fair is what has you surviving. Clear?"

Drake nodded again. "Yup."

Jack beckoned to him. "All right. Drake, come at me. Don't hold back. Come at me however you want, with the goal being to put me on the ground. Don't deafen or blind me, but beyond that, anything goes."

"Are you sure?"

"Just do it."

Drake spun without warning and leveled a kick at Jack's chest, intending to follow it up with blows to his abdomen. The next thing he knew he was lying in the grass, blinking, the wind knocked out of him. Jack stood over him, breathing easily.

"Not bad. But you'd be dead. Now I'll show you what I did, so you understand what you did wrong, and how you should respond to that kind of an attack." He held out his hand to Drake, who took it shakily. Jack hauled him to his feet. "You okay?" Jack asked.

"Yeah. I'm just…kind of shocked that you were able to do that. I was thinking about how to pull the punches to avoid breaking your ribs."

"That was one of your first mistakes. I wasn't thinking about anything except how to take you down. And you'll notice I didn't waste any time trying to parry or block your blows. I avoided your kick and used your energy to allow you to turn past the point of no return, and then attacked. If I'd wanted to kill or blind you, you'd be dead or blind. Now let's take this in slow motion. You do your kick, I'll demonstrate how to avoid it and neutralize the attacker."

Drake did as asked, and paid close attention to the sequence of blows Jack used – only two, with a sweep kick that knocked him flat. They practiced a few more times, with Jack taking the role of Drake, allowing him to perfect the timing and the strikes, and then they separated and drank some water.

They continued throughout the day, pausing only to eat a fast lunch, and by the time the sun was sinking behind the green hills, Drake was bruised and panting, exhausted – although now he was landing as many blows as he was taking. As they made their way back to the house, Jack patted his shoulder, Allie padding alongside him.

"You did well. Tomorrow we'll concentrate on knife work, then some more hand-to-hand, and then I'll show you some knots that could save your life in a pinch. Obviously the hope is that you'll never have to use any of this. Especially the knife work. Because I can tell you firsthand, the scariest thing in the world is someone coming at you all out with a knife. Mainly because there's almost no way to defend against it."

Allie smiled when Drake caught her eye. "Which is why he's not going to focus on defending against a knife attack. More on how to deliver one that will inflict maximum damage. Only problem is that if your adversary has a knife, too, you're probably not going to come out of it all that great, no matter what happens."

"Sounds like avoiding a knife fight should be rule number one," Drake said.

Jack chuckled. "Damn right. But you've got that machete of your father's, so might as well show you how to use it. Thing's almost big enough to cut a man in two. If you get into a pinch, it could save your life. But only if you know the basics."

"Which would be, get a gun and shoot first. Early and often," Drake replied.

"You're actually not far off. That's exactly what I'd advise." Jack paused. "The only other problem being that when people are shot and stabbed, they don't just fall over dead. I mean, they can, but more often than not, they keep coming. Because unless you get a clean head shot or one right through the heart, it takes time for the body to realize it's hit. When you have a ton of adrenaline racing through your system, it actually numbs you. A lot of combat veterans who were pretty horrifically wounded didn't even realize they'd been hit until minutes, or even hours, after it happened."

"So it's not like the movies, is what you're saying," Drake observed.

Jack laughed again. "You know what? Nothing in life is. And that's the end of today's lesson. Let's get cleaned up and make some dinner. I'm starving."

The house was quiet upon their return. Drake shed his clothes within moments of getting into his room, and then realized he didn't have a private bathroom. He rooted around in the closet, found a blue towel, and wrapped it around his waist before walking down the hall. He knocked on the bathroom door, and Allie's voice called out from inside.

"I got to it first."

"How long are you going to be?" he asked.

"Not long. Maybe an hour."

"Are you serious?"

"Okay. Fifteen minutes. I've got a lot of hair to wash."

Drake returned to his room and studied himself in the mirror. Bruising from the day's lumps was already appearing, but overall he looked fit, the wrestling and karate having sculpted his upper body.

He checked his watch, dropped to the floor, and forced himself to do a hundred pushups, the practice session having convinced him that he'd allowed himself to get soft. Bands of muscles on his arms and shoulders seemed to strain his skin, stretching it to the breaking point. When he finished, he gulped the remainder of the liter of water in his room and then returned to the bathroom, hopeful that Allie was done.

When the door opened, he almost gasped at how good she looked with her hair wet, sporting a towel wrapped around her body, smelling like floral shampoo and soap. She stood in the doorway for a few seconds as Drake moved aside, and graced him with a smile as she brushed past.

"You can put your eyes back in your head," she called softly behind her.

"They weren't doing much there," he said, not bothering to deny admiring her, any response but admission an obvious lie.

When she reached her bedroom, she tossed him a knowing look over her shoulder, and he decided to cut his losses and leave her to the dinner preparations. The warm shower was calling to him after a long day's exertions, and his better judgment was telling him that with Jack in the mix, he'd be better off sticking to deciphering the journal than exploring the rebellious look in Allie's dancing eyes.

Chapter Twenty

Thunderstorms moved through the valley while Drake and his companions ate breakfast on the veranda. Fortunately, the morning's downpours had tapered off enough to continue with their training by the time they'd finished eating.

Paolo's wife cleaned up the dishes as they returned to their rooms to collect their things. Drake's body felt every minute of the prior day's abuse: his shoulders and arms were stiff, and his muscles protested as he climbed the stairs. He withdrew the big knife from his backpack and strapped it onto his hip, the weight oddly reassuring. The knife seemed like a very real link between father and son, and he resolved to wear it for the duration.

The slog to the clearing took longer than the prior day. Flocks of birds rose into the gray sky as they passed, the air smelling like ozone and wood smoke, the tall grass rustling softly from stray gusts of wind, the trail now mud, pulling greedily at their shoes with every step. When they arrived, Jack stood by the same spot and gave a brief lecture on knife techniques, and then demonstrated them with a short length of dowel he'd found in one of the drawers.

It was immediately obvious why anyone with a functioning brain would want to avoid a knife fight at all costs. When Jack demonstrated the most effective attack, it was truly terrifying. He held the dowel low by his right side as he used his left to block any potential threat. Drake could see why no matter how skilled the defender, he was going to get cut – in most cases, badly cut.

"Add to the pure violence of a knife-wielding attacker your inability to do much to stop him, and you'll see why it's the absolutely last thing you ever want to deal with."

They continued, and after a morning focused on knives, they munched on sandwiches while Jack chatted about guns.

"Let's talk about silencers. Specifically, on pistols. First, they're called suppressors, not silencers, by anyone who knows anything about them. Second, with ordinary ammo they're still really loud. So if you're thinking you can be like one of those guys on TV and sneak up on your target and pop him without anyone noticing, think again."

Drake nodded. "What I'm getting out of all this is that it's hard to kill someone, hard to do so quietly, and hard no matter what method you use."

Jack grunted. "Yep. But at the end of the day, a gun's the surest chance you have, so if you can't dodge a fight altogether, which is what I keep coming back to as the smartest choice, it's how you want to take on your attackers. But the same things that will make you harder to shoot will work against you. Moving, for instance."

"I found that out the hard way back in the Rio slum," Drake affirmed.

"Five more minutes and we'll start on knots. Allie, this will be more interesting for you. I've never really shown you most of these."

Allie didn't look convinced. "How about some kind of super ninja skills? That's what I want to learn."

Jack grinned. "The takeaway from all this is that your best skill is the ability to stay calm under pressure. That's a very rare trait. Most soldiers can't manage it. So that's what we'll be practicing. Because to have a chance against professional killers, who *will* be calm, you need to match them, or you'll be dead before you know it."

A cloudburst hit in the afternoon and they had to run for the house, getting soaked by the warm rain in the process. When they arrived, Jack stood under the overhang, water dripping off his nose, watching the deluge.

"That's one of the things I remember about the trip with your dad. The rain. It hits out of the blue, and it soaks everything. That was the worst part about it. Worse than the bugs, the snakes, you name it. Constant rain. At least at this time of year, it might be a little better than when we were there – right in the middle of the wet season."

"How long were you in the jungle for?"

"Almost a month. Seemed like it was never going to go anywhere, and then your father discovered the remains of one of the outposts built along the trail from Peru to Paititi. We actually found that in the area that's laughingly referred to as their Matsés National Park. Don't let the name fool you – it's a frigging swamp. Mosquitoes the size of baseballs, venomous insects too numerous to count. Small wonder nobody's bothered to do much exploration there."

"Don't sugarcoat it, Dad," Allie said.

"Nothing I say will prepare you for the reality of that place – and the Brazilian side's as bad or worse. This is a vacation at the Ritz compared to what we're going to be going into."

A car bounced up the drive, both sides covered in mud up to the windows, and Jack squinted to make out the driver. "That's my meeting. You two get cleaned up. No point in trying to do anything more with this coming down. If all goes well, we'll be getting out of here soon."

Drake and Allie exchanged puzzled looks and she shrugged. Drake followed her into the house, both trailing puddles of water on the rustic hardwood floor. Allie climbed the stairs and looked over her shoulder at Drake with a small smile.

"You want the first shower?" she asked.

"I was thinking I could wrestle you for it. Sort of like combat practice."

"Haven't you gotten beaten up enough? If I didn't know better, I'd have said he wanted to torture you."

"I wasn't going to say anything. Plus, you looked way too amused by my misery."

"That's not true. I mean, not completely true. You risked your life to recover my purse. That earns a lot of points, Ramsey."

"Could have fooled me," he said, and then changed the subject. "Who's your dad meeting with, anyway? He's being very secretive."

"I don't know. But I wouldn't read too much into it. He's always like that."

Drake paused by his bedroom door. "You can take the first shower. I'm good."

"A real gentleman, I see. Tell you what, I'll buy you a beer in half an hour. In the kitchen. I saw they stocked a few six-packs."

Drake grinned. "Deal. Let me know if you need your back scrubbed or something," he tried, and immediately regretted it.

She took it in stride. "Did you make my dad the same offer?"

Drake recovered quickly. "You bet. Especially after he spent the last two days beating the snot out of me."

Her frank gaze met his with a look he couldn't read. "I'll leave you some soap. You look like you need it. Go on. I'll be out in a few."

He took the hint, his arms sore from hundreds of blocks, and pushed into his bedroom, wondering simultaneously at Allie's unreadable demeanor and the visitor who'd come in the middle of a rainstorm to the Brazilian hinterlands to meet with Jack on unknown business.

The rain beat a steady tattoo on the metal roof as he stripped off his clothes and wrapped a towel around his waist. The storm had blown through, the insistent percussive attack now little more than a drizzle. Drake stretched his arms over his head and yawned, and then moved to the window to look out. He squinted through the grimy panes of glass at the area beside the house where the newcomer was parked, and saw nothing but muddy puddles of water and two ruts already filled from the downpour.

The car was gone.

Chapter Twenty-One

Jack was quiet at dinner, wolfing down heaping mouthfuls of a delicious stew Paolo's wife had cooked up. When he finished with his bowl, he sat back and took a long sip of water before speaking.

"We'll be leaving tomorrow. Flying to Lima. My contact arranged for an introduction to someone who's familiar with the area and can get us whatever we need."

"What time do we leave?" Allie asked.

"Someone will pick us up at six. So, early. Back to Rio, then to Peru, which will take most of the day. I meet his guy tomorrow evening in Lima."

"How do you know you can trust him?" Drake asked.

"How can I be sure I can trust anyone here? He's being recommended by a friend. An expat who's been in country for a long time and has his fingers in a lot of pies. So he rubs shoulders with plenty of people who are, shall we say, helpful when it comes to niggling issues like crossing borders without paperwork, getting weapons…"

"Great. Who is this recommendation, exactly? What does he do?"

"The way my friend described it, he's a facilitator who does a lot of business in the tri-border area – Brazil, Bolivia, and Peru. Knows the customs, the locals."

Drake nodded. "He's a smuggler?"

"An ugly word."

"For an ugly occupation."

"The world here's different. It requires a certain…ethical flexibility. Corruption is endemic, and there are a lot of people who exist in a gray area that would be illegal in the States. Here, they make the machine work. They get things done. They arrange things."

"What else does the guy have on his résumé?" Allie asked.

"He's been in the region for over ten years. The jungles are his backyard. Speaks some of the local dialects. Most importantly, he likes money. And he's always hungry. My friend contacted his associates in Peru, and this was the only name that came back. So he's our only choice."

Allie and Drake shared after-dinner beers once Jack had retired for the night. They sat outside, stargazing, the clouds having blown west earlier. The trees around them buzzed and clicked and rustled with nocturnal creatures, and with all the lights off except for the one in the kitchen, the darkened compound could have been uninhabited.

"You think we'll actually be able to pull this off?" Allie asked, swinging one leg lazily as she reclined in an outdoor chair crafted from wood and hide.

"If anyone can, we can. Don't ask me why I feel that way, but I do. Maybe it's having read the journal, I appreciate the logic that went into my father's reasoning. Or maybe it's because I'm stubborn, and I always finish what I set out to do."

"Have you always been that way?" she asked, taking a pull on the bottle of beer.

"As long as I can remember. My mom said that's how my dad was, too. She said it probably ran in the genes. When she first told me that, I was about six. I ran around for a week wondering where in my jeans stubbornness was running – what it looked like and how she could see it."

Allie laughed. Drake took a swig from his brew and set it down by the side of his chair. "What about you? What does the trained archeologist among us think?"

Allie beetled her brow. "I don't have an opinion yet, because I don't fully know what we're up against. In a way, it's like a needle in a haystack. Worse, really. We need something that will narrow the odds. Hopefully the journal will help us do that. It would really help if I knew what you did. I guess that's what I'm saying."

Drake nodded. "The journal's really a set of deductions based on a careful examination of the oral and written histories that exist. Much of it's speculation, but it seems well founded. Remember that my father made at least four prior trips here, so he felt like he was onto something to make the final one. And your dad says that my father believed he was only a day or two from locating the treasure when he was killed. Really, all we need to do is get back to that last camp area and see if we can find any of the landmarks he mentions – waterfalls, a stone jaguar, an arch. Waterfalls near Paititi are consistently mentioned."

"Then it's really going to be more about thoroughness than any *aha* moment."

"That's how it sounds. Good old-fashioned grunt work," Drake agreed.

"If that's all it would take, I wonder why the Russians never found it."

"Because they're criminals, not critical thinkers or archeologists. That's my guess. If we see them, we can ask," Drake said.

"I wonder why they killed him. Your dad?" Allie said softly.

"Maybe he wouldn't tell them what they wanted to know. Or maybe he did, but it wasn't the truth – or simply wasn't enough to go on. I've come to grips with the idea that I'll never know. Whatever happened, only a few people were there. My dad. The two Russians. Maybe helpers, if they had any." Drake paused. "Or here's an idea that came to me a while ago: we've been assuming the Russians killed him. What if they didn't? I mean, we know they were in the jungle, but so were the local tribes, and probably smugglers, and who knows whom else. It's possible he was killed for reasons that have nothing to do with Paititi."

Allie shook her head, disagreeing. "I'll go with 'the murderous psychos chasing us killed your dad' as the most likely, though."

Drake finished his beer with a nod. "Seems the most obvious. But I'm also willing to entertain the possibility that he was killed and the

Russians either didn't do it, or didn't learn anything, and that's why any information they got didn't help them. It doesn't change much from our end, but one of the things that comes through loud and clear in the journal is my father's philosophy of keeping an open mind. Maybe that's not such a bad thing."

"It's never a bad thing," Allie agreed.

Drake went inside, retrieved two more beers and popped the tops off using his new knife. He handed one to Allie and returned to his seat.

"What about you, Allie? Seeing as we're going to be going into the deepest darkest reaches of the rainforest together. What are you all about?" he asked, his tone light but the question serious.

"What is there to tell? I'm just a girl. Grew up without a mother, for the most part. Spent most of my time working my ass off in school. And then trying to find a job. There's not a lot more. It's not like I have some fascinating hobby or anything. Just a girl out in the world trying to get by."

"That's it? There's always more. Come on. Give."

"Okay. I'm also a serial killer. Been abducting hot young male hitchhikers for the last five years, keeping them locked in the basement to pleasure me, and then offing them when I grow bored. Oh, and I cook 'em and eat 'em like that Hannibal dude."

"Sounds like you're not getting enough fiber in your diet."

"Or greens. It's really hard to prepare a balanced hitchhiker meal."

They sat comfortably, bantering easily for another fifteen minutes, but when they mounted the stairs to the bedrooms, Drake knew little more about Allie than he had that morning. A part of him wondered what she was hiding or defending against, but another cautioned against being too interested. He needed to work with Jack, and that would be almost impossible if Allie and he became a thing.

Morning came too soon, and he was still groggy when he descended with his bag. Allie and Jack were at the dining room table, drinking coffee and nibbling at their plates.

"Hey. Good morning. There are some more eggs on the stove. Just heat them up for thirty seconds and you should be golden," she said as he dropped his backpack near the door.

"Thanks." He helped himself, preferring to wolf his breakfast down lukewarm from the pan. Two minutes later he sat down across from them with a mug of steaming coffee and checked the time. "At least I'm not late."

"You'll find that once we're in the jungle, you'll be rising at dawn," Jack said. No greeting. Just a terse warning. Drake had already grown accustomed to his abrupt style, so he merely nodded.

A car approached the front of the house, its exhaust burbling from a deteriorated muffler, and they quickly finished their coffee and rose.

"I've got to take care of Paolo. Go ahead and load the stuff into the car. I'll be right back," Jack said as he moved to the door. Drake and Allie hefted the bags and followed him out into the bright sunlight. The heat was already rising and the atmosphere humid, as it had been since their arrival in the tropics. The driver, a tall black man with a shaved head, helped them load the luggage into the battered sedan, and when Jack returned they all piled in, Jack in the front seat, Drake and Allie in the rear.

The flight to Peru took five hours, and when they arrived they quickly passed through customs and caught a taxi to their hotel. They agreed to rendezvous for dinner after Jack's meeting with his contact, which was arranged for seven that evening at a nearby watering hole.

Now that they were nearing putting boots on the ground and heading into the rainforest, Drake was feeling a mixture of excitement and trepidation. The theoretical was about to become real, and the prospect of walking the same trails as his father was invigorating and terrifying. He tried to rest after eating a late lunch, but his mind raced, and after an hour tossing and turning he flicked on the light and reread his notes for the fiftieth time, hoping for some new kernel that had escaped him thus far.

He was disappointed. There were no revelations, no breakthroughs, and the task on which he was about to embark seemed as impossible as ever. He locked the notes in the room safe and returned to the bed, and spent the next hour trying to sleep. When he did finally drift off, his dreams filled with visions of fleeing through the jungle chased by invisible pursuers.

~ ~ ~

Jack stood outside the bar for several minutes waiting for seven o'clock to roll around, leaning against the red mortar façade with a casual ease as practiced as a streetwalker's, studying the neighborhood and calculating escape routes in case he had to bolt. The habit was unconscious, like so many of his survival instincts, honed over the years and now as indelible a part of his makeup as his crow's feet or the aches in his bones.

A beggar in tattered rags shuffled toward him with a grimy hand extended, and Jack fingered a couple of coins and dropped them into his palm, more for the sake of the skinny dog trailing him than out of compassion for the man. The beggar offered a muttered *gracias* and their eyes met for an instant. Jack immediately regretted his generosity – the vagrant's pupils were dilated with the telltale look of the drug-addled, and he was much younger than Jack had originally thought.

The man continued on his way and Jack checked the time again. It was still shy of seven, but he was impatient and decided to push his way through the double doors in the hopes his rendezvous was already there.

The interior was dark. A pall of cigarette smoke hung near the ceiling, where an inadequate ventilation duct battled to clear it. He walked to the long bar and took one of many empty barstools. A few desultory drunks were seated down the scarred wooden slab, their arms protecting their drinks as though they'd be snatched away if they let their vigilance slip. Several groups of locals stood quaffing beer in groups of two or three, occasionally laughing at a joke. An ancient television flickered a soccer match, and a bored bartender with the face of a basset hound watched the screen as though it was about to announce the winning lottery numbers.

Jack waved and waited for the bartender to approach, and ordered a mineral water with a twist of lime. The bartender's expression didn't change, but a subtle eye roll told Jack what he thought of his choice.

A tall man in his mid-thirties took the seat one down on the right, and Jack was about to move farther away for privacy when a dark-complexioned man, his hair an oil slick combed to the side, in a red dress shirt, as agreed on the phone, slid onto the stool next to his. The newcomer ordered a beer, and when the bartender deposited it in front of him along with Jack's water, he took a long pull before setting it down and leaning into Jack.

"You found the place okay, I see," the man said in heavily accented English. But not with a Spanish inflection – more Indian or Pakistani, which fit with the voice on the phone.

"Yeah. No problem."

"You were cryptic about what it is you need. Hopefully you can clarify for me. You mentioned weapons?"

"Correct. I'll want three fully automatic assault rifles, with flash and sound suppressors if possible. Four extra magazines and two hundred rounds of ammo for each. And three pistols. SIG Sauer P226s would be preferred. With holsters. Fifty rounds apiece, with at least one spare magazine per."

"Any particular caliber?"

"On the rifles, AKs will work. On the pistols, .40 caliber S&W would be preferred. But they all need to be in new condition. I know weapons, and I won't accept crap."

"Of course. How soon do you need them?"

"Yesterday."

"You have cash?"

"Some. Dollars. How much?"

The man took another sip of his beer and thought. "Twelve thousand. Half in advance."

Jack shook his head and tried his water. Flat. Tasted like metal. He set the glass down and turned slightly.

"I'm not a fool. I know the going rate. Six."

"If you know the rate, then you know for that you get a few thirty-year-old AKs in spotty shape, and maybe some Berettas that have seen better days. What you're requesting are top-shelf guns. Those command a premium. Eleven."

They settled on nine, and the little man finished his beer and motioned to the bartender for another. Jack waited for the next round to arrive, and with it the inevitable questions.

The man's voice struggled to make it over the din of the nearby conversation as a trio of workers entered and called to the bartender for drinks.

"You also mentioned a need for a guide. Someone discreet."

"That's right. A guide who knows the jungle and who can keep his mouth shut."

"Why do you want to go into the jungle? I don't involve myself in anything drug-related."

"It's not drug-related."

"Then what is it?"

"An archeological expedition."

"I see. What are you looking for?"

This was where the art would come in, Jack knew. Too much information and he'd compromise the operation before it started. Too little and the man would balk once he understood their real intentions. Jack cleared his throat and edged nearer his companion.

"Inca ruins."

The smuggler stared stonily at his beer as though it contained the answer to questions he'd long pondered in vain.

"Inca ruins. Any particular ones?"

"I have one site in mind. But that's not important. I need someone who knows the area and can assure us safe passage."

The little man nodded. "It's very dangerous, you know. A lot of trafficking activity. Primitive tribes who have no hesitation about killing intruders. It's not something to be taken lightly."

"I understand."

"Let me think about how much I'd need to help you with that. It won't be inexpensive."

"Nothing in life worth doing usually is. How long on the weapons?"

"One day. Maybe two. Go count out the money in the bathroom and then slip it to me when you return. I'll save your spot."

Jack rose and made his way to the back of the bar. The men's room was as vile as he'd expected, and he breathed through his mouth as he stood in a filthy stall and thumbed through a wad of hundreds. He slipped money into an envelope he'd brought for that purpose and slid it into the pocket of his light windbreaker before leaving the empty bathroom, a whiff of stale taint following him out as he returned to the bar. Another group of rowdies had arrived, and suddenly the room was moderately full, making Jack uncomfortable. He laid his jacket next to his new friend and lifted his glass to his lips. After another small mouthful of the bitter water, he set it down.

"It's in the pocket. Take the jacket. Have you thought through the other matter?"

"Not sufficiently to commit. But enough to guarantee that it will be at least triple what the guns will run. Is that a problem?"

"We can talk about it when I take delivery. I don't know you well enough to discuss that kind of money yet."

"Fine. Call me tomorrow and we'll see if I've been successful," the smuggler said as he stood. He took the windbreaker and left, sticking Jack with the bill.

The tall man on his right chuckled and shook his head. Jack appraised him surreptitiously. A Caucasian, dirty blond hair, his skin tanned to a leathery brown – the typical look of the traveler who'd arrived years past and stayed on for the plentiful cheap cocaine and inexpensive living. Peru, Brazil, and Bolivia were filled with down-on-their-luck expats, casualties of the drug trade or fugitives from the U.S. looking for a new start.

"Something funny?" Jack asked.

"Nah. None of my business," the man said in English. American English, Jack noticed.

"Correct," Jack said, wondering how much of the discussion the eavesdropper had overheard.

The man smirked and returned to his beer with a shrug. Jack pushed back from the bar, unwilling to engage, and then some instinct commanded him to turn to the man.

"You got a problem?" Jack asked, his voice soft, the menace obvious in spite of the volume.

"Hey, like I said, it's none of my business. But I'd say *you* do."

Jack considered possible responses as the man stood and faced him, taking Jack's measure, his gaze steady and unblinking. Jack revised his earlier assessment. This wasn't some casualty wasting away in an alcoholic fog.

The man dug in his pocket and extracted a business card. He handed it to Jack, who looked at it before palming it. A phone number. Nothing else.

"What's this supposed to be?" Jack asked.

"A lifeline for when Asad there screws you."

"What are you talking about?"

"He went off the reservation about three months ago. On the pipe. You're never going to hear from him again. He's got enough money to go half a year now, thanks to you. And by the way, he was right. What you asked for will cost more like ten to twelve, unless you want junk." The man finished his beer, threw a crumpled bill on the bar, and then edged past Jack and made for the door.

"We'll see. What's your name?" Jack asked, not moving.

The man turned and looked around before speaking softly.

"Everett Spencer. People just call me Spencer."

Then he was gone, the doors swinging behind him. Jack tossed some money at the bartender and followed him out, but when he exited there was nobody in view, the sidewalks empty other than a few couples hurrying along. Jack scanned the surrounding buildings and saw nothing but shadows. Wherever he'd disappeared to, Spencer was good. He'd managed to evaporate in seconds, leaving nothing in his wake but his card and a feeling of dread that Jack hadn't experienced in a long time.

Chapter Twenty-Two

Drake jolted awake and rolled over, sweating in spite of the air conditioner, and squinted at the alarm clock, which read seven p.m. He forced himself upright and, after getting his bearings, moved to the bathroom. Once the water was warm he took a shower, trying to expunge the memory of the troubling dreams with soap and elbow grease. The sense of unease that had seemed so vivid upon waking gradually faded, rinsed away in a spiral of suds down a rusted drain. By the time he toweled off and stepped out of the stall, he'd forgotten it, his mind occupied with more immediate concerns.

Nobody was downstairs yet, so he wandered into the lobby bar and ordered a Pisco Sour, advertised on the small menu as the Peruvian specialty cocktail. He watched the preparation with concern when the raw egg white was added, but quickly resigned himself to living dangerously. He was getting ready to head into one of the most hazardous stretches of jungle on the planet. The possibility of a little salmonella paled in comparison – and he had to admit, the concoction was tasty.

He was on his second drink when Allie joined him, and he convinced her after a taste to have one as well. When Jack showed up at eight, they were enjoying themselves, which abruptly ended when they saw his expression. He ordered a cup of coffee and, when the bartender brought it, sat at their table and filled them in on his meeting, as well as his concerns.

"Who's this Spencer character?" Allie asked when he finished.

149

"I don't know. He must have heard enough of the discussion to put two and two together. What he was doing there, I have no idea. Same with who he is."

"Do you think he was telling the truth?"

"We won't know until tomorrow, but he seemed pretty confident. In which case I just lost a tidy sum to learn that you can't trust anyone," Jack spat.

"What are we going to do if he's right?" Drake asked.

"We don't have a lot of options. Worst case, I call him and set up a meeting to learn more. I'd hoped that because my contact vouched for the Pakistani guy, he was reliable, but it could have been a while since he dealt with him." Jack took a long sip of coffee. "And a lot can happen in a short period around here. Occupational hazard in a country where pure cocaine costs four dollars a gram."

"Then you believe Spencer?" Allie asked.

"I don't know what to think," Jack said.

Dinner was a maudlin affair, and when they parted, Drake agreed to meet them the following morning to strategize. They'd still need to source the rest of their equipment and could occupy their time with that while waiting to see whether Spencer's prediction held true.

The next day was spent traversing Lima, buying camping gear and the various odds and ends they'd want for their jungle adventure. Their final stop was at a pharmacy, where they assembled a respectable first aid kit suitable for attending to any kind of emergency, including gunshot wounds and snake bites. Although from what the pharmacist explained, most of the local poisonous snakes would kill you long before the bite could be treated.

Asad didn't answer his phone, and after spending hours trying with no reply, Jack suspected the worst. He'd been taken, and there was no recourse – they didn't have the time to hunt down the Pakistani on the unfamiliar streets of Lima.

Spencer answered on the second ring and agreed to meet at six at a café a block from the hotel. He didn't ask what had happened. He'd obviously known when he'd handed Jack his card.

Drake accompanied Jack to the rendezvous in the empty café. When Spencer showed up, Drake instantly disliked him. The man's attitude was cocksure and smug, his good looks a little too smooth, his breezy assurance that he could help them insincere.

"I can get the guns. Peru and Brazil are crawling with them. But good condition weapons always command more, and fully automatic assault rifles come at a premium. So expect to pay. As to playing guide in the jungle, that's a different story. I'm not into risking my life for a few lousy bucks. You're going to need to make it worth my while. And no bullshit about secrets and need-to-know. You either tell me the whole story or I'm out, and you can take your chances with someone else," Spencer said.

"For a guy living in dope central, you have high expectations," Drake began, but Jack held up a hand, his gaze never leaving Spencer's.

"Why don't you convince me I should trust you? You're just some guy in a bar. Why would I want to hand you money?" Jack demanded.

"You called me. That means Asad screwed you. If you had a backup, he'd be here instead of me. So why don't we skip the posturing and cut to the chase? You need guns and a reliable guide. I can supply both. But I'm not dumb, and I'm not cheap. I make plenty with my little business. I don't need to die for chump change." Spencer paused, studying Drake before returning his attention to Jack. "But seeing as you got bent over by your man Asad, I'll answer some reasonable questions. Ask away."

"Who are you? What do you do in Lima?" Drake demanded.

"I'm a businessman. I arrange things. I fix things. I cross borders with anything besides drugs. Money, people, papers, whatever."

"Then you're a smuggler," Drake said.

"Sure. If it pays. Why – you have something against smugglers? Your grandpa here was trying to hire one of the most notorious in the area," Spencer replied evenly.

"Where are you from?" Jack asked.

"Central Valley, California."

"How did you wind up in Peru?"

"I spent some time in the service. When I got out, I realized that I wasn't cut out for standing behind a counter greeting people or pushing a mop. So I decided to travel until I found something that interested me. Peru interested me. That was twelve years ago."

"What did you do in the army?" Jack asked.

"I didn't say I was in the army. I said the service."

"How about you tell me exactly what you did. Because this is already sounding like make-believe to me," Jack said.

"Make-believe? Fine. After a stint in the navy I wound up as a SEAL. For four years. I won't talk about specific missions, but you look like a man who's spent time in the trenches. Figure it out."

"And now you're a lowlife in a third world backwater," Drake said flatly.

Spencer's expression didn't change, but his eyes narrowed. "You've got a pretty smart mouth. What's your claim to fame? Impress me."

"I don't have to impress you. I'm not asking for a job," Drake fired back.

"Neither am I. You called me, not the other way around."

Drake turned to Jack. "I don't like him. Let's find someone else."

Spencer laughed. "That's rich. You still don't get it. There is nobody else. Just cheats and addicts trying to con you out of your cash. You may not like me, but I'm the best chance you've got. Assuming I'm interested. Which so far, I'm not." Spencer sat back. "I can get you the weapons within forty-eight hours. The rest? Good luck. Better leave instructions on where to send your bodies, assuming anyone finds them. Because at the rate you're going, you're history."

Jack cleared his throat. "All right. Enough of this. We don't need to fall in love. We need to be able to work together. Why should we trust you?"

"Because you'll make it worth my while to be trustworthy. That's why." Spencer shifted. "Now I've got some questions of my own. But first, tell me why you need an arsenal – and why you want to go into the rainforest. And don't make it up. If you don't want to tell me, that's fine. I'll get your popguns, and best of luck. Although I've got to warn you – the jungle traffickers are loaded for way bigger bear than you, so you'll need more than what you've asked for to survive a week. They've got grenades. Fifty cals. Every conceivable weapon you can imagine." Spencer gave Drake a dismissive laugh. "And you expect to go into their backyard and walk out alive? Don't make me laugh."

"Fine. Get the guns. We'll take our chances," Drake said, the color rising in his cheeks.

Jack shook his head and glared at Drake. "Easy, huh?" He turned to Spencer. "Here's my proposal. Find us the weapons. We'll pay a reasonable amount. If you get them in a timely manner, we'll consider telling you what you want to know. How much do you need up front?"

Spencer laughed. "Five grand. Cash. But I'll tell you what. We can play a game. You can either give me the five now, and the price will be ten, or you can give me nothing, and when I have the weapons, the price will be twelve. Call it bridge building. You have to earn trust to get it. Your choice."

Drake and Jack exchanged glances. "We'll take the twelve. You sure you can have the weapons that quickly?" Jack asked.

Spencer stood. "I already have the AKs. They're the most requested weapon down here. More punch than M4s – better stopping power, even if not as accurate. But in the jungle you won't be sharpshooting, so an AK's a solid choice. It's the SIG Sauers that'll take a little creativity. Very popular, but getting three on short notice in new condition without any paperwork…they'd normally go for more like a grand apiece through legit channels, but seeing as you probably don't want to bother with reams of paperwork…"

Jack nodded. "That's right."

"Then it's a deal. You have my number. Call me tomorrow. I'll be around."

With a parting glare for Drake, Spencer left, leaving Jack and Drake alone with their coffee. Jack finished his cup and sighed.

"What do you think?" he asked.

"Should be obvious. I don't like him. It feels like he's playing us. Too slick. I feel like I need to check my wallet after talking to him for five minutes."

"I don't disagree. But perhaps he's confident because he knows what he's doing? You have to admit – ex-SEAL commands some respect."

"If what he said was true."

"I believe him. There's a look. You get to know it. He's got that look. And he recognized it in me the first time he saw me."

Drake shook his head and frowned. "You can't be seriously thinking about including him in this."

"We need all the help we can get. Having a seasoned player to guide us could be a lifesaver. When your father and I went into the jungle, it wasn't crawling with drug smugglers. But it is now, and without a guide that knows the ropes, this will be over before it starts. So I don't think we can dismiss him so easily. Let's see what he does with the weapons. If he performs, I say we tell him what we're doing, and cut him in on a share. The only way a guy like that's going to go all in is if he thinks he's going to get a home run out of it. Otherwise he'll just be hired help, and you'll always be looking over your shoulder."

"Of course, there's nothing to stop him from killing all of us once we find the treasure."

Jack eyed him with a small smile and stood. "I'm not so easy to kill. You can start with that."

Chapter Twenty-Three

Spencer answered his phone when Jack called the next day – a promising sign. They agreed to meet at a warehouse in the Comas district, on the northern edge of town, at 4:00 p.m. When the three of them piled into the taxi and told the driver the address, he looked at them with hesitation, then shrugged and flipped the meter on.

Allie had insisted on coming this time. She didn't like being excluded, and had made a compelling argument that since she was part of the expedition – and the only one with archaeology training, she pointed out – she wanted a say in who they took on as a partner. Jack tried to talk her out of it, but she wouldn't budge. Drake stayed out of the argument, although he didn't like her joining them for the meeting any more than Jack did.

Drake had found a wide-brimmed hat for the jungle, and was wearing it in spite of the ribbing he'd taken from Allie when she'd seen him with it on.

"Wow. Are you making a low-budget remake of *Raiders of the Lost Ark*? What's next? The whip?" she'd teased.

He'd ignored her taunts, figuring that he'd be glad for the protection it afforded from the sun.

The neighborhood degraded as they rolled over increasingly rough pavement. The downtown area storefronts transitioned to graffiti-covered eyesores with bars across the windows, razor wire circling the tops and rusting rebar jutting above the roofs. Groups of youths loitered on the corners, trash clogged the gutters, and Drake understood the driver's reticence when they'd given him their destination. Eventually the buildings gave way to large industrial warehouses, many of unfinished gray cinderblock, and the streets became more ruts and potholes than asphalt.

They pulled up to the curb, uneven and cracked, in front of a particularly unfortunate structure that looked like a run-down prison.

The driver pointed at it. "*Numero ochenta-dos,*" he announced, doubt written across his face.

Jack checked the address and nodded, then fished out a wad of nuevo sols, the Peruvian currency, and peeled off several bills.

"*Es possible esperar?*" Jack tried, asking the man to wait for them. The driver shook his head and pulled a card from a holder on the dash.

"*Llame,*" he said, holding his hand to his ear, thumb and pinkie extended, as though calling on a phone.

Allie leaned forward and batted her lashes at the driver, a slight pout trembling her bottom lip. "*Por favor?*" she pleaded.

He shook his head. He wasn't having any of it. Obviously, the neighborhood was one where any money to be had waiting was outweighed by the danger lurking in the long shadows.

They stepped out of the taxi and it roared away in a cloud of exhaust, leaving them on the sidewalk. A pool of noxious water nearby buzzed with a swarm of flies. Jack approached the black iron slab door and knocked.

"Let me do the talking, all right? Drake? We on the same page?" he asked.

Drake nodded. They'd discussed it before. He was not to say anything to ratchet up the tension – or the price.

The sound of a motor rumbled off the façades. An old American sedan crept along the deserted street and slowed as it neared them, fenders primered gray, a spiderweb of cracks glazing the windshield. Drake could make out four heads inside through the grimy glass. It was fifteen yards away and slowing when the building door swung open and Spencer's voice echoed from inside.

"Better get in here. The natives aren't very friendly."

Allie stepped over the threshold first, followed by Drake. Jack remained outside until they'd entered, and then pulled the door closed behind them as the car pulled even with it. Spencer appeared out of the gloom and reached beside him. The thunk of the bolt sliding home boomed in the dark space like a gunshot. He flicked a switch. Fluorescent light sputtered to life above them, and they found themselves standing on the concrete floor of a windowless warehouse half-filled with wooden crates.

Spencer gestured to a utility table near the closest wall, where the weapons lay disassembled. They moved to the table, and Drake caught Spencer admiring Allie out of the corner of his eye. He bristled, then choked it down. This was business, and even if the man was a pig, they were there for a specific purpose, not to make new friends.

Spencer tapped one of the rifle stocks with a finger. "You know how to assemble one of these?" he asked, throwing Allie a smile.

Jack didn't seem to notice, concentrating on the weapons. When Allie returned Spencer's smile, rage swelled in Drake's chest, but he focused on ignoring it. Allie could flirt with whoever she wanted. They weren't married. They'd only held hands, and even that had been innocent. At least on her part.

"I think I remember," Jack said, and inspected each part before expertly fitting the gun together. He nodded his approval. "Seems like it's in good condition."

"Lightly used by a little old lady on church visits only," Spencer said, deadpan.

Jack repeated the process with the other two rifles and next turned his attention to the pistols. "These seem new."

"Next best thing. Very few shots fired. You did specify you wanted nearly new."

"I did. And I see they're the .40-caliber versions, not the 9mm. They'll do nicely."

"What's that?" Drake asked, pointing at a nearby bag.

"A couple of night vision scopes and a set of NVGs. I was surprised you didn't ask for some, but I figured I might as well get them while I could. Might come in handy in the jungle. Sometimes the traffickers will be on the move at night, so that's when shooting could happen."

"I figured recharging them would be a problem," Jack said. "We'll probably be in there for weeks."

"They should hold a charge for at least that long. Just don't turn them on unless you need to. The new generation batteries will last for a while."

"That's good to know. Seems like you've thought of everything."

"I aim to please. The ammo and the holsters are in that bag. Feel free to inspect them, too. Just don't load any of the weapons. It's hard to build trust if the three of you are holding loaded guns."

"I presume you're carrying a loaded gun," Allie said. "What about that?"

"That's my business, young lady, just as it will be your business once you've paid me for the hardware and we've concluded our transaction. Once you're out of here, you can walk down the street waving your AK, for all I care. Until then, we play by my rules."

Jack nodded. "Fair enough. Let's take a look at what we've got."

He dumped out the bag on a wooden crate and opened each box of .40-caliber Smith & Wesson shells and inspected them, and then did the same with the 7.62mm cartridges for the Kalashnikovs. Satisfied, he checked each of the magazines and withdrew a stack of hundred-dollar bills from his pocket, which he set on the table near Spencer.

"It's all there. Feel free to count it," Jack said.

Spencer picked up the cash and hefted it, then slipped it into his jacket. "Don't need to. I can tell by the weight." He gave Allie another appraising look and then indicated a green canvas duffel. "You can put the guns and ammo in that. My compliments. If you want the NV gear, that'll be another five grand for the lot. Your choice."

Jack thought about it briefly and then reached into his back pocket and withdrew a smaller wad of hundreds folded in half. He handed it to Spencer. "Five thousand. Pleasure doing business with you."

"Likewise."

Drake helped Jack stow the weapons and ammunition. When they straightened up, Jack faced Spencer.

"Have you got a cell phone I can use? We need to call for a ride."

Spencer reached into his jacket pocket. He retrieved a small phone and held it up. "You have a number?"

Jack read off the card, and Spencer pushed the buttons and spoke in fluent, rapid-fire Spanish. When he was finished, he offered Jack the phone. "You can check the sent calls to verify I actually spoke to someone. It'll show the duration of the call next to the number."

"I'm sure that won't be necessary. You're going to wait with us till the cab arrives, right?" Allie asked.

"Normally I'd say no and send you on your way. But seeing as you asked so nicely, I'll make an exception," he said. "The driver said five minutes. Which gives you just about long enough to explain what you're up to, so I can decide if I'm interested. My advice would be to talk fast."

Jack fixed Spencer with a penetrating gaze. "Have you ever heard of Paititi?"

Spencer laughed. "Of course. Who around here hasn't? The lost city. That's what you're trying to find?" He shook his head. "Good luck. There's no such place. They've been looking for centuries. Guess what's been found? Nothing. Nada. It's a story. Nothing more."

Drake cleared his throat. "Maybe. But my father spent his life researching it, and thought he was close to discovering it when he died."

"Just because he thought he was onto something doesn't make it so. What evidence do you have other than his feeling?" Spencer asked, his voice reasonable.

"He was killed to get the information. He took it to his grave," Drake spat.

"Really? How do you know that?"

Jack told the story of the Russians. Spencer was in the middle of asking more questions when they heard a car pull up outside and honk.

"Let me think about this some. You have my number. Call me when you're ready to make full disclosure. And be prepared to fill me in on everything. I'm not interested in getting involved in anything half-baked. Which is what most of the expeditions I've seen are. Every couple of years some academics show up, go into the jungle, and come back a month later, exhausted, beaten, and empty-handed. That's of those that make it back. Quite a few don't."

Jack nodded. "In case you haven't figured it out, we aren't academics."

Spencer gave Allie a final long look. "I can see that. Let's talk later. Now get going before your car hightails it out of here. Taxis get nervous in this district. They won't even come into it after dark."

"What about you?" Allie asked.

"You worry about yourself. This is my turf. I know my way around."

Jack carried the duffel through the door and the cabbie popped the trunk. He placed the bag inside and shut it, noticing that the driver didn't offer to get out and help. Jack took the front passenger seat, Drake and Allie the rear, and their doors had barely shut when the driver accelerated, eager to get to safer turf.

Drake looked back at the anonymous building through the rear window. The last thing he saw was Spencer standing by the open door with an infuriating crooked smile on his face as he watched the taxi shoot down the street.

Chapter Twenty-Four

Jack stowed the weapons in his room and met Drake and Allie downstairs in the bar, where their only company were two Argentine businessmen at the far end having an animated discussion in Spanish. Jack took a seat and ordered a soda, then sat back with his arms crossed.

"It's decision time. Do we trust him, or do we keep looking?"

Allie frowned. "He came through on the guns. Just like he said he would."

Drake shook his head. "A bad idea. He's got something up his sleeve. And he's way too arrogant."

Jack's drink arrived. "I don't disagree that he comes off that way, but that doesn't matter to me. What matters is whether he's competent and whether he'll keep his word. So far he's done what he's said he would. But that was just sourcing us merchandise at a handsome profit. It doesn't require a lot of trust. If we tell him everything about how we plan to proceed…"

"He could sell us out," Drake finished the thought.

"How? In the middle of the jungle?" Allie asked.

"I don't know. But he could."

Jack took a sip of his cola. "So could anyone. That's a risk we take with any guide. It's the same no matter who it is."

"Then maybe we should do this on our own. Take our weapons and get going. Why do we need a guide, anyway?" Drake grumbled.

161

"If we blunder around, we're as good as dead. Think about the drug gangs. A seasoned smuggler's going to know their routes and how to avoid them. We don't. There's no question that we need a seasoned guide. The question is only, is this man our best bet?"

"He's our only bet so far," Allie said.

They continued the debate for an hour and finally agreed that they'd tell Spencer their plan and take their chances. Everyone was aware of the clock ticking, and that the Russians would figure it out sooner than later and be on their tail. Drake had been in favor of nosing around more to see who else they could find, but in the end he'd deferred to Jack's wisdom, even if he didn't like it.

Spencer agreed to meet them at a nearby restaurant after a late dinner. When he arrived he looked relaxed, as always, although Jack noted that his eyes did a complete scan of the room as he neared their table.

"How was the food?" Spencer asked as he pulled up a chair.

"Not bad. Little spicy, but that's what keeps it interesting, right?" Allie asked.

"True words." Spencer flagged the server down and ordered coffee. When the man departed, he leaned forward. "All right. I'm here. So spill the beans. Why do you believe you have any chance of finding a treasure that's gone undiscovered for five hundred years?"

Jack and Drake took him through everything that had happened, and Drake offered an overview of the journal's contents, keeping it general. In spite of Jack's assurances, his gut told him to hold back, so that was what he did. He fielded the pointed questions with honest if incomplete answers, reasoning that they'd all see whether they could depend on Spencer over time. If so, then he would learn more as they went. If not, Drake still had the most important information in his head.

When they were done, Spencer sat silently studying their faces. "You know it's nearly suicidal to go into the area you're thinking about, right?"

"We know what we're walking into. That's why we need someone who's familiar with the terrain and the people in it," Jack said.

Spencer frowned. "What do you make of the treasure's value?"

"It's anyone's guess, but based on what accounts there are, it may be in the five to ten billion range," Allie said.

Spencer whistled quietly.

"But if we inform them, the government of Peru will want the majority. We'll probably get five to ten percent as a finder's fee. Assuming we can keep the location known only to us until they officially recognize the discovery as our find," she finished.

"So you're hoping for a half a billion to a billion dollar payday?"

Drake nodded. "If we're lucky, that's how the math works."

Spencer eyed him without expression. "Fine. If I decide to do this, I want twenty-five percent."

Drake laughed. "Right. A quarter-billion dollars for the jungle guide." He turned to Jack. "I told you. We're wasting our time."

Jack's eyes narrowed as he held Spencer's gaze. "That's a little rich, don't you think?" he asked.

"Is it? You want me to risk everything to help you survive in a jungle that'll kill you as surely as a firing squad, but you don't want to share the proceeds evenly? Maybe you've got the wrong man. Find some local crook who'll agree to do it for fifty grand, and then find out the hard way that he was worth exactly nothing. You already got ripped off once. Why not try to bargain-shop for your parachute, too? Sure, it's the only thing between you hitting the ground at two hundred plus or landing safely, but why not shoot for a deal?"

Jack grunted. "I don't disagree that you should walk away with a lot of money. We were thinking more like ten percent. If our calculations are right, that's between fifty and a hundred million bucks. Are you going to tell me that's not enough for you?"

Spencer shook his head. "It's not about what's enough. If I join this little shindig, I join it as an equal, not as hired help. I'll pull my weight, and for that I expect an even cut. You want to hire a contractor, not take on a partner who will see it through, then best of luck. Remember that you have to come out alive to spend any of that cash you're sure is just lying around in the jungle. A bargain's not going to seem like one when you're dying a million miles from nowhere."

"How do we know you can guide us safely?" Drake demanded, his voice tight.

"Because I've spent ten years navigating that region and I'm here to tell about it."

"And how do we know that's true?" Drake fired back.

"Gee, I don't know. I got you exactly the weapons you needed within a matter of hours. Your contact Asad screwed you, just like I told Jack he would. So far I'm 100%, and except for your dealings with me, you've been taken. I'm telling you that I know that jungle well. And guess what? I'm not the one asking someone to guide them. You are. So here are your options: keep looking and hope you get lucky – not just with someone who actually knows what the hell they're doing, but who also won't cut your throat. Or take me on as an equal partner, assuming I'm willing to do it – which I have to tell you, decreases every time you open your mouth, kid."

Jack cut Drake's response off. "It's a lot of money, Spencer. A lot."

"Only if you find it. If not, it's just hot air. Which brings me to the next part. I want fifty grand up front."

"What?" Drake blurted.

"For expenses. And I don't take American Express."

"You're delusional," Drake spat.

Spencer shrugged. "Sixty grand. Keep talking."

"Completely nuts."

"Trying for seventy? That's next."

Jack interrupted the escalation. "Your point's taken. But I've got a serious concern. If the two of you can't get along, this isn't going to work."

Spencer nodded and glared at Jack. "I completely agree. I don't know what your buddy's problem is, but he's doing everything he can to queer this deal. I don't much care, frankly, because without me, you're not going to make it, and the chances of you finding Paititi are close to zero, anyway. So it's not like I feel like I'm losing much by walking away. Better powwow with your friend here, because he's about to talk himself out of a guide, and I can pretty much guarantee whoever you get, assuming you can find anyone crazy enough to bite at this, is going to do nothing but steal your money or get you killed – or both."

Jack turned to Drake. "Can I see you for a minute?"

"Sure," Drake said.

They walked toward the restrooms and Jack stopped in the access hall. "What the hell do you think you're doing?" he growled.

"I think he's full of it."

"You may, but all you're accomplishing is making him more expensive by the minute. Was that your goal?"

"I'm not giving him twenty-five percent of the take," Drake said adamantly.

"Which is how much, at the moment? Help me out. Because I'd like to understand what kind of jet I should be shopping for. How much have we found?"

"That's not the point."

"No, Drake, I think that's exactly the point. Right now this is all speculation. It's a wild card. Anything can happen. We may find this lost city, and the gold might be gone. Or it might have never existed, and the legend was just that – a story to pass the time. Or we could get killed before we ever find it. Or never find it. Because that's the most likely, given that five hundred years of explorers have failed – including your dad, God rest his soul. I had nothing but respect for him, but the fact remains he didn't find it either. He was excited and thought he was close, but that's like being close to being pregnant. On things like this, the world's binary. Black or white. Do you get that?"

Drake ground his teeth, about done with Jack's tone. "I do. But I still don't want to cut him in at that level. We discussed ten percent. If you remember, I thought even that was way too high."

"I remember. But here's how it's coming down. Either we agree to his terms, or he walks away, and we're right back where we started. We can try a little negotiation, but once we have, we either have to go with him, or start over and hope that the next guy isn't a complete criminal."

"Which Spencer could also be."

"Sure. But in my experience crooks don't deliver top-quality weapons, on time, with no deposit. So in the absence of any other info, right now he's the last blonde in the bar and it's closing time. The question is, do you want a date, or do you want to go home alone?"

"That's an apt metaphor, because I feel like we're about to get fu–"

Jack stopped him with a gesture. "Drake, this isn't about your feelings. I don't know what your problem is with Spencer, but my vote is we stop screwing around and close this so we can get to finding the city. Sometimes you have to do the best deal you can, not wait for the ideal one to come along. You don't have to love him. I'm not asking you to get engaged. I'm asking you to behave like a professional and do what has to be done in order to make this work."

Drake sighed. "Fine. Try to get him to fifteen. I'll swallow my pride and shut up. I promise."

"This time, for real, right?"

Drake put his hand over his heart.

"Good. Because we can't really afford any more bickering, in more ways than one."

"For the record, I also don't like the way he's checking out Allie. He's a slimeball. We'll live to regret this."

Jack's eyes narrowed. "Is that what this is all about? Allie? You don't want him around because you think he's going to put the moves on her?" Jack paused. "Or is it that you're afraid she'd be receptive?"

Drake's eyes darted to the side. "I don't care if you don't."

Jack's tone softened. "Allie's a big girl, and a handful, as you've seen. She can take care of herself. But some words of advice: Think with your head and we'll all do a lot better. You can worry about what Allie might or might not like after we've found the treasure and made it out of the jungle in one piece, okay? In the meantime, keep your eye on the prize. I think we've got more than enough drama without two rams butting heads over one woman."

Drake bit back the three nasty responses that sprang to mind, and merely shrugged. "Like I said. I don't care if you don't."

"Then it's settled. I can cover thirty of it from the gold I sold in Texas if you've got the other thirty. Now let's see if I can whittle him down some on the percentage, okay? And remember your promise. Not a word."

"I'm the third monkey. Silent as death."

Jack gave him a final stare. "I'm going to hold you to that."

They returned to the table, where Allie was chatting easily with Spencer, and Drake hated him all the more for it but kept quiet. Jack sat down heavily and cleared his throat.

"Now where were we? You were discussing giving us a discount?" he asked.

"Not exactly."

"Look, fifty grand is almost all our money."

"It's sixty, remember?"

Jack stayed calm. "If you're going to be a partner, why do we have to kick in cash? If everyone's getting a piece, you should actually be contributing to the pot."

"You're offsetting other jobs I have to cancel or farm out. Or you can wait until I'm done. Probably three weeks."

Jack decided not to push it. "We could go as high as fifteen percent. Maybe hundred and fifty million, if the stories are even close to being true."

"Not good enough."

They went back and forth, and finally Allie shook her head. "Gentlemen, here's my suggestion. Spencer? You seem like an honorable man. Let's not argue over this. We'll go twenty percent, and the final five percent you want will come out of my twenty-six and change percent. Does that make you feel better?"

"Why should you have to take the hit?" Spencer demanded.

"Because it's obviously more important to you to prove your point and do the alpha male dance than to just agree to a fortune and have done with it. If we're right, boohoo, I'll only get two hundred ten million or so instead of two hundred sixty-six. Guess what? I think I'll learn to live with that disappointment."

Spencer sat back, the tension seeping from his shoulders. "Fine. I'll take twenty. But I want the sixty up front. Nothing happens until I see that."

Jack nodded. "Where do you want to meet tomorrow morning? I can have the cash then."

"Same coffee shop. Nine a.m.," Spencer said. "I'll need some time to arrange everything on my end, but it shouldn't take that long. Figure we can start this shindig in a few days."

They discussed logistics, and then Jack rose, extending his hand. "I'll see you tomorrow, partner."

Spencer clasped it and shook after a wary glance at Drake.

"Done deal."

Chapter Twenty-Five

The handoff of cash took place without incident, leaving them with seriously diminished resources, but at least the outline of a plan. Spencer handed Jack a satellite phone for communication, and Jack told him to get to the tiny Peruvian town of Atalaya, in the Ucayali region of the country, smack in the middle of the eastern jungle, as soon as possible. Spencer agreed to join them there in three days – he said he needed to coordinate support for their journey – which gave Drake pause. But in keeping with his new philosophy of silence on the subject of Spencer, he didn't voice his misgivings: that Spencer would never appear, preferring to make off with a huge amount of their cash. In Peru, Drake figured a smuggler like Spencer could easily vanish for years, leaving no trace.

Jack didn't seem concerned, so Drake choked down his doubts and put on a brave face. Spencer arranged for a private plane to fly them to Atalaya, on the banks of the Tambo River, where they would be met by a car and driver to ferry them to their lodging.

The plane, an old Cessna 210, took off at 4:30 that afternoon, and after a bumpy ride over the Andes at thirteen thousand feet, by 6:00 they were dropping over the jungle and touching down on the distressed asphalt at the Lieutenant General Gerardo Pérez Pinedo Airport, a grandiose name indeed for a meager strip of battered pavement. When the pilot opened his door, the wet heat seeped into the tiny cabin with a vengeance, easily twenty degrees hotter than Lima on the coast.

They exited the plane and walked to a battered VW Beetle, where a man with deep brown skin stood waiting, a grin frozen in place. As they drew near, Drake realized that the man wasn't being friendly – he was disfigured, and one side of his face was puckered with scarring that pulled the lip up in a morbid permanent smile. The driver introduced himself as Benji, and told them in halting English that he'd escort them to their hotel. They quickly packed their bags into the small front trunk and wedged themselves into the Volkswagen, which was about the temperature of molten lead from sitting in the fading sun.

The engine sputtered to life and they bounced down a furrowed dirt road, Benji swerving to avoid the worst of the potholes, many of which were nearly the size of the car. A scorching breeze drifted through the small open windows, cooling the interior's infernal temperature to merely stifling. Benji was as talkative as the pilot had been, which was to say not at all, and the only thing he said in the entire trip was to confirm they wanted to go to the best of the three lodging choices in the small hamlet.

Atalaya was as shabby a town as any they'd seen, an impoverished outpost built just west of the riverbank. When Benji dropped them off at their temporary new home, Allie's face was a study in horror at the filthy street and crumbling buildings, although she quickly recovered and assumed her normally placid expression.

Jack gave the place a sour look and shrugged. "Doesn't look like much has changed in Atalaya since the last time I was here. Maybe a little bigger. But still about as welcoming as hepatitis. Come on. Might as well get some rooms. By the looks of this joint, though, we're lucky if it's got running water." He shouldered his bags. "Which is going to seem like impossible luxury once we're in the rainforest. So enjoy it while it lasts."

Allie and Drake exchanged looks and followed him inside, where a wizened old woman greeted them in Spanish, which Allie spoke passably well. Each room was the equivalent of eight dollars a night, which, while highway robbery in the ass end of Nowhere, Peru, they weren't in any position to argue about.

The rooms were more like jail cells than guest quarters, each with a creaky overhead fan and a second, smaller one sitting on a table near the open windows, whose mosquito netting sported gaps the size of a man's fist.

"Hey, at least the toilet's got a seat," Drake called out upon opening the bathroom door and seeing a mold accumulation that was more in keeping with a science experiment than human habitation.

"It's the little things," Allie agreed from her room next door, the walls scarcely more than cardboard thickness.

After settling in, they went in search of sustenance – an easier task than they'd expected given that there were only a few establishments in town that sold hot food, assuming you didn't want to eat from the back of a barbecue in someone's driveway. The family-style shack they eventually chose had six tables, of which three were occupied by workers, their faces tired after a long day fishing or logging.

Jack sat at the one closest to the open window and Drake and Allie joined him. The owner, a small woman with well-padded hips, wearing pink plastic sandals and baggy jeans cut off at the knees, approached and handed them a laminated menu before asking what they wanted to drink. They all opted for bottled water, the heat already working its dehydrating magic, and Allie read off the various choices, which unsurprisingly revolved around fish, with some chicken and pork thrown in – all of it local, they were sure.

When the woman returned with their drinks, Allie ordered, and the proprietress disappeared into the kitchen, where presumably she would cook the meal herself. An ancient standing fan blew eddies of moist air from one side of the restaurant to the other, and by the time the food arrived they were soaked with sweat. Flies orbited throughout the establishment, and Allie spent much of her time swatting at the pests in a futile attempt to dissuade them from their attraction to her.

"Get used to it. This is as good as it'll get. It's jungle, which means heat and rain, rain and heat. It's probably a good thing that we've got a few days to acclimate," Jack said.

"And I thought Rio was uncomfortable," Allie said.

"I told you then, that was nothing. This is like the Bataan death march compared to Rio, because there you have the wind off the Atlantic to cool things off. Here it's going to be miserable. Only question is how many hours a day it'll rain."

Drake tried a forkful of fish, and his eyes widened, then began streaming. "Oh my God that's spicy. My mouth's on fire," he said, reaching for the water.

"The locals do like a little bit of pizzazz to liven up their meals. I should have warned you," Jack said. "I remember that from last time. Probably kills the parasites, so be thankful."

Allie nodded after taking a bite of her chicken. "At least I don't have to worry about gaining weight. This will burn any fat off."

"Along with most of my stomach lining," Drake agreed, taking another soothing sip. "Which reminds me. How are we going to get food and water once we're in the jungle?"

"Water won't be a problem. I've got some treatment pills, although with the amount it rains, we'll probably just collect rainwater – that way there are fewer complications. As to food, other than our supplies, we'll catch fish when we're near a river, and hunt whatever we can. There's plenty of wild boar, different varieties of deer, snake, monkey…"

"We're going to be butchering Bambi?" Allie asked, frowning.

"Either that or chimp à la mode," Drake quipped.

"I'm *so* not going to eat monkey," she said.

"In some countries, it's a delicacy. Or at least a staple. Parts of Africa, for example. They call it bush meat there," Jack offered.

"Ew."

"How are we going to bring down a deer or a pig without alerting the whole jungle with gunshots?" Drake asked.

Jack chewed his fish, then pulled a long bone from his mouth and set it on the plate. "Fair question. I asked Spencer to source a couple of crossbows. They're accurate, good stopping power, and with a little practice, silent and deadly."

They ate in silence, the heat draining them of any enthusiasm they otherwise might have had at being so close to beginning their journey into the unknown. The flies were already an accepted part of the experience – the least of their worries and only a minor annoyance compared to the mosquitoes, which came out en masse as dusk arrived.

"I see what you mean by needing insect repellent," Drake conceded, glad he'd sprayed not only his skin but his clothes.

Jack nodded. "That's the thing I remember like it was yesterday. If you leave even one inch unprotected, you'll be eaten alive, and malaria and dengue fever are endemic to this area. Bug spray's more valuable than water in the jungle. I honestly don't know how anyone explored without it. Imagine being on a wooden boat five hundred years ago, going up the Amazon, wearing armor. Unbelievable, really, when you think about it."

"I suppose we don't have it so bad," Allie said, waving away a particularly persistent fly circling her head.

"It's all relative. The town's grown some, but it doesn't seem like prosperity's singled it out. Look at the place. The poor are really poor, and the shopkeepers don't have it much better. Amazing that people can live like this," Jack said. "At least some of the streets are paved now. That's progress."

They paid a pittance for their meals before walking to the *malecon* that ran along the river, ambling down the sidewalk that meandered the length of the town along the bank. Now that night had fallen, only a few of the buildings in town had lights on – most were dark, the next work day starting when the sun came up, the residents already asleep.

After a cursory constitutional they returned to the hotel, which wasn't any more inviting in the evening than it had been in daylight. On the street, two small motorized tricycles sat parked waiting for fares – the town's taxi force, hardly more than motorbikes with a cab on the back large enough to accommodate a couple, like the tuk tuks of Vietnam and Thailand. The drivers lounged by the corner, trading jokes and anecdotes, nowhere to go, no customers, buoyed by the eternal hope that someone would happen along and want a ride.

Upstairs in the room, Drake took a tepid shower and then coated himself head to toe with bug spray before pointing the fan at the bed and pulling back the single sheet to confirm there were no insects lurking beneath it to feast on him. Satisfied he was safe, at least for the moment, he switched off the light and rested his head on the flat pillow, the only sound the occasional laugh from the drivers on the street below and the atonal hum of the fan's motor.

Chapter Twenty-Six

"Again."

Jack's face was beaded with sweat and red from sunburn as he stood in a fighting stance, waiting for Drake to make his move. The field on the far edge of town was vacant in the late morning, the inhabitants all busy on the river that sustained them, be it with trade or food. They'd watched from their breakfast perch at a hut near the *malecon* as long, thin wooden boats eased into the flow of muddy brown water while young men tossed nets from their knee-deep positions along the bank, hoping to trap some of the fish apparently teeming in the noxious soup.

"Come on. That last pass was pretty good. Let's see if you can do it again," Jack said, having risen and dusted himself off after Drake had downed him for the fourth time that morning. Drake had improved as they'd practiced, to the point where he was now giving almost as good as he received. Allie sat beneath a tree fifteen yards away as the two men slowly circled each other, their T-shirts drenched with sweat as well as the remnants of a momentary cloudburst that had hit fifteen minutes earlier, before they'd had a chance to find cover.

The sun filtered from between the clouds, raising the already blistering temperature another few degrees. Drake eyed Jack, waiting for a tell – something that would give him an indication of what he was expecting, so he could do the opposite. The sparring had come naturally to him after years of karate and wrestling, yet he was consistently surprised by how fast the older man was.

Drake feinted left with a blow and followed with a sweep kick with his left leg, crouching as he spun, hoping to knock Jack's legs from under him with the sudden change in tactics. His shin connected solidly with the side of Jack's knee and he felt it buckle. Drake was already up as Jack tumbled backward, and it was over before it started as the ground knocked the wind out of Jack with a loud "oof."

Jack lay flat on his back and looked up at Drake. "Looking good. I never saw that coming."

Drake leaned over and offered his hand to pull Jack to his feet. "I got lucky."

"No, that was actually a great move. And it worked. My only caution would be that if I'd had a knife, it would have been sticking out of your back before you had a chance to finish the kick."

"Which is why we agreed that getting into a fight with a guy with a knife is a losing proposition."

"So you *were* paying attention."

"I told you, I have a good memory."

Jack checked the time and stretched his arms overhead. "Let's call it quits. I'm getting hungry."

"What about Allie? When does she get the crap beaten out of her?" Drake asked.

"Son, I wouldn't say that too loud. She's about as good as any I've seen, and I'm not kidding. Lightning fast, and a lot of power behind her strikes."

Allie's voice rang out. "I heard you. Just let me know whenever you feel like you've graduated, and I'll take you for a few rounds, tough guy," she called from her position, the smile on her face belying her words. "I used to take down Dad with regularity."

The two men gathered their backpacks, and Jack hefted the rucksack with the guns, which Jack hadn't thought prudent to leave in the room for whoever cleaned to discover. The last thing they needed was to land in a Peruvian jail for possession of illegal weapons. He shouldered it and led the way back into town, taking long, economical strides. Drake hung back and chatted with Allie, who'd apparently warmed up to him again and was being increasingly friendly as they spent more time together. But even as they walked, in the back of Drake's mind was the tension Spencer would bring with him. With an act of will, he decided not to worry about it – Allie was an adult, and if she preferred Spencer over Drake, that was her choice.

They tried a different place for lunch, a large *palapa* by the river, where several groups of laborers from the boats were digging into their food with gusto. Allie read them their choices and all three opted for the fish after eyeing the neighboring tables, where heaping plates of fresh catch were being devoured.

Training continued until another rainstorm passed through at 5:30, this one sustained. They soldiered down the muddy roads back to the hotel, soaked but at least not baking. That night passed much as the prior night had, and when Drake collapsed onto the bed after covering himself with a film of insect spray, every muscle in his body was sore. His last thought as he drifted off was of Allie taunting him.

The following afternoon, after another long session, this time with knives as well as more unarmed technique, Jack powered up the satellite phone just before they left the field and called Spencer. He had a hurried discussion and stabbed the phone off before rolling his head around to loosen the stiffness in his neck.

"Well? Aren't you going to tell us what he said?" Allie asked.

"He said he'd be here tomorrow. And to be ready to move out the following morning. That was it."

"At least he answered his phone. That's a plus," she observed, and Drake had to reluctantly, if silently, agree.

That evening, after dinner, Drake wasn't tired yet and decided to see what, if any, after-dark entertainment the town offered. He wasn't hoping for much, and when he bid Jack and Allie goodnight at the hotel, he was surprised when she offered to join him, ignoring Jack's stern look.

"Just remember, if anyone starts something, walk away. You can't afford to be on the radar. Keep a low profile."

"Yes, Dad," Allie said, her voice light.

"This is a really bad idea, just so you know," he warned. "These small working towns can get rough at night. But I know better than to try to talk you out of anything by now."

"We won't do anything. Just grab a beer, and hit it. I promise," Allie said, and she sounded sincere.

Occasional clouds drifted above them like luminous cotton painted against the night sky. They could smell the rushing water as they ambled wordlessly along the riverbank to a bar they'd noticed tucked away under two huge trees at the far end of town. When they made it inside the hut, they found a short, chubby man with an elaborately waxed black moustache tending bar. A dozen blue plastic tables sat crookedly on the hard-packed dirt floor, mostly empty. Seeing them, he left the small portable television he'd been watching and approached. Allie went back and forth with him for a minute, and when he turned away to get their drinks, he had a broad smile on his face.

"What was that all about?" Drake asked.

"I asked him why his establishment wasn't packed on a Thursday night. He said that the workers get paid every Saturday. They're out of money by now, so Thursdays and Fridays are usually dead. But look out come Saturday."

"That was it?"

"Then I asked if what I'd heard was true: that his bar served the coldest beer in town. That's when he laughed. He said he served just about the only beer in town, but that he'd do his best to find a couple of cold ones for us."

"I guess at some point I'll have to learn to speakee."

"We can add Spanish to your long list of learning experiences, if you like. I'm not fluent, but I'm pretty decent at it."

"Sounded fluent to me."

"That's because you had no idea what I was saying. A native speaker would know the difference."

The bartender returned with four bottles of beer in a bucket of ice. He sat the dented metal pail on the table and popped the tops off two, adding something in drawling Spanish. It was Allie's turn to laugh, and then they were alone, the proprietor returned to his TV program, the other patrons focused on their drinking and conversations.

"He said we get the special treatment because I'm so nice," she explained.

"A bucket of ice?"

"Yes. Because the beer would be warm thirty seconds after it sat out, and he didn't want to disappoint me." She batted her lashes.

Drake held his beer out in a toast. Allie clinked hers against it and took a long sip. She closed her eyes, leaned her head back, and emitted a contented sigh before opening them and setting the bottle on the table. Drake took a swig of his own, enjoying the icy bite in his mouth before placing it beside hers. They sat quietly for several minutes, watching beads of sweat form on the bottles and tear down the sides, and then he drained another third in two gulps and stuck the bottle back into the ice, which had already melted into a frosty soup. Allie did the same as she looked around the bar.

"Not really that lively a place, is it?" she asked.

"Maybe the band doesn't show up till later."

She shook her head. "How would you like to live in a dump like this? Most of these people will never leave this town. They'll spend their entire lives here, by the river, fishing like their parents did before them, living and dying oblivious to the outside world."

"Maybe there's something to be said for the simple life. I mean, we're from the outside world, and they don't look that unhappy to me. Perhaps they know something we don't."

"I'm not sure about that. I think it's about lowered expectations. If you don't know any better, then you're happy raising chickens and wearing rags. But there's more to life than eking out a sustenance existence."

"Sure there is. But at its essence, isn't this the same as anywhere else? Boys meet girls, they start families, they do the best they can, they raise their kids, and eventually get old and die. In between, they enjoy what they can, living off the land in a place time forgot. I'd say they have everything."

"The noble savage? Really, Drake? You believe that?"

"I'm not saying that their lives couldn't be better, but for the most part, they'd just be different lives, not necessarily improved ones. Okay, sure, modern health care would be nice, but do they really need the Internet and text messaging and designer everything? I mean, do we? What have we got to show for it? Everyone I know is kind of miserable. Maybe with a fifty-thousand-dollar car, but still, not all that happy. There's a certain simplicity to knowing your place in the scheme of things. A satisfaction that always wanting bigger, faster, better kills."

Allie studied him without saying anything, and then finished her beer. "You surprise me. That's unexpected, coming from a California boy raised in the heart of progress."

"I've been thinking about it a lot since reading my dad's journal. He didn't seem all that impressed by the modern world – it comes through loud and clear in his notes. That was part of the appeal of finding a big treasure. He wrote several times that if he wound up rich, the first thing he'd do was to move his loved ones someplace with a slower pace."

"Really? Like where? Did he say?"

"He mentioned a couple of islands. In the South Pacific. Away from the crowds, as he put it."

"And what will you do if we find a fortune, Drake? Have you thought about it?" She pulled the two sealed bottles of beer from the bucket and opened the first with the top of the second and handed it to him, then popped hers open on a section of the pail handle. "Cheers."

"Cheers. No, I haven't. Something about staying alive long enough to find it keeps intruding."

"Well, think about it. What would you do?"

He drank a large swallow of beer. "You know what? I have no idea."

"None? At all?"

He shook his head. "Pretty lame, huh?"

"No. It just means that maybe you aren't that motivated by money."

"What about you? What would you do?"

"Oh, that's easy. I'd start an archeology team and go in search of the most elusive legendary finds out there. And buy a really cool house and a super obnoxious car. And probably hire a dozen hot pool boys."

They laughed easily together. "Something tells me you wouldn't have to hire them," he said.

"No, that's the whole point. I'd want to. They'd have to wear little outfits with no shirts, and wander around the house barefoot, attending to my every need. Don't spoil the fantasy with them being free. I'd want to be ugly rich. Screw being graceful about it. Hot and cold running Sven and Zack. That's my speed."

"Would you really do that?"

She giggled, offering a flash of white teeth that made Drake's breath catch in his throat. "Probably not. It sounds dumb. But I want to buy something to prove to myself that I made it. Maybe a plane or something. That's what you should do, too."

He toasted her again. "Well, let's find it first. Then we can worry about how to spend it."

"Killjoy."

Drake held his beer up to the light and peered through the final dregs. "You think he's got any more of these cold ones back there?"

She gave him another long, appraising look, and stood. "I'll ask."

An hour later and two more beers apiece, they were feeling a glow almost as warm as the night air. Drake paid and they left the bar, the streets dark except for an occasional porch light and an intermittent glow from the moon as it silvered the surface of the river. They ambled along the waterfront in silence, two stray dogs ahead of them scavenging for scraps, and when they neared the halfway point to the hotel, Drake took Allie's hand and pulled her toward him. He stopped and drew her into his arms and kissed her. She pushed away initially, but then responded in kind, her fingers entwined in his hair as she met his urgency with her own.

Heavy footsteps sounded from the direction of the bar. Drake's eyes opened and he swiveled toward the sound. Three figures were approaching, sticking to the shadows. Drake disengaged from Allie and whispered in her ear.

"This could be trouble. Go back to the hotel. Now."

"No. Remember, we're supposed to avoid any drama. I'm not leaving without you."

She began walking hurriedly toward the familiar cross street a hundred and fifty yards up the bank, and Drake accompanied her. The footsteps increased their pace behind them, and then broke into a run.

"Go on. Move. I'll slow them down. You don't want to get raped, Allie. All they can do is rob me." He reached into his pocket and withdrew the last of his American cash and handed it to her. "Quick. Get to the hotel and tell Jack I'm in trouble. Get going."

Her eyes caught the moonlight and he could see fear in them. Then she was running, fortunately faster than the approaching footfalls behind him. He watched as she sprinted down the street, and turned when he judged that whoever was giving chase was ten yards away.

The three men were nothing like what he'd been expecting, which had been laborers from the bar, or possibly indigents looking for easy prey in a frontier town. Instead, the men were obviously Caucasian, well groomed, wearing reasonably expensive tropical-weight clothes. A tickle of fear crept up his spine as his eyes met those of the man in the lead – the cold, expressionless eyes of a predator.

Drake looked for weapons, but didn't see any. That was good. He might be able to take them with nothing but hand-to-hand, especially after all the training. He turned slightly and began bouncing on the balls of his feet as he prepared for their first assault.

The lead man, easily in his fifties, shook his head. "There's no need for that, Mr. Ramsey."

Drake maintained his stance, but the unaccented English threw him. He'd been expecting…Russian. This man sounded American. He squinted at them. "You know who I am. What do you want?"

The two other men drew abreast of the first and Drake stiffened. The speaker held out a hand to hold them back. When he answered, his words were measured, his tone reasonable.

"To talk. We have a proposition for you."

"I see. Why don't we start with who you are, and how you know who I am?" Drake countered.

The man shrugged. "Names are unimportant, but you can call me Gus if you like. As to how I know who you are, that's equally unimportant. Let's just say that we've been watching you for some time."

"Very dramatic and mysterious, Gus, but not an answer."

"Perhaps. More importantly, we know why you're here. We know your history, and we know what you're after."

Drake's eyes narrowed. "You may. Or you may be bluffing."

"Hardly. You'll find we don't bluff."

"We. Again with the we. Who's *we*?"

"Let's just say that we represent a powerful organization that shares the same interest you do."

"Could you be any more vague?" Drake asked, stalling for time. Allie would be back at the hotel by now. Given a few minutes to rouse Jack and for him to get dressed, Drake needed to buy himself four to five minutes, tops, before the cavalry came over the hill.

"Fine. We're with the Central Intelligence Agency." Gus paused for a moment to allow his words to sink in. "You haven't asked about the proposal."

"Maybe it's because I don't have important discussions while outnumbered three to one in dark alleys by people claiming to be American spooks."

"This is hardly an alley. In any event, we're interested in getting your assistance with a matter we believe you can help with. And we can guarantee your safety if we work together."

"Work together? Guarantee my safety? The CIA wants me to work with them, and had to come to the armpit of Peru to ask me?"

"I'm up to speed on the regrettable story of your father, Mr. Ramsey. I'm also aware that the same adversaries who were responsible for his death are closing in on your location and will be actively pursuing you."

Drake tried to blink away the fogginess from the beer. "What do you want?" he demanded.

"We want the journal, young man."

"I have no idea what you're talking about."

Gus's tone hardened. "Stop playing dumb. We want the journal."

"I don't have it."

Gus didn't flinch, but his voice dropped to a whisper. "You have no idea what you're playing with."

"I haven't broken any laws, and I'm not guilty of anything," Drake countered.

Gus gave an impatient shake of his head. "Drake, we'd like you to work with us. This is a matter that we've been pursuing for over twenty years."

"I'm not interested."

"Maybe that's because you don't know what you've gotten into. Drake, does the journal mention a man named Palenko?" Gus watched Drake's eyes for a reaction and saw nothing. "Your father was working with us when he went into the jungle the last time, you know."

"Working with you? Why?"

"He discovered a connection between Paititi and the Soviets. He met a Peruvian who'd been treated for congestive heart failure in the same hospital room as a Russian who was dying of encephalitis. A Russian who claimed to have lived in Paititi for two years."

"What? And he believed that?"

"Aren't you wondering why Russians are involved in this?" Gus asked softly.

"I have a feeling you're going to tell me."

"What I'm about to say is classified, do you understand? Never to be repeated."

"Do I have to sign something?"

"Believe me, we'll know if you talk." Gus eyed him. "At the end of the Cold War, a brilliant but unbalanced Soviet scientist – Grigor Palenko, one of the regime's top weapons developers – left Russia, taking with him a container of some ore he'd mined from a meteor he'd discovered in the Peruvian jungle decades before. He believed an element in the ore could be used to create new kinds of weapons of mass destruction; or if used for peaceful applications, might accommodate most of the world's energy needs. He'd spent years working to extract the element and refine it, and had created a theoretical technology that he believed had the potential to change the world order."

"What does that have to do with the journal, or my father? Or me, for that matter?"

"Palenko had been consumed by two passions in life: developing that technology and the legend of Paititi. But as the Berlin wall crumbled, it became obvious to him that Russia was no longer safe, and that he'd be persecuted by political enemies ascending to power. He slipped out of the country with the only twenty-four pounds of the element in existence, accompanied by several cronies, determined to locate Paititi and fund the development of his ultimate invention – the equivalent of cold fusion."

"And you believe he found Paititi? Doesn't that sound a little like a fairy tale to you?" Drake asked, his scorn obvious.

"The Russian, who we believe was Palenko's assistant, died shortly after telling the Peruvian his story. And the Peruvian died only a few days after selling your father the account for five hundred dollars."

"Sounds like there are con artists all over Peru. I can't believe anyone would buy that load of malarkey."

"Drake, Palenko has the ore, and we need to locate it at all costs. We've been looking for a long time."

"Right. For what did you say – twenty years? How's that going?" Drake asked. "And if it's so important, why not just come up with some excuse about shutting down drug trafficking in the region and send in the marines?"

"That's not how these things work." Gus paused. "The man's a lunatic, Drake. Lunatics can be problematic to track, but our mission hasn't changed. We have to find him."

"What do I have to do with that?"

"You're in considerable danger. The Russians are after the same thing, and they'll stop at nothing. The shooting in Menlo Park should have been your tipoff. You need to choose which side you're on. If you're on ours, we can protect you." Gus's eyes scanned the street. "We're back to your father's journal. We know you recently came into possession of it. We're willing to pay quite a bit to get it. That's where the proposal comes in."

"What's 'quite a bit'?" Drake asked, his curiosity aroused.

"Enough to do anything you want with your life. To live anywhere. Be anything you can dream of."

"I can dream pretty big."

"I'm sure you can. But I'm sure you know the old saying about a bird in the hand, right?"

"Of course."

"We're willing to offer you a very big bird indeed. Enough for you to take care of your associates and still be rich."

"How much?"

Gus stepped closer, but Drake detected no obvious threat. Gus leaned into him and whispered near his ear, "Fifty million dollars."

Drake swallowed hard, the beer fog now gone.

"Fifty…fifty million dollars?" he stammered. "Did I hear you right?"

"You did. You can give your friends five million apiece, and take thirty-five million and live a dream. Anywhere in the world. With no risk to yourself, and nothing to fear from the men who murdered your father. We'll deal with them."

"And all I have to do is give you the journal."

"That's correct."

"How do I know you won't kill me the second you have it?"

"If we make a deal, we'll arrange for a wire transfer to the account of your choice, anywhere in the world. Once you confirm that the funds have been received, you turn it over to us. There are more safeguards for us both, but those are details." Gus waved a hand. "The important thing is that you agree."

Drake hesitated. He had difficulty imagining actually having fifty million dollars. Even after paying off Jack and Allie, and throwing a small bone to Spencer, he'd still be filthy rich.

If.

If Gus wasn't lying. If Drake could figure out a way to guarantee his own safety.

Fifty million for doing nothing. No risk, no jungle expedition, no homicidal Russians, no possibility of coming up empty.

A smart man would take the sure thing and leave the risk to his new associates.

"The treasure's rumored to be worth much, much more than fifty million. Billions. Many billions. Possibly tens of billions," Drake said.

"Possibly. Assuming you locate it. And assuming the Peruvian or Brazilian government is willing to give you even a small percentage of it – which isn't a given, no matter what you've been led to believe. And of course, if the Russians don't get to you first. Besides which, we're not that interested in the treasure. It's Palenko we're after."

"Then why can't I turn over the journal and continue hunting for Paititi?"

"Because if you found it, you might lead them right to it, and we would have lost the advantage we paid for. That, and we can't protect you in the middle of the rainforest."

Drake said nothing. Gus made a compelling argument.

"How did you know about me?" Drake asked.

"Your buddy Jack contacted his friend to check up on the two Russians who were in prison – connected to this in the most intimate possible way. That flagged us. Figure it out. We have a lot of resources." Sensing his wavering, Gus stepped back, giving Drake more space to think, and tried a friendlier tone. "Think about what you could do with that kind of money. You'd be a king anywhere in the world. Nothing would be off-limits or out of your reach. Imagine it, and you can have it." Gus paused. "An opportunity like this comes along once in a lifetime, Drake. You're an intelligent guy. Do the right thing."

Drake glanced at his watch. Where was Jack?

"I…how do I know you're for real? Talk's cheap."

"All you have to do is say the word, and we'll put gears in motion to consummate. Then you'll discover we're as serious as it comes," Gus said, and Drake believed him. "Take the evening to think about it. We'll touch base tomorrow. I can assure you that you're not going to get a better offer. The Russians will…well, they play differently than we do."

"You know them?"

"We know everyone involved. They're a particularly nasty bit of business – you wouldn't want to meet up with them. They're crude and extremely brutal as a matter of course. As your father learned, unfortunately."

"You've mentioned him a number of times. Did you know him?" Drake asked.

"I didn't know him personally, but I was aware of his demise. A tragedy. Hopefully the same won't happen to you."

Drake registered the threat. "Not a very nice way to talk to your prospective partner, is it?"

"I'm being genuine. Enough people have already died. It would be a shame for you to be added to that list."

"But you're not concerned."

"No. I'm confident in our ability to protect you."

Drake studied Gus's flat eyes and saw the truth. As he looked away, he realized he was torn. It was an incredible offer. If it could be structured so it was foolproof…

"I need time to mull this over."

"Like I said, take the evening. We'll be in touch tomorrow."

"How will I contact you?"

"Don't worry about that. We'll find you." Gus fixed Drake with a hard stare. "Choose wisely, Mr. Ramsey. Don't do anything stupid.

There's no assurance that you'll find anything if you try this on your own, and there's a high degree of certainty that you'll never come back. Whereas with our proposal, you'll be a rich young man with an unlimited future. I've tried to frame this so there's really no choice. And I think that's the conclusion you'll arrive at."

Gus turned, apparently unconcerned about defending himself from Drake, and strode across the street, back toward the bar, his henchmen in tow. Drake watched them disappear into the gloom and heard something behind him. The scuff of a sole on pavement. He spun and saw Jack approaching at a trot, the unmistakable shape of one of the SIG Sauer pistols in his hand. When he reached Drake, he stopped. His gaze swept the deserted waterfront.

"Are you okay?" he asked, eyes roving over their surroundings.

"Yeah. I thought I was in trouble there, but it turned out all right."

"What happened?"

Drake considered telling Jack about the offer, but something made him hesitate. He shook his head and shrugged it off. "Harmless. Some drunk fishermen. I think they were just screwing around. They were more interested in asking me for a few coins than in rolling me."

Jack grunted. "That's a relief. But as you're discovering, taking these kinds of risks is a bad idea. You could have just as easily been hacked in two with a machete."

"Nah. I've been told to avoid machete fights. Oh. Wait. That was knife fights. I'd imagine machetes are worse."

"Okay, smartass. So you're no worse for wear?"

"Never better."

"Then let's get back to the hotel. I was fast asleep when Allie got me."

"Sorry."

"No problem. But we're up early, and I'm beat." Jack took a last look down the street before turning and heading back to the hotel with Drake by his side, the pistol now nestled in his belt at the small of his back, covered by his shirt.

Allie came out when she heard them opening their room doors and wanted to know how it had gone. Drake told her the same story he'd told Jack, and she seemed relieved, although still a little worried. He liked that – Allie worried for him. I could get used to that, he thought to himself as he entered his quarters. Very used to it.

The room was stifling, but that wasn't what kept Drake tossing and turning. His sweat-soaked sheets seemed to radiate his anxiety, and at two in the morning he sat bolt upright. He hadn't understood his impulse to keep the conversation he'd had from Jack, but he'd come to the conclusion that it had been the wrong call.

Drake pulled on his shorts and unlocked his door, then stepped softly down the hall to Jack's room, after pausing briefly outside Allie's, the memory of their kiss still vivid. He rapped on the door and, when he didn't hear any response, tried again.

Footsteps approached and Jack cracked the door open, his eyes red. "What is it?"

"We need to talk."

"Now?"

"Sorry. But yes. Now."

"Damn. Come in, then," Jack whispered, and pulled the door toward him. Drake slipped through and sat on the bed, and told him what had happened, as well as about Palenko. When he was done, Jack whistled softly. "Drake, this changes the entire game. This is way larger than a search for lost treasure. Now we're mixed up in something much more dangerous, and the best thing we can do is recognize when we're way out of our league."

"It doesn't really change our basic objective, though. Just throws another variable into the mix."

"Yeah, like the CIA. I wouldn't screw around with them, Drake." Jack hesitated. "Fifty million. That's a lot of money. A lot."

"They suggested I give each of you five million, then go have a nice life."

"Man, with five million I could disappear forever. The Russians would never be able to find me. More importantly, they wouldn't have any reason to. Wow. I mean, think about it. Thailand. Russia. Argentina. Fiji. With that kind of money…"

"I know."

"And Allie would never have to worry about anything again. She could pursue archeology to her heart's content," Jack finished.

"Which is why I needed to talk to you."

"What's there to talk about? You just won the lottery."

"I'm not sure I want to do it."

Jack looked at him in surprise. "Why the hell not?"

Drake stared at his hands in the dark. "Because it feels wrong. Like I'm quitting."

"Drake, listen to me. Fifty million isn't quitting. Really. You have nothing to be ashamed of. That's life-changing money. And as you just said, there's obviously more in play here than just the Inca city. With the CIA in the mix, it's bigger than anything you want to be involved with. You should take the deal and run."

"Maybe. What would my dad have done?" Drake asked quietly.

"Who cares? You're not your dad. And with all due respect, he made some pretty lousy choices. And look what it got him."

"No argument. But what would he have done?" Drake asked, steel in his tone.

Jack sighed in resignation. "You know what he would have done. He wouldn't have taken the money. That's just how he was. But that doesn't mean it's the right choice, Drake. You don't have to make the same mistakes."

"So you'd take the cash?"

"Damn right I would. I'm old enough to know a great offer when I hear it."

Drake sat silently for several endless moments and then stood. "I'm sorry to disappoint you, Jack. I'm not going to do it. I can't. I need to see this through to the end, whatever that is."

Jack looked like he wanted to protest, but nodded instead. "Okay, Drake, it's your show. I just hope you know what you're doing. That's a lot of money. For all of us."

"I know, Jack. Believe me, I know. Listen, I want to get out of here tomorrow morning, early, before they're even awake. I can meet you somewhere."

Jack appeared to think for a few seconds. "If you're willing to be up at five, we can see about having a boat take you up the river. But if you do that, I'll want you to go with Allie. I don't want her around if this gets messy once they find out you're gone."

"No problem. I don't mind. You'll be right behind us once Spencer arrives. Which reminds me – he's got to be the leak. I told you I didn't trust him, and then these guys show up. How else could they have known exactly where we were?"

"I wouldn't underestimate the CIA, Drake. But even if you're right, we still need him. Tell you what – I won't tell him where we're going, and then I'll take his sat phone from him once we're gone. That way he'll have no way of communicating. Sort of force him to be honest. And I'll go through his stuff when he's not around to make sure he doesn't have a tracking device on him."

"You think that'll work?"

"I don't see how we have much of a choice if we're going through with this."

"Damn. Okay, if you can manage it."

Jack winced. "There's not a lot I can't manage."

"I hope you're right."

~ ~ ~

Vadim looked up from his half-empty glass of vodka as a young Peruvian woman entered the bedroom wearing nothing but a smile.

"You have a call," she said in fractured English. Vadim grunted and tossed back the rest of his drink, savoring the familiar burn as it spread from his throat to his abdomen.

He rose and followed her into the other room, noting that she could give some of the Russian girls he'd paid for their hospitality a run for their money, and lifted the ancient black phone handset to his ear.

"Yes?"

"We just got word. They're in Atalaya." The voice on the telephone spoke heavily accented English, all no-nonsense, the words seasoned by years of hard living.

"I told you. They used that as jumping off point before. It made sense they would use it again."

"My contact is watching them. Not hard to do considering the size of the place."

"Very good. We will be on our way tomorrow. Do nothing overt. I do not want them warned that they are under surveillance. Is that clear?"

"Of course. We'll know when they decide to leave. They suspect nothing."

"See that it stays that way. Have you sourced the equipment I requested?"

"Yes. We're ready."

Vadim checked the time. It was later than he thought. "We will be there by the middle of the day."

"I'll be waiting."

Vadim hung up and eyed the young woman, who was seated at the coffee table, helping herself to a line of the local cocaine. Vadim approached her, weaving slightly, the vodka having gone to his head, and clumsily grabbed her, which she pretended to enjoy as she giggled and squirmed. A bruise on her face had taught her not to question the customer's strange demands, and the drugs at least blunted some of the pain she knew would follow.

Vadim pulled her to her feet and led her back to the bedroom, shuffling like an old bear. She teetered after him on precarious heels that snicked on the tile floor as she went to earn her keep, a professional smile frozen on her face, dreading what was to come.

Chapter Twenty-Seven

Allie seemed grumpy when they met in the lobby at five. She had every reason to be. Her trip was starting a day earlier than she'd expected, and Jack had apparently told her why.

The fishermen were already working at the river in the predawn gloom, preparing for another in an endless string of long, hard days. Within a few minutes Allie had persuaded one of the men to skip fishing in exchange for making ten times what his catch would bring to take them to Puerto Mapuyo – the small hamlet where they would wait for Jack and Spencer to join them.

Money changed hands and they climbed aboard a battered wooden skiff, their backpacks bulging, each with a SIG Sauer in a waterproof pocket and their AK-47s hanging from shoulder straps. Drake had his father's knife dangling from his belt, and both of them wore knee-high rubber boots for the rainforest's perennially wet soil. The fisherman traded some of his pay for two jerry cans of gasoline before he started his outboard with a sputter and guided them into the river. They were the only boat on the water as the sun struggled over the jungle horizon, and Drake was confident they weren't being followed.

The trip took all day, and by the time they arrived at their destination it was nearly dark. Puerto Mapuyo turned out to be a small collection of shacks with a few families living by the sloping bank, sustaining themselves with fishing. They regarded the

Caucasian newcomers with curiosity before heading back inside their dwellings as twilight faded, with no electricity to light their way.

Drake withdrew a flashlight and they walked to a clearing near the river. He hurriedly pitched their tent, which thankfully had mosquito netting incorporated to protect them from the swarms that clouded the air, thick as smoke.

"Your father wasn't kidding about the bugs, was he?" Drake said.

"He warned us. Too bad we didn't take the CIA's deal. Could have spared us a lot of grief."

"Allie..."

She shrugged. "Hey, nobody asks me what I think, so no problem. Let the men make all the decisions, right? I'll just smile and clean up after you. Maybe sing to entertain you if you're bored."

"We didn't come all this way just to sell the journal. We're going to find Paititi. You'll be famous. And rich. Don't worry."

Allie looked at him doubtfully. "I'm glad you're so confident. Because last time I checked, we came all this way because we've got some killers that want to cut us into pieces to get their hands on the same journal you just declined an easy fifty mil for."

"Which should tell you it's worth a lot more."

She gazed into the distance. "Maybe you're right. It's just an awful lot of money"

"I know, Allie. It was the hardest decision I've ever made."

Allie pounded in the final tent stake with a stone.

"You know, it's not just the money. It's...why do you get to make all the decisions, alone? Don't my father and I get any say, after all we've been through? Because of you? Do our opinions count for nothing?"

"Allie, I'm sorry I turned down the money."

She shook her head, obviously conflicted. "These mosquitoes are driving me crazy. I'm going into the tent. Dinner will be an energy bar. Hope you don't mind if we hit it early."

He finished with his side and nodded. "I didn't get any sleep, so no problem."

She hesitated. "Drake, just so you know, I like you. But I'm not stupid. I'd like to be consulted every now and then, especially on life-and-death matters. And last night? On the river? That was nice, too. But we're going to keep it strictly business while we're on this trip, okay? That means you stay on your side of the tent."

Drake controlled his expression, showing nothing. "Allie, of course. I'm not going to maul you or anything."

"Damn right you're not. I just wanted to get clear on that so there are no misunderstandings, all right?"

"I'm completely clear on it. Crystal."

"Good." She lifted her backpack with one hand and unzipped the entry netting, and then ducked into the tent with her gear before zipping it back up, leaving Drake standing outside wondering how everything had gone so wrong in the blink of an eye. He decided that he didn't know anything about women, and chalked it up to experience – he'd thought there had been some real heat between them, a powerful connection, but apparently not strong enough. She'd just made clear she wanted nothing to do with him romantically, and it hadn't seemed ambiguous.

Drake hoisted his backpack and resigned himself to a difficult evening, and decided to give her time to prepare her part of the tent to her liking. It was still unbearably hot, so there wouldn't be any sleeping bags, and his only hope was that the small netted window flaps would allow sufficient ventilation so they wouldn't roast inside. After the constant warnings about snakes and poisonous insects, sleeping outside the tent wasn't an option, but he was under no illusion that inside would be pleasant.

Ten minutes later he ducked inside and secured the flap. Allie had already rolled onto her side, either asleep or pretending to be. He set his bag down, removed the SIG Sauer and chambered a round, and used the backpack as a pillow. He lay down only a few short feet from Allie – the woman who wanted nothing to do with him. The realization that he was now fully committed to a potentially disastrous course hit him with the force of a pile driver as he wiped sweat from his face, trying to get comfortable in the swelter.

The last sounds he heard as he drifted off to sleep a half hour later were her soft breaths and the symphony of night creatures chittering and chirping in the trees around them.

~ ~ ~

Spencer arrived in Atalaya in the afternoon and checked into the hotel, noting that he and Jack were the sad little establishment's entire guest roster. They met in his room and he distributed his finds – two crossbows, a collapsible camp stove, and a host of odds and ends that would come in handy in the bush. By the time he finished, it was obvious that they'd be as loaded as they could manage and still make their way through the jungle.

Jack was turning to leave with his gear when Spencer handed him a wad of dollars. Jack took the money.

"What's this?" he asked.

"I ran into Asad. He saw the error of his ways. He'd already burned a few hundred, but he wanted me to give you back the rest of the money."

Jack blinked. "Did he, now?"

"People can surprise you."

"Every day. Thanks for that. What are the odds?"

"Serendipity, isn't that what they call it?"

"That's one of the things."

Dinner was more fish, spicy as ever, and they turned in early, having agreed to meet at six a.m. to take a boat up the Urubamba, and then farther east on a tributary until they arrived at Puerto Mapuyo and rendezvoused with Drake and Allie.

Dawn was breaking as they met in front of the hotel and walked down to the river, where Spencer had hired a boat. Clouds blanketed a granite sky as they arrived at the waterfront, the air thick with the smell of runoff and marsh. A slim wooden skiff, easily thirty-five feet long and no more than five wide, waited by the bank, captained by a middle-aged man with a coffee complexion and half his teeth. Spencer and the captain exchanged pleasantries as he handed him their bags. They climbed aboard and settled in for the seventy miles of winding water that Spencer had said would take them all day to navigate. The plan was to camp out near the river for the night and then begin hiking to the spot where Ford Ramsey's body had been found.

Neither man spoke much on the trip, preferring to stay silent as the boat puttered along. They only saw two other people the entire day, both natives on the banks, throwing nets into the water, their canoes beached under bowed trees. The fishermen waved as they passed and the captain returned the simple gesture; the rainforest was an environment where anyone might be a valuable ally if they ran into mechanical trouble in the middle of nowhere.

The overcast burned off by late morning and Jack drowsed as the sun beat down. The slight breeze from their passage offered slim relief from the heat, but he managed a few hours of rest in spite of the discomfort. Spencer appeared unfazed by the experience, and was asleep within minutes of getting underway.

Drake and Jack had agreed not to discuss his run-in with the CIA with Spencer, and Jack spent most of the day trying to figure out how to make good on his promise to disable Spencer's satellite phone. He finally opted for the direct approach and asked Spencer to let him use it to call his Brazilian contact.

"Why can't you use the one I gave you?" Spencer asked, clearly annoyed.

"Drake has it."

Spencer dug the phone out of his backpack and handed it to Jack, who pretended to fumble it as he lost his balance. The phone splashed into the mocha water and disappeared out of sight.

"Damn," Jack exclaimed, almost falling overboard himself, which he could tell from Spencer's glower would have been fine with him.

Spencer frowned and shook his head. "You owe me a grand."

"I'm sorry. I…damn. There's nothing to say. At least we have another one. I'll give you the money when we're stationary."

"I'll hold you to it."

They spent the rest of the trip without speaking, Spencer obviously angry, which was okay with Jack. He'd done what he set out to do. Spencer didn't seem suspicious, but rather disgusted in his new companion's idiocy, which was the way Jack wanted it. He preferred to be underestimated and believed to be a fool by Spencer, especially if he was a turncoat.

When they arrived at dusk, Jack saw Allie and Drake sitting on the bank, waiting for them to arrive. Drake was fishing with a hand line while Allie watched him. When Drake saw the boat, he waved and pulled a stringer of fish from the water and held them aloft. The skiff ran up onto the sandy slope, and once beached, Spencer and Jack got out and unloaded their gear. Once they were finished, the captain wished them luck and reversed the motor, off to make as much progress on the return as he could before spending the night in the boat, tied to a tree.

"You made it," Allie said as they approached. "The great white hunter caught dinner. He's a wizard with fish."

Drake shrugged. "Not really. The water's teeming with them. I could practically throw a rock and hit a dozen."

"We need to get our tents set up before it gets late. We've got about a half hour of light left. How many do you have?" Spencer asked.

"Five. Pretty decent size."

"That's good. I'll cook them once I'm done with my tent. Unless you feel like playing chef tonight."

"I'm easy. You're probably a better cook than I am, considering I'm hard-pressed to boil an egg."

Spencer looked to Allie. "Would you see if you can find some relatively dry wood for a fire? I'll make it once I'm finished."

"Aren't you going to use the stove?" Jack asked.

"Negative. I don't want to waste limited fuel and get a pan dirty. It's easier to roast them, skewered on sticks like the natives do. I've done it a million times. Not half bad if you're hungry enough."

"At least it's stopped raining. It's been going most of the day," Allie said.

"Do what you can on the firewood. If we have to, I have a jar of petroleum jelly and some cotton, but if you find some dead branches that aren't soaked through, that would be best."

Spencer had his tent pitched in ten minutes and a fire going in another fifteen, coaxing a reluctant flame from the soggy wood Allie brought. It was dark by the time the fish were done, but Drake had to admit that a meal had never tasted so good.

Jack moved into the large tent with Allie, while Drake took the small one Jack had brought for him. An hour after sundown the camp was still, the fire out as the patter of raindrops splattered against the fabric enclosures, a drumbeat that was to be a constant in the days ahead. The only positive was that the intermittent storms cooled the air, and Drake found himself drifting off more easily than the prior night, which if they were lucky would be the norm as they progressed on their journey into the rainforest.

Chapter Twenty-Eight

Drake awoke to a deluge pouring from the lead-colored clouds that brooded over the river valley. A machine-gun torrent of wind-driven rain hammered at the flimsy tent with the aggression of an attack dog as thunder roared overhead. He rolled over and looked at the glowing dial of his watch. Five o'clock; dawn still an hour off. He lay listening as the downpour thrashed against his shelter and tried to fall back to sleep, but to no avail.

Resigned, he sat up and drank the rest of his bottle of water as his thoughts turned to the day ahead. Hopefully the rain would abate, but even if it didn't, they couldn't stay on the riverbank – they needed to find the site of his father's final camp so the real search could begin, ideally well ahead of any pursuit from the CIA or the Russians.

Twenty minutes later the cloudburst let up, slowing to a steady drizzle, and he forced himself out into the rain to begin his daily routine. Spencer was already breaking down his tent, and Drake did the same, water streaming off his hat brim. They worked in silence, and then Jack and Allie emerged from their tent. Jack began collapsing it as Allie went off for some needed morning privacy.

"So what's the drill?" Drake asked as he folded the support rods.

"Rain or shine, we need to make twelve miles a day if we're going to get there within three days," Jack said. "That means we start hiking early, and try to get most of it done by 1:00. Better to spend the hottest part of the day resting than trying to slog through when it's blistering out."

Spencer nodded. "He's right. By noon, it'll feel like we're being boiled alive. So up by daybreak, and go hard till it's too hot to keep moving."

"Sounds like a plan," Drake said as he knelt and carefully rolled up his tent.

Allie returned, looking uncomfortable and wet, but she gave no indication she was anything but game to go. They were loaded up in five minutes, and as the rain continued to fall, they entered the rainforest, Spencer in the lead with a machete in hand, the first rays of light providing just enough illumination to see.

The first hour was miserable, but as the storm blew past and the sun came out in force, the second and third were worse. Steam drifted from the wet canopy, and the area they trudged through became a muggy sauna, every breath like inhaling soup. Spencer led them at a moderate pace, obviously used to the conditions, Allie and Drake following him carrying their rifles, Jack bringing up the rear. Spencer warned that they were now in a no-man's land where the drug traffickers operated with impunity, a law unto their own, so the Kalashnikovs were their only option if they came into a conflict situation.

Jack echoed the sentiment in a hushed voice. "This ain't Kansas anymore. If we see anyone, the best option is to go undiscovered, because whoever we come across in here is likely to be hostile. If someone's in this jungle, they're probably here for a reason, and it's not to make new friends. Don't shoot first, but if Spencer or I do, be ready to follow suit."

"Wouldn't that bring consequences? I mean, if we killed someone?" Allie asked.

A corner of Spencer's mouth pulled upward in a smirk. "Out here, it's survival of the fittest. There's nobody to help and nobody to tell. Forget everything you know about civilization. We're on our own. What's that saying? What happens in the Amazon, stays in the Amazon…"

"So we shoot people, nothing happens," she said.

"Well, hopefully they die. Either that, or you do. Other than that, no, nothing happens."

Drake had begun to notice that Allie was friendlier to Spencer than to him, which had quickly gotten under his skin. Even in the middle of the jungle, it wasn't lost on Drake that she had curves in all the right places, as he admired the fit of her cargo pants beneath her backpack. Whatever he'd done to distance her had worked, because she was almost flirtatious with Spencer, who seemed not to notice, whereas whenever she'd addressed Drake it was no-nonsense, with all the warmth of a fast-food drive-through window attendant.

A screeching echoed through the trees, and Spencer slowed, pointing overhead.

"Howler monkeys. They're usually quiet during the day, but in the early mornings and evenings, they'll make a lot of noise. They live in large groups. Harmless but annoying."

"I don't see anything," Allie said, shielding her eyes with her hand. "Ooh, no, wait, now I do. Up there. Fast, aren't they?"

"Yes. They're a good early alarm system. If we hear them during the day, it could be because they've spotted someone moving through the bush. Just as anyone listening now knows we're here."

"Double-edged sword, then," Drake observed.

"Everything is, here."

They resumed their pace, making decent time along a game trail. Their boots were nearly soundless against the wet ground, which was covered with leaves. At nine they took a break by a tiny stream. Allie ventured off to refresh herself as they sat in the shade of a towering tree, soaked with perspiration, drinking greedily from their canteens.

"How often are you in these parts?" Drake asked quietly, now accustomed to speaking in a murmur.

Spencer closed his eyes and leaned his head back. "Often enough."

"When was the last time?" Drake persisted.

"About a month ago."

Spencer wasn't more forthcoming, so they settled into an uneasy silence, the only sounds around them an occasional bird call or the crackling in the canopy of an unseen animal flitting from branch to branch.

Allie's scream shattered the calm, and Jack was instantly on his feet, weapon at the ready. Drake leapt up, as did Spencer, and they moved into the underbrush in the direction she'd gone. Drake almost ran into Jack's back as he came to an abrupt stop, his arm out to the side to keep them from moving forward. Spencer stood next to him and, after assessing the situation, began speaking to Allie in a low voice.

"Calm down. Stop struggling. It's quicksand. Any movement will only make it worse." Spencer shrugged off his backpack and retrieved from it a tightly coiled roll of black nylon rope. He turned to Jack and Drake and whispered, "If she can get her legs and arms separated and concentrates on leaning back, she'll eventually float to the surface, but that could take all day, and she doesn't look like she's calm enough to do it. It's doubtful that she'll completely submerge, but we need to slide her out before she makes it any worse."

Allie had sunk in viscous sludge up to her armpits, a look of terror on her face. Her backpack lay near the spot where she'd slipped when she'd hit the edge of the patch.

Jack removed his pack and set his weapon against it, and spoke in even, measured tones. "Honey, he's right. Take it easy. We'll get you out. But don't struggle. Save your strength, and if you want to try to help, shake your legs just a little. That should free them slowly, and you should start to float to the surface."

Spencer held up the rope. "I'm going to toss this to you, okay? Grab it, and we'll pull you out. If I don't get it within reach, don't panic or try to get to it. I'll just throw it again, all right?" He didn't wait for Allie to answer and, after taking a quick look at her position fifteen feet away, tossed the wound-up line toward her, using the bundle's weight to carry it through the air.

It landed about three feet from her right arm, and she slowly moved her hand toward it, but was a foot short. She tried to stretch to grab it, but it was no good. In the process of trying, she sank another six inches, the ooze now almost covering her shoulders. She let out a low moan as Spencer hurriedly wound the rope back toward him.

Drake removed his backpack and dropped his gun on the ground. "Give me one end of the rope. I'm going in after her. She's not going to make it," he said, and before Spencer could protest, he grabbed the free end of the cord and skirted the edge of the quicksand as Spencer played out line.

When he slipped at the edge and slid into the muck, he almost dropped the lifeline, but he reacted quickly and latched onto it. Spencer and Jack pulled on the rope and he managed to get clear. He continued along the rim until he was near where she'd gone in. The sludge was now up to Allie's neck – an ominous progression.

"Let out about five feet of line," Drake instructed, and as they did, he tied the rope to his belt, freeing up his arms. With a final glance at Allie, he backed up and took a running jump. When he hit the surface, Allie's head went under, and he groped where she'd disappeared. He felt an arm and latched onto it, and then yelled to Jack and Spencer. "I've got her."

The two men immediately pulled, and Drake slowly edged through the goop to the firmer edge of the sinkhole, trying to get Allie to the surface, but failing due to the resistance of the wet muck. As he felt his back move against the harder ground, he took a deep breath and heaved with all his might, the veins in his neck and forehead bulging from the effort. Slowly, Allie rose to the top, and then her arms were around him and she was gasping, covered with sludge, her eyes clamped shut as she spit out clumps of quicksand. Spencer wrapped the end of the rope around his waist twice, faced away from them, and began plodding like a plow horse. Jack also pulled on the line with all his might, and Drake and Allie slid out of the treacherous mire onto firmer soil.

"All right. We're clear," he called out, and Jack moved along the perimeter of the swampy section to where they both lay covered in muck. He knelt down and lifted Allie to her feet and, after hugging her, held her away from him as she wiped wet ooze from her eyes.

"That was close. I thought we discussed quicksand back in town," he said quietly.

She nodded. "I know. I didn't see it. I...maybe I wasn't paying close enough attention."

Drake got to his feet, doing his best to shake off the clinging slag. Allie turned to him and hugged him as well, pressing her full breasts against his chest.

"Thank you," she said simply, and he nodded, figuring words weren't necessary.

Back at the stream, Allie and Drake used one of the cooking pots to scoop water and clean themselves as best as they could while Spencer and Jack stood watch, alert for anyone their commotion might have attracted. The rainforest's customary tranquility had descended again, a deathly stillness in the damp air, not even the monkeys making noise. They hurriedly finished with their field showers and pushed their way farther into the brush five minutes later, keenly aware that they'd made far too much noise and anxious to put as much distance between themselves and the site of the near-disaster as possible.

Another rainstorm hit an hour later, and for once both Drake and Allie welcomed the steady stream of water, which rinsed them as clean as if they'd gone for a swim.

By Drake's reckoning, they were nearing their target point for the day's camp when Spencer held a hand up in warning and slowed, head cocked to the side and listening intently. Everyone froze, ears straining for whatever he'd heard. The only thing Drake registered was the incessant patter of raindrops on the surrounding leaves. After a few moments, Spencer backed up as he slipped his machete into its belt sheath and freed his rifle. He leaned toward them, eyes locked on the trail.

"I heard voices up ahead. We need to get off the track. Follow me. Hopefully the water will erase our footprints by the time they get here," he whispered. He cast his eyes around, selected a sparsely vegetated area to their right, and moved through it into the denser underbrush beyond.

They pushed past tangled vines and stepped over fallen trees until they were fifty yards from the track. Spencer made a curt hand gesture and knelt by a rotting log, his weapon pointed at the trail, which was no longer visible through the thick foliage. They spread out, guns in hand, and lay next to any cover they could find.

Stillness enveloped the jungle, the rain splattering on the surrounding leaves as the seemingly never-ending drizzle continued while they settled in to wait. One minute went by, and then another, and then they all heard the sound of several sets of boots on the trail. Spencer glanced to the side at Jack, who had positioned himself ten feet away, and held a finger to his lips. Drake nodded understanding and turned to where Allie lay next to him, repeating the gesture, but froze when he saw the look on her face – raw, unbridled fear. His eyes traveled down her body lying on a bed of wet leaves, until he saw the reason. A brightly colored snake was making its way for her, slithering along the forest floor, no more than two feet away; one of the deadliest creatures on the planet – the coral snake, whose neon coloring was nature's warning of its lethal venom.

He shook his head in warning. "Don't move. Not a muscle."

Allie's eyes flickered understanding, but the mask of panic on her face belied her apparent calm. The footsteps from the trail continued past their position as Drake watched the serpent make its way to her, and his stomach did a flip when she closed her eyes, her trembling barely perceptible. It reached her gun and paused, then wound toward her torso, three deadly feet of bright red, yellow, and black bands.

Drake stood in a crouch as the snake hesitated by Allie's side and, after a couple of lightning flicks of its tongue, began moving down toward her legs. She gasped but remained still when it eased up her right thigh, apparently interested enough to want a closer examination of the life it sensed.

In a second Drake was at her side. Using the barrel of his AK, he flipped the toxic creature off her and through the air, where it landed harmlessly six feet away and slipped into the undergrowth. Allie's exhalation was audible, and Drake again held his finger to his mouth, urging caution. She struggled to slow her breathing as the fright seeped from her eyes and, after squeezing them closed again for a moment, nodded and resumed her watch of the trees near the path.

Five minutes passed like an hour. Hearing nothing more, Spencer stood and signaled for them to follow him back to the trail. They took careful steps, now hyperalert to the hidden threats lurking beneath the carpet of brown leaves on the wet forest floor, Allie's near miss fresh in all their minds. Once at the muddy track, Spencer leaned over and studied the fading imprints that were already disappearing as the rain washed them away.

"Looks like a half dozen, maybe more. Stay quiet and let's move. I want to be far away from them as quickly as possible," he murmured, and then hurried away in the direction they'd been headed, still with his rifle in hand instead of the machete. The group matched his pace, which he kept up for a half hour before slowing. The heat was now oppressive as the clouds drifted east and the rainfall eased and then stopped.

When he arrived at a brook engorged by the recent runoff, he paused. After scanning the area, he whispered to Jack, "How far have we come?"

Jack searched in his backpack for his handheld GPS and powered it on, squinting to read the small screen's information. "This says thirteen miles. But we drifted south some. So really only about twelve in the direction we're headed."

"Close enough, I'd say. Let's follow the stream until we're well away from the trail and, at the first hospitable looking area, set up camp. I don't like that we had company, so I want to get clear of it. Follow me."

The brook was only five feet across and no more than three or four feet deep most of the way, but around the second bend it deepened to where they couldn't see the bottom anymore. Spencer stopped and pointed at a flat area twenty yards away, under the dense growth suspended from the tops of the tall trees. "That looks good as any."

They pitched their tents, exhausted from the first day's exertions, and lay in the shade. The heat drained from them any desire to move. In spite of the swelter, Allie decided to spend the remainder of the afternoon in the tent – a reaction to coming within a hair of being killed by the coral snake; everyone understood.

Eventually the sun dropped behind the distant mountain peaks, and Drake took his fishing line and a few small shiny spoons to see if the brook held anything promising for dinner. Allie emerged from the tent several minutes later and wiped the sweat from her face before moving in the opposite direction along the stream, rifle in hand, eyes roving over the ground in front of her, now fully alert to the myriad menaces the jungle held.

Drake returned with three fish – each at least a couple of pounds. Spencer looked them over and grunted. "That'll do. I'll cook them on the stove. I don't want to risk a wood fire drawing anyone to our position. Let's wait until dark. Nobody's going to be roving around the jungle at night well away from any trail – there are way too many threats. Jaguars and snakes being the least of them."

After nightfall they feasted on Drake's catch, silent except for the sound of their chewing, the day's events having reinforced the need for stealth and the suddenness with which danger could savage them. Jack argued for a three-hour guard shift during the night, and nobody had any objections. He would take the first watch, Drake the second, Allie the third, and Spencer the final that would lead into dawn, each waking the next when their stint was over.

When they retired for the night, the rainforest pitch black around their position, it was with a new appreciation for the hardships they'd taken on in their quest for the Inca city. As Drake shifted in his tent, trying to get comfortable, he was sure that the others were equally restive, and resigned himself to a long night with little sleep as the jungle around them rustled and creaked with unimaginable dangers.

~ ~ ~

The afternoon was drawing to a close when the wooden skiff beached itself on the riverbank and the captain killed the engine. He rubbed his face and yawned, glad to be home after the long day on the water following an uncomfortable night sleeping in the boat with one eye open. He was disconnecting the scarred red metal fuel tank when he raised his head and saw three Caucasian men moving cautiously down the path that led to the river's edge. The area was deserted, the other fishermen gone, and for a moment a tingle of apprehension ran up his spine.

Gus sized up the old boat with a seasoned eye and nodded to his two younger associates. One of them stepped forward and fixed the local with a hard stare.

"You took some passengers up the river?" he asked in Spanish colored with a slight American accent.

"Yes…" the captain answered truthfully, his expression puzzled.

"We need you to help us. We're supposed to join up with them, but we were delayed."

"I can take you where I dropped them off. For a price…"

"How soon can you be ready to leave?" the American asked.

"Tomorrow at first light."

The younger man relayed the information to Gus, who frowned. "We're going to be too far behind them. Find out where he left them, and we can see about getting a helicopter. Worst case you can take him up on it tomorrow, but I'd rather get a bird in the air this evening." Gus stared at the darkening sky with a sinking feeling, knowing that the odds of being able to arrange for transportation for a team into the Amazon at night were less than slim.

The man took out a wad of bills and peeled several high-denomination notes from it, and then handed them to the captain. "Where exactly did you drop them off?"

Chapter Twenty-Nine

The next day began much as the previous one, up at dawn, trudging through the undergrowth trying to find a viable game trail, locating a promising one, and following it deeper into the jungle. It didn't start raining until ten, and when the heavens opened up, everyone was relieved, the heat having built to an almost intolerable level in the interim. They marched along silently, occasionally pausing when Spencer would point out an animal or bird moving through the thickets, the downpour denting the leaves around them as they marched steadily forward.

They spotted several more snakes, most notably a large bushmaster, easily six feet long, that they startled as they came around a bend in a trail as they forged their way east. Spencer froze when he saw it, and held them back until the drowsy serpent had moved off the trail, preferring a less trafficked spot for its slumber.

At noon they entered an area with numerous waterfalls and took a break near one of the largest as Jack made calculations on his GPS.

He glanced at Drake as he entered coordinates using the keypad. "This area looks familiar. We're half a mile from the first outpost your father and I located. It's a little northeast of us, and as I recall, it was close enough to a stream to camp in."

"Then that's our target for the day," Spencer said. "Half a mile shouldn't take us more than an hour, unless everyone would prefer to stay here. Is there any reason we should go on to the outpost now, Jack?"

"Not really. There's not a lot to see. A few remnants of stone walls overgrown with vegetation. I'd say this is as good a place as any to stop. We're sixteen miles west of the spot where…where the final camp was located."

Allie shook her head. "I want to see the outpost. We've come this far."

"Why?" Drake asked.

"Because I trained my entire life for this, and I may see something that everyone missed."

Jack nodded. "I suppose we can afford another hour. Let's keep at it."

The slog took forty-five minutes. When they made it to the outpost, everyone but Allie took a break while she explored the ruins. The stone outcroppings appeared unremarkable to Drake, but he went to join her later as she was still clearing an area beneath two piles of stone.

"What do you think?" he asked.

"This would have been the stone arch. It's collapsed, but for our purposes, it'll do."

"Does it fit with my Dad's theory about the paver stones that ran through the arch pointing to the next spot?"

"It's interesting how they aligned them. A continuation of the path, but with enough variation so that anyone trying to chart a straight line between the outposts would be stumped – if you didn't know that the pavers exiting the arch indicated the new bearing, you'd be wandering in the jungle forever. My guess is they used the stars as an orientation – you can see grooves cut into the arch base that probably coincided with the angle the sun would hit at a certain time of the year."

"Were they advanced astronomers?"

"Yes, actually. They built observatories and timed their harvests based on celestial observations – often solar, but also of stars and planets, like Venus and the Pleiades," Allie explained.

"Interesting. But how precise would that be for the purposes of plotting a course to the next outpost?"

"There would be a margin of error, sure, but it would be slimmer than you'd think."

Spencer and Jack approached. "So? Anything unusual?"

Allie shook her head. "No, but the layout confirms we're on the right track." She pointed to where the stone arch had stood. "That would have stood about twelve feet high, and it would have established the direction of the next outpost." She turned to Drake. "How far are we from the campsite?"

Drake did a quick calculation. "Seventeen miles." He regarded Spencer. "Do you think we can make that tomorrow?"

"It'll be a push. We've been averaging twelve per day so far. It really depends on the terrain. If we get lucky and there's a clear trail most of the way, and it's not too hot, it could happen. But it's a long trek in these conditions. Don't get your heart set on it." Spencer looked around. "Do you want to stay here or keep going?"

"Let's keep at it," Drake said. "Maybe we can get another couple of miles under our belt before we stop for the afternoon. Every day of delay is another that the Russians have to catch up to us."

"He's right. We should keep moving," Jack said. They spent another ten minutes resting before continuing east, leaving the outpost behind. Half an hour later they encountered a fair-sized game trail, and they were able to make it to a shallow stream two miles farther before stopping. It had begun raining again, which they were now used to, and they made short work of raising the tents far enough from the stream so anyone following it wouldn't spot them – although the chances of that were slim given the overgrowth on both banks.

Once camp was set up, Spencer spent some time at the water's edge. When he returned, he had a smile on his face – the first since the trip had started. He approached Drake, who was preparing to drowse in the shade of his tent.

"You got that big knife of yours handy?" Spencer whispered.

"Sure. Why?"

"I want to make a couple of spears. We're going to eat well tonight."

Drake unsheathed the knife and handed it to Spencer. "What are you planning to spear?"

"Pirarucu."

"What's that?"

"Big catfish. I saw a couple of them near some rocks. The smaller one looked like a good eighty pounder."

"Eighty pounds? Are you kidding?"

"They get up to four hundred. But they're not bad eating. And anything we don't finish, the animals will take care of. Nothing goes to waste in the Amazon. I want to find a few sturdy saplings I can sharpen so once it gets closer to dusk we can spear one for dinner. Your knife's got a better edge than my machete after a long day of hacking."

Spencer returned in a half hour with three eight-foot staffs, their tips whittled to sharp spikes. He gave Drake back the knife, leaned the spears against a nearby tree, and wiped the sweat from his face.

"There. After *siesta*, we'll spear us a fish."

"Sounds good."

Birds called to one another up in the canopy as the day wore on. The rain eased for an hour and then resumed with renewed vigor. Drake slept lightly for much of the afternoon, his prior night having been difficult, especially after his shift, when his adrenaline had been pumping with every stirring in the brush.

At five, Spencer's voice called through the tent fabric. "You ready to play hunter?"

Drake roused himself and poked his head out. "Sure."

They made their way down to the stream, spears in hand, and Spencer picked his way onto a jutting outcrop of boulders as the cloudburst eased to a drizzle. "There are three here," he called softly, and Drake hurried to join him. Spencer pointed to the long, dark shapes in the water, the closest only four feet from the rocks.

"How do you want to do this?" Drake asked.

"Let me go first, and if I get him, you spear him too. Then we haul him out before the piranhas can get him."

"Piranhas?"

"Of course. Water's teeming with them. They're attracted to blood, so we won't have much time."

"All right. Go for it."

Spencer turned his attention back to the fish, which was immobile. Its odd tail waved lazily, keeping it stationary headfirst against the mild current. He hefted the sapling, as if testing its balance, and then drove it through the catfish's flank in a fluid stroke. The creature bucked like a bronco as the water turned bright red. Drake followed Spencer's lead and skewered it with his spear, and then they heaved the big pirarucu out of the water and up onto the bank.

Spencer went to work on the catfish with his machete, cutting long filets before tossing the carcass into the water. They carried the big slabs back to the camp and again used the stove as night fell. Everyone overate, the fresh protein a welcome change from the dry food they'd munched on throughout the day, and by the point Allie took the first watch, they were ready for sleep.

~ ~ ~

The sky was darkening when the captain pulled the fishing skiff onto the beach and pointed to the nearby jungle with a gnarled finger. The three hardened CIA operatives gathered their rifles and packs and followed the local guide they'd hired out of the boat – an expert in tracking who claimed to be as familiar with the rainforest as with his backyard. The captain reversed the bow off the sandy slope and returned down the river, leaving the four men staring at a wall of dense vegetation.

The guide walked along the edge of the jungle until he spotted a trail. He studied the surrounding branches, nodding and muttering to himself, and then turned to address the team.

"They went this way. But this won't be easy. Too much time has passed."

"How can you tell this was the route they took?"

"Some of the bark is scraped from that sapling where a pack or a rifle rubbed it."

The leader relayed the information to his men. After a hurried discussion with the guide, he shook his head and shrugged out of his pack. He retrieved a satellite phone and placed a call as his men prepared to make camp.

"We should have gotten the helicopter. They're a day ahead of us now, and the guide says that may be too much of a lead."

"We tried. There was nothing available on short notice, and nobody who would risk setting down near there," Gus said.

"We'll do the best we can, but the guide's already equivocating. Says he's the best, but there may have been too much rain. And that if they're sticking to game trails, it could make it impossible."

Gus's tone hardened. "I don't need to tell you what's at stake here. Best efforts won't cut it."

"Yes, sir."

Chapter Thirty

Morning brought an eerie mist that blanketed the rainforest, and when they set out, visibility had fallen to twenty yards, making the first hours on the trail otherworldly. Spencer seemed especially apprehensive and stopped several times to listen attentively before waving them forward. The fog eventually burned off and they were treated to more of the humid heat that was now their norm, the daily rain that had made it at least somewhat bearable nowhere in evidence.

Just before lunchtime Spencer stopped them again and, after peering through a clump of plants ahead of them, backed away and shook his head.

"Trouble. A few shacks in a clearing. There's nothing I know of out here, so I'd bet that's where our friends from the other day were coming from. Meth labs are a big moneymaker these days. Let's backtrack and give this a wide berth," he whispered. "There are two men by the larger building. Armed. So stay quiet."

They retraced their footsteps, and when they found a smaller track that led south, Spencer took the lead again and they made their way through the almost impassible brush, wary of anything more accessible – the last thing they wanted was to meet a returning group of drug traffickers on a heavily traveled route.

An hour later they'd made a half circle around the encampment and found a tributary to one of the larger rivers, which they followed for six miles before it turned south. A thunderclap sounded at two o'clock and the rain came shortly after, torrential but welcome, and it continued until Jack took a bearing on the GPS and announced that they were only a quarter mile from the site.

There was no clearly defined track for the last leg. They had to hack their way through, Spencer in the lead, tirelessly swinging his machete to clear a path. When they finally reached the riverbank, they were all spent, dehydrated in spite of the steady downpour, physically exhausted from the long march.

"This is it? You're sure?" Drake asked Jack when he set his backpack down on the brown bed of wet leaves of the jungle floor.

"Absolutely. This was our final camp. I still remember it well. That outcropping of stones near the bank. Those trees," Jack replied.

"Where did you find him?" Drake whispered.

"Over by that grove of palms."

"Show me."

Jack nodded. When they arrived at the spot, both men stood staring at the rainforest floor, which looked exactly like all the other ground around it, creeping vines intertwined as they crawled up the sides of the trees, streams of rain runoff trickling from the leaves. "He was lying here. What was left of him. I wound up burying his remains along the river, using my machete to scoop the dirt. There was no way to get his body out of the jungle – you've seen what we went through to get here."

"Where, exactly?"

Jack shook his head. "I don't know for sure. North along the bank. There was nothing to mark the spot with other than a few small rocks and a cross I made out of two branches – but there's no way it would still be here. In the end it was just a place. Like any other." Jack hesitated. "I'm sorry, son. I never thought anyone would be returning to pay their respects. Least of all you and me. But he's out here, where he chose to spend his final days. That's the important thing. The exact place doesn't matter that much. This whole rainforest was his grave, the trees his tomb. He would have approved. He wasn't big on ceremony."

"Walk down there with me. Maybe there's something you'll recognize – that'll jog your memory."

Jack nodded. "Sure, Drake. Why not?"

They plodded to the river and made their way up its bank, wary of snakes, the game track that ran parallel barely passable. After fifty yards Jack slowed. "I don't think it was any farther than this. So somewhere between the palms and here. That's about as close as we're going to get."

"You don't see anything that stands out?"

Jack stopped. "Look around you. This is jungle. I doubt anything stays the same for a month, let alone two decades."

They spent a couple of minutes watching the rain flow in veins to the river, and then Jack turned and began walking back. Drake stayed planted, and Jack stopped and turned to him.

Drake shook his head. "Go ahead. I can find my own way back."

"You sure?"

"Yeah. Pretty easy. Follow the river, make a right at the palms. A cinch."

"All right." Jack left him alone, understanding Drake's desire to commune with his departed father, and inspect every bump or irregularity in the bank for a clue as to his final resting place.

Drake took his time, the big knife in his hand, cutting away plants to get a better look at anything he thought promising. After a half hour he came across a lump of blackened leaves that yielded four softball-sized river rocks in a pile. There was no cross, the wood having rotted away, but Drake didn't need that final marker to know that he'd finally found his father. He stood staring down at the spot for a long time. Then he dropped to his knees, his tears mingling with the rainwater on his face, the salty drops falling onto the stones, the sadness soaking into the silent earth as he sobbed, as sons had been sobbing for their departed fathers since time began.

Chapter Thirty-One

The first night at the riverside camp was a rainy one, making guard duty miserable. By morning the front had moved beyond them, and a stillness settled over the small clearing as the sun rose, the endless rhythm of the falling rain finally abated.

Drake and Jack caught breakfast at the river, several three-pound specimens that looked like large piranha. They fried them over the stove and the group ate unhurriedly while discussing their plan of attack for the day. Drake believed his father had been looking for the final outpost along the theorized secret Inca route that would point them in the direction of the lost city. If he was correct, the fourth outpost lay ahead, perhaps near…and beyond that, Paititi.

"I want to go with you," Allie announced, back in her usual high spirits.

"I don't have a problem with that, do you?" Drake asked Jack.

Jack tried to hide his dislike of the idea. "I'm thinking we should all go together."

"That's fine. But we should spread out in a search pattern, each of us every twenty to thirty feet," Allie said. "That way we won't miss anything."

"What about the camp?" Drake asked.

"Two choices," Spencer said. "Either one of us remains here, or we pack it all up and cart it with us every day. I don't feel comfortable leaving everything unguarded."

"I agree," Jack said. "But I don't want to lug our entire camp through the jungle. My vote is to rotate who stays on guard until we pick up and move the whole mess."

Drake nodded. "I'll second that. Jack, you have the GPS location of the last outpost find. What about the other two?"

"Sure. I've got them."

"What's the trajectory? Straight line, or no discernible pattern?"

Jack looked at Allie. "Time to earn your keep."

Allie activated the device and checked the screen. "Other than east, it's not a straight line. The outposts were directional. Knowing the orientation of the last one we found, our best bet is to search in a triangle northeast from this point. If you look at the spacing between the outposts that have already been found, they're about two days of hard hiking apart, or twenty to twenty-five miles from each other. If this last one holds true to that pattern, the final one would be within a few miles of this camp. Of course, there's no way of being sure until we find it."

"I was going to say, then why don't we just skip past that outpost, assume it's around here, and look for Paititi twenty to twenty-five miles from here?" Spencer said.

"We could. But where, exactly? We can't assume it's east. It could be any direction. Without that final bearing, we're talking months or years of searching with just the four of us. With no guarantees. That's the big problem: without the final outpost, we've got nothing."

"How do you know it's the final one?" Spencer asked. "Why four after the river? Why not six? Ten…?"

"That's not what the journal concluded," Drake explained. "My father was convinced there were only four after the river. There were eight before, and all have been discovered over the years. My dad extrapolated that series of finds, connected the dots, and developed the theory of a sacred path for the faithful to follow. A yellow brick road."

Spencer finished his breakfast and sat back. "Okay, then. What exactly are we looking for?"

Allie squinted at him. "All of the outposts were built out of stone, and had an arch that was a symbolic threshold for the next phase of the journey. I'd expect the final one to look much like the one we saw yesterday."

"An arch? That was a pile of rubble. How do you get a bearing on direction if the arch isn't standing?"

"Each arch had paver stones running through it. Symbolizing the road," Allie explained. "Even if it collapsed, the pavers still point the way. That's what I confirmed yesterday. You can still see them."

Spencer shrugged. "Fair enough. So the question is, who wants to stay with the camp today?"

"Not me," Allie said. "I came all the way here to look for this damned thing. I'm not going to sit and watch the grass grow while everyone's out doing what I trained for…"

"And I think it's pretty obvious I'm going to be on the hunt," Drake said.

Jack caught Spencer's eye. "I suppose that leaves either you or me. Want to flip a coin?" he asked.

"Nah. I have a feeling we'll both have plenty of chance to ferret around in the jungle before this is over. You can have first whack at it," Spencer said. "What time do you want to target for getting back, so I'll know if we have a problem? We could have stayed in contact by phone, but that would have required two sat phones."

Jack ignored the barb and tapped his watch. "I think the same rule as the hike. We stop by one, two at the latest. If we're not back by around two thirty, there's an issue. That will give us at least seven or so hours to look for the outpost each day without killing ourselves."

Allie nodded. "Works for me."

"All right then. Good luck. You can leave most of your stuff here. Just take what you'll need for the day. Guns, water, food, that sort of thing," Spencer advised. "I'll watch over the rest."

They were on their way within fifteen minutes, each with a rifle and a machete in hand. Allie had argued for fanning out and working a methodical grid pattern using the GPS for guidance, so they wouldn't waste time repeating an area they'd already inspected. They crossed the river at an area downstream where the water was only knee deep, and soon were hacking their way into the wilds. It was slow going, made worse by the lack of trails and the constant worry that they'd come across another poisonous snake or attract the attention of some predator, human or animal. By 1:30 their arms were leaden and they'd found nothing. Jack recorded the end point on the GPS so they could go straight back the following day, and they returned to the camp, ready for rest.

The following day brought more of the same, with the added drama of Allie twisting her ankle on a vine. To Drake's chagrin, Spencer stepped up and supported her all the way back to the camp as she limped along, her arm around his shoulder for stability. Back at the river, Jack did a cursory examination of the swollen appendage and shook his head.

"You should be fine in a few days. But you'll need to stay off it so the swelling can go down. Looks like a doozy of a sprain."

"It hurts," Allie confirmed. "I was so busy watching for snakes I missed the vine entirely. Just stupid."

"Not really. It could happen to any of us. Yet another reminder from the Amazon that one misstep and things can go badly wrong," Spencer said. "You can stay here with me tomorrow. Take it easy."

Allie frowned. "No, we need three people on the search or it will take almost twice as long. I'll be fine. I know the drill. If I see anyone, shoot them, right?"

"Never a bad idea," Jack confirmed, nodding.

Spencer looked troubled. "I don't know. I don't feel good about leaving you alone."

"I can stay with her," Drake said.

Eventually they agreed that they'd break down the camp the next morning and conceal the gear to avoid detection, and that Allie would remain to guard their possessions against what had so far turned out to be nothing.

They awoke at dawn to drizzle, but mild compared to some they'd endured, and made short work of the tents, stowing them in a thicket near the river. As they left for another long day of searching, Allie waved to them from her concealed resting place between two tall trees, nearly invisible in the dense foliage.

They'd already covered a swatch that stretched almost a full mile from the camp. Jack had calculated that at their current rate they'd be ready to do a return run on another ninety-foot-wide section within two more days. The enormity of their task became obvious as they resumed hacking through the jungle at yesterday's stopping point, every hour seeming to drag by in slow motion with nothing to show for it.

At 1:00, just as they were preparing to call it a day, Drake chopped his way into a clearing where he found a number of green mounds. He approached the overgrown irregularities and poked at the nearest one with his machete.

The blade clanked against stone.

Drake fought to stay calm as his pulse pounded in his ears. He retraced his steps to where he could see Jack and Spencer.

"I think I found it," he called in a stage whisper.

Spencer appeared a few moments later, Jack behind him. Drake led them through the flora into the clearing. Jack peered at the faint outline where the lone building's walls had stood, and then moved to the smaller of the lumps beside it and began scraping away the accumulated soil and vegetation. Minutes later they could plainly see the remnants of square columns that had supported an arch, and between them, the rectangular stones set together to form a threshold and path. Jack stood between the columns with his GPS and recorded the spot, and then made a notation to record the direction the path pointed.

Distant gunfire shattered the quiet of the surroundings – the distinctive staccato chatter of an AK-47. Jack swung around, his normally flushed face pale.

"Allie!"

Spencer took off at a sprint, and it was all Drake could do to keep up with him as he ducked and weaved through the path they'd cleared. Jack was right behind him, his boots thumping against the ground as he ran.

When they neared the clearing ten minutes later, Drake was gasping for breath, pouring sweat. Spencer held his arm out and motioned for Jack to move to the right, separating to provide a less obvious target. He pointed to the left and Drake nodded, fighting the urge to vomit from the exertion and heat.

They crept to the riverbank and looked over the camp area. It was quiet, with no evidence of a struggle. If it hadn't been for the shooting, they would have believed it was just another afternoon following a tedious search.

Except there was no sign of Allie. She wasn't in her hiding place between the two trees.

She wasn't anywhere they could see.

After several minutes of watching, waiting for any movement, Spencer emerged from the brush and moved down the bank to cross the river. When he'd made it to the camp side, Jack followed, Drake waiting until they were both out of the water to join them.

When they reached the campsite, a quick hunt through the bush yielded nothing. Their gear was still hidden, undisturbed, but there was no sign of Allie.

She'd vanished without a trace.

Chapter Thirty-Two

The evening meal was a grim one. It was as though Allie had disappeared into thin air, leaving only three brass shell casings and nothing else. All three men had their pistols strapped to their belts and their rifles by their sides, and Spencer and Jack had been quietly discussing how to proceed, with no agreement.

The final rays of waning sun streamed through the overhead canopy as they ate surplus MREs, none of them having the will to fish, their imaginations working overtime on what might have happened to Allie.

A muffled thud sounded from nearby. They were instantly on their feet, rifles at the ready. The vegetation across the river rustled and Drake was drawing a bead when Spencer pushed his gun barrel aside.

"No. Look. Over there." He pointed to a white square fastened to a grapefruit-sized rock.

Drake retrieved it. A folded sheet of paper was tied to the stone with twine. He unsheathed his knife and sliced the cord, and then unfolded the note. The handwriting was neat, the message brief.

Greetings Drake Ramsey. We have the girl. We want the journal. A trade. The journal for her.

Think long and hard about refusing this. The girl will die, and you next.

Do not fire on my man when he come there tomorrow morning for your answer. Do not attempt any ambush. You and your two companions be where you sit now. Any deviance will result in the girl's immediate death.

The note was unsigned.

"What the hell..." Drake muttered and gave it to Jack, who read it once and handed it disgustedly to Spencer.

"The Russians." Jack spat his contempt on the rainforest floor.

"Are you sure?" Drake asked.

Jack squinted at the far riverbank. "They tend to favor the brute-force approach. No finesse. And kidnapping is about as brute force as it gets." Jack thought for a moment. "We need to figure out a way to deal with them and get her back."

"Deal with them?" Drake asked.

"Of course. They're going to kill her no matter what. Even if you give them the journal. That's how they work."

"But I don't have it."

"Right. And at that point, they'll want you. What's in your brain. They'll torture it out of you and then kill you, too. It's their standard operating procedure."

Spencer's eyes narrowed. "Seems like you know an awful lot about these Russians."

Jack nodded. "I should. I made it my mission to find out everything I could about them after they killed Drake's father. You could say I'm an expert on their behavior by now."

"How did they know we were here?" Drake asked.

"I told you we were racing the clock. They obviously recorded the spot, just like I did, and bet that we'd come back to it eventually. Turns out that was a good bet," Jack said.

"What are we going to do?" Spencer asked, deferring to him.

Jack paced, fingering the trigger guard of his rifle as he did so, a nervous habit he was unaware of. Eventually he stopped and turned to Spencer.

"How good are you at tracking?"

~ ~ ~

The next day they rose before dawn and sat around the stones they'd circled to create a fire pit, their faces drawn from a night with no sleep. Nobody spoke, their demeanors serious, dark circles beneath their eyes evidence of their fatigue as the gray shower fell around them, the silence broken only by an occasional bird or a monkey screeching overhead.

When the messenger arrived on the far side of the river, they bristled, guns in their laps. The man on the other bank was reed thin, Jack's age, dressed in tropical camouflage pants and shirt, his gray hair trimmed tight to his skull. He had a Kalashnikov of his own slung over his shoulder, but seemed completely calm. Jack was almost certain it was Sasha, but it had been a long time…

"Drake Ramsey," he called, his Russian accent obvious.

"That's me," Drake said, standing.

"You read note?" the Russian asked, the words more a statement than a question.

"Yes."

"Good. You give me journal, yes?"

"No."

Sasha looked puzzled, but only for a moment. "Then girl dies."

"I don't have the journal."

"Lies."

"It's true. I don't. I left it in the United States."

"I don't believe."

"Doesn't matter what you believe. I don't have the journal, and I can't give you what I don't have."

"Then why are you here?" Sasha fired back.

"To find the Inca city."

"Using journal…"

"No. Using the *information* in the journal."

"Is same thing. Where is it?"

"The info? It's right here." Drake tapped his head with his free hand.

They stood staring at each other for a few beats. "You write it down. Give to us."

"I can try. But there's no way of guaranteeing it will be complete. Just what I can remember."

The Russian seemed to make a decision. "Then girl is dead."

"And you get nothing," Drake said, his tone mild. "Seems stupid to me. Are you an idiot?" He tapped his forehead with his hand while scowling.

Sasha's eyes narrowed. "We keep the girl till you remember everything."

Drake shrugged. "Hey, do whatever you want."

The discussion obviously hadn't gone the way the Russian had expected, and he seemed unsure of what to do. A sly look flashed across his face and he nodded.

"Then we wait until you find city."

"That might be a while, buddy," Jack said, speaking for the first time. "It's not like youngblood here has a map where X marks the spot."

Sasha didn't understand. "We trade girl for map."

Drake nodded. "I can try."

"No try. Do it."

"I'll need some time."

"You have one day."

"Wait…"

But the Russian had spun and run back into the jungle, obviously distrustful of them.

"How much of a head start do you want to give him?" Jack whispered.

Spencer looked at his watch. "Five minutes. He doesn't look like he knows much about negotiating the jungle. Wrong kind of boots, for one. And his hat. He didn't have one. Which is poor planning in a rainforest for a host of reasons."

"You're confident you can track him?"

"As long as it's fresh, which is why I advised against killing him and trying to follow his trail back to the camp. And assuming it doesn't rain hard and erase his footprints. As it is, the ground's soft and moist, so he should leave a trail as obvious as an elephant."

"Okay. We'll be right behind you," Jack said.

"It's smarter for me to track him on my own and return once I've located their camp. Why don't you give me the GPS and I'll set a waypoint when I find it, and then sneak back?" Spencer suggested.

"I don't like only one of us going," Jack said.

"Even if a slip from one of you results in your daughter being killed?"

Jack brooded for a moment and then pulled his GPS free from his backpack and handed it to Spencer. "You win. But for God's sake, be careful."

"I will." Spencer eyed them both. "But don't try to follow me. I need to know that if I hear something behind me, it's an enemy. I can't be second-guessing. Clear?"

Jack and Drake nodded. "Clear. You really think you can do this?"

"I'm positive." Spencer bent down, hefted his backpack, and slipped his arms through the straps. He adjusted his hat and, after taking a last look at his watch, jogged down the bank to the shallow part of the river. "I'll be back. Stay put."

Chapter Thirty-Three

The anxiety coming off Jack was palpable, creating an unpleasant aura as he and Drake waited for Spencer's return. An hour after the Russian's disappearance it began raining again, and Jack's shoulders slumped – if Spencer hadn't found the enemy camp by then, he likely wouldn't at all, and their gambit would have been for nothing.

They never heard Spencer – he just appeared in the middle of the river, like a specter in the gray downpour, seeming to glide across the surface of the water with no visible effort. Jack jumped to his feet and moved to meet him. Drake remained where he was, figuring that if there was bad news, he'd rather Jack heard it first so he could digest it alone.

When they approached, Spencer looked grim but determined.

"There are eight of them. They're about a half hour from here. By the same river, from what I can tell. Looks that way on the GPS. Anyway, I made out six locals and two Russians, counting the one that showed up here. So…difficult, but not an impossible number for us to take."

"Did you see Allie?" Drake asked.

"Yes. She's tied to a tree. They've got two tents set up. But if they're smart, they'll have a guard posted at night. Especially at night. Everyone's armed to the teeth, so it won't be easy."

"How do you think we should do it?" Jack asked.

"We wait until dark. We've got night vision scopes, hopefully they don't. But I'd rather not go in heavy – a lot can go wrong when the shooting starts." Spencer appeared to consider the problem. "There are a few ways to approach it. For my money, the best will depend on where the guard's sitting. Assuming he doesn't patrol the perimeter." He returned his attention to Jack. "You'll need to see the layout. I say we head over there an hour before dusk, scope it out, and be ready to hit them once everyone's asleep."

"How competent do the locals look?"

Spencer frowned. "They look hard. My guess is they work with traffickers. They know how to handle their weapons. You can tell."

"That would figure. The Russians would want seasoned help. Men who wouldn't bat an eye about kidnapping or murder. Birds of a feather." Jack looked around their camp. "We better pack everything up. We won't be able to stay here if we get Allie back, unless we kill everyone – and that might not happen. So we should move our gear now while we have downtime. Probably stash it closer to the final outpost. That clearing looked as good as any."

Spencer nodded. "We can go in light, with just weapons and whatever else we deem necessary. The bare minimum." He studied Jack's drawn face. "You have an idea?"

"Tell me about the river and the layout."

~ ~ ~

The cloudburst stopped twenty minutes before they arrived at the Russian camp. The air felt thick as they crawled to a position upstream, the vegetation hiding them as they eyed the gunmen, who were eating dinner – fish, by the smell. Drake's mouth watered as the aroma wafted on the breeze, and he was reminded that he hadn't eaten anything but an energy bar since choking down a few mouthfuls of breakfast twelve hours before.

The Russians sat near the fire, with the natives grouped nearby, eating separately. Allie had a bandanna tied around her mouth, muzzling her so she couldn't cry out, and nobody made any attempt to offer her food. As the late afternoon light faded, the natives finished their meal and went to relieve themselves. The taller of the two Russians approached Allie and pulled the bandanna down. He poured a few gulps of water into her mouth before putting it back in place. Drake's anger swelled at what she'd probably been through all day, tied to the tree, no food, at the mercy of her captors. He had to force it down, and emulate Jack's dispassionate precision.

The sliver of sky overhead turned vibrant orange and red, high wisps of clouds like trails of white smoke as the sun set, and then it was dark, the transition from twilight taking only a few minutes. The Russians entered the two tents, leaving the native gunmen to sleep outdoors under a tarp they'd strung from several trees on the opposite end of the grotto. One of the men took up a position on the perimeter near the fire pit, his gun across his lap as he sat cross-legged beneath a smaller tarp.

They waited an hour and a half. Jack watched through his rifle's night vision scope as the locals rolled into sleeping positions and dozed off. Unfortunately, even after a long wait the guard still looked alert, which didn't bode well for a surprise attack.

Jack put the gun down and faced Drake and Spencer, his voice barely a whisper. "Here's how we'll play this. I'll go in and take out the guard. Spencer, you cover the others. I want to avoid shooting unless we absolutely have to, but if we do, make every burst count. Drake, once I've neutralized the guard, get to Allie and cut her loose. Take her to the river and follow the bank to where we are right now while Spencer and I cover you. We'll be able to move faster than they can once we're clear of their camp. I didn't see any NV gear on their weapons."

Spencer nodded at Drake. "Take the night vision goggles so you can see what you're doing with Allie. We've got the rifle scopes," he murmured. He extracted the goggles from his backpack and handed them to Drake. "The strap goes around your head. Try them on. Get used to them, because when it's showtime, they'll be your lifeline."

Drake did so, and Spencer flipped a small switch on the side of the goggles. "There."

The night lit up in a yellow-green haze. Drake's eyes adjusted, and soon he could make out the guard and the sleeping gunmen – and Allie, who looked like she'd also fallen asleep.

"I can see pretty well."

Jack nodded. "All right. Spencer, follow me in. Don't get too close – let's try to do this without waking anyone up."

"How are you going to eliminate the guard?" Spencer asked.

"Knife. The old-fashioned way."

Spencer nodded in the gloom. "Too bad we can't use the crossbows."

"Too much noise. And if for some reason I didn't get a clean headshot, he'd go berserk, and then we're in a firefight. No, I'm going to circle around, come up behind him, and put him down before he can make a sound. It's the only way."

A low rumble of thunder sounded and Spencer grimaced. "Damn. That's going to wake them."

"Nobody said this would be easy."

The sudden downpour fell heavy from the night sky, fat drops the size of marbles pelting the trees around them. Drake watched through the goggles as the natives awoke and made hasty adjustments to their shelter before crawling as far under it as they could and resuming their slumber. The guard sat impassively, rain streaming off his tarp. As the downpour intensified, he stood and walked through the rain to Allie's position. He looked down at her for a long time before moving back to his original spot, where this time he squatted, squinting into the dark as sheets of water rained down on the camp.

Jack nodded at Spencer and left without a sound. Drake and Spencer watched as the guard bounced on his haunches and then stood again. He paced back and forth before easing himself into a seated position beneath the drooping fabric square, seemingly unruffled by the cloudburst.

Jack appeared at the edge of the clearing behind him, moving in a crouch, each step carefully placed, the falling rain masking any sound his boots made on the wet ground.

Spencer leaned in to Drake. "When he drops the guard, don't hesitate. Get to Allie, cut her loose, tell her to stay quiet, and get to the river. If something goes wrong and there's shooting, don't stop, don't try to join in...don't do anything but get her clear. Understand?"

"Got it."

Jack prowled through the tall grass toward the sentry. Drake watched through the goggles, fascinated, his stomach in a knot as the older man closed the distance to the guard. Twenty feet, then ten, then five, and then he was on him, one hand across the man's mouth as he drove his combat knife into the base of his neck, instantly severing his spinal cord. Spencer nudged Drake into action, and he sprinted from behind the plants and across the clearing as Jack gently lowered the guard's inert form to the ground. His first errand complete, Jack swiveled with his rifle, watching for any movement from the sleeping gunmen.

Drake reached Allie and she started awake, obviously surprised by his sudden proximity. He saw panic in her eyes and realized that she couldn't make out who it was, especially with the night vision goggles covering most of his face.

"Allie, it's me. Drake. I'm going to cut you loose and we're getting out of here. Don't say anything, stay quiet." Drake realized as he spoke that she couldn't talk with the bandanna gag. He pulled it out of her mouth and sliced at the rope binding her wrists, careful not to slash her with the big knife's razor-sharp blade.

"Wha—"

"Shhh. Are you hurt?" he murmured.

"No."

"You think you can run?"

"Damned right I can."

"Okay. Quiet as possible. Take my hand and follow me," Drake said, sheathing the blade and gripping his rifle.

They rose and, after a final look around, crept to the river twenty yards down the bank. They were three-quarters of the way to the water when Allie stifled a cry. She'd landed on her bad ankle the wrong way, sending a streak of blinding pain up her leg.

A grunt sounded from beneath the tarp, and one of the men called out a query in Spanish.

When no response came, the gunmen scrambled for their weapons as Drake practically carried Allie the rest of the way to the river. Gunfire exploded behind them in the night, instantly answered by the percussive bark of Jack's rifle. After that, everything seemed to happen at once. Muzzle flashes lit up the clearing as the guards fired indiscriminately at the perimeter. They were quickly joined by the two Russians, who emerged from their tents spraying lead with their AKs on full auto.

Spencer picked off one of the guards, and Jack another, and then a stray round struck Jack in the chest. He went down hard, coughed, and scrambled to his feet, returning fire as he made his break for the jungle's cover. Spencer lay down measured volleys as Jack stumbled toward him.

Jack threw himself into the undergrowth as rounds whistled by, and then Spencer had his arm around him and half dragged him farther into the jungle. Spencer held his AK in front of him, using the scope to see, and soon the hiss of slugs tearing through the leaves died as they moved deeper into the brush.

"We…need to…get to the river…Allie…" Jack said. Spencer heard the telltale burble of blood in his breathing, as well as the sound of air sucked through Jack's chest wound.

"Okay. We will. Save your strength. The river's off to our right. Come on. You can make it."

They stumbled through the undergrowth, Jack's legs barely supporting him as he tried to keep up with Spencer. After what seemed like an eternity, they saw a ribbon of water, rain rippling the surface in the darkness.

"We're here. Now all we have to do is wait," Spencer hissed. Jack collapsed in a heap on the bank, his lifeblood seeping from his chest, his shirt soaked with its inky stain.

They heard splashing from their right. Drake and Allie materialized out of the night. When Allie saw Jack struggling to breathe in the dim moonlight, she dropped to her knees next to him.

"Oh, God. What happened? Are you..." She looked up at Spencer.

Spencer shook his head. "He's hit. Bad."

Allie put her hand on Jack's cheek. He felt cold. His eyes flitted open and he took her in.

"We...got you out...of there."

"Yes. You did."

"Took a couple of them with us, too." He coughed, and she could see the crimson trickle from his lips. He groaned and shut his eyes again. "Get moving. I'm done for."

"No. I won't leave you here," Allie cried. Drake squeezed her hand.

"Shhh. They'll hear you, and then we're all dead."

She bit back her response and nodded, her eyes welling with tears as the rain washed Jack's blood into rivulets that strained down to the river.

Jack hacked, an ugly wet sound. "Drake...I'm....sorry about...your dad..."

"You did everything you could. Don't worry about it, Jack. It's over."

Jack shook his head. "No. You...don't...understand."

Drake leaned in closer. "What don't I understand?"

"I...he wasn't...supposed to get...hurt..." Another cough, this one accompanied with blood and wheezing through the chest wound. "Something went...wrong."

"What do you mean, he wasn't supposed to get hurt? By who?"

"I'm...sorry. The...Russians. They...promi–"

Drake had never heard a death rattle before. It wasn't so much a rattle as a long, gurgling moan. Jack stared heavenward, his final regret dying on his lips, gazing into eternity as droplets of warm rain fell into his open eyes.

"We need to get out of here. Grab his gun and his backpack. Hurry," Spencer whispered, breaking the spell. Drake picked up Jack's rifle and slipped his backpack off, his movements wooden, his mind reeling from Jack's revelation. The bastard had sold his father out. No doubt for a handsome figure – enough so he'd never had to work again. But something had gone wrong. Dad hadn't cooperated and things had turned ugly, robbing Drake of his father.

They plodded down the side of the river until Spencer stopped and turned.

"The goggles. Give them to me. Quick."

Drake handed them over. Shots rang out behind them, and slugs smacked into the wet dirt. Spencer scrambled up the bank and growled at Drake and Allie. "Follow me."

Allie crawled to Spencer and he pulled her to her feet. Drake was right behind her, his boots slipping in the slick mud as he fought for a foothold. Then they were moving along a trail, branches tearing at his skin as he pushed through them, Jack's confession burning in his ears as they plunged deeper into the jungle's embrace.

Chapter Thirty-Four

"It's still pretty swollen," Drake said as he inspected Allie's ankle in the hazy morning light.

They'd made it to the outpost and tried to rest, adrenaline from the nocturnal escape still coursing through their systems. Jack's words and the reality of his death had made it impossible to sleep. Allie had been quiet, and Drake left her alone with her thoughts.

Drake's mind was racing now that he knew his father's best friend had betrayed him. For all of Jack's remorse, wasn't it equally possible that he'd betrayed Drake as well, only this time to the CIA? No wonder he'd been so adamant about Drake taking the offer. He wondered what Jack had been offered to encourage him to jump at it? Ten million? Twenty? Had he still been planning to betray them later on?

The rain had ended at some point during the night, and once dawn had broken he'd gone to check on Allie, who looked puffy and red-eyed, her ankle still swollen.

"It hurts, but not as much as when I first sprained it." She hesitated. "Thank you for risking your life to rescue me."

Drake felt color rush to his face and looked away. "You would have done the same for me."

"Easy to say after the fact. But I want to tell you that I appreciate everything you did. I wouldn't be here if you hadn't put it all on the line for me."

Drake's voice softened. "I'm a sucker for a damsel in distress."

"I'll have to remember that."

Drake hesitated. "I'm sorry about Jack."

She closed her eyes and nodded. "And I'm sorry about your father. I couldn't believe my ears."

"That was a long time ago. And it sounds like he was surprised they killed him." Drake shook his head. Excusing Jack's treachery didn't come easily, even if it was to make Allie feel better.

Spencer approached from where he'd been standing at the edge of the clearing, his AK at the ready.

"We should probably give your ankle another day to heal before we try to move," Spencer said. "Keep it elevated. That'll reduce the inflammation."

"What are the odds they can find us?" she asked in a small voice.

Spencer shook his head. "Pretty low. With the rain, they wouldn't be able to track us easily, and since we're not on any trails, it would be almost impossible. Having said that, we still need to be careful and quiet. No point in making their job any easier. And remember that they're not the only bad guys in this jungle." He stared at the remnants of the Inca outpost. "By tomorrow afternoon, we'll be miles away. I like our chances."

"We can get going today. My ankle really does feel better than yesterday."

"Don't sweat it. Give it time to mend," Drake echoed, which seemed to settle it.

In the late afternoon Drake and Spencer tried their hand at hunting with the crossbows, as there were no nearby rivers. Spencer showed Drake how to cock the bowstring, and they practiced firing at a tree for an hour. Drake found that he was pretty accurate with the weapon – surprisingly so at up to thirty yards – more than with a pistol.

When they finished practicing, they screwed hunting tips onto the carbon shafts and headed into the brush.

"What are we looking for?" Drake whispered.

"Anything we can eat. Python, deer, monkey…"

"I thought you were kidding about monkey."

"Do I strike you as a kidder?"

"What about—"

"Shhh." Spencer stopped and cocked his head to the side, listening. He stood frozen, then leaned into Drake as a light breeze dented the canopy above them. "Get ready. I think we got lucky."

"What?"

Instead of answering, Spencer opened his mouth and slapped one cheek, making a hollow *ponk* sound. He repeated the odd performance several times before raising his crossbow and pointing it into the brush. Drake narrowed his eyes, trying futilely to make anything out. He was just about to say something when he heard grunting and snorting from ahead. He froze, waiting. Spencer was tracking something with his crossbow, and Drake was just raising his when Spencer fired. His bowstring snapped, and Spencer whispered to Drake.

"Give me your bow. Quick."

Drake did as instructed and Spencer fired again. Drake heard movement racing through the brush, as if a herd of deer were tearing away. When it had grown quiet again, Spencer pushed branches aside and led Drake to their prize: what appeared to be a small boar, with a quarrel embedded in its side and another in its skull.

"What is that?" Drake asked as Spencer knelt beside the dead animal.

"White-lipped peccary. This is a juvenile. Maybe thirty pounds. Adults can get up to more than double that. They're good eating. What we heard crashing through the brush was the rest of the herd. They travel together in large groups – up to a hundred or more." Spencer eyed Drake's knife. "Give me that shiv of yours and I'll dress it right here. No point in hauling the carcass back to camp."

Drake handed it to Spencer, who expertly carved steaks and slipped them into a plastic garbage bag he'd brought. He cleaned the blade with some of his canteen water and wiped it on the peccary's bristly coat. The whole procedure took no more than five minutes, and they were soon returning with ten pounds of meat for dinner.

"We can cook it tonight and it should keep for breakfast. Unfortunately in this heat it won't last longer."

"How do you cook it?"

"Very carefully."

Allie was sitting under a tree when they arrived, her Kalashnikov beside her for companionship, a look of relief on her face when she saw them.

"Did you get anything?"

Drake told her about the peccary, and she made a face. "Tell me it didn't look like Bambi."

"I can swear it looked absolutely nothing like Bambi. Honest," he said, hand on his chest.

The steaks smelled mouthwatering when Spencer cooked them, and they tasted like butter after days of eating nothing but fish and dry food. He slipped the leftovers into another bag and wrapped it carefully, then sealed it in yet another bag.

"We want to ensure that nothing comes sniffing around in the middle of the night. I wouldn't want to try to take on a jaguar in the dark. Or at any time, but especially not at night," he warned. Drake believed him. He didn't want to ask him how he knew.

Morning brought more hiking, but tougher going due to the absence of trails. Spencer studied Jack's GPS and calculated the route direction, and then zoomed out and studied the satellite image, which showed a solid field of green.

Using the trajectory from the final outpost's paver stones, their goal for the day was a barely visible stream eleven miles east. While they were in uncharted territory now regarding what to expect, their hope was that the same general pattern would hold and that they were no more than twenty-five miles from Paititi – or two days' hard push from their current location.

Allie pushed along without slowing them down, determined to not be a hindrance. Her limp lessened through the morning, and by the time they reached the stream where they would camp for the night, she seemed greatly improved.

They spent most of their daylight hours the following day slogging through the rain, following game trails through the jungle as they pressed on. In the early afternoon they heard the crashing of a nearby waterfall – a promising sound, because the journal had theorized that Paititi would be located in an area surrounded by waterfalls and a river.

At the base of the waterfall, they took a break while Spencer studied the GPS. "We're two miles short. You want to keep going, or have you had enough for today?" he asked.

Drake eyed Allie. "It's up to her. I could go on. But if there's no pressing reason to, this is a pretty nice spot."

Allie pursed her lips. "Oh, sure, make it all about me. I'm fine."

"This is a good place to camp. And the rain's letting up, so it'll get hot soon. I vote for stopping here today," Spencer said.

The river below the small waterfall proved to be full of fish, and they feasted on several different types that they roasted over a fire. The rain had stopped an hour after they set up the tents, and Spencer had used his petroleum jelly to ignite a small pile of damp branches in order to dry out an armful of others.

They spent the next two days exploring their surroundings, using their new camp as base, but their efforts yielded nothing but exhaustion. As their second evening by the waterfall drew to a close, Spencer's skepticism about their chances of success grew more pronounced. Drake tried to ignore him, but the doubts had an insidious effect. He could tell Allie was also wavering, but they had no option B.

On the third afternoon, Drake was chopping his way through some particularly dense jungle, his machete heavy in his tired hand, when he heard the roar of falling water ahead – another waterfall, but bigger than the one they'd camped by. Allie called out softly from behind him.

"Do you hear that?" she asked.

"I do. Follow me. It can't be much farther," Drake answered.

"Lead the way," Spencer said, his tone morose.

Drake hacked at the foliage with renewed vigor, and in a few minutes he emerged onto a ledge overlooking a breathtaking sight – easily five stories of water tumbling over a cliff edge into rushing rapids below.

"I'd say that qualifies as a waterfall," Drake said, inching along the rock outcropping to get a better look at the pool below.

When his feet went out from under him, slipping on moss he hadn't seen, it felt like gravity was suspended for a brief moment, and then the wind was knocked out of him as he landed on his back, though his backpack absorbed the worst of it. He shook his head groggily and tried to stand as Allie edged closer to help him, but felt himself sliding inexorably toward the precipice, the slick growth covering the rock accelerating his fall.

Allie and Spencer watched in horror as Drake's expression went from confusion to fear in a kind of slow motion. Desperate, he clawed at the rock, trying to find a hold. Blood stained the surface of the stone as he tried to latch on to it to break his slide, and then he was gone, sucked into the roaring vortex.

"No!" Allie yelled, pushing forward. Spencer restrained her, knowing that if she made it much farther onto the ledge, the same fate awaited her.

"Stop screaming. Unless you want to draw every hostile for ten miles," Spencer warned, his tone sharp.

"Oh, God. We have to help him…"

"Not by joining him. Come on. Let's find a way to the bottom."

Spencer backed away from the edge, pulling Allie with him. Farther in the brush they found a faint track that led down the side of the slope. After some rough terrain, they emerged at the base of the waterfall, where the cascading water exploded into a deep pool before frothing along a narrower channel that transformed into whitewater rapids. Spencer shrugged off his backpack and removed his shoes, and then dove into the pool as Allie watched.

He bobbed to the surface after almost a full minute, like an otter, and then went under again. He repeated the process several times, with no success. When he came back up for the final time, he swam to the edge of the pool and climbed out, gasping for breath. Allie studied his glum expression with shock written across her face. She tried to speak, but the only sound she produced was a dry rasp. He shook his head and looked away, unable to meet her gaze.

Drake was gone.

Chapter Thirty-Five

Pinpoints of light floated in Drake's consciousness, his senses numb. He coughed reflexively and water exploded from his mouth and nose. He choked and sputtered, hacking more as fluid streamed down his chin as his body tried to clear his lungs. Pain seared through his head and he retched, and then instinctively he tried to reach up and touch the raw spot on his skull.

His arms wouldn't move. As he regained full consciousness, he realized that his wrists were bound over his head and secured to something. He opened his eyes and instantly winced – one of them was almost swollen shut from the battering he'd endured in the rapids after dropping into the pool and being flushed down the river. Vision in his other eye was blurry, but as he strained to focus, he could make out figures near him.

As his eyesight cleared, he could make out faces – indigenous tribal features burned deep brown from the sun, the vaguely Asian cast to the eyes and flatter nose typical of the Amazon rainforest's primitive inhabitants. His gaze stopped at a young woman around his age, her animal-skin tunic soaking wet, like his clothes. She held his stare unflinchingly, and then one of the young men next to her emitted a whoop, and he felt something pulling at his belt.

The man held up Drake's knife, unmistakable malice in his gaze. After waving the weapon around, laughing along with his companions, he turned to Drake with an ugly expression and approached, his grip on the knife tightening as he prepared to put it to use. He held it over Drake's head, and then a warning shout barked from beyond Drake's field of vision. The man hesitated and stepped back, his black eyes locked on Drake's, obviously not happy. Drake passed out, his last impression a lightning bolt of agony shrieking through his skull as he tried to pull free.

When he came to again, his head was less tender, and when he tried to move his arms, he was able to. He tentatively cracked his eye open. The young woman was sitting nearby, looking at him. Next to her was a wizened elder with long gray hair, his complexion the color and texture of rawhide, the skin wrinkled from a lifetime in the rainforest.

They were in some sort of structure. He could make out thatch overhead, the dried fronds supported upon a crude framework of wooden poles, saplings that had been stripped and tied together to form the roof. Rain dripped from the sides, but inside they were dry.

Drake tried to sit up. His head swam, and along with the disorientation the pain returned with a vengeance. Supporting himself on one elbow, he reached up to his head and felt some sort of muck lathered on his skull. He brought his fingers to his nose and sniffed, and gagged at the odor.

The woman stood and approached on bare feet, her bronze legs lithe, no trace of embarrassment at her nearly nude form. She shook her head and pointed to his skull, and then hers. He understood. He wasn't to mess with whatever they'd put on his head.

The torrent of questions that flooded his awareness brought another wave of nausea and dizziness, and it was all he could do to keep from passing out. The woman made a sign with her hands like someone sleeping and pointed to him. His attempt to nod was ill advised, and he barely got his head back onto the cushioned softness of whatever they'd placed beneath it before he blacked out.

This time when he regained consciousness it was dark out. A small fire by the side of the structure provided the only illumination as its flames licked at the sky, the dim light flickering off the drying poles that supported the roof. The woman was sitting in the same place. When she saw his eyes open, she stood and moved to him with a bowl and a gourd. He pushed himself up on his elbow again and drank greedily, the water in the gourd tasting sweeter than any he could remember. Finished, he eyed the bowl distrustfully. Judging from the smell, it appeared to be some sort of a fish stew. He ate small bites of the pungent mixture, but couldn't manage much due to the pain that sliced through his skull each time he opened his mouth.

She seemed to understand and removed the bowl from his grasp before pointing at his backpack, which was lying nearby, his knife resting on top of it, his belt rolled up neatly next to it. He grunted and cursed his inability to communicate. He wanted to ask her where he was, how he'd come to be there, why he'd been spared when the young man had seemed an instant away from eviscerating him, but he didn't know how.

The energy seemed to drain from his limbs from the effort of supporting himself, and his frustration drifted into a dreamless sleep as the fire's glow faded, the cooking over and the tribe already down for the night.

Morning brought with it the familiar Amazon heat. Drake awoke sweating. The woman knelt by his head, applying more salve to his wound, and he was pleased to discover that the swelling around his eye had receded somewhat during the night and that he could now see through it, albeit with the remaining puffiness causing discomfort when he opened it.

She spoke several words, which he interpreted as instruction to stay still, and he allowed her to press the goop in place, wincing as she did so. When she was done, she moved to the edge of the hut and placed the bowl next to another, and again brought him food and water. This time he was able to choke more of the gruel down, driven by hunger and his body's efforts to repair itself. The mixture of an unfamiliar fruit and fish wasn't as unpleasant as the prior night's concoction, and he finished the bowl to the woman's smiling approval.

When he was done, the old man appeared at the far end of the hut and approached him on unsteady legs. Drake guessed he was someone of importance within the tribe by his elaborate bone necklace and his ornately carved walking stick, its top sculpted into a likeness of a jaguar head, mouth open to reveal its teeth, the dark stone polished to a bright sheen. He moved slowly and deliberately to the backpack and picked up Drake's knife, still in its sheath. He slid the blade free and held it up to the light, examining the sharp edge before turning his attention to the scarred leather and studying it for a long time. After a pause, he edged to Drake's position and sat beside him, the knife clutched in his gnarled hand.

He regarded Drake as if memorizing every detail. After a seeming eternity, he nodded and slid the knife back into the sheath, which he placed by Drake's side. Drake tried a smile, but only managed a sharp intake of breath from the pain the expression caused. The man's eyes danced with merriment. He patted Drake's shoulder reassuringly and pointed at the knife, and then at Drake. Drake nodded, ignoring the lance of discomfort the action brought.

The man pointed at Drake again, and at the knife, and then did a pantomime that left Drake baffled, circling his face with one finger and pointing at Drake, then the knife. Seeing the lack of comprehension, the elder went through the same routine again, this time gesturing to Drake's chest, then his own, then touching his wrinkles and pointing to Drake again.

A light bulb went off in Drake's head and his eyes widened in disbelief. "My father? You're saying me, but older?" Drake pointed to the old man's face and then himself.

The elder nodded and offered a puckered smile. To be sure Drake understood, he repeated the pantomime a final time and then gestured to the young woman. She approached and sat near him. He patted her head and pointed at her, then at Drake, then touched his own lined face before waving to the girl again and making a swimming motion. Seeing no recognition, he repeated the gestures and added a fair depiction of someone thrashing around. He ended with an arm grasping at air, the fingers waggling while he had a look of distress on his face, and then he pointed to Drake and touched his face with a leathery finger, and then the woman.

A vague recollection stirred in Drake's memory. Something Jack had said. About his father saving a drowning native girl and the locals leaving them in peace as a result. Was that what the old man was trying to communicate? That this was the child he'd rescued, now grown, in her early twenties? The woman smiled again and patted her chest, then reached out and patted Drake's, and he couldn't help but notice that she was attractive when she smiled, her face illuminated with an inner radiance and tranquility that was beautiful.

The old man patted his necklace and then the woman. She did the same, and Drake got it. She was the man's daughter, and he was the chief. He'd recognized not Drake but his father's knife, and figured the rest out from their strong resemblance.

They spent the remainder of the morning exchanging primitive signs, struggling through a discussion of sorts. After more water and food, Drake was exhausted and slumbered, this time his dreams filled with visions of his father swimming in rapids to save a young child who would grow up to save his son. In the dream the child transformed into the woman, and he awoke with a start when she stepped out of the water, naked and smiling, her smooth skin golden in the warm sunlight.

The woman was by his side, blotting sweat off his forehead, and when she saw he was awake, offered him more water. He was parched and felt hot, even considering the tropical surroundings – feverish. A chill ran through him and he trembled, and the woman put a soft hand on his cheek before wiping away the perspiration that beaded on his face.

Day merged with evening, and the fever worsened. He faded in and out of consciousness throughout the night and the next afternoon, his skin sizzling to the touch, and during one of the brief lucid periods, he wondered whether the gash in his head had gotten infected and somehow spread to his brain.

When the fever broke on the third day, he was so weak his guardian angel had to steady his head as she poured water into his mouth. The old man made an appearance and ground several types of roots and leaves into a slurry before adding more water and making Drake drink the bitter concoction. When he'd consumed it all, he drifted off again and didn't wake until the next morning – but stronger, the fever gone.

This time when he tried to sit up he managed, and his head didn't come off. The ever-present woman and the old man sat in their customary spot near the edge of the hut's floor, watching him without expression. Drake realized that he was naked. He could see a drizzle coming down outside, and debated trying to stand, but decided against it. The woman stood and brought yet another meal, and he tried to concentrate on eating and ignore his nudity, which wasn't helped by the young woman's proximity.

That afternoon the elder reappeared and sat near Drake for another sign discussion. At the end of it, he offered Drake a small depiction of a jaguar head, carved out of a piece of bone and suspended on a leather lanyard. Drake noted that the carving was surprisingly detailed, and the old man slipped the leather cord over Drake's head. He patted Drake's chest and flexed one of his scrawny biceps, and Drake understood – the amulet would make him strong. Next, he gestured at Drake and shrugged his shoulders, then pointed at the surrounding jungle. Drake didn't need an interpreter to understand the question: What the hell are you doing out here?

Drake pointed at his knife, then at himself, and then did his best charades version of searching for something. The old man nodded.

Drake then pantomimed structures, and when the old man didn't understand, Drake scratched out an illustration on the dirt floor – his feeble attempt at a city. The man sat staring at it for some time before nodding and pointing to the depiction and then off into the jungle. Drake felt a thrill of hope. Jack had told him his father had been excited after saving the girl, but also tight-lipped about why, other than to say that he felt that they were close. Was it possible that this ancient shaman held the final clue?

He held his breath as the man extended his hand and called to his daughter, who went into the cloudburst and returned moments later with a short stick. The elder brushed away the depiction of structures and drew a snaking line, and then a passable illustration of a waterfall.

Then another waterfall a few inches away from the first, and a circle between the two with a crude recreation of Drake's buildings. Satisfied with his handiwork, he sat back, pointed at the second waterfall and then at Drake. Drake shook his head, not getting it. The old man drew a stick figure in the waterfall and gestured at Drake.

Understanding flashed across Drake's face and he whispered to himself, "That's the waterfall where I fell? Then…Paititi is between these two waterfalls, down a different river…?"

Drake's breathing accelerated as he pointed to the first waterfall and shrugged his shoulders, signaling, "Where?"

The old man sighed and stood, then pointed at the young woman, then at the waterfalls. His meaning was clear.

His daughter would show him the way.

~ ~ ~

Gus stared at the phone as though he was holding a steaming handful of dung and struggled to maintain his composure.

"I thought I was clear. Failure on this is not an option."

"Yes, sir, you were. But we haven't been able to pick up their trail, and the guide says at this point he's not going to be able to."

"That's not good enough."

"Agreed. But I'm not sure that staying out here is going to accomplish much after almost a week. And we've already run across some drug traffickers we had to neutralize in self-defense, so we're leaving tracks."

Gus sighed. "Keep at it. Try not to kill everyone in the area, though. We really don't want to have to answer difficult questions from the Peruvians."

"We'll do our best. This is just to warn you that the trail has gone cold."

"I don't want to have to report that to the director."

"Understood."

Chapter Thirty-Six

Vadim swallowed another antibiotic pill with boiled water and tested his weight on his leg. One of the rounds exchanged during the raid on their camp had hit the exterior of his left thigh, and while the wound wasn't life-threatening, it was certainly painful enough, although mending. His leg twinged when he walked, but was much improved, and while he wouldn't be playing soccer anytime soon, he was ambulatory.

Sasha looked up from his position under a tall tree as Awa, one of their native guides, stepped into the camp. He shook his head as he approached, toting his Kalashnikov in one hand with a walking stick in the other – good for probing the ground in front of him while moving through the jungle to ensure he didn't step on a surly snake.

"No sign of him," Awa said in barely understandable English.

"What do you make of that?" Sasha asked, looking at Vadim.

When they'd caught up to the trio, Awa's tracking ability having proved invaluable, the three were now two, camped beside a waterfall, with the Ramsey boy nowhere to be seen. At first they'd believed he was out exploring, but after watching the site in shifts, they realized that wasn't the case. The remaining man, whom they didn't recognize, and the girl left the camp every morning to root around in the jungle, presumably looking for Paititi, but Drake had yet to reappear.

And Vadim had no interest in the pair beyond their ability to lead him to Ramsey.

"This I do not understand, Sasha: why would he go off on his own? That makes no sense."

"Perhaps he met with some kind of misfortune?" Sasha suggested.

"Anything is possible in this hellhole, but you had better pray his good fortune still remains. The Ramsey boy is the only connection to the journal, and if it was all in his head, we have a big problem if he fails to materialize. This is a big jungle, and he was our best chance. Without him, we could spend ten lifetimes looking for the city and never find it."

Sasha knew better than to continue the discussion. When Vadim became enraged, he could lash out unpredictably, as they'd discovered twenty years earlier when the older Ramsey had steadfastly refused to share his knowledge. Sasha could still remember it like it was yesterday. Ramsey had been beaten and burned with cigarettes, and through it all, had remained silent, refusing to reward them with even a word. When he had spoken, it had been to utter a Russian curse involving Vadim's mother and her son, and he'd punctuated it by spitting a bloody tooth in Vadim's face.

Sasha had tried to stop Vadim, but by the time he'd reached him, it had been too late. The point-blank shot to Ramsey's head killed him instantly.

Sasha had also seen that brutal streak when they'd been in the gulag together in Siberia. Any prisoner who crossed him would be in mortal danger, and more than one body had been found over the years, stabbed dozens of times, frozen in the snow. Vadim was wildly bright, but as with so many who had served in the KGB on its secret wet teams, unbalanced; his anger could flare to the surface without warning, with deadly consequences.

Vadim took several cautious steps toward the stream they'd camped beside and stared into the underbrush, as though the plants held a solution to the quandary he faced. When he returned, sweat beading down his unshaven face, his mood had darkened further. He glowered at Awa and barked an order.

"We continue watching and waiting. We have no choice. They are our only option."

"Maybe we should take them and interrogate them," Sasha said.

"If we do that, we lose the chance to catch Ramsey. No, for now, we wait."

Sasha waved off an ever-present mosquito and nodded with an enthusiasm he didn't feel. He despised the infernal jungle, with its never-ending parade of poisonous insects, deadly reptiles, diseases, heat, and rain. Always rain, and the mud it created. He would gladly have traded it for the icy climes of Siberia. At least there were no bugs there.

Awa moved to one of his men and had a hushed discussion in their native tongue. The man rose and walked soundlessly to the trail to take up the surveillance of the pair a scant mile away.

Awa watched his subordinate go without expression. The crazy Russians were paying a king's ransom for their services, and if they wanted someone watching the two gringos by the waterfall as they blundered around in the surrounding jungle, then that's what they would get. Round the clock. Pointless or not.

It was all the same to him.

~ ~ ~

Spencer leapt to his feet from his position by his tent, AK-47 in hand, when the bushes near him rustled from something large moving through the undergrowth. Allie fumbled for her weapon as he flipped the firing selector to active mode, and gasped when Drake emerged, supporting himself on a staff, the cuts on his face healing and his black eye now faded to a dull purplish yellow. Spencer slowly lowered his gun, an expression of astonishment widening his eyes before his face resumed its usual unreadable set.

"What's wrong? You'd think you've never seen someone come back from the dead before," Drake said with a smile. Allie rose and rushed to him. She gave him a long hug before standing back and studying him.

"You look like you fell off a cliff or something," she said.

"Yeah. Remind me not to do that again. It's a lousy way to see the sights."

"What happened?"

Drake dropped his backpack onto the ground and sat down stiffly, not completely recuperated from his injuries after a week, and filled them in on his near-death experience and his time among the natives. They both listened to him with rapt fascination as he described his salvation and fever, ending with his trip from the tribal longhouse and into the jungle, escorted by the chief's daughter.

"That's amazing, Drake. An incredible story," Allie said.

"Yeah. I was lucky. If you call falling off a cliff lucky."

Spencer moved to the circle of river rocks where he'd stacked some wood. He spread petroleum jelly on the pile and ignited it with his lighter, refraining from commenting on Drake's ordeal.

"I caught some fish for dinner. Luckily, big ones, so more than enough to go around," he said.

"That's good. I have a feeling we're going to work up an appetite over the next day or two," Drake said, noting Allie's body language, which was becoming more distant by the minute. He wondered vaguely whether, in her grief, she had turned to Spencer in his absence, and realized that he didn't care with the same burning urgency he'd had before his fall. Something had changed inside him, as if the placid calm of the shaman and his daughter had somehow seeped into him.

"Oh yeah? I have to tell you, we've been looking since you went for your swim, and haven't found anything," Allie said, her voice resigned.

Drake nodded. "I'm not surprised."

Something about Drake's inflection or tone caused Spencer's antennae to quiver, and he stopped what he was doing and stared at Drake.

"Yeah? Why's that?" he asked.

Drake walked over to where the gathered branches were crackling, the fish waiting to be skewered and broiled whole over the fire, and kicked at the leaves on the ground before looking up at Spencer and meeting his eyes.

"Because you're looking in the wrong place."

Allie moved over to where the two men were facing each other. "What? What are you talking about, Drake?"

He sighed and touched the scab over his eye. "It's not here. It's about three miles from here. Nearer a smaller waterfall to the southwest."

"How do you know?" Allie exclaimed.

Drake offered a small smile.

"Easy. Someone drew me a map."

Chapter Thirty-Seven

"They did what?" Spencer demanded.

"I just got back from the other waterfall. I was going to suggest we move the camp tomorrow morning, because it would be dark by the time we made it if we tried tonight," Drake explained.

"You were just there?" Allie demanded, surprised, her tone skeptical.

"Yup. Or close enough."

He told them about the shaman and the daughter leading him to the waterfall yesterday, but refusing to go near where they'd indicated Paititi lay. The daughter had stayed with him that night and guided him back to Allie and Spencer the following day after drawing Drake a map in the dirt. He'd tried to convince her to accompany him to the city, but she'd made it clear that she didn't want to go any farther, and the fear in her eyes had been all too real. She'd drawn more pictures, but these were of hideous creatures, demonic. Even though they didn't speak a word of the same language, he understood that she was terrified of whatever inhabited the ancient Incan ruins.

"Then you know how to find it?" Allie asked.

"I think so. It may take some doing, but with the GPS we should be able to get there a lot faster. Once we find the other waterfall, which is where I just came from, we follow the river that leads from that one, and when it forks off into a smaller one, we follow that."

"You can't see the city from that river?" Spencer asked.

"Apparently not."

"But the local tribes know where it is?"

"I'm not sure they have any idea what it is. To them, I got the sense that it's a haunted or forbidden place. The daughter looked like I was trying to get her to eat live scorpions when I wanted her to take me there. She was okay showing me with a drawing, but refused flat out to go anywhere near it. It was apparent they think it's cursed, or evil. Or some kind of sacred ground they keep secret. I don't know. Our communication was sign language, and even then, it left a lot to be desired."

"You say the natives had no modern clothes? No rifles or shoes? Nothing?" Spencer asked.

"No. They looked like they could have been from a thousand years ago. The land that time forgot."

"Then it's quite likely they're one of the Amazonian tribes that's had no contact with modern civilization. If that's the case, it would explain why the secret's still a secret. There's been no one to tell."

Drake grew silent, his mind elsewhere as he stared off into the distance, and then he snapped back to the present. "Any signs of trouble here?"

Allie shook her head. "Nothing. So it looks like we're in the clear."

"That's good. Tomorrow, at first light, let's break camp and head for the waterfall. We'll be able to make it in a few hours. Paititi will take longer, but by afternoon we should be camped there," Drake said.

"It'll take a while to explore if it's big."

Drake nodded. "Probably. Although my father had some theories about where the treasure could be located once he found the city. But who knows whether those were accurate or not…"

"So you really think you can find it?" Allie asked.

"We wouldn't be here if I didn't," Drake said, confidence in his voice. He still hadn't put it all together, but he had a good idea that the fabled riches of the Inca Empire wouldn't be located in an ordinary building. It would be in something that would survive the years. Something that would defy the casual adventurer who stumbled across the city, or any raiding conquistadores. He was sure that if there was a pattern to spot, he'd do so once he had seen the city's layout.

Which all assumed that the mysterious Palenko hadn't gotten to it. But Drake didn't want to get ahead of himself. Based on the legends, there were anywhere from two hundred and fifty to five hundred tons of gold. Not the sort of weight you loaded on a few carts and hauled around the jungle. That meant that the treasure was still mostly, if not all, there.

Drake hoped so. The only wild card was the depictions of the demons his escort had drawn. While they could have been superstitious nonsense, Drake had felt a definite stab of unease when he'd looked into the daughter's eyes, her expression clearly conveying fear for the first time since he'd seen her.

They sat around the fire munching on fish while discussing the following day. Spencer and Allie had innumerable questions about what he'd seen. Drake did his best to answer them without giving too much away.

When he crawled into his tent for the night, he was tired but at peace, the feeling of having crossed an important threshold while with the indigenous tribe stronger than ever. He had no concrete reason for it, but it was as palpable as the heat.

As his eyes fluttered shut, his imagination filled with visions of the old shaman and his daughter. That now seemed like a lifetime away, and the entire encounter had the aura of a dream, a surreal fantasy induced by the remnants of his fever.

~ ~ ~

Awa's radio crackled softly, and after a short discussion, he went to where Vadim and Sasha were sitting, preparing to eat.

"The young man returned. He's at their camp."

"What?" Vadim exclaimed with a start, almost cutting himself with his knife.

"He's there. But it will be dark before we can reach it. What do you want to do?"

Vadim frowned. "This is our chance. I do not want to ruin it by acting rashly. Let me discuss this with my associate."

Awa nodded and moved back to where his men were cooking the fish they'd speared, leaving the two Russians to scheme in their mother tongue.

"We could wait until they are asleep and then take them," Sasha suggested. "They are expecting nothing. It is the perfect time."

"Perhaps. But also it introduces the possibility that the young Ramsey decides to emulate his father and go to his grave without disclosing his secrets."

Sasha gave him a lupine smirk. "I can be very persuasive."

Vadim didn't comment. He had every faith in Sasha's abilities. He'd watched him torture enough prisoners during difficult interrogations to know his skills were formidable. But even so, they hadn't been sufficient to convince the elder Ramsey to capitulate, and he didn't want to take the chance that the son was made of the same stuff as his father.

His stare moved to the fire, and he seemed to drift away before returning his attention to Sasha.

"At this moment they believe that they are in the clear. And so they will continue their search. To allow them to do the hard work is the smartest – wait until they find Paititi, and then move in. At that point they will be of no use to us any longer, and we can end their troublesome existences with a bullet and conclude our unhappy business with them."

"True. All we have to do is remain undetected."

"Which we have easily done for days. We will watch, and they will lead us to city, and then we will dispatch them. It is cleaner this way."

"Agreed. Although I would like a day or two with the girl before we kill her. I hate to see her go to waste," Sasha said with an ugly smile.

"Ah, of course. If you have no objections to sharing, I think this can be arranged," Vadim confirmed.

The two Russians laughed together, and Vadim removed a small metal flask from his pocket and took a long pull from it before passing it to Sasha. "A little celebratory vodka, *da?*"

Sasha took it and held the container aloft in a toast. "*Na Zdorovie.* To a better tomorrow."

Vadim studied his charred slab of fish and swallowed hard.

"After this, I never want to eat fish again. I have had my fill of seafood. Enough to last a lifetime."

"What do you think the odds are that Palenko left a trail we can follow?" Sasha asked, his voice quiet.

"There is no real way of knowing. He was a lunatic. Perhaps he stayed in Paititi and died there. But what I do know is that once we have found the city, we are much closer to finding him and his ore, and getting our lives back."

Sasha nodded. "And the rumored riches?"

"If we locate the Inca gold, as the Americans say, it is icing on the cake. Nobody else need know."

"It would be a wonderful problem to have, wouldn't it?"

"Indeed it would. Now stop hoarding the vodka."

Sasha passed him the flask. Vadim swallowed another large gulp before capping it and slipping it back into his pocket.

Sasha finished his fish and sat back. "Twenty years. A long time."

Vadim shrugged. "Over and done with. What is that annoying American saying? All is well that ends well."

"For us, anyway."

Vadim stared at the guides, who would also be meeting their fate when they found Paititi. They wouldn't need the natives any longer, and planned to execute them at the first opportunity. Then it would be just the two of them, with their support a satellite phone call away.

"To the victor goes spoils, *nyet?* Now let us get some sleep before the infernal rain starts again. Ahead of us, we have a big day," Vadim said, the alcohol and a full stomach making him drowsy.

"We do indeed. For the Americans, perhaps, their last day on earth," Sasha said with a malevolent grin. "Which I will do my best to ensure is also their worst."

Chapter Thirty-Eight

Spencer patted Drake's backpack, the tents rolled up and stowed along with the rest of their gear, and with a final look around the tranquil waterfall area, peered into the surrounding jungle. The early morning sun was just beginning to climb high enough to afford light.

"Lead on, Bwana," he said.

Drake nodded as he slipped his AK-47's strap over his shoulder and drew his machete. "It's about three hard hours away."

"You sure you can find it again?" Allie asked, approaching from the pool at the base of the waterfall, looking radiant in spite of having been in the rainforest for weeks.

"You bet. I'm really getting the hang of this whole jungle-adventurer thing."

"That's good, because it looks like it's going to start raining again soon," Spencer said, eyeing the thunderheads parading across the sky.

"Wouldn't be the rainforest if it didn't rain, would it?" Drake quipped, making for the faint game trail he'd used the day before.

The clouds erupted with a shattering roar an hour later, and the tepid rain poured down on them as they slogged through the dense foliage, this time with Drake in the lead and Spencer bringing up the rear. The journey took longer than Drake had promised due to the difficult conditions, but by eleven they were standing at the base of an even larger waterfall as the last of the rainstorm spent itself around them. Drake pointed at the river, perhaps thirty feet wide, its brown water swirling with a strong current, and turned to Allie.

"Thar she blows. We follow that, and when we hit a smaller river branching off to the left, that's our path to Paititi."

Allie nodded as Spencer removed his backpack and set his rifle against it.

"Let's take fifteen, refill our canteens, and then get on with it. I'd like to be near the city by the time the heat really gets ugly."

"Which it will, as always," Drake agreed.

"How sure are you that it's only a few more miles?"

"That's an approximation. I'm assuming that the map the daughter drew was close to scale, but there are no guarantees. However, based on the distance between the two waterfalls, we're in the ballpark."

The riverbank was slippery from the rain, but they found a game track that ran roughly parallel, so they were able to set a reasonable pace. Two hours later they came to the branch in the river, and Drake's pulse quickened as their destination seemed as close as around the next bend. He mopped sweat from his face as he considered the smaller tributary, and after another break, they set off, the heat now oppressive as any cooling effect brought by the rain evaporated with the drying droplets trembling on the leaves around them.

A little over a mile farther, Drake stopped, extending his arm so Allie wouldn't walk past him. He felt her move closer and signaled for her to remain quiet, and then pointed to a spot a few yards ahead of him. A pile of human bones rested beside a thicket, skulls grinning from between the vines, sightless eye sockets dark in the bushes. Allie gasped and grabbed Drake's shoulder, and stabbed a trembling finger at another skull impaled on a crude pole to the side of the trail.

Spencer took the lead. They set off, now moving considerably more slowly, clutching their weapons, the sense of menace palpable as they moved cautiously forward. A hundred yards farther they came to another skull, this one with a large crack running along the top and the front teeth almost all rotted out. Spencer chambered a round as they walked by, and a bird flapped away in the overhead canopy, the unfamiliar sound of the rifle loading startling it into flight. A troop of monkeys leapt from branch to branch near a break in the trees by the river, their grunts and cries echoing in the forest. Drake checked to ensure his weapon was also loaded and ready for use.

A quarter mile along the bank, Spencer stopped and pointed into the jungle at what appeared to be ruins, much like those they'd found at the outpost – but far more of the mounds, invisible from the river, the rainforest hiding the remains, having long ago reclaimed them. Spencer motioned for them to stay quiet; and then, from the direction of the ruins, they heard voices.

They froze as the sound of soft male voices drifted nearer, though the exact spot they were coming from was impossible to pinpoint. Drake slowed his breathing and crouched low in the brush, hoping that any snakes were taking the afternoon off. Allie gave him a scared glance, and then the voices were moving away, deeper into the jungle. They waited motionless for a few minutes, not daring to tempt fate. Spencer eventually crept back to their position and whispered to them.

"We've got company."

"What do you think? Traffickers?" Allie asked.

Spencer shook his head. "No. Too quiet. My guess is natives. But you can see why Drake's tribe would view the area as off-limits. Those skeletons aren't just for display – they came from somewhere, most likely from other natives who stumbled across the city."

"So what do we do?" Drake asked.

"Try to avoid getting killed while we see what we're up against."

Spencer stopped talking, his head tilted at an angle, listening. A faint thumping sounded in the distance, rhythmic, its beat echoing off the trees. Spencer began moving toward the sound in a low crouch, his rifle in front of him, pushing the bushes aside. Allie and Drake followed him, the wet leaves beneath their feet absorbing any noise from their boots as they edged along another trail, this one more defined. Drake saw footprints in the wet mud – bare feet – which confirmed Spencer's guess that the voices belonged to tribesmen.

They approached a particularly dense thicket, and the drumbeat seemed only a stone's throw away. Spencer slowed and eased a branch aside to peer into an open area beyond. Drake edged alongside him and did the same, Allie right behind them, and froze at the spectacle that greeted his eyes.

Two dozen dark-skinned men with their faces painted like skulls waited with spears, bows and ten-foot-long blowguns, watching a stone podium where a figure straight out of hell stood gazing at the drummer, who was beating on a hollow log. The figure was naked, as were the tribesman, but white as a ghost, his hair matted with pale mud that coated his entire body. Streaks of black darkened his eyes, giving his face a cadaverous look. Drake's skin crawled instinctively at the apparition.

Then the figure moved, and Drake could see it was in actuality an old man, his body thin and frail, the mud lending him an even more skeletal aura. The man barked something unintelligible, and the drummer stopped, waiting.

From the edge of the clearing another tribesman entered, dragging a small figure. Drake saw it was a boy, no more than ten years old. The boy stumbled. His ankles were bound with a leather cord, as were his wrists, and another leather tether had been wrapped across his face, blinding him and muffling any cries. His captor pulled him by the arm, and Drake could make out a wound on his abdomen, blood crusted around it. When they reached the stone podium, Drake realized with a jolt that it was an altar.

Allie inched next to him and watched in horror as the boy struggled to stand, obviously in agony, trembling and tiny as the collection of natives observed in silent witness. The white-clay-covered man leaned his head back and emitted a blood-chilling moan at the sky, only vaguely human in timbre, and then spread his arms wide, as if welcoming the boy.

What happened next caused Allie to grip Drake's arm and press her head against his shoulder, tears streaming down her face.

The captor struck the boy in the back of the head with a heavy wooden club, and he collapsed in a heap at the man's feet. The man knelt down, lifted the boy ceremoniously, and placed him on the stone altar.

The mud-smeared elder brandished a shining metal blade over his head – what looked like a machete ground down to a sharper point for more sinister duty than clearing brush. The captor took it from the elder and bowed, and then turned to the boy's prone form and held the blade above it with both hands.

Drake flinched and turned away as the captor brought the knife down in a violent arc, and didn't need to hear the murmur from the gathered men to know that the boy's life had been brutally ended. When Drake returned his attention to the altar, blood streamed down its sides, and the men were stomping their bare feet against the ground and pounding it with their spears. The mud-caked old man did a little jig as he moved to the boy's corpse. With a howl like a demented wolf, he plunged his hand into the new wound gashed wide by the knife, and with the boy's blood smeared a design on his muddy white forehead.

The eerie ritual went on as the mud-smeared shaman anointed each of the gathered natives with a smudge of the crimson. When he was done, two of the tribesmen approached the altar and dragged the corpse unceremoniously into the underbrush, likely destined for one of the bone piles on the perimeter.

Spencer held his finger to his lips and pointed the way they'd come, and Drake nodded. He put his arm around Allie, whose eyes were clenched tight, and leaned into her.

"We need to get out of here," he whispered.

He led her carefully back along the track, Spencer guarding the rear. As they arrived at the riverbank they paused, waiting for Spencer to catch up. When he joined them, he shook his head, his expression dour.

"I guess we know why your shaman's daughter didn't want to set foot near here," he said.

"Pretty obvious. Is human sacrifice common with the natives in these parts?" Drake demanded.

"No. This is some kind of an abomination. Craziness." Spencer paused. "Did you notice that the head of the party was considerably taller than the others? I made him for Caucasian. Hard to tell with all the mud, but he looked like a white man to me."

Allie's eyes met Drake's. "The Inca used to perform human sacrifices. The ceremony was called *capacocha*. But it was nothing like what we just witnessed."

"Really? I thought that was only the Aztecs," Drake said.

"The Aztecs were certainly the most flamboyant, cutting hearts out. But the Incas also had their savagery. Children, often of royalty, spent a year at feasts leading up to their sacrifice, stoned out of their minds on massive amounts of cocaine. At the end of the year, they would go to the highest points in the Andes and be buried alive, left to die." She swallowed hard. "This is nothing like what we know of those ceremonies. I agree with Spencer. This is some new ceremony that's only slightly drawing from the *capacocha* tradition."

"Could the shaman...be Palenko?" Drake asked, eyes on the jungle they'd just fled through.

"Who's Palenko?" Spencer asked, and Drake remembered he'd never shared that part of the story with him.

Drake sat down, Allie next to him, and gave an abridged version of the Russian's history, including the speculations about Palenko's technology. Spencer's eyes narrowed dangerously as he finished.

"So this is another little surprise you left out of the mix? A lunatic Russian with a doomsday weapon?" Spencer growled.

"It's not a weapon. We actually aren't sure what it is, other than some kind of ore."

"Our deal was full disclosure. Now I'm facing some Russian who's as nutty as a Christmas fruitcake, who's set himself up a death camp with an entourage of cutthroat natives. Did I miss anything?" Spencer seethed.

"It doesn't change much, does it? We found Paititi. Now we just need to locate the treasure."

"Right. While we've got a lunatic mass murderer defending the place."

Drake couldn't argue with the assessment, so he didn't try. "I didn't say it would be easy."

"You weren't honest about what I got myself into."

A crack sounded from the trees, and Spencer swung around, his weapon leveled in the direction of the commotion. A simian shape flitted among the branches, and they relaxed. When Spencer returned his focus to Drake, any trace of anger was gone.

"Whether or not their leader is this Palenko character doesn't matter. The natives are the only thing standing between us and the city, and I didn't come this far to turn tail and run. Frankly, I'll feel pretty good about taking out a bunch of child killers, so I say we watch, figure out their weakness, and then exploit it."

"That sounds fine, but how?" Allie asked.

"We'll start with surveillance. I want to understand whether that was the whole group, or if we'll be facing down more. The good news is that I didn't see any guns. Although we shouldn't underestimate the effectiveness of the blowguns. But in a straightforward assault, spears against AKs aren't going to fare well," Spencer said.

"It doesn't look like they're worried about being attacked," Drake said.

"No, any natives in the area are probably scared out of their minds. Like your shaman was. I bet everyone gives it a wide berth. Especially if the Paititi residents are poaching for sacrifices from other tribes, which would be my guess. I have to admit, it's an effective way to ensure nobody comes calling on your discovery."

"It's cold-blooded murder," Allie said.

Another rustling came from the trail leading to the city, and Spencer turned to face the dense underbrush before whispering to Drake and Allie, "Let's get moving. I don't like being this close to an enemy camp with no plan."

Drake was rising when something whizzed by his head. He wasn't sure what it was, but Spencer didn't hesitate. He grabbed Allie's hand. "Run. They're firing darts at us."

Spencer and Allie sprinted along the water's edge. Drake was scrambling to his feet when a dart hit his backpack with a thump and another brushed his cheek. He didn't wait to find out whether the next volley would be better aimed, and bolted after Spencer and Allie, who were now thirty yards down the river.

Drake's foot hit a slippery stone and he lost his footing. Tumbling sideways, he slammed against the ground. A bolt of agony shot through his ribcage as he felt something crack – he'd fallen against his elbow, breaking a rib. Drake gasped for breath and tried to get up, but the pain was momentarily blinding, each inhalation sending spikes of agony through him. He was fighting to stand when something struck his head, and everything spun and went dark.

Allie's and Spencer's footsteps thumped along the bank as they ran, putting as much distance between themselves and their attackers as possible. Not sensing Drake behind them, Allie slowed and looked over her shoulder. Spencer tried to pull her along, and she jerked back, hard.

"Stop. We've lost Drake," she said.

Spencer slowed, rifle gripped in his right hand, and looked back over his shoulder before coming to a halt. They'd rounded a bend in the serpentine river, so they couldn't see more than a dozen yards behind them.

"Damn."

"We have to go back," she insisted.

Spencer hesitated, but Allie made the decision for him when she began retracing her steps. Spencer caught up with her and grabbed her arm.

"You can't just go charging in, or you'll wind up dead. Do you understand? If Drake ran into trouble, getting yourself killed isn't going to help him."

"Fine. But we have to get him."

Spencer grunted and nodded. "Stay behind me. Keep your finger off the trigger unless you need to shoot. Which you shouldn't unless someone's trying to kill you."

"Got it."

They crept along the riverbank, Allie six paces behind him, their senses tingling, ready for an attack that never came. When they reached the spot Drake had been sitting, there was no sign of him. Spencer scanned the jungle, the barrel of his weapon searching the undergrowth for any hint of a threat, as Allie knelt by the river.

"Spencer, this is bad," she whispered, holding up two fingers red with blood. "They've got him."

He squinted at the leaves and saw the red droplets on the dirt, already coagulating in the heat, and returned to his scrutiny of the surrounding jungle. Allie stood and he shook his head, annoyance coming through his whisper.

"Allie, just hold your horses. We need a plan. Otherwise, even with superior firepower, we could fail, and it'll cost us our lives."

"Then start planning. Because based on what we know, we were out of time the second they got their hands on him."

Chapter Thirty-Nine

Drake came to slowly, his skull throbbing, his shirt wet with blood from his head wound. The tribesman who'd whacked him with a club stood over him as he gradually regained consciousness – and was the first thing Drake registered when his eyes opened, the lids heavy, reluctant to cooperate. Drake peered around the native and saw that he'd been carried to the clearing, near the altar, and laid on the ground there. The clay-covered man was rooting through Drake's backpack as the natives stood guard over him. The man held up Drake's pistol and studied it with interest before dropping it on the ground next to Drake's rifle and continuing to remove gear from the pack.

Drake's bindings cut into his wrists, but he knew better than to struggle – an exercise in futility, given that he was outnumbered over twenty to one. Pain seared down his neck as he tried to turn his head, and he cursed silently. This was the second time in a week he'd been tied up by natives, suffering from a head wound. And something told him that this time his experience wouldn't end with him being led to safety by a shaman's comely daughter.

His blurry gaze drifted to the altar, still stained rust-colored from the blood of the sacrificed boy, and locked with the clay-smeared man's, who'd spread out Drake's meager possessions in front of him. The man approached and Drake could see that his eyes were bloodshot, with a crazed, manic look. Some kind of drug, perhaps from a hallucinogenic plant, Drake thought...and something more.

Something deeper than a chemical reality, more akin to barely controlled blind fury.

The man spoke in halting Spanish, watching Drake for a reaction, and when he didn't get one, he moved closer. Drake could smell him now – a dank, primitive stink, like an animal used to sleeping in filth. The man barked the same words, this time more clearly, but they meant nothing to Drake.

He felt a tug at his belt. The man had his knife and was staring at it as if possessed, his grin displaying diseased gums with only a few teeth left. Drake watched as he keened an atonal hum and then did a little dance to music only he could hear, brandishing the knife like a trophy. For some reason, the display frightened Drake more than anything so far, and his breath froze in his chest as he watched the bizarre performance.

The man seemed oblivious to Drake now, completely entranced by the play of light on the oversized blade. Just as suddenly as his focus had shifted to the knife, he whirled with a cry and moved back to where Drake lay. He screamed, his voice a shriek, holding the knife above Drake's throat, repeating the gibberish.

Drake clenched his eyes shut and cried out, "I don't speak Spanish!"

The man stopped, the wicked blade only inches from Drake's neck. His smell was overpowering, and for a moment Drake thought he would pass out again. Then he sensed the man moving away, and he opened his eyes. The mud-smeared figure was grinning demonically, the boy's blood still caked on his face as he regarded Drake, the knife hanging loosely at his side, his arms only bone, thin to the point of being emaciated.

"You...speak...English." The words sounded unfamiliar on the man's tongue, heavily accented and coarse, as if he was just learning them, the notes different than those he was familiar with – than his native Russian.

"Yes."

The man's eyes narrowed. "Ah. American."

"Yes."

The man nodded as though he'd discovered a great secret, and the tribesmen around him watched with interest as their leader communicated with the captive.

"Why...are you...here?"

"I'm looking for Paititi," Drake said, seeing no point in lying.

"Paititi? Paititi! Paititi!" the man cried, and then sang the word over and over in his eerie falsetto. He began his shambling jig again, and Drake saw that his toenails were long, yellow, and cracked, like a wild animal's. The odd song faded as he seemed to lose steam, ending with a wet cough before he stared at Drake again. "This...is lucky day, then...for you. You...found...Paititi."

"Who are you?" Drake asked, playing for time, praying that Spencer and Allie had registered his absence and returned for him.

"Me? I...I am...called...many names. They mean...nothing...to you. For I...I am ruler...of Paititi. The lost city, *da?* I am king. A god...here...in earth's womb."

"Grigor Palenko?" Drake tried.

Something shifted behind the man's eyes, and a look of sly cunning returned to them as he licked his lips. "*Da.* That...was...one of my...names. But he...he is dead. Reborn as...as a god. Risen like phoenix, yes?"

Drake didn't know how to respond. Palenko had obviously crossed an important line beyond which reason had been abandoned, and now inhabited a dark world of shadows where he was a deity, with the power of life and death in his grasp, worshipped by the men around him. Drake waited for him to continue, wary of saying anything that would set him off.

Palenko shambled to the backpack, knife still clenched in his hand, and picked up Drake's flashlight. When he clicked the light on, the tribesmen gasped in astonishment as he played the beam into the darkness of the brush.

"See? I am bringer of light. I rule this city...of the dead. Of riches...beyond...imagination..." Palenko seemed to deflate, his train of thought lost. He stopped, defeated; a tired, old, sick man. Turning to his followers, he flicked the light off and raised it over his head, like a high priest preparing to sprinkle holy water upon a crowd.

Drake tried to recapture the Russian's attention. "Then you found the treasure?"

Palenko's cackle was maniacal, a half shriek, deranged beyond imagination. "Treasure? Oh, foolish boy. *Da*, I found. But…real treasure…is in my head…in city of the dead…encased in lead…while rivers run red…" His voice rambled off until Drake couldn't make out his words any more. Palenko shifted from bare foot to bare foot, his leg muscles also wasted to nothing, and Drake began working his wrists around, trying to free himself.

Palenko seemed departed for another plane, but returned to the present as he tossed the flashlight on the ground near the rest of Drake's things. He cocked his head from side to side like a bird of prey, the light glinting off the knife blade as he moved it slightly, enraptured by the reflection. Then, without warning, he hurled it at Drake. The blade plunged into the ground barely six inches from Drake's head. Palenko's laugh rang through the trees, and then he called out to the assembly in a native dialect.

The same tribesman who had dragged the boy to the altar approached Drake and grabbed him under his arms. He said something to one of the others, and a second native hefted Drake's feet. They carried him squirming to the altar and set him on top, facing the sky, as Palenko hummed tunelessly to himself, mumbling nonsense as he shuffled his feet in the wet leaves.

The pounding of the nearby drum sounded like cannon fire to Drake as the nightmare performance he'd just watched played out again, only with him as the intended victim this time.

Drake fought to free himself, but it was no good – the one tribesman pinned his shoulders to the altar while the second man gripped his feet, and the bindings on his wrists combined with his head wound and broken ribs had effectively immobilized his upper body. Drake turned his head to where Palenko was standing with the knife and called out to him.

"If you're going to kill me, tell me where the treasure is. So I know my journey wasn't in vain."

"Where? Why…beneath our feet. In cool water…where it remains. Holiest of holies, riches of lost time. And my own…contribution. The world…is unfit…for any of it. If there is…a world…outside of this place. I am…not so sure. Maybe it was…all…dreams. As are you…as am I. All…invention. Of…pretention." He looked up at the sky. "They're destroying the rainforest…you know? Eighty percent…the world's oxygen…comes from…plants. And they're cutting…they're cutting down…the trees. Idiots. Unfit to survive…killing my planet."

"What about your technology?" Drake asked over the drumming, trying to engage the madman and pull him back to reality long enough to survive a few more minutes.

"Mine? Ha. They would use it…to destroy. I demonstrated…potential to create…and all they wanted…was to make death. They are unfit. Unfit to…rule…"

The drumming stopped and Palenko returned his focus to Drake, the Russian's bloodshot eyes crimson gashes in his skeletal face. Palenko nodded at the tribesman standing by the head of the altar, and held the knife aloft, as he had with the machete. The native moved forward, took it from him, and turned to Drake. He stepped to the altar and, after saying a few soft words, perhaps a prayer or a curse, held the knife overhead and tore Drake's shirt open.

The man gasped and murmured something as he reached out with a trembling hand to touch the jaguar amulet on Drake's neck – the carving the shaman had given him, still on the leather lanyard. He turned to Palenko, fear in his eyes, and shook his head.

Palenko barked at him, but the man remained frozen. Palenko took the knife away from him, seeing that he wasn't going to carry out the execution. He backhanded the native across the face and spit on him, and the man cringed like a child. Palenko held up his hand and pressed the knife blade against it, and sliced his palm with a swift cut. Blood welled and pooled from the gash. He rubbed it first on his own face, then on the cowering native, and then finally on Drake's forehead. Drake tried to pull away, but couldn't, and pain again shot through his skull as his head wound ground against the stone.

Chastised, the native moved back to the altar and accepted the knife, and this time his eyes held a trancelike quality, as though he were sleepwalking. He held the blade over Drake's chest with both arms extended over his head, and Drake winced as he saw the man's muscles tense.

Drake heard a thwack followed by a gurgle, and a warm gush of blood splattered his cheek and neck. The knife-wielding native's face was distorted by puzzled pain, his mouth opening and closing like a carp's, the brightly colored feathered tufts of a crossbow bolt sticking out of the center of his naked chest. He coughed and more blood sprayed from his mouth, and then he slumped to his knees. The knife fell with a clatter on the altar next to Drake.

The tribesmen stood frozen, bewildered, and before they could react, another crossbow bolt streaked from the jungle and impaled the native holding Drake's shoulders with a *thwack*, dead in the center of his forehead. He tumbled to the ground, and the other natives sprang into action, their blowguns and bows brought to bear on the invisible threat.

Palenko ducked behind the altar as an automatic rifle opened fire from the perimeter, its lethal chatter hurling burst after burst of rounds into the natives, the slugs shredding through them as they fired futilely at the jungle with their bows.

Twenty seconds after it started, it was over, Palenko's followers dead or dying on the ground. Palenko had slunk away into the undergrowth when the shooting started, and there was nobody left alive in the clearing when Spencer and Allie stepped from the brush with their weapons. Allie ran to the altar and stopped when she saw Drake, his shirt crusted with drying blood. Drake took in the vision of Allie, gripping her AK like a seasoned fighter, eyes wide with adrenaline, and managed a weak smile.

"For a minute there I was getting worried."

"How badly are you hurt?" she asked.

"They knocked me out, but I'll live. Cut me loose, would you? I can't feel my hands anymore."

She scooped up the big knife and leaned the rifle against the altar as Spencer moved among the dead natives, ensuring there was no further threat. She pushed Drake onto his side and sliced the bindings, freeing his wrists. He flexed his fingers as circulation returned, and she handed him the knife. Drake sat up, leaned forward and cut the cord around his ankles, and then sheathed the blade as he slid off the rough stone surface. Everything tilted and faded for a moment, and he grabbed the altar for support as he got his bearings.

Allie eyed his shirt and whispered to him, "You've lost a lot of blood. Are you sure you're okay?"

"Just give me a second. Don't worry, most of this blood isn't mine."

Spencer approached the altar, and giving the two tribesmen killed by the crossbow bolts a once-over, he inspected Drake's head.

"Looks like you got yourself a nice gash there."

"Yeah. Seems like my head's a popular spot for those lately."

"At least it's clotted. How weak are you?"

"So-so. Like I told Allie, I'll live." He looked around. "Where's Palenko?"

"The mud-covered nut's definitely Palenko?" Spencer asked.

"None other. Seems like he went round the bend a long time ago. He was babbling all kinds of nonsense about being an Inca god."

"I thought I saw him duck through there," Allie said, pointing to a dense thicket of bushes behind the altar.

"Do you see my pistol anywhere?" Drake asked, alarmed.

"Your pistol? Where was it?"

"In my bag. He dumped it out," Drake said, pointing at his things.

Allie kneeled down and double-checked the backpack before stuffing his gear back inside and standing with it. "Nope. Now what?"

Drake shouldered the backpack on with a wince, and Allie handed him his rifle. He caught Spencer's eye. "We follow Palenko. He's out there with my pistol, and he probably still remembers how to use one."

Spencer frowned and nodded. "Agreed. Let's finish this."

He ducked below the vines hanging across the faint trail and eyed the ground. Satisfied with whatever he'd seen, he moved deeper into the jungle, Drake behind him, Allie in the rear. They passed a ruin on the right, and Spencer slowed as he studied the muddy track in front of him.

Birds flapped overhead, and Drake followed their flight with his gun barrel. Spencer's gaze never left the trail as he edged forward, his rifle gripped in both hands.

They entered another clearing, this one encircled by large overgrown structures that had collapsed at some point in the distant past, and Spencer stopped. Palenko stood thirty yards away, Drake's pistol in his hand, the weapon pointed at them.

"Spread out," Spencer whispered. Drake moved from behind Spencer to his right, and Allie to his left. When they had ten yards between them, Drake called out to the Russian.

"It's over. Drop the gun. We're not going to hurt you."

Palenko howled his laugh to the trees. "Hurt me? You can't hurt me. I'm god!"

Spencer shot Drake a warning look. "Yeah? Then you don't need the gun, do you?" he said.

"Do you…not understand? I rule here. This is…my kingdom. You…you are insects. Unworthy."

"Sure thing, buddy. Put down the gun. You can tell me all about how you're a god," Spencer replied.

"You…know…nothing. Nothing. I will return, stronger than ever," Palenko screamed, and before any of them could react, swung the pistol at Allie and fired twice.

Spencer's rifle barked and Palenko tumbled to the ground as the shots reverberated through the clearing. More birds took flight, terrified by the unfamiliar sound. Spencer moved cautiously toward the Russian. When he reached him, Palenko was gasping for breath, two entry wounds in his chest the only eulogy he was going to get, the pistol lying harmlessly by his side.

"You...are...nothing..." Palenko hissed, blood running from the grinning corners of his mouth.

Drake screamed from behind him. "Allie."

Spencer turned to see Allie crumpling as Drake ran toward her. He heard a groan from Palenko and twisted as the Russian raised the pistol to shoot him. Spencer didn't hesitate, firing two short bursts from the hip, shredding Palenko's sternum and extinguishing his life.

He watched the Russian shudder and lie still. Spencer ejected the spent magazine and slapped another into place as he moved to where Drake was cradling Allie's head. When he arrived, her blue eyes connected with his, their beauty shining through the pain, and a tear rolled down her face. Spencer knelt and gently pulled her hand away from her shoulder. After inspecting the wounds, he caught Drake's eye and gave him a dark look.

Spencer shrugged off his backpack and dug into a pocket for the first aid kit and, after opening it, removed one of the syringes. He clenched the cap in his teeth and pulled the needle free and, after another look at Allie's contorted face, slid it into one of the veins in her forearm. Her eyes began to glass over even before he'd finished emptying it, and when he was done, he stood and threw the needle away, defeated.

Drake wiped dirt and sweat from Allie's forehead as her eyelids drooped. She reached up and clutched at his arm with a weak grip.

"Oh...Drake..."

"Shhh."

She coughed and grimaced, then relaxed; the spasm of pain passed as the morphine took effect.

"Save your strength. We'll call a helicopter. We'll get help. You'll make it."

"You're so sweet. It almost makes me wish we'd..." She trailed off, her voice dreamy.

"You're going to be all right, Allie." Drake looked up at where Spencer was standing, gazing off into the jungle. "Spencer, call someone. The sat phone's in her backpack. Come get it."

Spencer turned, a vicious expression clouding his face, and began trotting toward them, raising the ugly snout of the AK-47 as he neared.

"No. What are you doing–" Drake screamed, and then the clearing was shattered by the eruption of gunfire as Spencer pulled the trigger.

The jungle behind Drake exploded as rounds shredded the vegetation. Spencer threw himself sideways onto the ground as he continued firing. Drake reacted instantly, rolling away from Allie and grabbing his rifle before shooting at the gunmen firing at them from the jungle. The closest of the three natives near the tree line dropped his rifle with a groan as Drake's rounds punched into his torso, and the man next to him fell backwards as the top of his head tore off from one of Spencer's volleys.

Spencer continued to squeeze off measured bursts at the attackers as he crawled to a nearby ruin for cover. The ground in front of him churned as bullets sprayed into the damp earth, and he fired blind at a third assailant just as he made it behind an outcropping of rock – the remnants of an ancient wall.

Drake saw a muzzle flash from deeper in the brush. He loosed three bursts at it and was rewarded with a scream of pain. He was shaking as he pulled himself behind a slight rise, scanning the jungle for more gunmen. Spencer's rifle burped from Drake's left at targets in the dense foliage. A divot of wet dirt ripped out of the ground near Drake's head. He squeezed off a shot at the shooter, praying as he did so that none of the rounds would hit Allie, who was lying exposed, out in the open.

Out of the corner of his eye he saw Spencer sprint for the far tree line. Drake did what he could to lay down covering fire, emptying the gun. He grabbed at his backpack for another magazine, and swallowed hard when his hands felt the pocket the spares had been in

– empty, dumped out by Palenko when he'd been rummaging through it.

Drake ejected the magazine in frustration and looked around for anything else he could use as a weapon. His trusty knife might have been large enough to row a boat with, but it wouldn't be much good against automatic rifles. He peered over the rise and saw Allie's AK lying where she'd dropped it when she'd been hit by Palenko's rounds. It was only ten feet away, and he could make it if he was fast – but it would be the longest ten feet of his life.

His head pounded, each throb of his pulse delivering a starburst of pain. He tried to ignore it as he listened to the sporadic distant gunfire from where Spencer had disappeared. After a deep breath, he launched himself to his feet and bolted for the rifle.

His lower leg shrieked in white-hot torment as a round caught his calf, and he landed hard, wincing as his ribs radiated agony – too far to reach the gun. Another round sprayed dirt and leaves on his face, and then a voice called out from the trees.

"It is over, Mr. Ramsey. One more move and I will shoot you." The Russian accent was as thick as maple syrup.

Drake froze, the few feet between his hand and the rifle a cruel joke. The two Russians emerged from the brush, Sasha limping badly from where one of Drake's slugs had hit him in the thigh. Vadim held his machine pistol almost casually as they neared to within fifteen feet of Drake, who was still trying to gauge whether he could make it to the rifle before they cut him in two.

"Do not even think about it. I will blow your head off and enjoy it," Vadim snarled. "Move away from the gun. Now."

Drake glared daggers at him but did as instructed, retracting his arm and pulling himself a few more feet from Allie's rifle. Vadim chuckled, his barrel never leaving Drake, and moved to the weapon before toeing it out of reach. He gave Allie's comatose, pale form a once-over and issued a terse command to Sasha before he returned to Drake. Sasha focused on the jungle where Spencer had disappeared, in case he'd survived and tried a surprise attack.

Vadim sneered at Drake. "So. Thank you for leading us straight to Paititi. Something your father was not willing to do."

"You killed him, didn't you?" Drake growled.

"Your father? Of course. In the end he cried like a baby. As he begged for his life, he whimpered like a little girl."

Drake closed his eyes, his leg on fire. "You're lying. I can tell. You killed him because he wouldn't give you what you wanted."

Vadim laughed, a dry, ugly sound. Sasha took the opportunity to unfasten his belt and fashion a tourniquet around his wounded leg, which was streaming blood, his attention still on the tree line.

"I owe you thanks for exterminating our little group. You saved us the inconvenience. Now, tell me – where is the treasure?"

"I don't know. We just got here."

Vadim eyed him suspiciously. "Never mind. We will find it. We have all the time in the world. But not you, perhaps, or the whore." Vadim grinned, his features contorting into those of a gargoyle.

Drake spit at Vadim and gritted his teeth. "You're a miserable bastard, aren't you? This is a big area. I hope you never find it. And with most of your men dead, you'll be easy pickings for the other tribes."

"This is such big talk for a boy with only seconds left to live. You are about to meet your idiot father in hell. Say hello from me when you get there." Vadim raised his gun and pointed it at Drake's head.

Drake didn't blink, didn't flinch.

A shot rang out. Vadim's shirt blossomed with a crimson stain from an exit wound. He stood, frozen, staring at Drake unbelievingly, his eyes uncomprehending.

Drake wrenched his knife free and hurled it at Sasha, who was whipping his gun around to fire. The handle struck him in the face, buying Drake the time to dive for Allie's rifle and fire six rounds. Sasha jerked like a marionette from the bullets pummeling him before he collapsed in a heap.

Vadim seemed to move in slow motion as he brought his weapon to bear. Drake squeezed off a burst that knocked Vadim off his feet and slammed him backward. The Russian groaned as he hit the ground, his gun tumbling harmlessly beside him, and then he shuddered and lay still.

Allie still clutched her SIG Sauer in a bloody hand, the barrel shaking as it pointed at Vadim's inert form. Drake dragged himself over to Allie and took the pistol from her.

"You did it. You saved my ass again. That's twice in an hour," he said softly.

Her eyes searched his face. "Drake...I..."

"We'll get a helicopter to haul you out of here," Drake said.

"Have...Spencer...look at the...wound. He'll know what...to...do." Allie's eyes drifted shut, the morphine hitting full force, carrying her with it to a warm, welcome numbness.

Drake pulled closer and took Allie's hand, the jungle around them now quiet. He looked at his calf. The bullet had seared through the muscle and exited cleanly. But he knew that infection would be only a matter of time. For them both.

They had to get out of there.

Allie shifted next to him, her breathing slow and steady, her top soaked with her blood. Drake considered trying to do something, but realized he might cause more harm than good. He felt so helpless and impotent as he moved closer to her and pulled a shirt out of his backpack, which he held against the wound, trying to keep pressure on it. He stayed like that for several long minutes, mind working over their alternatives, and then jolted back to reality when he heard a rustle from the brush – a heavy body moving through the undergrowth.

"I see you didn't need much help here. How's she doing?" Spencer's voice called from the jungle behind him.

"You kill everyone?" Drake asked, his tone flat.

"Pretty much. I see you did the same."

"Allie got one of them. Saved my life."

Spencer walked over to the Russians and turned them over, confirming that they were dead. He picked up Drake's knife and handed it to him, his eyes on Drake's wounded leg. "Looks like you got nicked there."

"Yeah. Hurts like a bitch."

"They'll do that. How is she?" Spencer repeated.

"Out cold. And bleeding a lot. You need to look at the wound and see if there's anything we can do."

Spencer moved to Allie and Drake rolled away, wincing at the pain in his leg. Spencer removed Drake's bloody shirt and studied the entry, and then lifted her gently and looked at her back.

"That's a little bit of luck. The slug looks like it ricocheted off her shoulder blade and exited there, on the side."

"But all the blood…"

"I can deal with that. I need to clean the wound and stitch it up after making sure no arteries were hit. I've dealt with worse."

Drake's voice sounded strangled. "We need to get a helicopter here."

"Sure. And set down where?" Spencer looked up at the canopy over the clearing, the sky only visible in patches overhead.

"They can lower a stretcher or something."

"Maybe so," Spencer said, not wanting to argue. "But we're hundreds of miles from the nearest chopper, assuming we can get one to fly into this area. I still have to work on her, or she'll be dead by the time it could get here. She'll have bled out." He sat down heavily next to Drake. "What a frigging mess."

"You said it."

"Palenko, dead. Jack, dead. Enough natives to fill a small town. Dead."

Drake shrugged. "Those 'noble savages' were child murderers and hired killers."

"I'm not mourning them. I'm just saying it's a mess."

"That it is." Drake hesitated, dizzy. "When you're done with Allie, think you could do something about the scratch I got?"

Spencer sighed. "Gonna be a busy evening, I see."

"Work on Allie first."

Spencer nodded, glanced at her, and then back at Drake. "It's gonna hurt, you know."

"Yeah. I guessed." He paused. "Maybe you can stitch up my head while you're at it, too?" Drake was about to say something else, something important, when the sky spun and he blacked out. He never felt Spencer catch his shoulders as he fell back, keeping his battered skull from hitting the ground.

Chapter Forty

Spencer stood watch as Drake slept fitfully through the night, the half syringe of morphine having dulled the worst of the pain. The rain had started a few hours after dark and continued until morning. When Drake awoke and crawled stiffly out of the tent, Spencer was sitting with his plastic parka on, his back against a tree, water running off his hat as his eyes roved over the jungle.

"You wanna get some sleep while I keep watch for a few hours?" Drake asked. He took a long pull on his canteen, his throat parched, and looked over at Allie's tent, which was set up next to his.

"I can sleep when I'm dead. How's the leg?"

"I'll manage. Thanks for doing that. And Allie?"

"All part of the platinum-level service I provide. You might want to take a day or two to let it heal." Spencer stared without speaking for a moment at Allie's tent. "She'll make it. She got very lucky on the path the bullet took – it was messy, but ultimately didn't do a ton of damage."

"And a helicopter?"

"We need to talk about that. Right now, she's sleeping, and there's no point in waking her up. But once she comes to, I want to see how she's doing. That will determine our next step."

"In what way?"

"The second we contact the authorities for a helicopter, Paititi's blown. Assuming they're even willing to come this far into the jungle, which isn't a given. And there are going to be a lot of questions about gunshot wounds – questions we might not want to answer."

"So…what? The answer is to risk her life so we can try to find the treasure?"

"Her life's not at risk anymore is my point. But that brings up the big question: you got any ideas where it could be?" Spencer asked.

"Some."

Spencer tossed Drake an energy bar. The rain eased as they sat together munching on yet another dry breakfast, silent. Drake's head was splitting and his leg felt like someone had taken a hot poker to it, but he was alive. They heard a stirring from Allie's tent, and both rose and approached it.

Allie looked pale and weak, but her eyes were open, though foggy from the morphine. Spencer had fashioned a bandage from one of his clean shirts and the gauze from the first aid kit, and as she tried to sit up, she reached for it, wincing.

"God, this hurts," she said as Drake climbed into the tent and handed her a full canteen. She drank from it greedily and then lay back. "What happened?"

"We got all the bad guys. And Spencer did a little emergency surgery on both of us," Drake said. "How do you feel?"

"Like a truck ran over me."

Spencer ducked his head into the tent. "Any fever? Shakes?"

"No, just really weak."

"That's because of the blood loss. You'll feel stronger as the day goes on. But you need to eat something, and drink plenty." Spencer tossed Drake two breakfast bars, and Allie reluctantly ate them as he summarized their situation and options.

"So there's no danger from the wound?" Allie asked, finishing the second bar.

Spencer shook his head. "Nothing immediate. You're on a high-dose antibiotic that'll control infection, which is the biggest danger."

"Then I vote we find the treasure before calling for help," she said, her voice stronger.

"That's not such a hot idea," Drake said.

"We didn't come all this way just to hand the location to the Peruvians. We need to locate the treasure, or this will have all been in vain," she countered.

Drake shook his head. "Allie, some things might be worth risking your life for. But this isn't one of them. We found the city. That's already a huge win."

"You heard Spencer. I'll make it. You just need to get busy and locate the treasure." She closed her eyes again and smiled. "Slackers."

After a few more minutes of back and forth, Allie terminated the debate, threatening to crawl off into the jungle if they called for help before they'd located the Inca gold. Spencer went into the brush and emerged with a branch for Drake to use as a staff. After a short discussion about the dangers involved in leaving the tents pitched with Allie waiting by herself, they agreed that she'd keep one of the pistols, for the unlikely event a native appeared to challenge her.

"Anything shows up, shoot it," Spencer said, handing her the gun.

"I kind of got that. Thanks."

"You sure you're going to be okay?" Drake asked, eyeing her skeptically.

"Go on. Get out of here. Make us all rich. I'll be fine," she said, her blue eyes flashing at him.

Drake backed out of the tent and looked around the clearing and, after hoisting his backpack, set off with Spencer to hunt for the treasure.

"What are we looking for?" Spencer asked.

"I'll know it when I see it."

Spencer gave him a sidelong glance. "You're kind of grumpy after getting shot and brained, you know that?"

"It'll do that to you."

Drake limped, supporting himself on the branch, and he realized as they walked through the ruins of the sprawling city that Spencer must have carried Allie and him after tending to their wounds and setting up the tents.

Although it pained Drake to admit it, it occurred to him that he'd misjudged Spencer. Those weren't the actions of a traitor.

They took their time walking what had at one time been wide boulevards. The temples on either side of them were now eroded lumps of vegetation, most of the structures having been built out of timber that had long ago rotted away. Drake's leg ached, but when Spencer had shown him how to change the dressing, there had been no sign of infection, and he'd gulped down several more antibiotic pills and injected a quarter of the morphine in the syringe before getting underway.

The day stretched on and they found nothing, and by afternoon they were both exhausted and hot. They returned to the clearing to wait out the worst of it, and found Allie dozing but safe. After a brief report on their lack of progress, Spencer went to the river to get water. Drake gave Allie another half dose of morphine for the pain, and she drifted off in a narcotic sleep after drinking more water and eating another bar. When Spencer returned, he sat down on a log and shook his head.

"This is a big place. There must have been thousands living here at one time."

"The last holdout of the Inca Empire. I wonder how many years it lasted, and what brought it down?" Drake said.

"We'll probably know in time. Once you register the find and teams of archeologists descend on the place, they'll figure it out. They always do."

"Let's hope I don't have a problem registering it. When big money's involved with a third world nation that's got plenty of corruption, anything could happen."

"That's always a danger. But I may have a way around it. One of my drinking buddies is the curator at the Museum of Natural History in Lima. He went to school in New York and has deep connections with the Smithsonian. If we actually find the treasure, I can reach out and see if he can assemble a team that's bigger than some bureaucratic larceny. If the Smithsonian announces the find, with your name on it, and flies a bunch of pencil necks out here to catalog the treasure, that'll go a long way toward eliminating the chance that big chunks of it disappear, or that you get cut out of a reasonable finder's fee."

Drake appraised him. "You'd do that?"

Spencer waved nonchalantly. "It's purely driven by self-interest. I can't collect my cut if you get screwed, now can I?"

Drake nodded, not entirely convinced by Spencer's gruff demeanor. "I suppose that's one way to look at it. Good thinking."

"Yeah. Now, why don't you tell me everything you know about the mad Russian? Seeing as we're sharing openly and honestly? Because I'm getting a bad feeling about this the longer I'm out here, you know?"

Drake sat back and took a deep drink of water before beginning. When he was finished, Spencer whistled.

"Boy, you don't do things in half measures, do you?"

"Look, I have no idea whether Palenko has a nuke or something, but whatever it is, the CIA is interested enough to send a team to keep it out of unfriendly hands. So they believe it's worth pursuing. Whether or not it is, who knows? Did he seem like he'd be able to design a working toilet, much less something that could provide energy for the planet or destroy it?"

"Hey, Howard Hughes had a similar look, and he managed some amazing feats. I wouldn't let that fool you. Besides, who knows what made him flip out and start the Inca god thing? For all we know he was schizophrenic. Heard voices. Maybe he went off his meds. Or maybe the voices got so loud once he was in the Amazon, he had to obey. You can't try to figure out crazy. Because you're not nuts, so you have no idea what was going on in his brain."

Drake nodded. Spencer was right. About a lot of things, apparently. Spencer was more than his appearance would suggest, and there was considerable thought behind the stone-faced façade.

"You know, something just occurred to me. If we find the treasure, we might also run across the mystery ore. If we do, what would you like to do with it? Drop it in the river so it's lost for all time? Or turn it over to the CIA?" Spencer asked.

"Beats me. I hadn't thought about it much."

"As I see it, you have two choices. Either you hand it over and you're off the hook; or you don't, in which case you're always going to be a marked man. Did I miss some nuance you left out?"

"But I haven't done anything wrong."

"Yeah. I get it. Unfortunately, being innocent hasn't ever meant going unharmed when you're dancing with elephants. If they step on you, you're squished just as badly as the guilty."

"Why are you harping on this?" Drake asked, annoyed at Spencer's tone.

"Because I might be able to help with that, too."

"In what way?"

"I know a few people at the CIA."

Drake fought to control his outrage. "Damn. I knew it. You're a plant," he said as he struggled to stand.

"Whoa, there, Nellie. Why is it always so black and white with you? If I didn't know better, I'd say you don't trust me."

"You just said…"

"I said I know some people. You don't spend a decade doing what I do for a living without making connections, you know? Someone needs to get across a border, or an agency needs some intel on the latest movements of a drug-trafficking gang, or some friendly rebels need a few cases of grenades without any accountability…it's an imperfect world, is all I'm saying. So yeah, I have contacts. If you decide you want to hand it over, I could negotiate a deal for you. Sounds like you could name a pretty high price."

"It's not about the money."

"It's always about the money. Are you kidding? If you're sitting on something they've been looking for that long, you're in the driver's seat."

The fight had gone out of Drake. He sat back down.

"What would you do?"

"Personally? Let's think it through. If you ditch it somewhere else, once they know the Inca city's here, they'll spare no expense on divers, sonar, whatever it takes. And you'll never be safe, no matter how much money you get from the treasure. Someone, either them or the Russians or someone else, will always think you know more than you're saying. So it's just a matter of time till they come for you. You'd be fighting the whole world. I don't like those odds."

Drake frowned. "That sounds about right."

"What's the downside to handing it over? Uncle Sam gets the ore and builds a death star with it? Guess what. They've already got enough nukes to kill everything on the planet a thousand times over. So I highly doubt that's the end game. Maybe it might have been when Russia was the evil empire, but now? Not so much. So it's more likely it's used to develop a power source, assuming Palenko was onto something. Or it could be he was completely off-base, in which case nothing ever gets built. I'm just saying that behind door number two, you have inevitable death, probably painful, and behind door number one, a way out with a potentially big payday."

"When you put it like that..."

Spencer squinted at him. "You have something against the U.S.?"

"No more than any other government, I suppose."

"Then what's the beef?"

Drake thought about it for a while. "I don't like being told what to do."

"Right. Join the club. But unless you left something out, they didn't order you to do anything."

"That's right. But it felt like I had no choice."

"Hey, do what you want, but I kind of like breathing, and I'm sure Allie does too. And the problem I see is that if we're associated with you, and you decide to bury it in your backyard, the bad guys will be coming for us, too. I didn't sign up for that. If you'd have come clean before, I would have made turning it over a condition of my help."

Drake shrugged. "You did miss that we haven't found anything."

"Yet. You found the frigging city. Everyone else has been hunting for it for hundreds of years. I'd say that should inspire some confidence. My money's obviously on you. Besides, if I didn't..." Spencer's voice trailed off. Drake had gotten to his feet and wasn't listening anymore.

Spencer rose too, rifle in hand. "What?" he whispered.

"I think I know where the treasure is," Drake said, and limped off into the jungle without another word.

Spencer glowered at his back as he disappeared into the brush, and with a groan and a glance at Allie's tent, followed him, wondering what had just clicked in Drake's head.

Chapter Forty-One

Drake approached the altar area, his gun in one hand and the staff in the other, and slowly turned to study the topography. The bodies had disappeared, either dragged away by Spencer to avoid attracting larger predators or taken by the jungle's hungry to be feasted on in private. He limped to the altar and gazed at the stone surface, the blood washed away by the prior night's rain. On it was a lateral line he'd believed had been a channel for blood, but which now appeared to be pointing across the clearing to a rise in the terrain, a bulge that jutted from the vegetation like a massive tumor.

Spencer edged to his side and followed his stare to settle on the outcropping. "What is it?" he whispered.

"My father speculated in the journal that the Incas wouldn't have just left their treasure exposed, where it could be easily found. And something about what Palenko said, that it was beneath our feet…"

"You think they buried it? That'll take forever to locate."

"Maybe. But what if…come on. Do you have your flashlight?" Drake limped to the rise a hundred yards away, its bulk growing as he neared it. Palm trees dotted its base, their trunks contorted in impossible directions as they sought elusive sunlight.

When they arrived at the bottom of the small hill, the stone reddish brown where it wasn't covered with creepers and plants, Drake began probing around the base with his staff, thrusting it into the brush like a man possessed.

"What are you doing?" Spencer asked, doubt in his voice.

"Looking for something that doesn't belong here. That isn't natural."

"Sure. Like what?"

"I don't know, but–"

Drake stopped and thrust the staff again, and heard the same sound.

Something hollow behind the plants.

"Let's get to work. Still plenty of light out," Drake said, unsheathing his machete from its place on his backpack frame.

Ten minutes later they'd cleared a six-foot space where they could see the underlying rock. Drake tapped one area with his machete blade and began scratching the dirt from the surface. A crudely built wall emerged, the mortar crumbling as the steel scraped at it, and Spencer joined him working at the joints in the rock – river rock, not the iron-rich ore that formed the outcropping.

After half an hour, the first of the stones fell into an empty space behind the wall, and Spencer renewed his efforts as Drake took a break, still not fully recovered from the prior day's blood loss. A second rock tumbled into the cavity, followed by a third and fourth, and Spencer stood back, studying the dark hole he'd bored.

"Looks like a cave to me," he said.

Drake offered a pained grin. "That's what we're looking for. How much longer you figure till it gets dark?"

"Maybe two hours."

"Plenty of time," Drake said, pulling his flashlight from his pack and turning it on. Spencer did the same and then invited Drake to lead the way.

"This is your dance. I'm just the window dressing."

Drake's calf flared pain as he climbed through the gap and stood in the cavern, the mouth no more than six feet high and ten wide. He took several cautious steps, playing his beam over the stone floor, which dropped below ground level as far as he could see. Spencer stepped in behind him. His boots scraped on the chunks of mortar and rock as he directed his light at the ceiling.

"Looks like plenty of bats, so there's got to be another entrance," he whispered.

Squeaking greeted his comment, and then the entire cavern seemed to come alive as the air thickened with hundreds of furry bodies beating tiny wings, screeching as they headed for the new exit. Drake ducked and covered his head as the swarm fluttered over and around him. Spencer did the same, the frenzied squeaks building to a crescendo and then fading as the bats departed, leaving them open-mouthed and shaken.

"You did say there were plenty of them," Drake said dryly. He took a tentative step farther into the chasm's gloom. Spencer moved to his side, and their combined lights glowed off the cave walls.

"Feel the temperature change? It's cooler already."

"At least that's a relief. I wonder if there are snakes in here?" Drake asked.

"I think we have to assume the worst."

"I was afraid you'd say that."

The area expanded as they traversed the sloping floor. The narrow passage became a large cave with a ceiling at least twenty feet high. Spencer grabbed Drake's arm and leaned into him, pointing at a far wall, his light moving across the stone.

Pictographs adorned the space, carvings of deities and dignitaries in elaborate gowns and headdresses, riding on carts pulled by jaguars and mythical beasts. In the background, atop a hill framed by two waterfalls, a huge form, part feline, part human, spread its arms heavenward, where an oversized, stylized sun beamed down on the procession.

Drake nudged him and moved forward to where a different scene depicted Inca warriors battling caricatures of bearded men with armor, bodies on both sides piled up, decapitated and otherwise mutilated. His light seemed inadequate to highlight all the carvings, which stretched to the ceiling – a graphical history of the Incas.

"Look at this," Spencer whispered from another wall. Drake made his way to him, where he was staring at a carving of a large gathering of men and women standing around a lake. A deity hovered over it, arms filled with icons and jewels.

"That could be El Dorado. The legend of the golden man," Drake said, his voice hushed. He directed his light at the mouth of a dark opening on the far side of the chamber, the squeak of an occasional bat reminding them that they weren't alone. Water dripped somewhere in the distance, wearing away at the stone as it had for eons to create the cavern. They approached the gap and stopped short at the final image carved into the wall – a grinning skull atop a robed figure, which clutched a snake in one bony hand and a war club in the other.

"Not much of a welcome committee, is it?" Spencer said.

"You can take the point position anytime you want."

"This is your movie. Lead on, Dr. Livingston."

Drake moved forward into the new cave and a low moan greeted him from its bowels. His flashlight beam flashed on the floor in front of him, and he hesitated as a large white scorpion faced him, tail raised, its pincers opening and closing furiously, clearly annoyed at having been disturbed. Drake sensed Spencer behind him, but kept his eyes locked on the creature, mesmerized by its menacing dance.

He jumped when Spencer tapped his arm and whispered in his ear.

"Looks like we found the cemetery."

Drake raised his beam from the creature and slowly played it over the wall, where hundreds of skulls leered at him. Spencer turned slowly, taking in the countless skeletons in the burial vault, and stopped where the oily brown exoskeleton of a centipede was worming through the eyehole of a skull with a feathered helmet on it.

"Okay. This is officially really creepy," Drake murmured, and returned his attention to the floor, where the scorpion had scuttled off into the recesses of the massive crypt.

"Agreed. Although the good part is that they're dead, so they don't pose much of a threat. I could take ten of 'em with one arm tied behind my back," Spencer said.

The moaning sound echoed through the cave again, and Drake pointed his light at the ceiling. "Wind's blowing somewhere above us."

"Probably where the bats get in."

"You're going to tell me to keep going, aren't you?"

"I don't see any treasure yet, do you?"

"Did I mention this is freaking me out?" Drake asked.

"Not yet."

"Okay, then I won't." Drake touched the hilt of his knife and felt the odd calming effect flood through him as he made his way through the floor-to-ceiling piles of bleached bones. They pushed thick cobwebs aside, the gossamer strands hanging from the stalactites above like ectoplasm. Rows of skulls fixed him with sightless stares as he put one silent foot in front of the other, and he wondered whether the experience would haunt his dreams forever, like the memory of Palenko's Saint Vitus dance, and the last light of life in Jack's eyes before he closed them the final time.

They reached the end of the crypt and entered an even larger one, legions of skeletons observing their progress, mute sentinels in the hall of the dead. The air smelled leaden and damp, with a musty odor of decay. The wind's moan followed them like a curse as they made their way toward the narrow gap at the far end, the aperture as black as the devil's heart. A distinct feeling of unease twisted in Drake's stomach as they neared it, and the odor in the air changed again – this time, a whiff of methane mixed with the unmistakable scent of water.

Drake and Spencer stopped at the threshold together, their lamps illuminating four mummified guardians in full battle gear framing the opening. All of the warriors had copper chest plates and bronze helmets adorned with elaborate multicolored feathers. They stood with round wooden shields and wooden clubs studded with stone spikes, their bodies positioned to give the impression of an attack, their leathery skin, protruding teeth, and gaping eye cavities as menacing in death as in life.

"I've had nights like that," Spencer quipped. The tension in the vault evaporated with the sound of his voice echoing off the stone walls.

"You ready to do this?" Drake asked.

"No time like the present."

The cavern they entered was smaller than the last but with the highest ceiling yet, and Drake estimated from the slope that they must have traveled forty feet below ground level, if not more. The temperature seemed cool as a wine cellar after the heat of the jungle above, and the endless rows of skulls gave way to bare walls. In the center of the cave was a hole in the floor the size of a truck, the rim around it crusted with small emeralds embedded in the smooth stone.

"It's a cenote," Spencer whispered, pronouncing the word *see-no-tay*. "See how steep the edges are?"

"Forgive my ignorance, but what's a cenote?"

"A Mexican term. Think of it as a really deep sinkhole filled with water. I'd guess that this one was formed by the roof of a cavern below us eroding away and finally collapsing, creating the hole we're looking at."

"I don't see any water dripping into it," Drake said as they approached the edge.

"That could have been fifty thousand years ago. But you can smell water."

Drake blinked as he looked around the cave. "Am I losing my mind, or do the walls in here seem to be…glowing?"

He extinguished his flashlight. Spencer did the same. A vertiginous disorientation hit Drake, and then his eyes adjusted and he could make out thousands of tiny pinpoints of light.

"What the hell?" He felt his way to one of the walls and examined it, and then pulled away in revulsion. The lights were moving, ever so slightly, and he could see that the neon points were the tips of gelatinous tubes.

Spencer's voice greeted him from a few feet behind him. "Glow worms. That's a first. I've seen fireflies and beetles with glowing tails, but never these. Apparently we can add them to the discoveries for the record books we've made today. The Amazon never fails to surprise, that's for sure."

"What do they feed on?"

"Any kind of flying insects. Wanna bet the water attracts mosquitoes, and when they hatch, they buzz around, attracted to the lights, and get stuck in that stringy goop?"

"Nice. I won't be eating dinner tonight."

They turned back to the sinkhole and switched on their flashlights again. "This seems like it's where the treasure would be. Look at the number of emeralds. There's a small fortune right there," Drake said.

Spencer nodded. "Promising. But how do we find out for sure?"

Drake pointed his light down the sheer walls of the sinkhole and saw water twenty feet below. He hesitated and then turned to Spencer.

"You have that rope in your backpack?"

"Of course. Why? What are you planning to do?"

"Did you know I was on the swim team in school?" Drake asked as he slipped the straps of his backpack off and set it on the stone floor.

"That's nice. I always wanted to be a cheerleader. What's your point?"

"I once won a bet for being able to hold my breath underwater for over three minutes. I mean, that's nothing compared to some free divers, who can go ten, fifteen minutes, but still, it's longer than most. It was a while ago, but I bet I could still manage two minutes, even if I was swimming. But this would work way better if I didn't have to."

"Didn't have to swim?"

"Exactly. I'm thinking if I could hold sixty or seventy pounds of rock in my arms, that would help me sink with the least amount of effort."

"You're going to dive into...that?"

"Not dive. You'll lower me down with the rope attached to my belt, and then I'll drop to the bottom and see what I can feel. My only question is about my wounds. You think that will increase my infection risk?"

"It might. But you're taking horse pills of antibiotic. And cenote water is supposed to be very clean. I forget why."

"How do you know so much about them?" Drake asked.

"I read about the famous ones in Mexico, and got curious." Spencer held up the coil of rope. "A hundred feet of nylon. Hopefully that will be enough."

"If it isn't, I can always untie the rope and keep going. Coming up's way easier than going down."

"Good to know if I ever have to do hundred-foot free dives."

"Come on. Let's go back and get a couple of those rocks at the entrance. Those should do it."

Spencer shook his head. "You're in no shape to carry heavy rocks that distance. I've got a better suggestion. Those four guards have copper breastplates. Want to bet each one weighs at least ten or fifteen pounds?"

"And a helmet should add some weight, too."

"Tell you what. You wait here and do breathing exercises or whatever you need to do to prepare, and I'll go do a little grave robbery."

Five minutes later Drake was at the edge of the cenote, stripped down to just his shorts, the breastplates slung around his neck and an Inca ceremonial helmet on his head. He tugged at the rope tied to his belt and nodded, his flashlight on the floor throwing light toward the opening.

Drake gave Spencer a thumbs-up. "Let me down easy, and once I'm in the water just feed the rope out until we're out of line. If I have to disconnect, leave the rope down and brace yourself, because that's my lifeline out of there."

"You ready?" Spencer asked, studying Drake. "I do wish I had a camera…"

"You sure you'll be able to support all this weight?"

"No problem. Just hope the rope holds."

"You're not giving me a lot of good vibes."

"That's why most people don't go cenote diving in the middle of the Amazon. Bad vibes."

"Okay. Here we go." Drake concentrated on taking deep breaths to oxygenate his blood, and then lowered himself over the edge, his arms straining from supporting himself with the additional burden of the copper. He dropped below the edge and felt himself descending as Spencer, true to his word, controlled his drop.

When his feet touched the water, he was surprised by how cold it was.

"I'm in. Hold me for a minute while I work on my breathing, and when I clap my hands, let the rope drop as fast as I can sink."

"You're the boss. Good luck."

Drake filled his lungs, expanding them as far as he could, held his breath, and then forced more air in using his mouth. He exhaled loudly after ten seconds and repeated the process four times. On the fifth, he clapped, and began to sink as the tension on the rope vanished.

Once fully submerged he dropped less rapidly than he would have liked, and focused on keeping his heart rate slow so that he would consume minimal oxygen. His leg wound stung as he sank, and he mentally counted off ten seconds, then twenty, then thirty, as he continued to drift lower while clearing his ears every ten feet. The water grew colder as he plumbed the depths, and then at sixty seconds, his feet touched something.

Drake opened his eyes, but couldn't see anything. He looked up and saw a faint glow from the surface – Spencer's flashlight playing over the water. His bare feet rubbed against a sharp edge and he almost exhaled, but forced himself to remain calm and concentrated on turning so he could feel around with his hands.

His fingers sank into the muck at the bottom, which was slimy and thick, and grasped a shape that had the hard edges of metal. It was heavy, and when he tried to pull it free, it wouldn't budge. He groped along next to it and grabbed the next shape, this one slimmer and smaller. He wrenched it from the mud, and even underwater he could tell it was extremely heavy. Holding it with his left arm, he reached down with his right and drew his knife, then carefully slipped it beneath the leather ties that secured the first breastplate to his chest and sliced upward. The copper plate slipped free and dropped to the bottom.

Drake repeated the process until he was free of the weight, and removed the helmet, leaving it to sink. He began kicking to the surface, his lungs starting to burn as he ascended, his muscles placing an instant demand for oxygen that wasn't available. The statuette was harder to maneuver with than the copper breastplates had been. The light on the surface beckoned to him like a distant mirage, and he kicked with all his might, ignoring the searing pain from his brutalized calf as he neared the sweet relief of air.

When he broke the surface he gasped, splashing, gulping in as much oxygen as he could as he treaded water. Spencer's head appeared at the rim and his voice echoed from the steep walls.

"Took you long enough."

"You going to haul me up, or am I going for an endurance test here?"

The rope slid by him as Spencer wound it up. He felt his belt tighten, and then he was inching higher at a snail's pace. When he reached the lip, he heaved the object he'd pulled from the bottom over the side and grappled for a hold, his arms shaking as he hoisted himself over the edge, cushioned by the glass-like facets of the emeralds as he lay on his back, breathing deeply, his vision blurry in the gloom. He turned his head and saw a deep orange glint in the dim light.

Spencer's boots crunched against the hard stone floor.

"I'd say you hit the jackpot with that, Drake."

Drake turned the statue over in his hands, a highly stylized llama cast from solid gold, eighteen inches tall, its expression a cross between a pout and a smile. "That was the smallest I felt down there. It must weigh thirty pounds."

Spencer hefted it and set it back on the ground. "More like fifty."

"What's that worth, you reckon?"

"Just the gold alone, for melt value, is probably over a mil. As a historical artifact? Sky's the limit. It's priceless. A collector would probably pay five million, easy. I've never seen anything like it, even in a museum."

"I'd say that should establish that we found the treasure, then."

"Oh yeah." Spencer grinned. "How was the swim?"

"Cold."

"Don't worry. You're going to be so rich you can afford to have your blood heated by burning hundred-dollar bills."

"Still got to pull off some pretty big stunts to get paid, though."

Spencer eyed the llama again and shrugged. "Like I said. Now that we know we hit the mother lode, I'll carry the heavy end of the log." He paused. "But this still doesn't solve your CIA problem."

Drake coughed and then smiled.

"*Our* CIA problem."

Chapter Forty-Two

Spencer and Drake moved Allie and the rest of the camp just inside the cavern mouth, seeing no reason to pitch tents outside as yet more rain drizzled at the opening. The three of them sat out of the rain and dined on a celebratory slab of fish Spencer returned with on the end of his spear after a twenty-minute hiatus. They sat with full stomachs, watching the last of the day's light drain from the ashen sky, minds racing over the successful conclusion of the quest of a lifetime. Drake had changed his dressing and was relieved to see that he was still clear of infection, and decided that he might just make it after all. Allie's shoulder looked battered but was also free of the redness and puffiness that would have signaled a problem, for which they were all grateful.

"You think the ore is down there with all the gold?" Spencer asked, his AK lying next to him like a sleeping lover.

"Who knows? Although I have a hard time imagining Palenko dropping his most valuable possession into a well."

"Then where do you think it is?" Allie asked.

Drake shook his head. "I have no idea. But if I were him, I'd have wanted it close at hand."

"I agree he'd have kept it nearby. Maybe where he could stare at it when he felt down."

"Assuming that it's not so radioactive it would fry your skin off," Allie said.

Spencer frowned. "Did the CIA goons go into any detail about the ore's properties?"

"No. Just that Palenko thought it could power or destroy the planet, depending on how it was put to use."

"This from a guy who looked worse than Keith Richards," Allie said.

"My guess is that it would have to be really radioactive, then, don't you think?" Spencer asked.

Drake shrugged. "Could be. Or it could be that Palenko devised some process using it, like cold fusion. It's all guesswork. The only thing that matters from our standpoint is that the CIA thinks it's important."

A surge in the downpour splattered against the wet blanket of leaves just beyond the entrance, the water running down the slight slope, away from the gap, the sound now as familiar as the sound of their own breathing. Spencer turned on his flashlight and leaned back against the cave wall after checking to ensure there were no critters nearby waiting to sting or bite him. Allie retired to her tent, and after giving her two more pills, Drake returned and sat next to him.

"So what are you going to do with all the money?" Spencer asked, his voice fatigued.

"I don't know. What about you?"

"Depends on how much it is."

"It'll be a lot," Drake assured him.

"I kind of figured when I saw the emeralds on the rim."

"Yeah. Just those alone, you could retire on."

Spencer laughed. "Maybe I'll buy an island someplace quiet."

"If it isn't quiet before you buy it, you can make it that way after."

"But no white mud smeared all over me."

"Not that there's anything wrong with that."

They both chuckled, and Drake patted his rifle. "You sleep. I'll take the first watch. No way I'm getting any rest after today."

"Is it because you've got a few thousand dead Incas watching your back?"

"Nah. Like you said. They're dead. It's the living that you have to worry about." Drake lifted the rifle and laid it across his lap, his legs extended out in front of him, and exhaled noisily. "This wasn't worth the price. My dad. Jack. Makes you wonder whether there's a curse or something."

Spencer spat into the night. "The curse is called greed. Greed killed them, whether it's for money or for the power of Palenko's technology. I've been around long enough so I don't believe in curses. There's no need for them. Humans create enough misery without involving the supernatural. Look at Palenko. He wound up butchering children to feed his craziness, and the natives he recruited helped him. Curse? Nope. Just human nature."

Spencer crawled into his tent and zipped up the mosquito netting, and Drake settled in, watching the entrance, his weapon by his side, a round chambered and the safety off.

At some point in the early morning hours, Spencer awoke and took over guard duty, and Drake gratefully slept. His dreams were unsettled, visions of a dark hall full of parading skeletons, their bony fingers grabbing at him as he was carried aloft toward the black pool, Palenko's maniacal grin drooling blood as he danced by the rim, his feet shredded from the emeralds. The mad Russian howled, baying at an unseen moon, and then skeletal hands pushed Drake closer and closer to the edge, until he was staring down into the void...

Drake bolted awake, gasping, sweat beading down his face as dawn's first rays filtered through the cave opening. Spencer was nowhere to be seen, and there was no sound from Allie's tent. Drake felt for his rifle and clambered out of the tent. Water dripped from the edge of the cave mouth, residue from the night's rain, but there was no drizzle outside. He stepped into the faint light and looked around the clearing for any sign of Spencer, but saw nothing.

"I got us breakfast," Spencer called from the edge of the tree line, and emerged carrying one of the crossbows and a fish, at least six pounds. "Like shooting fish in a barrel. It's amazing the amount of life in the Amazon. We'll never starve here, that's for sure."

Spencer prepared the meal over the dwindling gas of the stove after checking Allie's dressing again and changing it. She looked stronger than the previous day and had a healthy appetite. They took their time eating together as they discussed their next move.

"I'm going to call my friend at the museum, if that's okay. I don't see any point in delaying that, do you?" Spencer asked.

"Other than bringing the CIA down on us? None at all," Drake said.

"It'll probably take him some time to figure out how to set up a team to verify the find and record it. He'll know the best way to approach it. In the meanwhile, we can keep searching for Palenko's ore. I'll tell him that the find's sensitive, and to only share the information with trusted friends. He'll read between the lines. He's very discreet."

"How do you know him?"

"We were roommates in college. In New York. He's the original reason I wound up in Peru, in fact. I helped break up a smuggling ring that was trafficking in pre-Columbian artifacts. It's a long story, but it ended well."

Drake nodded. "Then you can level with him?"

"Absolutely. I trust him like a brother."

"Hopefully the satellite phone still has a charge."

"I already checked. It's low, but it's got enough to last a few more days."

"Do me a favor, Spencer. Don't give him the exact coordinates until he confirms he has the group ready to move. Call me suspicious, but I don't want anyone dropping in unexpectedly, you know?"

"I'm way ahead of you. I like breathing, too. Gotten kind of used to it."

"Exactly."

"What about arranging for some transport for Allie?" Drake asked, eyeing her.

"I'll tell them we have an injury that will need to be air evacuated when they arrive."

"Are you in that big a hurry to get rid of me?" she teased.

Drake offered a smile and a shrug. "More fish for us."

Spencer's friend, Jorge Esquival, was excited by the news that Paititi had been discovered on Peruvian soil. After a hurried discussion, he agreed to assemble an international team of archeologists to explore the site as soon as possible, and to put into motion preparations for the official registering of the site, listing Drake Ramsey as the discoverer, with Allie getting a co-discovery credit.

Jorge was puzzled that he didn't recognize Drake's name. "Drake Ramsey? Who is he? I've never…is he an archeologist? Physical anthropologist?" Jorge asked.

"No. He's…an adventurer and explorer. One I'm sure you'll be hearing a lot more about," Spencer said, and Drake felt himself blushing as he listened in.

"Ah. Very well then. Nationality?"

"American."

"Well, my friend, you're right that his name will be recognized after this. It's the biggest find in South American history. Maybe world history, if the legends of the treasure's value are correct."

"I'd say they are." Spencer briefly told him about the statue and the emeralds, as well as the mass crypts.

"Truly remarkable. I can't wait to see it. I'll start contacting colleagues as soon as I hang up. How can I reach you when I have everything arranged?"

"I'll call you in a day or so to coordinate. This phone's low on juice, so I want to leave it off until I need it."

"Okay. I suspect those I call will jump at the chance to be first on the ground for a find like this. I'll tell them to hop on planes."

"Please do. And also get some scuba gear and some industrial diving equipment."

"The treasure's underwater?"

"Assume that's the case. You'll want enough gear to allow divers to work around the clock. And Jorge? We're talking big pieces, so think block and tackle."

"I see. Very well. All quite mysterious, but that's fitting given Paititi's history. I'll do as you ask."

"And remember. Keep it confidential."

"Will do. Although I intend to call in a favor once the team's assembled. I know the president of Peru, and for news of this magnitude, I want him on our side. I'll arrange for a meeting and fill him in. That will prevent any underlings from scheming to cut in on the find."

"Good idea. And thanks, Jorge. I owe you one."

"Sounds like you'll be in a position to pay off all your debts soon enough, *amigo.*"

"That's good to hear. What do you think Ramsey will see as a finder's fee for the discovery?"

"I should think…perhaps ten percent of the value would be in keeping with other finds like this. Would that be acceptable? I'll discuss it with the president and get his approval."

Spencer looked at Drake. "Ten percent?" he repeated. Drake and Allie nodded, and Drake gave him an okay sign. "That would work. More than enough to go around, right?"

"If this is as large as legend suggests, yes, more than adequate to start one's own country."

"All right. Again, many thanks, Jorge. I'll buy the first drink."

"And the second, and the third…"

"Deal."

Spencer hung up and powered the phone off. He returned it to his backpack and spoke to Drake.

"So what now, Mr. Ramsey, sir?"

Drake ignored him. "We need to concentrate on finding the ore. Sounds like we've got a couple of days, tops, before all hell breaks loose."

"Yeah. And you become a rich celebrity."

"You too. You'll wind up bathing in pink champagne, or whatever, too."

"That's going to be my plan," Allie said.

Spencer rolled his eyes. "Unfortunately, we have to live to spend it. Any ideas on where to start looking for the ore?"

"I think we work from the sinkhole out. We obviously can't dive until the team gets here, but we should assume that he stashed it somewhere else. Maybe among the skeletons. Or it's possible he buried it…"

"When he ran, he stopped in that other clearing. Maybe there was a reason. I'd say we should start there," Spencer said.

"Okay. Twist my arm. Not that I'm not looking forward to digging through several thousand dead Incas."

"I thought you might like that suggestion. Come on. Grab your gun. Let's see whether there's anything over there. Will you be okay here alone, Allie?"

She waved them away. "Go on. Get out of here. Do what you need to do. I've got my boyfriend SIG Sauer to keep me company…"

The search took all morning and yielded nothing, and that afternoon they began on the sinkhole chamber, hunting for anything suspicious or any cavity they might have overlooked the day before. As they were finishing with the largest cavern, Drake cried out. Spencer came running.

"What?"

"Look. You see that?" Drake asked, pointing into the darkness behind a mound of bones.

Spencer squinted and directed his fading flashlight beam where Drake had indicated – a recess in the cave wall a foot off the floor.

"Yeah. It's a plastic tackle box. Hold my flashlight. I'll get it."

Spencer picked up a tibia from one of the skeletons. He got down on his hands and knees and slowly eased the shinbone into the cavity as Drake held the light steady.

A lightning-like blur struck at the bone, nearly jolting it from Spencer's grip. Spencer pulled back as a triangular brown-scaled head with malevolent black eyes glowered at them from the recess.

"Damn. Viper. Another reminder of why you don't want to stick your hand in dark holes," Spencer said. He prodded the snake again.

It struck at the bone two more times before slithering off along the wall in search of more tender prey. Spencer leapt to his feet and backed away, as did Drake, and they watched the six-foot-long serpent disappear into the bone garden.

"That was close," Drake said, shaken.

"The Amazon has a way of reminding you who's boss, doesn't it?" Spencer said, his voice even, his composure unruffled by his brush with death.

He got back on his knees and slid the bone under the plastic handle, and pulled the container from its hiding place. It was a dull blue plastic tackle box, no markings, held shut by a single corroded clasp. Drake unsheathed his knife and used the tip to unhook it, and flipped the clasp open. Spencer inched his toe under the lid and kicked it wide, wary lest another surprise await him inside.

They stared at the contents: A single piece of animal hide with unfamiliar symbols on it.

"What do you think? Inca?" Spencer asked.

"Could be. Too bad neither of us can read it, huh?"

"They left that out of my high school curriculum. Obscure pre-Columbian glyphs."

"You think it could tell us where the ore is?"

"No way of knowing until an expert looks at it."

"Crap."

"Close it up. Palenko obviously thought it was important enough to want to protect it from the elements."

By evening they were dusty from looking through piles of skeletons, and had nothing more to show for it but sore backs and spiderwebs stuck in their hair. The next day brought more of the same, and by nighttime they were both disillusioned, the enormity of the task weighing heavily on them as they ate in silence, mulling over other possible hiding places – assuming Palenko hadn't tossed the ore into the river or secreted it many miles away. The only positive was that Allie seemed to be recovering, and was strengthening with every passing hour. She'd already begun weaning herself off the morphine as the worst of the pain diminished.

Dusk brought with it the rumble of thunderheads approaching from the west, and they resigned themselves to another rainy night. Darkness descended quickly, and Drake volunteered to take the first watch, his mind too wound up with the puzzle of where the Russian might have hidden his treasure to sleep. Spencer was slumbering in his tent within minutes, the storm's approaching fury not fazing him. Drake tried to get comfortable on the hard stone floor, his muscles tense, long hours of watching the rain fall his only relief from the tedious duty.

A flash of lightning lit the grotto and the gray stone of the altar seemed to glow for a split second against the inky backdrop of the jungle before fading into darkness, followed by explosive thunder. Drake shifted, his head still sore, his calf aching dully, and resigned himself to a long, wet night. When the rain came, it arrived in heavy sheets, drops the size of golf balls pummeling the ground. Another tree of lightning seared the night sky, and looking out of the cave, Drake was suddenly seized by a conviction so strong it was like a physical assault.

He contemplated going into the downpour with his machete, but decided to wait for morning. If his intuition was right, they'd have plenty of time before the team was in the air. He sighed, a feeling of peace settling upon him as he peered into the gloom. He absently fingered the hilt of his father's knife and watched the celestial pyrotechnics as he waited for the new day to arrive, and with it, the end of his odyssey.

Because he knew where Palenko had hidden his ore.

He was suddenly as sure of it as he was of his last name.

Tomorrow, the last puzzle piece would fall into place and the jungle would reveal its final secret.

Chapter Forty-Three

Drake and Spencer walked across the clearing, their boots sliding on the wet grass, machetes in hand, rifles hanging from their shoulders, as Allie watched from the shelter of the cave. They slowed as they approached the altar, and Drake circled it, eyeing the base – two square stone columns supporting the slab top.

"I don't know. I mean, I respect your hunch and all, but what's your best guess? He buried it somewhere around here?" Spencer asked skeptically.

"Could be. But the altar's the key. I'm sure of it. He chose it for the sacrifices. It was important to him."

"So was rubbing mud all over himself and doing the world's worst tap dance routine. That doesn't necessarily mean anything."

"You take that side, I'll take this one. It's probably buried near the base."

Fifteen minutes later they'd excavated a trench around the altar and were working on the ground between the pillars. Spencer set down his machete, already soaking with sweat, and shook his head.

"Sorry, man. Looks like a false alarm."

Drake jammed the machete blade into the wet ground and rose before taking a long drink from his canteen. "I would have bet anything it's here. It has to be."

"Yeah, well, unless it's ten feet down, I don't think so."

Drake stepped away from the altar, staring at it, and began pacing as he examined it from every angle. He was about to say something when he stopped mid-stride. After another glance he retrieved his machete and tapped on the top, and then the two columns, with its handle. He turned to Spencer, who was watching him like he was demented.

"How much do you think this thing weighs?" Drake asked.

"Probably thousands of pounds."

"Then how did they get it here? From wherever it came from?"

"Beats me. Maybe they carved it out of some of the local stone."

"What kind of stone does it look like to you?"

"I don't know that much about rocks. Granite?"

"No. It's not granite. More like some of that lighter-colored stone from deep inside the cave where the iron deposits peter out. By the sinkhole."

"Whatever. What's the difference? It's stone."

"Right. But some stones are softer than others."

Spencer regarded the altar. "Softer," he repeated.

"Right. Do you see any engravings on that side? Pictographs?"

"Well, not really. I mean, yes, but they're eroded from the weather. Faint. More like bumps."

"Right. Because the stone's soft."

"Uh-huh. So you said. And that's important because...?"

"Because one of the ways you might make it easier to move from the cave to its present location might be to hollow the biggest pieces out."

Spencer's eyes narrowed and he nodded. "Okay...I follow you. You think the columns are hollow?"

Drake tapped the nearest one again. "Hard to tell. But my bet is, yes. It would make sense to do if they had sufficient time. Might cut the weight by half, or more, making it way easier to drag from the cave and assemble."

"Still thousands of pounds, though. As in tons. Damned thing probably weighs as much as a Chrysler."

"Right. But what if Palenko had time on his hands and was thinking of an original hiding place? He was a genius. What if he arrived at the same conclusion?"

Spencer grinned. "Then you're both crazy?"

"Maybe." Drake got back on his knees and began energetically scraping more dirt from the base of one of the columns. With a roll of his eyes, Spencer reluctantly joined him.

"You really think Uncle Nutty tunneled beneath this to stash his ore? Why not just leave it in the cave?" he asked.

"I don't believe he left it there."

Two hours later they'd excavated from beneath the center of the first column sufficiently for Drake to lie in the trench and poke his head under it with his flashlight.

"Well? Anything?"

Drake edged back out and shook his head. "Nope. But I was right. It's hollow."

"Great," Spencer said, his tone dry.

"Let's do the other one."

"Sure. My blisters need blisters. They're getting lonely."

The heat of the day rose as they worked, and by the time they'd cleared another trench, the air was stifling. Both Spencer and Drake poured sweat, their torsos slick with it. They took a break to rehydrate, and Drake pulled on his filthy T-shirt and grabbed his flashlight.

"Time to see whether this has all been worth it," he said.

Spencer waved in assent as he swallowed more water.

Drake lowered himself into the depression and slid beneath the column. Spencer set his canteen down and took a couple of steps toward him.

"Anything?"

"This one's not hollow. No. Wait. It is. There's something stuck in the cavity."

Drake unsheathed his knife and began chipping away. A few moments later he pulled his head out just before a loud thump issued from the base.

He looked up at Spencer, dirt and flecks of mortar on his grinning face. "Bingo."

Spencer got into the ditch with him, and together they manhandled a fiberglass container from under the column, scraping more dirt out of the way so it could clear. Spencer hoisted the box, veins bulging in his forehead as he strained under the weight, and set it on the ground.

"Damn. Must be at least a hundred pounds. Maybe more like one-twenty. I thought you said he made off with only twenty pounds of ore," Spencer said.

"I did. Twenty-four."

"So what now? You thinking about opening it, just to take a little peek?"

Drake scraped a coating of moist dirt off the container, where the universal radiation hazard symbol was embossed in yellow, and tapped it with his finger.

"Might be a really bad idea to open it. Pandora's box and all. Unless you've decided you never want to have children and want to join the worms glowing in the dark."

Spencer nodded in comprehension. "That's why it's so heavy. Lead shielding."

"Yup. And a lot of it. Maybe we should just wait for the experts on this one...?"

"Not a bad idea."

"I have them every now and then."

They stared at the container, unsure of how to proceed now that they'd accomplished the impossible. Drake caught Spencer's eye.

"I'd buy you a drink to celebrate if there was a bar within five hundred miles," Drake said.

"And I'd let you. But no dancing."

"Right. Got to establish boundaries."

"Exactly."

Drake brushed dirt off his arms. "You going to call the CIA?"

"And Jorge. I'd say we're ready for the onslaught now, wouldn't you?"

"Not that I don't enjoy hanging out in a cave full of ghosts and sleeping in a tent, praying no snakes get me."

Together they dragged the container into the cave, and Spencer got on the sat phone while Allie examined the box. He gave Jorge the coordinates and they agreed that the first group would arrive the following day. The next call was to Spencer's contact at the embassy, who passed him to someone who called himself Mr. Smith. Spencer described Drake's meeting with the three agents in Atalaya, and Mr. Smith acted noncommittal. As the phone ran low on juice, Spencer lost his patience.

"Get on the horn with this Gus guy, and tell him we've located Palenko. I'll call back in two hours. Write that down. Palenko." Spencer stabbed the off button and looked around the grotto with annoyance. "Idiot. I hate the way these spooks try to say nothing and milk you for information. It's infuriating."

"I'd say you handled that well," Allie said with a smirk.

"Yeah, well, I have a little problem with authority. We all have our crosses to bear."

Allie retired for her afternoon rest, her energy still low as the heat rose outside the cave. When Spencer called back later, he was immediately patched through to someone different, and Spencer could hear an engine in the background.

"Who is this?" Spencer demanded.

"Gus. You wanted to talk?"

Spencer handed Drake the phone.

"Hello? Gus?"

"Yes. Mr. Ramsey?"

"Speaking. The battery's low, so I'll make this quick. I have what you're after. We need to do an exchange."

There was a pause on the line. "You found it?"

"Correct. I have it in my possession. That should be worth a hell of a lot more than fifty million after everything I've been through."

"Name your price."

Drake covered the mouthpiece with his hand. "He said name your price," he whispered.

"Damn. Um, tell him a hundred million. And we split it three ways, all right?"

Drake looked at him like he was crazy, but Spencer didn't flinch, and Drake decided he could learn a thing or two from him.

"Gus?"

"Yes."

"The number's a hundred."

"You have it with you?"

"Yes."

"Fine. Done. Where do you want the funds sent?"

Drake gave him his bank account number and bank name. "It's the Menlo Park branch."

"We'll figure it out. Son, you wouldn't be pulling a fast one, would you?"

"Do I sound particularly playful right now, Gus? I've got a gunshot wound, and one of my group is dead. You want to make it two hundred?" Drake had already learned one lesson from Spencer.

"Slow down. I was just asking. Because you don't want to screw us over."

"A deal's a deal. It's yours for a hundred. Going once. Going twice…"

"We'll do the wire today."

"And I don't want any tax problems."

"We'll handle that."

"Okay. Once I verify the funds arrived, I'll tell you where to find the container."

"You aren't going to meet me with it?"

"Gus, I'm in the middle of the frigging Amazon rainforest. Not that I don't trust you, but no, I'm not going to stand out in some field while you helicopter in, hoping you don't take a sniper shot at me. You pay, you get the box, and you do whatever you want with it from there. That's the deal. And then we're done. Agreed?"

Gus paused, and when he spoke, Drake could have sworn there was a smile in his voice.

"Done. Here's a number. Call me once you've verified the funds. I'll arrange for a helicopter. And leave the sniper at home." He rattled off a U.S. number, and Drake repeated it back to him.

"How long will it take?" Drake asked.

"A few hours."

"Fair enough. Oh, and forget about triangulating this phone. I'm nowhere near the ore. If the money's not there by the end of the day, I'll assume you double-crossed me, and you can spend the rest of your life looking for it."

"That won't happen."

"Make sure it doesn't."

Drake shut the phone off, then pulled the battery and put it in his pocket. Spencer looked at him with new respect.

"They went for it?"

"Just like you said. Although I would have given it to them for free."

"I know. But that's not how these guys work. If you don't make them pay, they start thinking maybe you're holding out on them. That's just the way they are. They're slippery, so they assume everyone else has an angle, too. Now they believe yours is money, and they'll like that, because they understand it, and money's nothing to them. They make a phone call, a bank somewhere with an operational account does a wire, and that's it. There's plenty more where that came from, and a hundred million won't even get you a decent jet fighter, so in the scheme of things, it's chump change. You could have asked for a billion, but then they might have had trouble doing the deal quickly."

"A hundred million's not chump change to me."

"Me either. Partner. Remember, thirty-three of it's mine."

"Only if you help me drag this thing along the river until we find a clearing."

"That's a tough one. Thirty-three mil for an hour's work…"

"I thought you'd see my side of it."

Drake and Spencer improvised a sled for the container using two saplings and one of the backpacks, and spent the remainder of the afternoon lugging the ore down the river to a small area of beach a half mile away. It started raining as they arrived, and they slid the box into the backpack and zipped it closed. Drake entered a waypoint into Jack's portable GPS and they made their way back to Paititi, the rain having already erased most of the sled tracks.

The phone was blinking a low-battery indicator when Spencer called Jorge and gave him the coordinates for the city. The next call to the international operator got the bank's phone number, and after one minute on hold Drake confirmed that the money had hit.

When Drake called Gus back, the phone was beeping every twenty seconds to alert him that it was about to shut down. He gave Gus the location, wished him well, and then the phone went dead in his hand. Drake tossed it to Spencer, who dropped it into his backpack and grinned at Drake.

"Fish for dinner? It's on me."

Chapter Forty-Four

The Sikorsky helicopter's huge blades beat at the air like a jilted bride as it hovered over the clearing, the surrounding trees shaking from the downdraft. The winch operator leaned out the door as he lowered the final wooden crate through the canopy at the end of a steel cable. The container set down next to five of its twins, and two workers ran to it and disconnected a large hook from the harness. The other fourteen men stood in a loose ring around the boxes, watching the display while Jorge chatted with Spencer and Drake near the cavern mouth.

Six hours later Allie had been airlifted to a military hospital, the area quiet except for the footsteps of the armed men guarding the perimeter. Deep inside the cave, a generator powered oversized work lights in the sinkhole chamber as the first of the divers lowered himself down a rope ladder to the water's surface, lights on either shoulder mounted to his buoyancy control vest. A second joined him and, after several seconds, dropped into the inky pool. When they slipped beneath the surface, the hush of the surroundings seemed to weigh heavier on the gathered men – Jorge, Spencer and Drake, and four archeologists from Lima who had accompanied the multinational team.

"There will be another dozen divers arriving tomorrow. The military's flying them in. Sorry about the soldiers everywhere, but it's a necessity. We don't want one of the cartels thinking about grabbing an easy payday," Jorge said, explaining the two dozen heavily armed

Peruvian Special Forces commandos, who had arrived shortly after the scientists and immediately mounted armed patrols.

"That seems prudent. Better them than the alternative," Drake said, thinking about the CIA.

"The mass burial site is stunning. This is an unprecedented opportunity to study every aspect of a functioning Inca city's society. So much was eradicated by the Spanish that almost all of our understanding of Inca civilization is based on fragments and hearsay. And of course, the reports that the clergy created – the codices that purport to tell about the Inca Empire."

Spencer shook his head. "As you said earlier, those are highly questionable. Likely a great deal of distortion based on bias and inaccuracies."

"Yes, but now we have thousands of skeletons, and each is a kind of historical record that will offer invaluable information on everything from diet, to medicine, to life expectancy…and that's not even counting what we could encounter once we begin excavation of the ruins." Jorge paused. "This is the most important single find in our history, for that reason alone. Never mind the Inca treasure, although that will certainly also afford unique insights into the culture."

Drake shook his head as if to clear it. "It was my father's dream to find Paititi. I'm humbled I could fulfill his ambition."

Jorge nodded. "I'd say you more than did so. You'll be quite famous before long. I'm green with envy, actually. And thrilled to be working with you."

A radio crackled, and one of the scientists lowered a huge steel basket into the water, suspended on a cable hanging from a portable crane that had been assembled and secured in place on the rim after the archeologists had photographed the stunning emerald ring and painstakingly cleared a section for the workers, laying down plywood for protection. The radio emitted a burst of static and the crane operator engaged a lever. The high-pitched whine of an electric motor filled the chamber, and the conversation ebbed as everyone waited to see what would emerge from the depths.

The cage broke the surface and the lights glinted off a huge gold ornamental headdress, easily four feet tall by six wide, ornately crafted and stunning. Emeralds the size of tennis balls adorned the crest, and Drake could hear a collective gasp from the assembly.

"My…God…it's incredible," Jorge whispered as the crane swung slowly and three men reached out to guide the basket to a position on the cave floor. Cameras flashed, memorializing the amazing find, and it took all three of them to remove it.

Spencer, Drake, and Jorge approached the relic as the crane operator moved the basket back over the pool and lowered it back into the water. Jorge reached out with a tentative hand and touched the glistening surface of an emerald in obvious awe.

The archeologist with the radio walked over as more pictures were taken and leaned into Jorge. After a brief discussion, Jorge nodded and returned his attention to Drake and Spencer.

"The divers say that the entire bottom is filled with artifacts, and that we'll need more equipment to get some of it out. They spotted part of the legendary Lost Chain of Huayna Capac, and that alone will require a larger crane. This…I can't describe to you what this means to our country," Jorge said, his eyes gleaming in the bright glare of the work lights. Unable to contain himself, he hugged Drake, who looked at Spencer out of the corner of his eye as he endured the embrace, obviously uncomfortable.

Spencer smiled and turned away. When Drake joined him, Spencer whispered to him as the crane began whining again, "Dude, you're a hero. And this goes with the territory."

"My head still hurts. They didn't warn me about that in hero school."

"Yeah, they probably left out some parts. Don't worry. You'll adapt."

They watched the steel cable vibrating as the winch reeled it back in, and Spencer shook his head. "Who woulda thunk, huh?"

"It's pretty surreal."

"Wait until the parade."

Drake gave him a look of alarm. "You're kidding, right?"

"Only a little. They take this kind of thing seriously. You and Allie are now national treasures. You don't get to just slip away with a fat check. You're a celebrity. The man of the hour."

"Well, so are you. You helped discover it, too. You're a partner, remember?"

Spencer shook his head. "I'm just the hired sidekick. This one's all yours. Although I still want my cut…"

"I figured."

~ ~ ~

Two weeks later the last of the treasure had been raised, and a conservative estimation had established the value at in excess of twenty billion dollars. Paititi now had more than a hundred workers and double that many soldiers guarding it as word of the find had spread. News crews had descended on the area in spite of the best efforts of the administration, and Drake had been hounded for interviews, finally limiting his public contact to an hour every morning. Allie, now fully healed and back at Paititi, seemed more fascinated by the archeological aspects of the find than the prospect of becoming rich, which surprised neither Spencer nor Drake.

Confirmation had come from the Peruvian president that they would receive two billion dollars as a finder's fee for the discovery, and that additionally, a new museum would be built to house the incredible riches on land near the presidential headquarters in Lima. That morning, Drake had been informed that they would all be honored at a groundbreaking ceremony at the end of the week, where they would be awarded Peru's highest honor before a crowd of thousands.

Drake had blown coffee out of his nose and down the front of his newly fitted tropical-weight shirt when Jorge had broken the news, and it had taken a full minute for him to stop coughing as he tried to catch his breath.

"Two billion dollars? That's…that's insane," Drake managed, his voice hoarse.

Spencer cleared his throat. "I believe that will be only one billion for you, Mr. Ramsey." They had discussed it earlier and decided that Spencer and Allie would both get twenty-five percent cuts. Drake had protested, but they'd insisted Drake would get half, and they'd split the rest.

"Only one? How am I going to get by on that?"

Jorge's eyes widened as he studied Spencer's smirk. "Wow. Spencer, you're rich! I mean, New York-level rich!"

"Well, not like some Wall Street crooks, but that does sound like I'll be able to get a good table at Nobu whenever I want."

"I guess I won't be going back to any administrative positions when I go home," Allie said, smiling.

"I...I don't know what to say. Congratulations. All of you. You deserve it. This is the achievement of a lifetime," Jorge said, obviously impressed.

"Wait. Can we go back to the part about the crowd of thousands? I don't really do well with public speaking..." Drake said, and Spencer and Allie exchanged a smile.

"Don't worry. You don't speak Spanish, so you won't be expected to say anything. Just smile when they pin the medal on," Spencer said.

"Sounds like you'll be right there next to me," Drake fired back.

Jorge nodded. "Yes, my friends, all of you are to be decorated. The president has already declared this Friday a national holiday. It's a big deal. And there will be a state dinner afterward, where you will be the guests of honor. The American government is flying the Secretary of State in to represent your country. This is international news."

Drake looked increasingly concerned as the morning wore on. When Jorge excused himself and Spencer went to get another refill of strong black coffee, Allie rose and approached Drake, one eyebrow cocked.

"Can I speak with you?" she asked, her tone revealing nothing.

"Sure."

"Alone."

Drake eyed Spencer, who was busying himself with the coffee pot. "Okay."

Allie took Drake by the hand and led him away from the clearing down to the river. When they reached the bank, she turned to him, her blue eyes flashing in the sun. "Looks like our quest is over now."

"Except for the dinner."

"You have to stop freaking out about that. You'll do fine."

"I know. I just get..."

Allie moved closer and stood on her tiptoes. Her full lips met Drake's and they shared a long kiss, electricity crackling between them. When she pulled away and sighed softly, Drake felt dizzy for a moment. She took his other hand and kissed him again, and then looked up at his strong jawline and deep tan.

"I'm glad you didn't die going over the waterfall," she said softly.

"Or any other time. For the record, I'm glad you didn't die, either." He kissed her again and then regarded the rushing water. "What about Spencer?"

Allie laughed. "Spencer? Nothing's going on between us. What...you thought we were...?"

"No. I mean, you thought I was dead. I'd totally understand..."

"Spencer's a fine specimen, but he's not my type."

"What's your type?"

"I'm hoping we can find out after this is over."

Drake swallowed hard. "I'd like that."

"There's no reason to be nervous about the dinner. Seriously. I'll be right there with you." She nuzzled against his chest, and then they both started when they heard the underbrush behind them rustle. Spencer stepped out, a sheepish grin on his face.

"Well, looks like it's Drake's lucky day in more ways than one," he said. "Sorry. I wasn't being nosy. I just wanted to make sure you two were okay."

Drake locked eyes with Allie, and they smiled together before turning to face him. Allie pushed a lock of dark hair out of her eyes and winked at Spencer.

"Never better."

Chapter Forty-Five

The award ceremony went by in a blur: countless dignitaries shaking hands, kissing cheeks, bowing and scraping and patting Drake's back like he was a new father. As he sat at the head of the long table in the position of honor, trying to remember which fork to use while avoiding spilling wine all over his tuxedo, he was struck by a sense of dissociation, like he was sitting apart from himself, watching someone who looked like him going through the motions, smiling and nodding at the right points. The sensation heightened as the dinner progressed, and he wondered whether he was having a seizure of some sort, brought on by the blow to his head. Then he seemed to get sucked back into his body, and he was looking out through his own eyes again as the Secretary of State's charming wife recounted a practiced story with just the appropriate amount of irony.

He took another sip of wine and considered the gathered faces, some jaded, others bloated with privilege and the ennui of the powerful, still others hungry with avarice or envy, all eyes on him like a sacrificial lamb. His gaze drifted to Allie sitting a few seats down the table across from him, looking radiant in a white sequined dress with a high collar, its contours hugging her curves with every move. Flashes of light sparkled from the massive chandeliers as a string quartet played Mozart with Latin zest, and he was struck by how silly his fellow humans were, how enamored with trappings of power and wealth, and how little of it actually mattered. He resisted a powerful urge to bolt from the hall, and instead chuckled at the right moment, the woman's diverting tale at an end.

"I hear that you're going to start a charitable foundation," the Secretary of State said after a bite of salmon poached in a champagne sauce.

"Yes. I'm having a great deal of the Peruvian government's generosity donated to create an organization in my father's memory. It was he that did the research that enabled me to find Paititi, and he would have wanted the money to go to furthering similar pursuits, I'm sure."

Polite applause greeted his statement, and Drake despised them all for a moment before choking down his volatile emotions. This was a necessary part of being a hero, Spencer had said, whether he liked it or not. The only thing he had to do was get through the evening without vomiting on the white tablecloth, and he'd be remembered as a hit: young, handsome, gracious, sunburned, and appropriately rakish – the perfect embodiment of the successful adventurer.

The only problem was that it felt like a lie. All he'd done was stumble around in the jungle following his father's clues. He didn't deserve any of it.

He offered a wan smile to the beautiful starlet the organizers had seated next to him and took another gulp of wine. Drake might have felt like an empty suit, but if he looked at this public appearance as a job, part of an act, he could get through it. He wouldn't embarrass himself and tarnish his father's name.

Spencer caught his eye from his position halfway down the table and grinned a warning. He'd spent enough time with Drake to know he was in trouble. As the entrée was removed to make way for dessert, Spencer excused himself and approached Drake. He bowed deferentially to the gathering and addressed them like trusted conspirators.

"I'm sorry. Would you excuse us for a moment? I need to ask Ramsey here for some investment tips."

Everyone laughed, the wine having flowed like water, and Spencer led Drake out onto a balcony overlooking the twinkling city lights.

Spencer leaned close to Drake. "Are you all right? You looked like you were about to yack on the hottie they set you up with."

They were interrupted by a servant carrying a humidor filled with Cuban cigars. Drake shook his head. Spencer took one and, after a slight hesitation, took a second, and slipped them both into the breast pocket of his tuxedo.

"I can't wait for this to be over," Drake said.

"Yeah, well, it shouldn't be much longer now. Just don't stab anyone with the silverware and you'll be okay."

"I know. But I'm having a lousy time."

"Welcome to the lifestyles of the rich and famous."

"So far it sucks."

"Yeah, but the hours are good, and the food's not bad."

"I want to get out of here."

"You're the guest of honor, Drake. You don't get to disappear."

"I know. That's the problem."

"What's up? We talked about this. You just need to smile. They don't even care if you pick your nose. You're a rock star. A blinding supernova. You can do no wrong."

"It just feels...wrong."

Spencer nodded. "Maybe so. Tomorrow it will be over. You can get on a plane and go anywhere in the world. You're set. So man up, grin and bear it, or I swear I'll personally bring a scorpion to your room and have it bite you on the ass."

"I'm pretty sure scorpions sting."

"Whatever."

"All right. Hell, if I can brave the Amazon, the least I can do is tackle a few geriatrics in monkey suits."

Spencer slapped him on the back. "That's the spirit."

Spencer turned to rejoin the dinner, and Drake stopped him.

"Thanks, Spencer. For everything. I couldn't have gotten through any of this without your help."

Spencer paused. "Bullshit. You nailed it every time. If you're beating yourself up because you think you didn't do your part, that's idiocy. You found Paititi, Drake. Not me. Not Jack, not your dad, and not even Allie. *You* did. You located the treasure. You tracked down the ore. I just held your gun for you." Spencer looked off at the city and then fixed Drake with a hard stare. "You're frigging Drake Ramsey, you found Paititi, you're world famous, and Goddamn it, you deserve every bit of it, and more. So suck it up and deal with it."

They stood facing each other like gladiators, breathing heavily, the music drifting from the ballroom like tendrils of curling smoke.

Drake nodded and smiled. "I have issues." Spencer pulled one of the cigars from his pocket and sniffed it appreciatively.

"Welcome to the human race, dude."

Chapter Forty-Six

Drake opened the door of his apartment's refrigerator and grimaced. The milk had gone bad and the bread was a science experiment. But strangely, being back home, packing his things, centered him, something he needed after two days in Lima before returning to California and what passed for real life. That had all seemed fake, including sitting in first class, the pod seats, polite flight attendants and warm bowls of mixed nuts impossibly luxurious to his pedestrian eye.

Drake stared down at his torn jeans, worn running shoes, and No Fear T-shirt and shook his head. It felt like a mistake. This was reality, not the jungle, or state dinners, or luxurious suites. Reality was a fridge with two cans of cola, a six-pack of beer, some frozen waffles that had been there longer than the TV, and dairy products that qualified as hazardous waste.

He rinsed off one of the sodas and popped the top and, after a swig, returned to pouring products down the drain in preparation for the movers. They'd arrive within the hour, and he wanted to hand them the keys and be out of there, no love lost for his sad collection of furniture and few electronics. The only things he was taking with him were a duffel bag with most of his clothes and the new laptop he'd bought. The rest could rot in storage while he figured out what he wanted to be when he grew up.

The morning had been busy. He'd stopped by New Start Bail Bonds and made arrangements for Betty to work for him as his assistant. Not that he needed one, but she'd declined his offers of financial help, making clear that she didn't want charity. So they'd reached an agreement where she'd find suitable offices and act as the manager for his new foundation – which at present would largely involve fending off the near constant media inquiries.

The knock on the door startled him. He flipped the switch for the garbage disposal and, satisfied that the worst of the refrigerator's contents were now either in the sewage system or the garbage, went to the door and twisted the knob.

Spencer took in his ratty clothes and extended his hand. "Nice outfit," he said.

"Thanks. I thought I'd put on something special," Drake responded, shaking it.

"It's not every day you cut a check for thirty-three mil. I hardly recognized you with shoes on."

"They don't cut checks anymore. They do wire transfers."

"Nobody likes a know-it-all."

Spencer followed him inside and closed the door behind him. He tossed Drake a newspaper with a photo of Drake at the award ceremony on the front page. Drake groaned as he read it. Spencer sniffed the air disapprovingly.

"So how you been?" Spencer asked.

"Good. I just landed this morning. Got out on a red-eye."

"You could have hired a private jet and flown whenever you felt like it."

"I wouldn't know how to book one. Seriously. I've never done it before."

"Neither have I. But it seems like the kind of thing you should start doing."

"I'll add that to the list. You get your money?"

"Yeah. Courtesy of Peru. Thanks again. Five hundred big ones. I'm still trying to get used to the idea."

"I know what you mean. Like, where do you start?"

Spencer shrugged. "You heard from Allie?"

"Yeah. She's back in Texas. Dealing with ranch issues. I'm supposed to head out and help her tomorrow."

Spencer nodded. "Did you ever figure out what you were going to do about the shaman and his daughter?"

Drake had debated donating some of his cut to providing health care and other essential services to the tribe.

"In the end, anything I did would just destroy what they have, so it's one of those situations where if I tried to help, I'd do more harm than good. I decided to just let them be. They've managed for thousands of years without me. Who am I to play god and change everything for them?"

"The beginnings of wisdom." Spencer surveyed the apartment. "Can't see why you're moving. It's got walls and everything. Electricity. A view of that hedge."

"Time for a change, I guess."

"I'm kidding. It's a dump. And it smells like ass."

"Don't hold back. Tell me what you really think."

"So where are you moving *to*?"

Drake paused. "I haven't figured that out yet. Sort of trying to get the hang of my new lifestyle."

Spencer eyed him. "Maybe Texas?"

"Too flat."

"What about Florida? It's warm there."

"Too many hurricanes."

"Ah. Right. Then what about Southern California? San Diego? Malibu! You could go full-tilt *Baywatch*. Get a place on the beach. Bug your famous neighbors for Grey Poupon. Walk around naked. Surf."

"Surfing sounds fun. I used to do it out by Santa Cruz, but it's been a while."

"You should pick it back up. Everyone's doing it. It's the new 'I'm not a yuppie' yuppie thing to do."

"Good to know."

"I read that in the in-flight magazine."

"You should have taken a private jet."

Spencer smiled. "And the pupil becomes the master."

Drake went into his bedroom, slipped his computer into his duffel and shouldered it. "You ready to hit it?"

"Sure."

"Just a second. I need to leave a note for the movers." Drake pushed by him, scribbled on a piece of binder paper, and carried it to the door, where he tacked it on the outside after closing it. Spencer glanced at the note.

"Nice. 'Door's open. Haul everything to the dump. There's five hundred dollars in the drawer by the fridge. Enjoy the six of beer.' Why get tied down with material stuff?"

"I was going to put everything in storage, but I realized just now that I don't care about any of it. So why keep it?"

"Right. Better to start fresh. In Malibu. Surf's up, dude."

Drake nodded. "Cowabunga."

"I rented a car. We can take mine," Spencer said.

"Sounds good. Let me throw this in my trunk. Just give me a lift back, would you?"

"You expect a lot for thirty-three million. I already hauled that damned ore box for you. My back still hurts."

The afternoon sun filtered through the trees, warming Drake as he walked to his car – another possession he couldn't wait to get rid of, he realized. He absently wondered whether it would start, and decided that it didn't matter. Part of him hoped it wouldn't. It would make it easier for him to leave it there, to be towed whenever the city tired of it collecting dust. He threw his bag into the trunk and met Spencer at the curb, where he was sitting in a red economy sedan.

Drake slid into the passenger seat and ran a hand over the dash. "Wow. Real plastic. You're living large, aren't you?"

"Screw you. I got the extra insurance. I know how to spend money, too. You're not the only one, big shot." He paused. "Where's the bank?"

"Go west to the El Camino and hang a right. Eight blocks up. Can't miss it."

Spencer signaled and pulled into traffic, the engine whining like a chained dog, expensive luxury cars flying by them as they made their way to the main drag.

"Have you figured out what you're going to do?"

"Allie and I talked after the award ceremony. There's still that smaller Inca city just waiting to be found. I haven't had time to look into it yet, but there has to be a thread to follow on that…"

Spencer smiled. "Told you so."

"All right. Fine. You were right. There. Happy now?"

"Couldn't be happier."

Spencer found a spot a quarter block away from the bank. The manager escorted them into her office and handled the transaction, wiring thirty-three million dollars to Spencer's account without comment. The two men in front of her looked more like pizza-delivery boys than multimillionaires, but she was used to everything this close to Silicon Valley. They were done within ten minutes, and when they stepped out onto the sidewalk, they both seemed unsure of what to do next.

"You got time for a beer?" Spencer asked.

"You buying?"

"Cheapskate. Sure. But no imports. Domestic only."

"Deal."

They walked down the block to a small tavern and entered the dark room, its polished wooden walls evoking a time long past. Drake selected one of the many empty tables and ordered from a bartender who offered them a sour expression. He brought their beers and Spencer toasted with his bottle.

"To the future."

"Hear, hear," Drake agreed with a clink of glass. "Although I still hate all the attention. Don't people have anything better to do?"

"You're a celeb. Enjoy it while it lasts."

"Yeah, right. *Enjoy it*. I'll remember that."

They discussed vague ideas about how they would spend their time now that they were of secure means. Neither noticed the two men who entered until they approached the table. Drake looked up and his heart skipped a beat. It was Gus, accompanied by an older man in a gray suit who looked like he'd lost one too many street fights.

"Mr. Ramsey, what a small world," Gus said, pulling up a chair.

"What do you want?" Drake demanded, his voice tense.

"To congratulate you on your success. And introduce you to someone who wanted to meet you. This is Jed Abby. He's with the same outfit I am. But higher up."

Abby sat down and crossed his legs, studying both Spencer and Drake before speaking.

"Mr. Ramsey, I wanted to meet you because I had an idea, and I wanted to see your reaction to it. Call it a proposal, if you like."

"I'm not in the proposal market. Thanks anyway. Is that all?" Drake snapped, annoyed that the CIA still seemed to want more out of him.

"You haven't heard it."

Spencer eyed Drake and tilted his head in warning.

Drake took the hint. "Fine. But make it quick."

"Of course – you're obviously a busy man. Here's the proposition. There might come a time when we need someone like you to help us, as you did this time. Someone who isn't a pro. Money obviously won't be the motivator anymore, because now you're rich. And you apparently think we're liars and cheats, so I can't appeal to your patriotism."

"You can't buy me or pump me up."

"Exactly."

"Then why would I want to help you?"

Abby took a long time to answer. "Because I'll tell you the truth about what's at stake so you can decide for yourself. And because it will be the right thing to do. Like with Palenko's ore. It might take another twenty years, but we'll figure out how to replace power plants with it. Not make bombs. There's no need for bombs anymore. Now it's all about economics. Cheap resources to power a hungry planet." Abby paused. "If I get in touch, it'll be because I need you, and only you, to do me a favor."

"And what do I get?"

"I could say you get to live, but that's old school. What you get is the chance to do the right thing. Plain and simple."

"The right thing? What are you talking about?"

"You're famous. And I presume from your statements to the Secretary of State that you intend to pursue other…adventures. Since that's the case, there may come a time when we need help with something, well, delicate. Where having someone with a rock-solid résumé could prove useful. It's just an idea. That's all. There's no specific event at present. But there could be…in the future."

"I see. And if I agree, you'll leave me in peace?"

"Why, Mr. Ramsey, I'd like nothing better than to never speak with you again. You have my word that if I call, it'll be because I have no other alternative."

Spencer and Drake exchanged a glance.

"Do you have a card?" Drake asked. "I'll think about it. That's all I can promise."

"I don't carry cards."

Gus and Abby pushed back their chairs and stood. "Good luck with your future ventures, young man," Abby said.

"Wait. How will you get in touch? I don't even have a cell phone."

Abby smiled, a humorless gesture with the warmth of a freezer. "Oh, don't worry about that."

The two men left as abruptly as they entered, leaving Spencer and Drake staring at their backs as they pushed through the door.

Drake took a long pull on his beer and shook his head. "Tell me that wasn't freaky."

"Sorry. No can do. It was completely freaky."

"I know. I mean, how did they know we were here having a drink, or that I wired money…" Drake's prior suspicions about Spencer's relationship with the Agency flitted back through his thoughts, but he kept his expression neutral.

"They're the CIA. I told you. Just assume they can do anything. Because they can." Spencer finished his beer. "But it doesn't sound like they want to hurt you. It was actually interesting. I wonder what they have in mind?"

"Whatever it is can't be good for me. I'm pretty sure of that."

"Maybe. But it sounded pretty open-ended."

"I don't like either of them."

"I got that. It didn't seem like they have you on their Christmas list, either. But in my experience, if the CIA comes knocking, it's best to pay attention. That's all I'm saying."

Drake signaled to the bartender and a second round arrived. They watched the game on TV, silently nursing their drinks, lost in thought. When they finished their beers, Spencer paid the tab. As they walked to the car, Spencer took a deep breath, the spring aroma of blossoming flowers heavy in the air.

"Well, buddy, you gotta admit. Life's interesting, if nothing else."

"That it is."

"Are you going to think about the Southern Cal thing? Or do the nomad bit for a while?"

"I could check it out. I really have no plan."

"Sometimes having no plan is the best plan." Spencer stopped and felt in his jacket pocket. "Oh, before I forget. Jorge made me promise I'd give this to you." He handed Drake a manila envelope.

Drake opened it and slid a large color photo out. It was one of the pictures from the treasure chamber. Spencer had his arm around Drake's shoulder, and they were both beaming as one of the gold relics was craned from the cenote in the background. Drake read the inscription across the bottom: two words scrawled in black felt pen.

He shook his head. "I wish they wouldn't call it that. It's embarrassing."

"What?"

Drake turned the photo so Spencer could see it.

"Ramsey's gold," Drake said, tapping the script with his fingertip.

Spencer grinned.

"Get used to it, *Señor* Hero. That's how everyone refers to it. Ramsey's gold. Not the Paititi treasure. Not the Inca treasure. Ramsey's."

Drake stopped and gazed at the traffic rolling down the wide boulevard. Just another blustery day with ordinary folks going about their business, hurrying to whatever important destinations they'd filled their lives with, immersed in their individual dramas.

"My dad would have been…" He couldn't continue, his voice cracking.

"Yes, he would have," Spencer said, eyeing the photo of the magnificent artifact, a depiction of the Inca sun god, Inti, rising from the water like an avenging spirit, its stylized glower seeming to fix on the two tired men as they smiled for the camera. "Yes, he would."

About the Author

Featured in *The Wall Street Journal*, *The Times*, and *The Chicago Tribune*, Russell Blake is *The NY Times* and *USA Today* bestselling author of over thirty-five novels, including *Fatal Exchange*, *The Geronimo Breach*, *Zero Sum*, *King of Swords*, *Night of the Assassin*, *Revenge of the Assassin*, *Return of the Assassin*, *Blood of the Assassin*, *Requiem for the Assassin*, *The Delphi Chronicle* trilogy, *The Voynich Cypher*, *Silver Justice*, *JET*, *JET – Ops Files*, *JET – Ops Files: Terror Alert*, *JET II – Betrayal*, *JET III – Vengeance*, *JET IV – Reckoning*, *JET V – Legacy*, *JET VI – Justice*, *JET VII – Sanctuary*, *JET VIII – Survival*, *JET IX – Escape*, *Upon a Pale Horse*, *BLACK*, *BLACK is Back*, *BLACK is The New Black*, *BLACK to Reality*, and *Deadly Calm*.

Non-fiction includes the international bestseller *An Angel With Fur* (animal biography) and *How To Sell A Gazillion eBooks In No Time* (even if drunk, high or incarcerated), a parody of all things writing-related.

Blake is co-author of *The Eye of Heaven* and *The Solomon Curse*, with legendary author Clive Cussler. Blake's novel *King of Swords* has been translated into German by Amazon Crossing, *The Voynich Cypher* into Bulgarian, and his JET novels into Spanish, German, and Czech.

Blake writes under the moniker R.E. Blake in the NA/YA/Contemporary Romance genres. Novels include *Less Than Nothing*, *More Than Anything*, and *Best Of Everything*.

Having resided in Mexico for a dozen years, Blake enjoys his dogs, fishing, boating, tequila and writing, while battling world domination by clowns. His thoughts, such as they are, can be found at his blog: RussellBlake.com

Books by Russell Blake

Co-authored with Clive Cussler

THE EYE OF HEAVEN
THE SOLOMON CURSE

Thrillers

FATAL EXCHANGE
THE GERONIMO BREACH
ZERO SUM
THE DELPHI CHRONICLE TRILOGY
THE VOYNICH CYPHER
SILVER JUSTICE
UPON A PALE HORSE
DEADLY CALM
RAMSEY'S GOLD

The Assassin Series

KING OF SWORDS
NIGHT OF THE ASSASSIN
RETURN OF THE ASSASSIN
REVENGE OF THE ASSASSIN
BLOOD OF THE ASSASSIN
REQUIEM FOR THE ASSASSIN

The JET Series

JET
JET II – BETRAYAL
JET III – VENGEANCE
JET IV – RECKONING
JET V – LEGACY
JET VI – JUSTICE
JET VII – SANCTUARY
JET VIII – SURVIVAL
JET IX – ESCAPE
JET – OPS FILES (prequel)
JET – OPS FILES; TERROR ALERT

The BLACK Series

BLACK
BLACK IS BACK
BLACK IS THE NEW BLACK
BLACK TO REALITY

Non Fiction

AN ANGEL WITH FUR
HOW TO SELL A GAZILLION EBOOKS
(while drunk, high or incarcerated)